Race to Tibet

A NOVEL

Sophie Schiller

Gabriel Bonvalot

The author wishes to acknowledge the superb research of Peter Hopkirk (1930-2014), Great Game historian extraordinaire who passed away during the writing of this novel.

"Scientific research will mask the political goals of the expedition and remove any suspicions in the minds of our enemies…The aim of the study will be Tibet. In addition to scientific research, we have proposed to gather intelligence about the political system of Tibet, to tie and strengthen our relationship with the Dalai Lama."

—Major-General Nikolai Prejevalsky

Gabriel Bonvalot and Prince Henri d'Orléans'
1889—90 Expedition to Tibet

DRAMATIS PERSONAE

FRANCE
Prince Robert, Duke of Chartres
Jean Louis de Quatrefages, *Geographical Society*
Gabriel Bonvalot
Henri Lorin
Professor Philippe Édouard Foucaux
Baron Maurice de Hirsch
Prince Henri d'Orléans
Camille Dancourt
François Raymond

CHINESE TURKESTAN
Col. Uspensky, *Russian consul at Kuldja*
Father Constant Dedeken, *Belgian Missionary*
Bartholomeus, *Dedeken's servant*
Hakim of Korla

THE CARAVANEERS
Rachmed
Abdullah
Timur
Isa
Parpa
Mahmud
Imatch
Niaz
Tong-Kia

TIBET
Princess Pema
Amban
Grand Amban
Grand Lama
Jamyang, *Interpreter*
Lama Tashi Thubten, *Grand Lama of Sok Lamasery*
Lobsang, *lama guide*

PART 1

CHAPTER 1

Paris, France
December, 1888

The Duke of Chartres eased himself into his arm-chair and listened to the crackling of the fire. He took a sip of sherry and opened up the newspaper that was lying on a side table. When he saw the headline, his monocle fell in his lap:

WHAT PARIS TALKS ABOUT
Prince Henri d'Orléans Dropped By Many French Royalists Over Opera Singer's Lawsuit. Woman claims the prince drugged her and seduced her.

"Good Heavens!" The Duke threw down the newspaper in disgust. He called for his valet, who promptly appeared from a side door wearing a quizzical look on his face.

"Yes, your Grace?"

The Duke shook an angry fist. "This is an outrage! A scandal! Send for my lawyers at once."

"Is something the matter, your Grace?"

The Duke pointed to the newspaper. "Have a look."

Picking up the newspaper, the valet read the story, his face turning colors and contorting with each sordid detail. When he had finished, he handed the newspaper back to the Duke.

"Are you planning to sue the newspaper?"

"No, I wouldn't waste my time," said the Duke with disdain. "That would only give them more fodder to print. I have no choice but to track down the little tart and pay her off to keep her quiet."

"Hmm...that has never worked in the past," said the valet. "These actresses rarely keep quiet. They often make more money by selling their stories to the highest bidder. I think it would be more prudent to spirit the prince out of the country as quickly as possible. In a few weeks, the story will die down."

"Where do you propose I send the little wastrel?"

"Oh, it will have to be very far away indeed," said the valet. "Someplace where there are no reporters, no newspapers, no race tracks, and apparently, no opera singers."

The Duke of Chartres buried his face in his hands. It pained him that Henri would never amount to anything. He had been the black sheep of the family since the day he was born. He was a dilettante, an idler, and combined with his drinking, gambling, and consorting with the lowest element of society, he had become a fixture in the gutter press. He had long ago been expelled from all the English clubs to which he'd belonged, including the international club, the diplomatic club, and the St. James's. One of the most important noblemen in the country, the Marquis de Beauvoir, who was for many years the Comte de Paris's private secretary, upon hearing of Prince Henri's scandalous conduct, transferred his allegiance to the Bonapartist camp. No, with troubles like these there was no place on earth the Duke could send Henri that would keep him out of trouble. And with the latest fiasco, when Henri was caught running for his life across a race track, chased by a furious English trainer who was calling him every insulting name in the book in full public view, it was only a question of time before Henri's antics resulted in a tragedy.

The Duke walked over to the fireplace and stared at the flames, lost in his thoughts. Behind him, the valet twitched his whiskers and scratched his head.

"Perhaps there is one possibility you haven't considered," said the valet. "You could send him on a voyage of exploration to a place so far away he won't be able to do any damage."

The Duke's eyebrows shot up. "Brilliant idea! I should have thought of that myself. Where's the little good-for-nothing now?"

"He's playing baccarat in the drawing room with your nephew, the Duke of Orléans."

"Good. Send for my lawyers immediately. I'm going to draw up a legal document that will strip Henri of his rights to inherit the family estate and the title if he refuses to agree to my terms."

"And what terms are those?"

"That he leaves the country immediately and agrees to stay out of trouble for at least a year."

"Very well," said the valet. "And have you given any thought as to who should lead this expedition?"

The Duke looked pensive for a moment, then he snapped his fingers. "I've got it. That chap that just returned from India. The one who was featured in the latest bulletin of the Geographical Society. What was his name? Oh yes, Bonvalot. Gabriel Bonvalot. Get me his address right away."

"Very well, your Grace."

Smiling, the valet turned and left. He had no doubt the Duke would be sending the young prince very far away indeed.

CHAPTER 2

At the same time the Duke of Chartres was planning to spirit Prince Henri out of the country, Gabriel Bonvalot was about to make the biggest gamble of his career.

He was ensconced in the sacred halls of the Geographical Society where the members were fêting him at a dinner party held in his honor. The president, Jean Louis de Quatrefages, had called the meeting to honor Bonvalot's successful crossing of the Pamir and the Hindu Kush Mountains in the middle of winter, a feat that had never before been accomplished, and to toast his escape from the Mehtar of Chitral's dungeon with his head still attached to his shoulders. And as often happens during such festivities, Bonvalot had imbibed too much booze and was liable to a slip of the tongue.

At forty-five minutes after midnight, Monsieur Quatrefages lifted his glass.

"I wish to propose another toast to Monsieur Bonvalot."

Monsieur Hervé lifted his droopy eyelids and said, "Any more toasts my dear Quatrefages and you'll find yourself married to the gent."

The members roared with laughter while Bonvalot responded with a good-natured upward curl of his lip. At the present, he was too tipsy to care.

"What are you toasting this time, Quatrefages," chimed in René Goblet, the Minister of Foreign Affairs. "You've already toasted his courage, his gallantry, his extraordinary horsemanship. I believe you've even toasted his *horse*."

More laughter erupted from the audience.

Undaunted, Quatrefages motioned with his free hand to quiet the assembly.

"Gentlemen, I'm sure you didn't come here tonight to hear your beloved president give another one of his long-winded speeches." Here he raised an authoritarian eyebrow to a few scattered guffaws. "You came here on this cold and windy night to hear the inside scoop of how Monsieur Bonvalot beat the wily old Mehtar of Chitral at his own game. So, let's raise our glasses once again in honor of our esteemed colleague and congratulate him for his resourcefulness, fearlessness, and unsurpassed ingenuity in escaping the Mehtar's dungeon. Now, if you would be so gracious, Monsieur Bonvalot, kindly stand up and tell this esteemed audience how you managed to secure your freedom."

Silence descended over the room. All eyes turned to Bonvalot, who downed the remainder of his drink and shoved his crumpled speech into his coat pocket before standing up.

"Thank you, Monsieur le Président," said Bonvalot, stifling a cough. "And thank you members of the Geographical Society for your warm welcome. Suffice it to say I won't bore you with details about the cold, the privations, the hunger, the mountain sickness, the constant threats to our lives. These are the challenges an explorer expects to encounter on a journey through hostile and hazardous terrain. Much to my chagrin, I discovered that it wasn't until we were captured by the Mehtar's soldiers that we faced our most difficult challenge. Do you care to hear more?"

The crowd erupted in cheers.

"Good, because as long as Monsieur Quatrefages is paying for the booze I can keep talking all night."

While Bonvalot rambled on about sword-wielding guards, well-placed bribes, and a sympathetic native messenger who raced to Simla to deliver a message to the Viceroy, his mind began to wander. It may have been the effects of the alcohol or the portraits of so many famous dead explorers lining the walls that broke down his normally staid demeanor, but at that particular moment he felt certain he was destined for greatness.

The proceedings carried on for another hour, during which time the members debated various points of exploration and discovery while Bonvalot contemplated his next great conquest. It wasn't until Quatrefages had called Bonvalot's name several times before he returned to the discussion at hand, and by that time, there was no turning back.

"Well, Monsieur Bonvalot? We are waiting to hear your thoughts."

"My thoughts?"

"As we were saying Monsieur Bonvalot, the members would like to know which part of the world you plan to explore next."

"Gentlemen, I'm going to Tibet."

"Excuse me, would you mind repeating that?" said Quatrefages.

Bonvalot cleared his throat. "Over the entire globe there is only one country that is completely sealed off from the rest of the world. It is a country so hidden that their only wheel is the prayer wheel and their inhabitants are ruled over by a God-king. It is a land so secretive it has long been the stuff of travelers' dreams. This country as you know is Tibet and my goal is to breach her walls of isolation."

Monsieur Hervé's eyes loomed large behind his pince nez. "Excuse me, Monsieur Bonvalot, but did I hear you correctly? Did you say *Tibet*?"

There was an audible hush in the lecture hall

"Yes, indeed," said Bonvalot, sitting up straighter. "I may as well announce it right now. My dream is to be the first living European to reach Lhasa. And I intend to achieve this goal by next year."

A great stir erupted among the members, interspersed by a few hecklers and naysayers.

"Balderdash!" said Monsieur Goblet. "No explorer has succeeded in reaching the Forbidden City in over fifty years! No man can breach the impenetrable wall of the Himalayas. It's impossible!"

"Hear, hear," chimed in the audience.

"Difficult maybe," said Bonvalot, straightening his tie. "But not impossible. I've been reading up on the subject and I believe I can do it."

"Have you not heard of the sad fate of Messieurs Krick and Boury, two missionaries who were slaughtered by hostile tribes when they attempted to enter Tibet?" said Monsieur Hervé.

"Well, I…"

"Monsieur Bonvalot, an expedition such as this would require a great deal of planning," said Monsieur de Quatrefages, adjusting his spectacles. "Are you sure you're ready to undertake such an arduous journey so close on the heels of your most recent one?

After all, with an average altitude of 16,000 feet, Tibet is the highest country in the world. They don't call it the Roof of the World for nothing."

By now Bonvalot was so dizzy, he was struggling to keep his head steady. "Absolutely. I'm certain I can do it."

The stern-faced Goblet locked eyes with Bonvalot. "Would you care to elaborate on that, Monsieur Bonvalot? All of us members are, as you know, well-versed in the area of geographical exploration."

"Gladly," said Bonvalot, loosening his collar. "And thank you for asking, Monsieur Goblet, as I have every intention of sharing my plans with you in due time. But for right now, I have much work to do and I don't believe in rushing things."

"Very well then," said Quatrefages, returning his attention to the audience. "I'm certain our esteemed members would love to have you back so you can share your ideas with us."

As the members cheered and applauded, Bonvalot broke into a cold sweat as the full weight of his announcement came crashing down on him.

CHAPTER 3

The next morning Bonvalot awoke with a throbbing headache, the aftereffects of a night of heavy drinking. When he opened his eyes, he recalled the stunning announcement he had made the night before and fell back against the pillow, moaning. The idea of launching an expedition into Tibet when he'd barely recovered from his last journey left him feeling numb. Even by the standards of the world's greatest explorers, Tibet was a risky venture. It was tantamount to suicide.

He focused on the clock on the wall: ten o'clock. The growling in his stomach reminded him it was time to eat. Fighting the effects of gravity, he sat up in bed, groped around for his pants and shirt, and stumbled over to the wash basin. After washing his face and running a comb through his hair, he grabbed his top hat and overcoat, and staggered outside to the blustery cold. He made his way over to Café Tortoni to contemplate the matter over a hot meal.

As France's most celebrated explorer, Gabriel Bonvalot was obsessed with traveling to the four corners of the globe. And when he wasn't riding on some windswept pass high up in the Himalayas, he was thinking of ingenious ways of getting there. Even ill health couldn't stop his mind from wandering to far-flung lands. While confined to bed during a lengthy recuperation from rheumatic fever, Bonvalot's greatest pleasure was to leaf through his trusty Schrader Atlas and watch the pages spring to life. From the volume's dusty maps, mountains would burst forth, followed by vast forests of pine, oak, and deodar trees swaying in the breeze, while shimmering streams of glacial water snaked down from the heights to water fields of apricot, almond, and apple trees: an entire world pulsing with life. And when his eyelids grew too heavy, and sleep was about to overtake him, a fine dusting of Himalayan snow would fall across his bed, prompting Bonvalot to pull up the covers and drift off into a deep, restful slumber.

When pressed, Bonvalot would always insist that geography was more than the mere study of maps and charts as found in dusty volumes languishing in libraries around the world. Geography was, in fact, an adventure waiting to be explored. A *costly* adventure, to be sure, but one that filled all his waking and sleeping hours. As always, Bonvalot's greatest worry was money. The art of coaxing funds out of fickle coffers was almost as difficult as extracting gold teeth from reluctant mouths. An expedition of any size was an expensive endeavor and after his near-fatal encounter in the Pamir Mountains, the price of high risk travel was greater than ever. Bonvalot knew he needed an extraordinary success to seal his name in the annals of geography.

This time he would go for the grand prize.

Bonvalot's dream was to be the first living European to reach Lhasa, the mysterious capital of Tibet. In fact, Lhasa had been closed to foreigners for so long it was called the forbidden city. But it would not be easy. Times were hard; money was scarce. Even the Royal Family had had their share of money woes. There were rumors that the young pretender to the French throne, Prince Henri d'Orléans—an idler and a dilettante—had amassed such a large gambling debt that his father, the Duke of Chartres, had been forced to beg his patron, Baron Maurice de Hirsch, for the money to cover the young numskull's debts of honor. Bonvalot shuddered at the thought of having to beg for the privilege of doing what he loved best.

Down the street, a crowd had gathered around his favorite newsstand, with all eyes glued to the latest edition of *Le Figaro*. Bonvalot quickened his pace, and when he spotted a familiar face splashed on the front page, he froze. Snatching the newspaper off the stand he stared at the headline with a mixture of shock and incredulity, his hand gripping the paper so tight his arms shook with excitement:

General Prejevalsky Dead

Bonvalot's pulse quickened. *Can it be true? Is that Russian braggart really dead?*

He threw down a few centimes and tucked the newspaper under his arm, certain that the news would send shock waves through every Geographical Society in Europe. Indeed, Bonvalot even expected the announcement would raise eyebrows at the highest echelons of British military intelligence. Rumors had been circulating for years that General Prejevalsky had been involved in intelligence gathering activities under the guise of geographical exploration. As it turned out, the two occupations were not mutually exclusive.

Dodging the onslaught of horse-drawn carriages, Bonvalot dashed across the street to Café Tortoni, his home away from home during the cold Parisian winter.

As he entered the café, the maître d'hôtel rushed over to greet him. "Monsieur Bonvalot, what an honor to see you," he said, removing the famed explorer's coat as if he were the Duke of Magenta himself. "I've saved your favorite seat—the best in the house."

"Actually, I'd prefer that quiet table over there."

"As you wish."

Bonvalot sat down and spread the newspaper over the linen tablecloth. Before he could look up, the wine steward was already at his side bearing the pride of the house: Chateau Lafite Rothschild 1883. He waited for approval, then proceeded to pop the cork.

"Compliments of the house," said the steward, filling a sparkling glass to the brim, after which he bowed and disappeared.

Bonvalot lifted the glass and inhaled the wine's fragrant bouquet. After tasting the libation, his eyes once again feasted on the article:

Major-General Prejevalsky, whose death was recently reported in the cablegrams was the most distinguished of all the Russian scientific explorers and one of the greatest modern authorities on Central Asia. He was a trusted officer of the Czar and had a well-earned reputation for being a bold, determined, and enthusiastic pioneer of travel. He broke fresh ground in Turkestan some fifteen years ago, traversing the

Pamir, skirting the Chang Tang, Tibet's great Northern deserts, and penetrating the Lob-Nor. Although he succeeded in exploring portions of Northern Tibet, he was unable to make his way south into Lhasa. At the time of his death from typhoid fever on the shores of Lake Issyk-Kul, he was about to embark on another attempt to reach Lhasa. The sudden death of Prejevalsky on the eve of another journey to Tibet will send shock waves throughout the scientific world.

Shock waves is an understatement, thought Bonvalot. With Prejevalsky dead, his biggest competitor in the race to Lhasa was out of the picture. But he was certain there were others: ambitious British soldiers seeking fame and glory outside the regiment, as well as the more covert kind of explorer, those who entered the Forbidden Kingdom disguised as Buddhist pilgrims or traders. The British had devised a plan to send pundits to map and explore Tibet incognito, using rosary beads with one hundred instead of the usual one hundred and eight beads so they could count their paces, compasses hidden inside of prayer wheels, and thermometers to gauge altitude smuggled inside a walking stick. Some of the pundits suffered unimaginable cruelty at the hands of the Tibetan authorities when their disguises were unmasked; others simply disappeared without a trace.

Aside from the danger of traveling in Tibet, organizing an expedition cost a small fortune. Bonvalot would need to find a sponsor who was fabulously wealthy yet wouldn't make too many demands. In time, he was sure he would resolve that problem as well. By the end of next year, Bonvalot hoped to be climbing the steps of the Potala Palace to meet the famed Dalai Lama, raise the Tricolor for the glory of France, and secure his place in the annals of exploration for all time. Success would be sweet.

Bonvalot sipped his wine and smiled. At the age of thirty-five, he had made a name for himself in the competitive world of exploration. But until now death had been an abstraction, like the sun-bleached skeleton of an ibex nestled along the shores of a Siberian lake. Prejevalsky's untimely death made him think hard about his own life. How long would his streak of good fortune last?

Bonvalot chuckled at the irony of it all. Prejevalsky, the larger-than-life Russian Hercules was dead while he was still alive. It was almost too ironic to believe. It was, in fact, a miracle. He stared at the frozen image of Prejevalsky in the newspaper. "So, my friend, your dream of Lhasa is over. You failed miserably."

"What do you know about my dream of Lhasa?"

Shocked, Bonvalot looked up. Sitting across from him was a disheveled tramp who had appeared out of nowhere. The skin on his face was cracked and bruised, his eyes sunken and bloodshot, and his arms an unnatural shade of purple and covered with festering sores. His clothes, if they could be called that, were in tatters—worse than a beggar's. His hair was a tangled, filthy mess more resembling fodder than human hair. And, most troubling of all, the man smelled of the sewers, of death.

Bonvalot recoiled. "Must you sit here? Find yourself another table."

"Not so fast, Monsieur Bonvalot," said the beggar in a voice that grated like wheels over gravel. "I didn't come here to ask you to open your purse. I came here to offer *you* something. And when you hear what I have to offer, you'll be glad I did."

"I'm not interested in anything you have to offer. Now get out you filthy beggar."

The stranger's face turned menacing. He grabbed Bonvalot's arm in a vise-like grip.

"I think you'd better sit back quietly, Monsieur Bonvalot, if you don't want to cause a scene."

Bonvalot pulled his arm out of the stranger's grasp and glanced around to make sure nobody was watching. The restaurant was filled with diners laughing and joking, waving their forks in animated conversation while an elderly Gypsy meandered around the tables serenading the diners with soft violin music. To Bonvalot's relief, no one had noticed that a filthy beggar had wormed his way into one of Paris's most famous restaurants and commandeered Bonvalot's private table. Even the maître d', who wasn't more than twenty feet away, was completely oblivious to the matter at hand. Bonvalot squirmed in his seat, trying to control his mounting anger.

The stranger continued, "As I stated before, I came here to make you an offer."

"I told you to leave."

The beggar narrowed his eyes. "Shall I raise my voice and cause a scene?"

Bonvalot glared at the intruder. "Then get on with your little speech and get out."

"You said before that I failed," continued the beggar over the din of the café, "but in many ways I succeeded beyond all measure. During my third journey, I penetrated deeper into Tibet than any other European explorer in modern times. I came so close to reaching Lhasa, I was sure we would make it. At our southernmost point, I calculated our position to be no more than one hundred and sixty miles away. This is a remarkable achievement given the odds we were facing. Even those celebrated Indian pundits the British sent into Tibet only managed to survey the southern and western portions of the country; they were never able to infiltrate the interior before disaster struck. But alas! Our camels held us back; those faltering beasts were completely useless at high altitudes. They grew sick and feeble, growled incessantly, and refused to get up no matter how hard I beat them. It was on account of these circumstances that I was forced to abandon the entire expedition or risk dying among those savages. But that was then. This time it can be different. I came here to offer you my services as guide on your expedition to Tibet. And if you're smart you'll accept it. I'm giving you the chance to use all my wisdom and experience. It's all up here." The beggar tapped his head. "Where I failed you can succeed. I guarantee it."

"Who the devil are you?" said Bonvalot, fighting to keep his voice contained. "I don't need your help or anyone else's."

The beggar smiled, showing teeth that were cracked and stained. "I am the greatest explorer in the world. The toast of Russia. The favorite of the Tsar. At least, I *was* all those things."

"Yes, and I'm Lillie Langtry, but that doesn't answer my question. *Who* are you and *how* do you know so much about Tibet?" said Bonvalot, his heart now racing.

The beggar smiled wryly. "I think you know."

Bonvalot dropped his spoon. He bent down to retrieve it and noticed the beggar was wearing boots that appeared to be made of yak fur and were caked with a strange yellow mud. He slid his pocket knife out of its sheath, cut a sample of the fur, and wrapped it in his handkerchief.

"I entered a region that was less known than the darkest Africa," continued the beggar. "But my men and I suffered terrible privations for our heroism. Dozens of horses and camels collapsed from sheer exhaustion. Some of them simply froze to death. The Hami desert that separates the Tian Shan from the Nan Shan was so hot at night that you couldn't sleep on the ground. There were no animals, no plants, no civilized life, just salt clouds that formed into mirages that mocked us and tormented us. The wind knocked us off our feet and tore at our eyes. There was no fodder for the animals, no water to drink. And the inhabitants! They mirrored the cursed terrain with their games of treachery. They refused to sell us food, refused to provide us with guides, called us foreign devils behind our backs and sometimes right to our faces. They used every means of deceit to rob us blind. Central Asia is a lawless, godless land, and only European rifles and Krupp guns can do any good there. Missionary preaching is like howling in the wilderness. The people are beyond saving."

Bonvalot's eyes grew wide. "Prejevalsky...?"

"The name is Nikolai Mikhaylovich Prejevalsky," said the beggar, bowing his head and twisting his lips in a gratuitous smile. "As you may have heard, I was never noted for my manners, never comfortable in polite society. I was only happy out there in the wilderness, far from wretched civilization. The only way you'll succeed is by taking me along. Without me, you don't stand a chance."

Bonvalot felt his neck grow hot. "Look, I've had enough of you. I don't know who you are, but I'm not the least bit impressed with your little charade. So get out before I call the gendarmes. Scat!"

All at once, the beggar erupted into a violent fit of coughing that was so loud, it drowned out the clanking of pots from the kitchen, the animated conversation from the diners, and the Gypsy's hypnotic violin playing.

Bonvalot whirled around, terrified the interloper would choke to death at his table and cause a hair-raising scene that would land him on the front pages of the gutter press. That the waiter failed to check on the situation only made him more agitated. It seemed, in fact, that no one else could hear the beggar's loud coughing, as if he wasn't really there. To calm the situation, Bonvalot gave the filthy tramp a few half-hearted thumps on his back.

"Is that all you can do after I came here to help you?" cried the beggar, shoving Bonvalot's hand away as he spat a large clot of blood into his napkin. "You worthless French bastard! You didn't even offer me a drink! Is this what you Frenchies call good manners? I should shoot you with my revolver to teach you a lesson. When I'm done with you, you'll never make it to Lhasa. Where is the damned thing?"

Bonvalot jumped out of his seat, heart pounding like a drum. The beggar rummaged through his tattered clothing for his gun with a fury that bordered on savagery. Lacking a weapon, Bonvalot searched in vain for help, but there was not a gendarme in sight. The other diners were eating and drinking to their heart's content; no one had heard the beggar's dire threat. No one knew his life was at stake.

The beggar gave up searching for his pistol and returned to his coughing spasm. Bonvalot breathed a sigh of relief, but felt his face grow hot at the humiliation of having a lowly street beggar encroach on his private table and lecture him about the rigors of Central Asian exploration. He called for the maître d', who came rushing over at once, corkscrew in hand.

"Yes, Monsieur Bonvalot?"

"Will you kindly escort this vagrant out of the café. He snuck in without permission, took over my table, and threatened to shoot me. He's stark raving mad and has no business being in this fine establishment."

"Certainly, Monsieur," said the maître d', who glanced at the table and saw only an empty seat next to Bonvalot. "Excuse me," he said, looking around with a baffled expression on his face. "but to which vagrant are you referring?"

Stunned, Bonvalot stared at the empty chair. Inexplicably, the stranger had vanished.

CHAPTER 4

For the next several days, Bonvalot tried to put the disturbing encounter with the beggar out of his mind, but found it was impossible. Ensconced in his apartment with a steaming mug of coffee, he pulled Prejevalsky's travel books off the shelves. One by one, he leafed through them, scarcely believing that this Russian giant had failed so miserably, dying of typhus at the foot of the Tian Shan Mountains before his final expedition to Tibet had even begun. *Now is my chance to succeed where Prejevalsky failed*, he thought. *I must reach Lhasa if it's the last thing I do.*

Prejevalsky's inexplicable appearance continued to haunt Bonvalot. He decided to find solace in the company of his best friend, Henri Lorin, an expert in colonial geography who sometimes dabbled in the branch of science known as psychology. Bonvalot tucked the newspaper under his arm and headed over to Lorin's apartment.

Henri Lorin leaned back in his chair and puffed on his pipe. He scanned the obituary for a few minutes as he scratched his chin in scholarly contemplation. Finally, he exhaled a thick plume of black smoke that curled up to the ceiling.

"There you have it," said Bonvalot, pointing to the newspaper. "That's the man I saw in Café Tortoni."

"Remarkable," said Lorin, meeting his friend's gaze. "A fascinating story. Even better than the one I heard about the lady on the Rue du Paradis who claims to receive visitations from the Archangel Gabriel and will gladly predict your future for a mere twenty francs."

Bonvalot raised an eyebrow. "I'm glad you find it amusing. But I assure you the vision I saw was not the least bit funny.

Especially when it tried to kill me. Henri, tell me the truth, do you think I'm going mad?"

"Mad?" Lorin laughed. "Good Heavens, no. I think it means you've been working too hard. How many hours did you sleep last night? Take a good look at yourself. Your skin is sallow and you look underweight. You've been under an enormous mental and physical strain since you returned from your last expedition. Not many men could have survived the dreadful ordeal you suffered in that dungeon. You're a lucky bastard. It was only on account of Lord Dufferin's intervention that you made it out alive. What you are describing sounds like ordinary hallucinations. I've been studying the latest *Manual of Psychology* by the eminent Dr. Friedrich Kirchner of Berlin. He writes that perfectly healthy men can occasionally experience visions such as the one you described. He claims they're caused by an excess of physiological stimuli."

"Physiological stimuli?" said Bonvalot. "You mean like opium and morphine?"

"No, those are pathological stimuli. Kirchner was referring to sensations or perceptions that you're probably not aware of."

"Are these hallucinations harmful to the spirit?"

"It is possible," said Lorin. "Think of them as sense deceptions, mental mirages if you will. If you recognize them as such—illusions—they lose all meaning and importance. But if you let them take hold of your mind, they can permanently cloud your judgment. When that happens, disease can set in rather quickly."

"A sense deception, you say?" said Bonvalot, furrowing his brow. "But to me it was real. I saw the man, spoke to him, saw him try to kill me. How can I convince myself that he was merely a hallucination?"

"Bonvalot, what I'm saying is that when you engage a hallucination you may cause it to return again and again, each time taking a stronger hold over the mind until it becomes a fixed idea. He who has once seen a spirit soon sees more. I've heard that individuals with strong imaginations can even call up a hallucination at will, but I strongly advise against doing this. You must fight these hallucinations or risk disaster."

"What may have caused it?"

Lorin leafed through the heavy volume on his desk. "It's hard to say. The latest theory suggests that hallucinations are spiritual disturbances, or abnormalities in the life of the soul to which anomalous physiological conditions correspond. This means that some faculty of the soul is malfunctioning. It says that people are particularly susceptible to hallucinations in times of great upheaval in the state, the church, and in science. Francis of Assisi and Joan of Arc are known to have experienced hallucinations. Luther claimed he saw the devil; Thomas Hobbes saw ghosts hovering around him in the dark, but that is what you'd expect from a man like Hobbes. Were all these people mad or were they merely experiencing sense deceptions that created an unseen metaphysical world? At the present, science does not have an answer to this question."

Bonvalot retrieved his handkerchief with the sample of yak fur. "Then how do you explain this?"

Lorin set his pipe down and reached for the handkerchief.

"How do I explain what?" said Lorin, looking perplexed. "There's nothing here." He had opened up the handkerchief but there was nothing inside.

The hair on the back of Bonvalot's neck stood up. "I put a sample of yak fur in that handkerchief. I cut it off the stranger's boots."

Lorin blanched. "Come now man, surely you don't believe that."

"I know what I saw," said Bonvalot, wiping the sweat from his brow. "Now do you see the strain I've been under? Nothing makes sense anymore."

"Then perhaps it wasn't a hallucination at all," said Lorin. "Perhaps the beggar you saw was real. An unemployed actor playing a sick joke to swindle a free meal out of you, and when his little charade backfired, he escaped through the kitchen door. It's an old trick, an unfortunate symptom of our present economic woes. Although I can offer no explanation for the mysterious yak boots."

"I suppose it's possible that the man deceived me with his costume and grainy Russian accent," said Bonvalot, walking over to the window and staring out at the falling snow. "Or maybe the hallucination has already started to take a physical form—a fixed idea." Bonvalot turned to face his friend. "Henri, tell me how to stop these hallucinations for good. I don't want to end up like that artist who died in the Charenton asylum, or another laughing stock on the front page of *Le Charivari*."

"Don't get carried away, nothing of the sort is going to happen," said Lorin, joining his friend at the window. "I'm sure there's a reasonable explanation for all these goings on. Try to relieve your anxiety a little. Perhaps a glass of sherry before bed will help. When the mind is agitated, the hallucinations give the fixed idea more time to catch hold. If you choose to ignore them, they will simply fade away. Have you thought about settling down? A life of domestic tranquility has been known to cure many ills."

"Not a chance. I could never give up this life of adventure. I'll probably remain a bachelor all my life."

"That would be a pity but I won't argue with you on that point," said Lorin. "Now, if you want my advice, get cracking. Start planning your next expedition right away. There must be some unexplored region of the world that beckons you."

Bonvalot's face brightened. "Now that you mention it, I do have an idea I'd like to share with you."

Bonvalot strode over to the bookcase and selected a Schrader Atlas. He set it down on Lorin's desk and whisked through the pages until he came to a map of Central Asia.

"*Voilà*," said Bonvalot, beaming with pride. "The voyage of a lifetime. I propose to mount an expedition from Paris to Tonkin that will penetrate further into Tibet than any other modern explorer has ever done. Further even than Prejevalsky. My goal is to reach the holy city of Lhasa and greet the Dalai Lama himself. With the photographs I will take and the fortune in gold and manuscripts I will bring back, this journey will be a monumental triumph for France. What do you think?"

Lorin let out a deep breath. "It certainly would be an extraordinary achievement, *if* you make it back alive. But I won't try to talk you out of it. Since you're intent on making this journey, I suggest you speak to a colleague of mine, a Professor Philippe Édouard Foucaux, a noted Tibetologist. He lives in the Latin Quarter on rue Guy Lussac, between a cobbler's shop and a bakery, the Boulangerie Luxembourg. But I must warn you, he's a bit eccentric. Thinks he's the reincarnation of a Buddhist deity."

Bonvalot laughed. "If he's a Buddhist deity then he should already be expecting my call. Do you think he'll agree to see me?"

"Without a doubt," said Lorin. "He's eccentric, but not reclusive. I'm sure he'll be happy to meet you. The only question that remains now is whether or not the Tibetans are ready for you. I hear they're not keen on foreigners trampling on their holy city."

"Ready or not it's time Tibet opened up her doors to the world," said Bonvalot. "And I intend to be the one to force them open. The Forbidden Kingdom with all its legendary riches and gold mines has been isolated long enough. Which brings me to my biggest concern—money. Without a patron, I don't have a chance of reaching Tibet."

"Leave that to me, old boy," said Lorin, pouring two more cognacs. "Where money's concerned, I'm sure something suitable can be arranged."

CHAPTER 5

The next morning, Bonvalot scribbled out a hasty note to Professor Foucaux requesting the honor of a meeting with him and was surprised to receive a reply the very next day.

At the appointed time, Bonvalot hired a cab to drive him to the Latin Quarter, and when he spotted the Boulangerie Luxembourg, he ordered the driver to stop.

He entered the building and after consulting with the concierge, climbed a dingy staircase to the third floor and located a green shabby door. He knocked and held his breath.

He heard a shuffling sound coming from behind the door, followed by a cough. After several more minutes of shuffling, the door was opened by an elderly gentleman with expressive eyes, tufts of white hair, and a full white beard; the beatific expression on his face and the hint of a smile at the corners of his mouth put Bonvalot instantly at ease.

"Pardon me, but are you Professor Foucaux?"

"Indeed I am," smiled the gentleman. "And you must be that famous explorer I've been reading about in the newspapers. Well, come in, come in, Monsieur Bonvalot, don't want to catch cold standing out in the hallway. I've got a nice fire going and the water's just about to boil. Pardon the mess but my housekeeper has been out sick for so long I fear she may have died. If you can find a chair please have a seat while I bring us some tea. You do drink tea, don't you?"

"Indeed I do, thank you, sir," said Bonvalot, making his way over to a rickety dining chair.

"I'll just be a minute."

Professor Foucaux shuffled off to the kitchen, giving Bonvalot a chance to study the elderly professor's apartment. As he scanned the room, Bonvalot was impressed by the number of rare-looking volumes in the bookshelves, some of which appeared to be written in Sanskrit and Chinese, and others that were written in languages too obscure to be recognized. Lining one wall was a collection of paintings of seated Buddhas in bright colors, steeped in Buddhist imagery; other paintings were scattered about depicting a variety of scenes, including animals, mandalas, and exotic musical instruments. The rest of the room was more mundane, consisting of a worn-out sofa, mismatched chairs, a dilapidated china cabinet, and faded curtains.

Several minutes later there was a sudden crash followed by a loud oath, after which Foucaux reappeared bearing a chipped tea service that rattled like a skeleton as he made his way across the threadbare carpet. The elderly professor dropped the tea service on the table, then proceeded to lift the teapot with shaky, arthritic hands, splashing most of the tea into little puddles on the table. As Foucaux attempted to pour some tea into Bonvalot's cup, it took all of the agility the explorer could muster to make sure the tea ended up in the cup and not on his lap.

"Excuse me if I seem untidy and disorganized," said Professor Foucaux, plopping himself in his chair. "But it appears I misplaced my glasses and I've been forced to rely on my remaining senses to keep the house running. So tell me, Monsieur Bonvalot, how can an aging Tibetologist with a nagging case of arthritis be of service to you?"

"Actually, you could be of great service to me, Professor. That's why I've come to see you. I'm planning an expedition to Tibet, the most important expedition of my life, and I need some information. Tell me everything you know about the Forbidden Kingdom."

"Ah," said Professor Foucaux, setting down his teacup. "So it's my wisdom and knowledge you're after, not my pleasant company."

Bonvalot smiled. "Actually Professor, I find you rather *fascinating*."

"Yes, I've been told that before," said Foucaux. "My students think I'm charming and delightful, and not the least bit eccentric. Well, if it's Tibet you're after, you've come to the right place. The only question is, where do I start?" He picked up a strange object that was laying on the table, a hand-carved wooden drum attached to a spindle of sorts. "This object you see is a prayer wheel. The Tibetans believe that if you spin it with great devotion, all your prayers will ascend to the gods. It also comes in a much larger size but I couldn't fit it into my valise and I was afraid the customs officials would confiscate it. Tibet, as you may know, is one of the most mysterious lands in the world. Beyond the Himalayas is a land of strange customs, golden Buddhas, fantastic murals, remote lamaseries populated by saffron-robed monks who live lives entirely devoted to serving the Buddha. Marching through the streets of Lhasa you will find medieval soldiers wearing chain mail armor, with jewel-encrusted scabbards and lances. Mystical magical things beyond our human comprehension. What makes you so interested in seeing Tibet, Monsieur Bonvalot?"

"Tibet has always been a dream of mine," said Bonvalot. "I grew up reading about the adventures of Fathers Huc and Gabet when they reached the Forbidden City. As you may know, the death of the Russian explorer Nikolai Prejevalsky set off a firestorm all over Europe. There's a veritable Race to Tibet underway, with every explorer worth his salt endeavoring to be the first to reach this Buddhist kingdom. I believe I was born to win this race."

Professor Foucaux rubbed his chin philosophically. "I see the sort of man you are, Monsieur Bonvalot, chasing after adventure, lost civilizations, buried treasure. It makes great fodder for novels. But getting there won't be easy. What makes you think you're ready for this adventure?"

"I'm a realist, professor. I know the dangers I'm heading into, but that doesn't deter me in the least."

"Your honesty is refreshing, Monsieur Bonvalot. Despite my present decrepit state, I was once young and adventurous like you. More than anything I yearned to see the world, to soak up all the knowledge and wisdom contained in ancient volumes and remote monasteries. I struck out on my own, trekking across India, Nepal, and most of Sikkim. I saw wonderful things, exquisite temples, met exalted people, fell in love with a beautiful Sikkimese girl high up in the Himalayas. She was like the snow lotus that grows high up in the mountains: delicate, supple, fragrant, and beautiful despite the harsh surroundings. But that's all gone now; there's no use bringing up the past. I'm old, useless, and forgotten. My heart is weak and my mind is going, but maybe, just maybe, I have something that I can share with you."

Bonvalot leaned forward. "I need your help, professor. Please tell me more, everything you can remember about Tibet."

Professor Foucaux stroked his beard. "I've heard it said that Lhasa means *The place of God.* If I was only thirty, no, twenty years younger I would offer to accompany you on this mountain trek. In truth, I came quite close to reaching Tibet all on my own, before I was forced to turn back due to illness. Despite the incredible hardships, I made an enormous breakthrough. During one especially arduous journey to a Tibetan lamasery in Sikkim in the summer of my fortieth year, a kindly lama took me under his wing, having divined by means of sorcery and astrology that I was the fulfillment of a prophecy concerning a Buddhist incarnation that would rise out of the West. The next thing I knew, the entire lamasery was convinced that I was Amitabha, the incarnation of a celestial Buddha from the West. Soon, the lamas began teaching me all the secrets of their sect, all the mysteries that had been shrouded from European eyes since the dawn of time. With this information, I traveled around the countryside visiting temples and monasteries where I went to work copying manuscripts and searching for texts that would enhance my own research. Due to my newly exalted status, I was able to witness strange rituals that no other European eyes had ever seen. I wrote everything down in a manuscript, but seem to have misplaced it. Haven't seen it in years."

Bonvalot was on the edge of his seat. "That is indeed an extraordinary story. Do you remember anything specific about the manuscript?"

Professor Foucaux narrowed his cloudy eyes. "Very little, I'm afraid. It comes and it goes. Some days I can remember everything; other days, just a few scattered remnants. As you can see, my memory is not very reliable."

"Think hard, professor. I'm about to tackle the greatest challenge of my life. I need an edge, something that will get me to the head of the pack. Tell me how to conquer Tibet."

Professor Foucaux laughed. "It's not possible for any one man to conquer Tibet. It would take a god or at least a massive army to reach Lhasa. However, if you're serious about this endeavor, I'll tell you what you need to know. Tibet is a land where sorcery and astrology walk hand in hand. Protected from the outside by an icy barrier known as the Himalayas, and on the inside by an army of warrior-like lamas who are sworn to keep out all foreigners on pain of death, Tibet is the most impenetrable country in the world. Even the most intrepid explorers have been barred from the Forbidden City for more than fifty years. The only reports that have leaked out have been mostly geographical in nature, produced by those celebrated pundits.

"The Tibetans give all their allegiance to the Dalai Lama, in whose hands rest all matters of state, and worship the Panchen Lama, in whose hands rest all matters of the spirit. The Tibetans believe that both the Dalai Lama and the Panchen Lama are reincarnations of different aspects of the Buddha himself. To the Buddhists, death does not symbolize a break in the continuity of life; it means his form has been altered but his essence or his spirit continues through rebirth in a new form. In the case of the Dalai Lama, the Tibetans believe that when a Dalai Lama dies, he is reborn as a baby, duly selected by a delegation of lamas who set off in search of him. Once he reaches the age of four, he assumes the attire of a monk and is installed on a golden throne in the Potala Palace. In this manner, the new Dalai Lama continues an unbroken chain which goes back through the ages."

Bonvalot stared intently in the professor's eyes. "Tell me Professor how I can infiltrate this mysterious country?"

"Over the years I heard rumors about a 'southern road' that leads directly to Lhasa," said Foucaux. "It's used mainly by Buddhist pilgrims from Mongolia as they head south on their annual pilgrimage. They say the 'southern road' lies somewhere on the outskirts of Bokalik, a place according to legend that harbors a secret gold mine. You'll know you've found it when you reach the Kizil-Sou River."

"Can you find this 'southern road' on a map?"

Foucaux's bushy eyebrows went up and down several times as he stared at some invisible object contemplatively.

"Do you see that magnifying glass on my writing desk? Bring it to me along with that large atlas."

Bonvalot retrieved the items and the elderly professor opened up the atlas from which he extracted a faded map of Tibet.

"From what I've read," said Professor Foucaux, locking his cloudy eyes with Bonvalot's. "Most of the explorers who made it into Tibet have come by way of Leh and Ladakh to the West, but their efforts did not bear fruit. They were stopped hundred of miles before reaching Lhasa. Here, look close. Can you see this?"

"See what?"

The professor pointed to a mountain range that cut through the center of Tibet.

"This pass here. The natives call it the Amban Ashkan Davane and it crosses through the Chimen Tagh mountain range. South of the pass you will come to the 'unfreezing lake,' a lake so salty it remains unfrozen the entire winter. Follow the trail south until you reach the gold mines at Bokalik, which is situated 120 miles southeast of the foot of the pass. From there, you can pick up the 'southern road' and follow it south until you reach the Dam Pass, which lies at the center of four large mountains. This is the final roadblock to Lhasa. If you can make it through the Dam Pass without getting stopped, you're as good as there. But be careful. The Tibetans will use every trick in the book to keep you out of their Holy City. I'll leave this old map in your capable hands, Monsieur Bonvalot."

Professor Foucaux handed the map to Bonvalot, who cradled it in his hands.

"This doesn't sound very promising Professor Foucaux. Perhaps I'm out of my league."

The professor laughed. "On the contrary, Monsieur Bonvalot, I know you're the right man for the job."

"How so?"

"Because you came to see me. It shows you're on the right track. Now, before you head out on your quest, there's something I must ask of you."

"And what is that?" said Bonvalot.

"While I was in Sikkim I heard of another prophecy, that of a reincarnated goddess, the earthly incarnation of Kali, the consort of the god Siva. I believe the implications of this prophecy are quite significant in this day and age. If you find evidence of the fulfillment of this prophecy, bring it back to me. I promise to reward you greatly for your efforts."

"Unfortunately, I know nothing about Tibetan Buddhism," said Bonvalot. "How will I know when I've discovered the fulfillment of this prophecy?"

"I suppose you'll have to rely on karma, Monsieur Bonvalot. A man of your stature should attract a fair amount of it. The good kind, I mean. In any case, good luck on your expedition. I hope I've been able to help you in your quest."

Bonvalot shook the elderly professor's hand. "In more ways than I can ever repay."

CHAPTER 6

Several days later, Gabriel Bonvalot and Henri Lorin drove down the cobblestoned Rue de l'Elysée and stopped in front of Number Two, the mansion of Baron Maurice de Hirsch. They paid the carriage driver and mounted the steps to the front door, noting the magnificent façade consisting of oval windows, ornate pilasters, and Spanish-style grillwork; the miniature potted trees that graced the stairway and at each side of the imposing front door were manicured to perfection. Lorin had arranged this meeting with the Baron in the hope it would solve Bonvalot's money problems and bring him closer to his goal of reaching Tibet. For his part, Baron Hirsch had hinted that there was an important individual who was eager to accompany Bonvalot on his next expedition. The implied quid pro quo was one of the necessary evils that existed in the world of exploration, adding an unnecessary element of surprise.

"It's now or never," mumbled Bonvalot. Lorin nodded in return. They rang the bell and announced their names to a butler, who led them up a winding porphyry staircase to the Baron's apartment. Lingering in the anteroom, they paused to admire the valuable paintings and rare antiques that rivaled the best works of art ensconced in the Louvre. Every now and then, they exchanged a worried glance as they steeled themselves to meet one of the richest and most powerful men in all of Europe.

At the age of fifty-seven, Baron Maurice de Hirsch had reached the height of his career. He regularly advised heads of state and was on familiar terms with royalty. The son of a wealthy Bavarian banker, Hirsch had parlayed his considerable business acumen to reach the pinnacles of fame and fortune, being now worth a reputed twenty million pounds. Baron Hirsch was also known for being the primary sponsor of a pretender to the French throne, Robert, Duke of Chartres, a grandson of King Louis Philippe I. Two years ago, Baron Hirsch had suffered the tragic loss of his only son from the ravages of tuberculosis. As a result, the Baron and his wife had turned to philanthropy as a way to ease their pain.

After an interminable wait, a butler finally showed Bonvalot and Lorin into the Baron's study.

As soon as they entered, Baron Hirsch rose from his desk and strode over to greet the visitors. Something about the baron put Bonvalot felt instantly at ease. Sporting an affable face, round, dark eyes, a receding hairline and a large, walrus moustache, Baron Hirsch didn't fit the image of a heartless banker. He looked more like a professor of Latin or Greek. He wore a black frock coat, a waistcoat, and a white shirt with a turned over collar and a silk ascot tie. The Baron, however, was not alone. Sitting sphinx-like beside the Baron's desk was a man they instantly recognized as Prince Robert, Duke of Chartres. Bonvalot shot Lorin a look of surprise as the latter's eyebrows rose in wonder.

Baron de Hirsch spoke first. "Gentlemen, thank you for coming on such short notice. Allow me to introduce his Excellency Prince Robert, Duke of Chartres. Excellency, allow me to present Monsieur Gabriel Bonvalot of the Geographical Society and Monsieur Henri Lorin, Professor of Colonial Geography at the University of Bordeaux."

"*Bonjour*," said the Duke, nodding in their direction. Bonvalot and Lorin bowed and shook the Duke's hand, noting the tired expression in his eyes and the premature grey hair that clung to his widening scalp; his gaunt frame and wrinkled face made him appear much older than his forty-nine years. The Orléans royal family was not without its share of woes. Years earlier, Emperor Louis-Napoléon Bonaparte, ruler of the Second French Republic, had confiscated all their property and sent them into a humiliating exile. To make matters worse, the Duke's son, Prince Henri d'Orléans had become a fixture of the gutter press with his hair-raising exploits.

"Gentlemen, please have a seat," said the Baron, pointing to a sofa and some chairs. "Let's have a brandy." The Baron opened a mahogany bar with gilded edges, and pulled out a crystal decanter and four tumblers, which he filled and passed around to his guests.

Holding up their glasses, the Duke offered a toast to France and the men drank, eyeing each other nervously. Finally, Baron Hirsch opened up a cigar box and, after selecting four of the choicest, passed them around and proceeded to light them for his guests.

The Baron puffed on his cigar and smiled. "Tell me, gentlemen, have you visited the Expo at night when it's all lit up with those magnificent new electric lights? And what is your impression of the Arab Fantasy with those splendid swordsmen on horseback? Or what about those veiled dancing girls clicking those tiny castanets with such precision? Have you ever seen anything quite so charming?"

"Indeed, it's all very amusing," said Bonvalot, smiling uneasily as he elbowed Lorin discreetly in the ribs, causing his friend to mouth, 'what' in surprise. "I can't get enough of it. I've visited the Expo at least a half dozen times already."

"And you, Professor Lorin," said the Baron, turning his attention to Henri. "What do you think of the Palace of Industry, with all those modern inventions?"

"Very impressive, my lord" said Lorin, smiling at the Baron. "It shows beyond a shadow of a doubt that in matters of science, France has been the great pioneer. And I believe that applies to architecture as well, which reminds me, you have a splendid view of the Eiffel Tower from that window over there."

The Baron turned to glance out the window. "Indeed. I watched them put the whole thing up. I don't care what the naysayers say, the Eiffel Tower is a credit to the Republic. And I don't believe it's chauvinistic to say that the splendor of Paris is unmatched by any other city anywhere in the world."

The Duke cleared his throat.

"Oh, yes," continued the Baron. "In the interest of time, I think we should get started. His Excellency has asked me to arrange this meeting so we can—"

"If you'll allow me," interrupted the Duke. "Gentlemen, thank you for coming. The reason why I've called you here today is on behalf of my son, Prince Henri. I have a proposal for you that I believe will be mutually beneficial for all parties. As you are probably aware, the Chamber of Deputies has passed the law forbidding members of the royal family from occupying public functions, which includes all aspects of military service. Like you, the aristocracy possesses strong patriotic feelings toward France, and as such, we have a natural desire to serve the Republic in any manner that is permitted to us, but because of this law, our choices are extremely limited. Unfortunately, this has affected Henri more than anyone else, as he greatly desired a career in the military. For this reason, I've been looking into other possibilities for him. And that, my dear Monsieur Bonvalot, is where you come into the picture. I need a man who can take my Henri under his wing and make something out of him. If you'll excuse my candor, the prince has a taste for pursuits that are beneath the dignity of his rank. What he needs is a proper mentor."

Bonvalot shifted uncomfortably in his seat.

The Duke let out a deep sigh and continued, "As you know, the House of Bourbon has suffered more than its share of tragedy. Every indiscretion, no matter how slight, ends up on the front pages of *Le Petit Journal* and *Le Charivari,* distorted beyond all reasonable proportions. I must protect Henri's honor, and keep our name out of the gutter press, no matter what the cost. And now, due to a recent scandal that ended up in the newspapers, I must ship Henri out of the country as quickly as possible."

"You could send him to Oxford University," interrupted the Baron, leaning back in his chair as he puffed on his cigar. "I hear they have an excellent fencing team."

"I'm afraid that's not quite far enough," replied the Duke, rubbing his forehead with the palm of his hand.

Bonvalot leaned forward. "Your Excellency, I think I understand where this conversation is heading, and while I sympathize with your plight, I don't think I'm the right—"

"Monsieur Bonvalot," interrupted the Duke. "It has come to my attention that you are seeking a patron for your next expedition. Is that not correct?" Bonvalot narrowed his eyes. "What I need for Henri is a mind-broadening activity, something that will improve his mind, increase his knowledge. He recently returned from a six month hunting expedition to India where he showed great promise as a marksman. He brought back dozens of tiger skins and numerous elephant tusks and rhino horns, but the minute he got back to France he wasted no time in embroiling himself in a pointless duel defending the dubious honor of an opera singer. Idle hands are the devil's playthings."

"I'm not sure I'm following you."

"To put it bluntly, Monsieur Bonvalot," said the Duke. "With the generous patronage of Baron Hirsch, I'm willing to finance your next expedition, provided, of course, you take along Henri as your full partner."

Bonvalot furrowed his brow. "With all due respect, Excellency, I'm not sure that's a good idea. A shooting party to India is one thing, but an expedition into dangerous, uncharted territory is something else entirely. My work is not for amateurs."

"I know all about your work," said the Duke. "And that is precisely why I called you here today. I believe you and Prince Henri will make a superb team. It's very costly to organize an expedition, isn't it? How much do you think it would cost? Ten thousand francs? Twenty thousand francs?"

"Fifty thousand francs."

The Duke let out a long breath. "Are you mad? Do you think you can raise that kind of money on your own? However, if you agree to take Henri along, your problem is solved. Your success will be guaranteed. This is the best chance for Henri to make something of himself."

"Your Excellency, that's most generous of you, and I'd love to help, but you must understand, an expedition of this sort entails numerous dangers and hardships. The risk would be far too great for a prince of royal blood. You remember what happened to the Prince Impérial when he fought the Zulus…"

The Baron chimed in. "Monsieur Bonvalot, we are not discussing fighting another Zulu War, but an expedition of scientific importance, which is exactly what France needs to reclaim her rightful stature in the world. I believe that's exactly what his Excellency is seeking for Henri."

Bonvalot bit his lip. "I see your point, but I have certain rules about how I run my expeditions."

The Duke eyed Bonvalot as he puffed his cigar. "Rules?"

"On any expedition there can only be one leader, and that is me. My decisions are final. Then there is the matter of assigning duties. Prince Henri will be expected to carry his own weight just like everyone else on the team. But before I agree to take him on, I would like to meet him first."

The Baron leaned forward. "That sounds fair, Monsieur Bonvalot. When you meet Henri you'll see he's a most agreeable young man. He'll make a splendid addition to your team."

"That may be correct but is Henri suited for the rigors of a lengthy expedition?" said Bonvalot.

The Duke slammed his cigar in the ashtray. "He's perfectly suited, Monsieur Bonvalot, this I can assure you. He's an expert marksman and horseman. When the Academy of Saint Cyr closed its doors to Henri, they doomed him to a life of idleness and wantonness. I know my son wants more out of life than horse races and casinos. The way I see it, Henri is the perfect candidate for this expedition."

"Then I shall just have to see for myself," said Bonvalot.

"Very well," said the Duke, grudgingly. "By the way, where do you propose to go on your next expedition?"

Bonvalot walked over to a map of the world that was hanging on a wall. He pointed to the white spot to the extreme northeast of India.

"Gentlemen," he said. "This blank spot is Tibet. It's the least explored region in the world. Even in this modern age, we know very little about the exact locations of major cities and the precise altitudes of mountain peaks. We have no reliable information regarding population, mineral resources, fresh water supplies, and locations of major rivers, lakes, and waterways. Please bear with me as I trace our intended route."

Starting in Paris, Bonvalot traced a line across the map to Berlin, Moscow, Kuldja, across the Tian Shan Mountains to Korla, then across the Taklamakan Desert and over the Kunlun Shan Mountains to the Tibetan plateau, also called the Chang Tang, then straight south to Lhasa before veering off into Yunnan where he followed the Mekong River all the way to Tonkin.

"There you have it, gentlemen, an overland journey of over 6,000 miles, from Paris to Tonkin by way of Tibet."

Baron Hirsch uttered a low whistle. "Very ambitious, Monsieur Bonvalot. But isn't an expedition of this nature very risky? To my memory, Tibet has been closed to foreigners for years. And what about those rumors that the Tibetan authorities put to death any citizen who helps foreigners?"

"Yes, this expedition entails a great deal of risk," said Bonvalot. "The natives will use every tactic to turn us around, including threats of violence and death. The only question is, does your son have the fortitude to withstand a trip such as this?"

"I've never heard of Henri shying away from risk," said Baron de Hirsch. "If anything, he embraces it."

"I will let Henri decide for himself, Monsieur Bonvalot," said the Duke of Chartres. "*After* the two of you become acquainted, of course."

"Splendid," said Baron de Hirsch. "I have no doubt the two of them will get along splendidly."

Later, when the Duke summoned Prince Henri to meet Bonvalot, the other three gentlemen excused themselves on the pretext of going off to inspect the Baron's prized collection of antique guns.

Prince Henri entered the Baron's study with the air of a self-possessed aristocrat. Bonvalot looked at him with amusement. Henri was a well-set-up young man, blond, athletic, with deep blue eyes, a sardonic wit, and a worldly, jaded air, but still possessing all the youthful enthusiasm one would normally expect in a bachelor of twenty-two, especially on the subject of guns and hunting. The young prince walked around Hirsch's office a bit, admiring the various souvenirs and curiosities that lined the shelves before snatching a cavalry saber off the wall and—after completing a hasty *en garde*—launching into some fancy thrusts and a superbly-executed lunge that resulted in a decapitated potted plant.

Finally, Prince Henri turned to face Bonvalot. "So you're Gabriel Bonvalot, the world-famous explorer," he said, thrusting the saber into the soil. "It's an honor to meet you. I've read all your books cover to cover. Or at least my valet Charles has read them— to me, that is. As far as valets go, he's very well-read. Useful chap."

The young prince opened the Baron's cigar box and selected a choice model. First he sniffed it, then he rolled it between his fingers before collapsing on the sofa. He kicked his feet up on the coffee table and lit the cigar with a stylish flick of his hand. Then he sat puffing it for several minutes as he ran his free hand absentmindedly through his blond locks. Bonvalot took a seat opposite the young prince and studied the young pretender with amusement.

"I hear you fancy yourself an explorer," said Bonvalot. "From what I've read in the newspapers, you're quite the man-about-town. Tell me more about yourself."

The young prince smiled effusively. "I prefer to call myself a man of the world. I've gotten the travel bug pretty bad, but lately it seems as though I can do nothing right. I can't take a quick piss without some blockhead journalist sneaking up on me and embellishing it for the entertainment of the masses. Most of it is complete nonsense. If they print rubbish about me in *Le Petit Journal*, the only guilty parties are those that buy it. I hope no one actually believes that tripe. Are people really so gullible to believe I would actually pay a clairvoyant to predict the outcome of a horse race?"

Bonvalot leaned back in his chair. "So those stories about the opera singer weren't true?"

Henri blew out a dark cloud of smoke. "That was supposed to be a private party. She was a lovely girl but she never told me she was married. There are certain inherent problems when you're a man in my position; people always try to take advantage of you, to enrich themselves at your expense. And there's another thing, if we decide to go through with this project, it's only on condition you agree to not go blabbing to the newspapers. I want to keep this discreet."

Bonvalot laughed. "I hear the English papers have dubbed you the *princely plunger*."

"Ha, ha. You're a funny man, Monsieur Bonvalot. But as they say, horse racing is the sport of kings. Fortunately or not, it's in my blood."

"Very well, now tell me about those six months you spent in India."

"We had a spiffing time, top notch. It was me, Charles, and Monsieur de Boissy, a former military officer my father hired to act as my unofficial chaperon. Jail keeper is more like it. We docked in Bombay and hired a team of coolies, two of the buggers splitting the minute they found out we were heading up to tiger country. Later we made our way over to Calcutta, where I chanced upon my cousin, the Duke of Orléans, who was anxious to accompany us, but the old windbag Lord Dufferin forbade him since he promised to join an Indian rifle regiment. Next we hit upon the Golden Temple, the Taj Mahal, and dined *al fresco* with the Rajah of Jodhpur, which was like a scene out of *The Arabian Nights*. But I didn't enjoy any of it since all I could think about were the tigers. They became a grand obsession. All my life all I ever wanted was walk with tigers, to line one up in my sights, squeeze the trigger, and watch the blasted thing writhing in agony. I must have shot over two dozen of them from the back of an elephant. I can't begin to describe what it felt like when I shot my first tiger. It was a sensation unlike any other I've experienced in my life; even better than opium."

"So you fancy yourself a good marksman, eh?"

The prince assumed a thoughtful look. "Hunting is more than just good marksmanship. The most important skill you need to be a good hunter is scouting. What good is expert marksmanship if you can't find the bloody game? If my trip to India taught me anything, it's that I know I'm perfectly capable of shooting in cold blood. I've got the trophies to prove it."

"Tell me more," said Bonvalot, putting his hands behind his head.

"Monsieur Bonvalot, if it's guns you want to discuss, I could sit here all day and discuss them with you. I've got a full arsenal at my disposal including a twelve-gauge shotgun, a Martini-Enfield 577 carbine, a 450 carbine, a Lee-Enfield No. 8, and a Winchester. I broke the bank when I bought the 577 from Purdey's, but I consider it a sound investment. For big game hunting, there's nothing better."

"I feel I should warn you, where we're headed there won't be any tigers or elephants."

Prince Henri raised an eyebrow. "And where exactly is that?"

Bonvalot leaned forward. "My friend, we are going to Tibet."

Prince Henri sat up straight. "You're not joking, are you? Tibet? That's absurd. I'm more inclined to go hunting crocodiles down in the Congo. If there's no big game hunting in Tibet, what the deuce do you expect me to do all day?"

"I'll teach you everything you need to know to be an explorer. You'll learn to take altitude readings with a hypsometer, and conduct field surveys with a theodolite. I'll show you how to collect biological samples and how to dry and store them. At other times you'll be expected to perform guard duty like all the others. There are no special privileges on my expeditions. Knowing all this, do you still want to go?"

Prince Henri snuffed his cigar out. "Do I have a choice? My father thinks this is the only chance I have to make a name for myself. As for me, I live for adventure and the thrill of the chase, but I'll do whatever it takes to raise the Tricolor for the glory of France. Yes, Monsieur Bonvalot, I would like very much to be a part of your team."

"Excellent, there's just one final thing you must understand. On any expedition there can only be one leader, which in this case is me. Got it?"

"Balderdash! That's going a little too far. After all, my father is sponsoring the entire expedition."

"With all due respect, your father's input ends the minute he hands me a bank draft for fifty thousand francs. Your job is to apply yourself and learn something. If we achieve this goal it's very likely we will be awarded the gold medal of the Geographical Society. Now, can I count on your full cooperation?"

Henri smiled wanly. "I suppose so. When do we leave?"

"July at the latest. I'll draw up an itinerary and a list of supplies you'll need to buy and send it over as soon as possible. I'm planning on making you official photographer. And in the meanwhile, I suggest you cut down on cigarettes and get out in the fresh air more often. Build up your lung capacity. I'll be taking along an Army Railway Medical Companion, but I'd prefer to not have to use it."

"Look here, Monsieur Bonvalot, I'm as rugged and able-bodied as you are. But if it's pushing, pulling, lifting, and hauling you're talking about—that's coolie work. For fifty francs per month, you can get a native to do practically anything."

"When it comes to traveling to the four corners of the globe, I need men who are not afraid of a little hard work."

Prince Henri's smile twisted into a sneer. "You have a lot to learn, Monsieur Bonvalot."

CHAPTER 7

During the next several weeks, Bonvalot scrambled to make the final preparations for the trip. One afternoon, as he returned to his apartment straining under the weight of his purchases, the concierge handed him a letter. Dropping the packages, he scanned the handwriting. *Unmistakably feminine*, he thought. Turning it over, he saw there was no postmark.

"Someone delivered this?"

"A young woman, about so high, reddish hair, an urgent manner," said the concierge, indicating about medium height.

Adding the letter to his cumbersome pile, Bonvalot climbed the stairs to his second floor apartment. He turned the key in the lock and dropped the packages on the dining room table. Curious about the letter, he shuffled through a stack of invoices and correspondence on his desk until he found his letter opener, then he sliced open the envelope. Out slid a letter written in a lady's elegant handwriting on fine linen paper:

June 1889

Dear Monsieur Bonvalot,

I have taken up and laid down my pen several times before finding the courage to write to you. My reason for writing this letter, Sir, is to request your assistance in a matter of life and death.

My husband Armand Dancourt joined a surveying party that was headed to Tibet when we lost all trace of him. Some travelers returning from Turkestan reported hearing a rumor about a party of Europeans that was ambushed by bandits and disappeared without a trace. While it is indeed possible that all the members of the caravan were murdered, I believe it's possible that Armand escaped, joined a native caravan, and may be somewhere in Tibet.

But after six months with no news, my heart has grown weary from the pain of uncertainty. Therefore, I find myself compelled to find out for myself exactly what happened to my husband.

Through a dear friend of my father's who is a member of the Geographical Society, I found out about your agreement with the Duke of Chartres to organize an expedition to Tibet. Therefore, I entreat you in the strongest possible manner to take me along with you as a member of your party. I intend to pay my way and will not be a burden to you in any manner. As wretched as I am, I no longer fear for my own safety, but seek only to uncover the truth about my husband. Indeed, I pray that I shall have the good fortune to find a kind-hearted person who knows something about my husband's fate and will take pity on me. My only wish is to know whether or not he still lives, and if he does not, that I should discover the circumstances surrounding his death.

I beg you to accept, Sir, the assurances of my highest consideration.

Yours faithfully,
Camille Dancourt

Bonvalot's brow furrowed. What this woman is asking for is completely out of the question. Surely Armand Dancourt is dead by now, yet she's brave enough—or foolish enough— to risk her life searching for him on the Roof of the World on the slim chance he may still be alive. Gallant soul! But regardless of her courage and steadfastness, I must decline her request.

Bonvalot went to the kitchen to boil himself a pot of tea. As he reclined on the sofa with his warm mug and plate of biscuits, he tried to put the woman's letter out of his mind as he checked and rechecked his packing list, crossing out those items he had already purchased:

Bulls-eye Lantern
Prismatic Compasses
Thermometers, min. & max. & regular
Pocket Chronometer
Hypsometer (Hicks)
3" Explorer's Theodolite (Cooke)
Micrometer

Pocket Compass
Army Railway Medical Companion
Boots, Ordinary Infantry Ammunition Pattern
Trooper's Saddles

Lying on the floor several feet away was a long wooden box marked DANGER FIREARMS that held the battery. In it were two double barreled 500 express rifles, one 12-bore shot gun, two cavalry regulation carbines, and three revolvers. A second box labeled EXPLOSIVES held three hundred rounds for the express rifles, two hundred for the shotgun, two hundred for the carbines, and a case of revolver ammunition. Bonvalot eased over to the boxes, tossed in more sawdust, and packed it down firmly. Then he sat back on the floor to reconsider the woman's heart-wrenching request.

After thinking the matter over, he got up and retrieved the letter. He read it again from start to finish, this time concentrating on the words, *As wretched as I am, I no longer fear for my own safety, but seek only to uncover the truth about my husband.*

He pictured a grieving widow in a black veil surrounded by crying children. Under the circumstances, they would need their mother more than ever. Shaking his head, he went over to his writing desk and pulled out a sheet of monogrammed stationary and a fountain pen. Being an impulsive man who often regretted his actions after it was too late, Bonvalot composed a terse but sympathetic response to the lady's query:

Dear Madame Dancourt,

I received your letter today and while I sympathize with your tragic situation, I regret that taking a woman on expedition is simply out of the question. The dangers of traveling across Central Asia and Tibet are far too numerous for me to guarantee your safety. As a rule, I don't even allow the wives of my caravan drivers to accompany us on expedition.

Therefore, I must respectfully decline your request. However, if you will supply me with a photograph of your husband, I will endeavor to make inquiries on your behalf with the intention of locating his whereabouts. Additionally, it would be helpful if you would provide me with information regarding the exact location of where your husband wrote to you last. With the help of Providence and some cooperative natives, we may succeed in bringing you some concrete news. You may forward the photograph to the same address.

Please accept, Madame, the expression of my distinguished sentiments.

Sincerely,

Gabriel Bonvalot

He sat back, satisfied that his response showed the appropriate level of concern without making any promises he would not be able to fulfill. He sealed and addressed the envelope, hoping this would be the last he would hear from Madame Dancourt.

Several days later, Bonvalot was dining in Café Tortoni when a shadowy figure approached his table. Startled, he jerked backward, splashing soup on his waistcoat.

"Forgive me, Monsieur Bonvalot, I didn't mean to startle you."

Looking up, Bonvalot was relieved to see a handsome, well-set-up young man of about twenty years old in a sack suit and top hat. Next to him was an attractive young woman a few years older. She was staring intently at Bonvalot with cerulean eyes that burned right through him.

"Don't worry, Monsieur. No harm done," said Bonvalot, using his napkin to mop up the soup.

"So it is you. You *are* Gabriel Bonvalot, the world-famous explorer," said the young man.

"Indeed," said Bonvalot. "Have we met before?"

The young man held out his hand. "I don't believe we've had the pleasure. My name is François Raymond, and this is my sister, Madame Camille Dancourt. I believe you received a letter from my sister recently about her missing husband."

Bonvalot's face dropped. "Yes indeed, how do you do? I was very sorry to hear about your sad plight, Madame Dancourt. Truly, I wish there was more I could do to help."

Camille stepped forward. "Actually, Monsieur Bonvalot, there *is* something more you can do. If you have a few minutes, I'll explain."

Bonvalot hesitated for a moment before gesturing toward the empty chairs opposite him. "Please have a seat." He watched as the siblings eased themselves into their seats, the young man holding the chair for his elder sister with remarkable tenderness. And then his gaze fell on Camille Dancourt. She was, in a word, lovely. With her elegantly curved face and reddish-gold hair coiled in ringlets, she looked more like a Renoir portrait than a grieving, matronly widow. She wore a fashionable high-necked dress with buttons running down the bodice on either side, and on her head was a plumed hat with feathers that brought to mind the ring-necked pheasant from Central Asia, a prized game bird. When Camille pulled off her gloves, Bonvalot saw delicate hands that were smooth and polished like marble, and she displayed unusual determination in the way she clenched them.

"Thank you for agreeing to speak with us, Monsieur Bonvalot," said Camille. "To be perfectly honest, my brother and I followed you here from your apartment." Her face flushed at this inadvertent confession, but she continued nonetheless. "The reason for our boldness is to ask you to reconsider my request to join your expedition. I am determined to find my husband in Tibet and joining your caravan is the most efficient way for me to accomplish this. And if that is not possible, then I will simply organize my own caravan."

Bonvalot stifled a grin at the young woman's naïveté.

"Madame Dancourt, organizing a caravan is no simple matter. And I certainly do not advise rank amateurs to go traveling in the wilds of Central Asia. Unfortunately my answer is still no. I can't risk taking on a woman. Aside from the matter of propriety, you must understand that I cannot guarantee your safety."

Camille refused to back down. "I don't think you understand, Monsieur Bonvalot, I'm not looking for guarantees. This is my best chance to find my husband. Please reconsider—"

"Madame," interrupted Bonvalot. "What you're suggesting is simply not done. Women do not join caravans nor do they organize them on their own. Perhaps if you were the wife of a Raja or an Amir it would be conceivable, but not for a European woman. The very idea of it is absurd. It's not like going to the Expo and paying five francs to ride a donkey down the Rue de Caire, or having a gypsy tell your fortune. We are talking about uncivilized, hostile territory thousands of miles from home. Please Madame, let the experts do the searching for you. Now, if you'll give me a photograph of your husband, I give you my word as a gentleman that I will make every conceivable effort to locate him. That's about as much as I or anyone else can offer. These situations must be handled delicately. Too much probing by inexperienced foreigners can land the novice in hot water. Do you understand?"

Camille shook her head. "No, it is *you* who must understand, Monsieur Bonvalot. I must find Armand. I can't sit back helplessly and leave my husband's fate in the hands of mercenaries."

"If I may ask," said Bonvalot. "What was your husband doing in Tibet?"

"He was part of a surveying party sent to map the Himalayas. Somehow he became separated from the others and joined up with a native caravan which we believe was ambushed."

Bonvalot switched to a sterner tone of voice. "Madame, do you not see the unreasonableness of your request? It's not suitable for a lady to travel to such dangerous territory. Please be patient and wait until I send you word."

Camille's eyes blazed with intensity. "I'm out of patience. I can't wait any longer to find Armand. All this waiting and hoping is torturing me. I have to get out of Paris before I go mad!"

Camille's brother put a sympathetic arm around his sister's shoulder. Tears welled up in her eyes as she fished in her purse for a handkerchief. When she couldn't find one, Bonvalot threw her his own, but he was not swayed by this overt display of emotion.

"Madame, all the more reason you should stay here," he said. "You're too emotionally involved to be of much help. I wouldn't be able to trust your judgment out there on the road. The slightest mistake can cause innocent people to get killed."

Camille pressed the handkerchief to her eyes.

"Forgive my bluntness," said Bonvalot. "But as the leader of this expedition, I'm responsible for the lives of my men. It's a duty I don't take lightly. We're heading to the Roof of the World, where altitudes are so high, we believe they may exceed the capability of a normal human being to survive. At night the temperature drops to fifty degrees below zero and the air is so thin, no matter how much air you draw in, you never get enough, and then water begins to fill your lungs until you slowly drown. The lack of oxygen makes even simple tasks like walking, cooking, and thinking so hard all you want to do is lie down and fall into a deep sleep from which you may never awaken, while all around the wind howls without mercy, tormenting you like a demon and snow and hail thrash your face like icy knives. When frostbite sets in, your limbs are rendered useless until they turn black and drop off. These are the conditions we'll be facing, Madame Dancourt. Knowing all this, do you still wish to pursue this foolhardy mission to Tibet?"

"I wouldn't be here if I didn't."

"Then that is why I'm certain I cannot take you. You're not thinking clearly and your lack of judgment might force me to take chances I wouldn't normally take."

The lady opened up her purse and pulled out a wad of banknotes.

"Monsieur Bonvalot, I've brought two thousand francs. Take it, it's yours *if* you'll agree to take me along."

Bonvalot pushed her hand away. "I cannot accept your money. You still do not understand the risks of such an endeavor. The price for retrieving your husband is very high, especially if he's no longer alive." The bitter look in her eyes told him to soften his tone. "Forgive me Madame, I didn't mean to be so blunt, but let me explain something. An expedition to Tibet is something men prepare for all their lives. It's not something we undertake lightly. I can tell you're a brave woman and I appreciate what you're trying to do—heaven knows, I *admire* what you're trying to do, but I'm certain your husband would be against you undertaking such a dangerous journey on his behalf. Certainly if he were a decent, honorable man."

"Armand *is* decent and honorable. That's why I must find him and bring him home. I fear he's in terrible danger."

Bonvalot shook his head. "Monsieur Raymond, please take care of your sister. I regret to say there's nothing further I can do. As for you Madame Dancourt, I advise you to stay here in Paris and think about your future. That's what Armand would have wanted you to do."

"You're more concerned with your own success than helping a lady in distress," said Camille, her eyes blazing. "I'm not giving up just yet. I *will* go to Tibet even if I have to go by myself." She stood up abruptly. "I'm tired of people not listening to me. I thought you of all people would understand my situation."

Bonvalot stared at her in shock.

François put his arm over his sister's shoulder. "Calm down. Listen to what Monsieur Bonvalot is saying. Think about maman…"

She pushed his arm away. "I will *not* calm down, François. Nobody knows what it's like sitting alone in my apartment day after day waiting for news, waiting for a letter that will never appear. I don't care what anyone says anymore. I'm going to Tibet and I'll get there before you, Monsieur Bonvalot. *Au Revoir!"*

Camille turned and stormed out of the restaurant.

"Madame, wait," said Bonvalot, knocking over a glass of wine in his haste to grab her hand. But it was too late. Camille Dancourt raced through the crowded café, knocking off a gentleman's hat and stepping on a lady's foot in her haste. Her brother gave Bonvalot a sheepish look, then dashed after his sister.

Bonvalot watched the young lady disappear out the front door, he felt a gnawing pit inside his stomach. When he returned to his soup, it was lukewarm. He pushed it aside. Minutes later, when the waiter appeared with a steaming plate of *coq au vin*, Bonvalot waved him away with the excuse that he had lost his appetite.

"I'm sure I haven't seen the last of Camille Dancourt," he said, tossing his napkin down on the table.

CHAPTER 8

On the sixth of July, 1889, Bonvalot was at the Gare du Nord early, his ticket tucked in his breast pocket, his maps, charts, and compasses secured in his rucksack. A hired cab brought the rest of the luggage, which consisted of crates of guns and ammunition, railway bags, sleeping-sacks, saddlebags, trooper's saddles, and folded tents. After loading the luggage, Bonvalot took out his pocket watch and frowned. Prince Henri was nowhere to be found. He paced around the platform, sweat building up around his collar as he scanned the faces of the crowd.

Approximately fifteen minutes before departure, Prince Henri rolled into the station with a royal entourage consisting of the Duke of Chartres, his mother, Princess Françoise d'Orléans, and numerous siblings and relatives; a gaggle of elegantly-dressed ladies promenaded down the platform whom Bonvalot vaguely recognized from the society columns. The ladies nodded vaguely in Bonvalot's direction while they presented Henri with boxes of food, bottles of wine, and assorted presents for the trip. For his part, Henri was only too happy to present his clean-shaven cheek for their tender embraces.

"There's no need for all this fussing," said Henri. "I'll be back before you know it."

Meanwhile, the Duke of Chartres pulled Bonvalot aside.

"Good luck to you, Monsieur Bonvalot," said the Duke. "I leave Henri in your capable hands. I fear that if I don't break him of his bad habits I will lose him forever."

"He'll be fine. I'm confident I can handle him."

"Tell me, Monsieur Bonvalot, is everything in order? Have you made all the necessary arrangements?"

"Everything's been taken care of, sir," said Bonvalot, smiling with confidence. "However, I must warn you that once we leave

Chinese Turkestan our communication will be sporadic at best. There are no telegraph poles in the Taklamakan Desert and once we enter Tibet, we'll be completely cut off from the outside world. You won't hear from us until we reach the French Embassy in Hanoi."

"Are you sure you can pull this off?" said the Duke.

"I do not wish to tempt the fates," said Bonvalot. "But I feel we shall have a great success. Consider it a *fait accompli*. Prince Henri and I will go down as the greatest explorers of the modern age. Together we'll conquer the Forbidden City of Lhasa."

"Then I shall leave it in your capable hands, Monsieur Bonvalot. And keep an eye on Henri. He's rash, reckless, and imprudent. When he starts drinking he's impossible. I hope you're up to the task."

"I've dealt with much worse in my career," said Bonvalot. "There's nothing a good fistfight can't fix. But if you're really worried about Henri's drinking, I will confiscate all his liquor."

The Duke smiled. "Do whatever it takes. I just hope that when Henri returns, he's a changed man. Well, good luck and bon voyage."

The two travelers were barely settled in their first class compartment when a disheveled vagrant with cracked skin, bloodshot eyes, matted hair, and a frayed overcoat entered the coach and shuffled down the aisle toward them. Bonvalot's stomach leapt in his chest. *Prejevalsky.* He struggled to remember Henri Lorin's advice. What was it? *When you engage a hallucination, you may cause it to return again and again, each time taking a stronger hold over the mind until it becomes a fixed idea. You must fight these hallucinations or risk disaster.*

By the time the vagrant reached their compartment, Bonvalot's heart was pounding and sweat was rolling down his temples, but he resisted the urge to look at the intruder. He turned to look out a window, but from the corner of his eye, he could see the vagrant stopping and peering inside their compartment, a devilish grin on his face. Gripping his armrest, Bonvalot turned and met the stranger's gaze and then, without warning, the vagrant attempted to enter their compartment.

Bonvalot leapt from his seat and jostled the vagrant down the aisle and onto the platform. The two men struggled, clashing violently despite the parade of onlookers. Prince Henri watched the unfolding commotion with mounting curiosity. The only thing he knew for sure was that Gabriel Bonvalot, France's most famous explorer, was standing on the railway platform arguing with someone, but he could not for the life of him make out who it was. He pulled out his flask and smelled it just to be sure. Nothing out of the ordinary there. Shrugging, he chalked it up to a misunderstanding over a tip and returned his attention to the society column.

Once outside the train, Bonvalot wasted no time in getting the upper hand with Prejevalsky. He pressed an index finger into the interloper's chest and issued a stern warning.

"Listen to me you bastard. I want no part of you. Get out of here."

"Don't be a fool," said Prejevalsky. "You can't make it to Tibet without me. You need me."

"That's a lie. I don't need you, now go away. You have no business being here."

"I have a ticket right here," replied his rival, waving a crumpled and stained ticket. "I have as much right to be here as anybody else. This time I'm going to make it to Lhasa."

"Go away and leave me alone!"

"I'm not going anywhere," replied Prejevalsky, smiling in his inimical Russian manner with the glint of gold peeking out his mouth. He opened his arms in the Russian fashion, as if to embrace the enraged Frenchman, but made no contact. "Why so suspicious? Everything I do is out of kindness and consideration for you. Let me buy you a drink."

"Keep away from me, you devil. Take that as a warning."

"Why do you have to resort to such language with a fellow traveler?" said Prejevalsky, feigning injury. "You've hurt my feelings. Aren't we both gentlemen? Come, let's have some vodka to toast your success."

"Not so fast Prejevalsky," said Bonvalot. "I've been reading up on you. All the experts say your travel books are loaded with inconsistencies. According to Baron von Richthoven, you never explored the Lob Nor."

A dark shadow fell across Prejevalsky's face. "Baron von Richthoven is a filthy liar. He knows nothing about my work. I should cut his lying throat!"

"It's too late for that. You had your chance and now it's my turn. I'm going to finish the job you started and I don't need you or anyone else meddling in my affairs."

Prejevalsky grabbed the lapel of Bonvalot's jacket and pulled him inches off the ground. "Don't be a fool you over-confident, stubborn little mule. You don't know the Asiatic mind like I do. They're bloodthirsty, cheating scoundrels. Get it through your thick skull. If you want to reach Tibet, your only hope is to take my advice. And why do you insist on hiding that little French pansy from me? When I take him under my wing, I will make him a first-rate explorer, a worthy successor to carry on my name and my work."

Bonvalot struggled to free himself from his adversary's grip, but it was impossible. He pounded his head, clawed at his face until the latter released him with a terrifying howl.

"I'm warning you," said Bonvalot, gasping for breath. "Stay away from my men. *All* of them, and especially Henri. If I catch you lurking around, I won't hesitate to shoot you."

Bonvalot turned and raced back to the coach, but before entering, he added, "Consider me armed and ready."

"You stupid Frenchman!" scoffed the hulking Prejevalsky as he pointed a menacing finger at Bonvalot. "I've had enough of you. I'll make sure you never make it to Lhasa. And moreover, I'll make sure you never make it out of Tibet alive!"

Bonvalot watched as Prejevalsky stalked off to the Third Class Coach, his hulking figure disappearing amidst the crowd. The train whistle blew and steam hissed, prompting Bonvalot to hurry to his seat. No sooner had he reached his compartment when he felt the grind of metal against metal as the train began to move. He sat down and let out a deep breath.

Henri glanced up from his newspaper. "What the devil was that all about? Who were you arguing with?"

"Nobody. Only a filthy beggar."

"A beggar? In First Class?"

"A delusional one, no doubt. Claimed to be the dead Russian explorer Nikolai Prejevalsky."

Henri burst into laughter. "Is that all? The streets of Paris are full of those deluded lunatics. Usually they claim to be Napoleon or Robespierre before he was guillotined. Good you got rid of him. The poor devil probably escaped from the Charenton asylum and the *flics* are out looking for him."

"Well, I don't expect he'll bother us again," said Bonvalot, fumbling to light a cigarette. "I gave the scoundrel the boot."

For the duration of the trip, Bonvalot kept a wary eye out for his ghostly rival, but there no more sightings. The strange apparition seemed to have vanished. Logically speaking, Bonvalot knew that Prejevalsky was dead, but the visions of his menacing figure were so real he couldn't ignore them anymore. He worried that the hallucinations had already started to take on a fixed form.

CHAPTER 9

July, 1889

During the trip to Moscow, Bonvalot spent the greater portion of his time studying maps and charts of Tibet while Prince Henri frittered away the hours in the smoking car, playing baccarat and drinking heavily with an endless assortment of shady Eastern European aristocrats of lesser nobility.

As Bonvalot sat in his berth late one evening he found his mind wandering back to that night in Paris when he had first laid eyes on Camille Dancourt. Her spirited eyes and childish vulnerability haunted him with nagging doubts about the way he had refused her request. Had he been too hard-headed? Too callous? Too blindly ambitious? While he knew that logically speaking he had done the right thing, he couldn't help but feel he had somehow blundered.

When they reached the Russian frontier, the passengers were taken off the train and led into a large hall for the examination of their passports and luggage. As soon as they were out of customs, Bonvalot and Prince Henri hurried to catch the next train to Moscow. All the while Bonvalot kept a wary eye out for the menacing beggar, hoping that by sheer force of will the hallucinations would end once and for all.

"I say old chap," said the Prince, once they'd settled into their seats. "How did you manage to get us through Customs so quickly?"

Bonvalot smiled as he lit a cigarette. "In Russia they have a weakness for the golden metal and all its charms. Otherwise they would have kept us waiting until *zavtra*, tomorrow. I had to speed up the process since we have someone important to meet in Moscow. "

"When do you plan on filling me in on the details or do I have to wait and read about it in the Illustrated London News like all the riffraff?"

Bonvalot exhaled a plume of smoke. "Patience my dear boy, patience."

They reached Moscow in the middle of July when the flowers and trees were in full bloom, and the sunshine sparkled like glittery jewels on the Moscow River. As they entered the lobby of the Central Hotel, they were greeted by a formidable giant of a man who greeted Bonvalot like an old friend. Bonvalot introduced him as Rachmed, his trusted Uzbek traveling partner.

Rachmed laid his embroidered rucksack on the floor and embraced Bonvalot, his swarthy complexion, Turkish eyes, and heavy accent giving no doubt as to his origins in the East.

"Praise be to Allah!" said Rachmed. "Bonvalot-sahib has found his way back to Moscow."

"Rachmed my old friend," said Bonvalot. "Once again our paths cross. Allow me to introduce my new traveling partner, His Highness Prince Henri d'Orléans."

Rachmed bowed. "Welcome Your Highness, it is my great honor and pleasure to serve you."

Prince Henri sized the man up and down. "I assume this is the man you hired to be my valet. He looks entirely unsuitable, but I suppose he'll have to do. I'll have to break him in first."

Rachmed's eyebrows shot up. "Perhaps there has been some misunderstanding. I am Bonvalot-sahib's caravanbashi, his caravan leader. It is my job to keep order in the caravan. At it is written, if the sheep go astray, they are led by an ill goat."

Before Prince Henri could respond, the hotel manager raced across the lobby to greet them.

"Ah, Monsieur Bonvalot, we've been expecting you," said the manager, shaking their hands. "And I see you've brought your special guest. Welcome, Your Highness. We are honored by your presence. Step into my office for a minute, allow me to offer you a suitable refreshment."

Bonvalot motioned to Prince Henri. "Go along, Henri. I'll catch up. I need to speak to Rachmed for a minute."

When Prince Henri was safely out of earshot, Bonvalot pulled Rachmed over to a quiet corner and spoke in hushed tones.

"Listen my friend, some things are going to be a little different on this expedition."

Rachmed narrowed his eyes. "What do you mean?"

"Please understand, Henri is a nobleman. They're a different breed; they're used to being treated like royalty, even after they've been deposed. They believe that those of lesser rank, which means the rest of us, were born to serve them. All I ask is that you be patient. Play along, as if it were a game. He won't know any better. But if he acts too haughty, put him in his place." Bonvalot lowered his voice a little. "He actually thinks he's going to be king of France some day. He's what they call a *pretender to the throne*, but he has about as much chance of becoming King of France as you have of becoming King of Kashgaria. Got it?"

Rachmed chuckled. "Have no fear, Bonvalot-sahib. I will control my tongue like a snake charmer controls a snake. The most beloved of Allah are those who remain silent. But his Highness sounds about as arrogant as a peacock."

"He's lovable when you get to know him. Just remember one thing: you work for me. I'm paying your salary, not the prince. He cannot dismiss you no matter what you do."

"I will play this little game. I know all the customs and habits of the sahibs and the prince will never know that I'm not really a valet. Now tell me this big secret of yours. Where are we going on our next expedition?"

"I don't think now is the right—"

Rachmed gave him a stern look. "It's now or never."

"Very well, since you put it that way," said Bonvalot sheepishly. "We're headed to Lhasa."

Rachmed's jaw dropped. "What? Are you mad? What happened, did a donkey kick you in the head? You want to go to Lhasa? I think I'd better leave. I have to catch the next train back to Tashkent."

Rachmed bent down to retrieve his rucksack, but Bonvalot grabbed it out of his friend's hand.

"Not so fast, my friend," said Bonvalot. "I've already thought this over. I believe we can make it. Do you remember that old saying that if a camel gets his nose in the tent, his body will soon follow? Well, you and I are the camel's nose and Tibet is the tent. But I can't do it without you."

Rachmed shook his head. "Tibet is farther than Pleiades. A thousand misfortunes may befall us before we reach the Forbidden City."

"This will be the most important expedition of the century. Every explorer in the world wants to be the first to reach Lhasa. This can get us the gold medal of every Geographical Society in the world. And there's a lot of money at stake, fifty-thousand francs. If we succeed, I'll reward you handsomely. But I need your help. Are you with me?"

Rachmed bent down to retrieve his rucksack. "Khoub! Very well. But do I have a choice? As they say in Tashkent, every bad has its worse."

Bonvalot clapped Rachmed on the back. "Glad to see my old friend is back in fine form. I knew I could count on you. Now let's get going. I've got to run over to the French Embassy to retrieve the letters of introduction for the Chinese officials. We leave for Zharkent in four days."

Rachmed sighed. "Four days? Just enough time for me to write out my will."

CHAPTER 10

Kuldja, Chinese Turkestan
September, 1889

With their letters of introduction in hand, Bonvalot, Rachmed and Prince Henri set out by train across Siberia. Upon reaching Semipalatinsk, Bonvalot hired a tarantass, a horse-drawn carriage, to transport them across the steppes to Zharkent, the last town in Russian Turkestan.

As the horses trotted, they watched the landscape unfold from barley, wheat, and corn fields, to wide, undulating steppes, to an endless desert punctuated every now and then by round Kirghiz tents and herds of grazing horses. During this time, Prince Henri complained of boredom, hinting more than once that what he really wanted was the thrill of the chase. He hungered after big game, and when none was available, he took to drinking whatever was handy and shooting at passing birds and small animals for amusement. Bonvalot left him to his devices, muttering to Rachmed that he had no patience to act as a nanny to an unmanageable princeling.

When they reached Zharkent, the three travelers dusted themselves off and checked into the most hospitable-looking caravanserai, the one whose roof looked least likely to cave in. They collapsed with exhaustion on the Oriental carpets while a veiled servant girl brought out pots of steaming Kazakh tea and filled their cups several times.

After resting awhile, Bonvalot and Rachmed hurried off to organize the caravan. In the distance, the Tian Shan mountains cut across the sky like a purple-blue curtain shrouded in a misty haze. Bazaar sounds filtered through the air: the call of the muezzin from a distant minaret mingled with the braying of donkeys and the cries of merchants. At last they were on the Silk Road. Soon they would be entering a world that was even more unknown.

In the bazaar, they found half a dozen unemployed men, some of whom claimed to be experts in loading camels, but who they suspected of being habitual opium smokers. They took them on, knowing that once they reached Kuldja they could easily cast them off and hire a new group. Their numbers now increased to ten, with double as many horses and camels, the little caravan started out.

Their next stop was the town of Kuldja, a Silk Road town nestled at the foot of the Tian Shan Mountains. Kuldja consisted of sprawling rows of sepia-toned clay houses with flat roofs, a telegraph station, and dilapidated buildings with signs in Chinese, Arabic, and Russian. There was also a Russian Consulate that hearkened back to better days when Kuldja was a part of Russian Turkestan. Along a dusty promenade, a line of barbers had set up shop and were engaged in a brisk trade shaving the prostrate heads of customers who appeared to be bowed in prayer. Men with Mongolian faces, brown skin, long beards, and unkempt tunics were seen leading sheep and camels to the livestock market; other men with black Uzbek sheepskin caps were busy conducting a brisk trade in Oriental carpets. At the center of town, a mosque that resembled a Chinese-style pagoda was humming with activity as a continuous procession of the faithful marched to and from prayer like bees to the beehive.

That evening, Bonvalot and Prince Henri paid a visit to Colonel Uspensky, the Russian Consul. They found Uspensky to be an affable, scholarly man in his sixties with a well-groomed moustache, and a face that showed the effects of a lifetime spent in a desert outpost. Sitting in a drawing room that was a blend of East and West, with sagging Russian couches, Oriental carpets on both the floors and the walls, and bookshelves filled with crumbling volumes in Russian and French, Bonvalot noticed a pile of yellowed newspapers moldering in a corner and understood his Russian host's lonely existence.

Colonel Uspensky poured three glasses of brandy and proposed a toast to his distinguished guests. "*À votre santé*," he said, smiling. "To your health, gentlemen." Their host took a long, thoughtful sip, then stared off in the distance. "Ah…this brings back memories of the good old days," he said with a tinge of wistfulness. "Please forgive the modest accommodations, gentlemen, but I've been operating on a shoestring budget ever since the treaty to return Kuldja to the Chinese brought our way of life to an unceremonious end. Before the ink was even dry, almost the entire Russian colony packed up and fled across the border to Russian territory. Even most of the Dungans, which are Chinese Mohammedans, and Taranchis, Mohammedans of mixed Persian-Mongol stock, ran away when the Chinese took over. They took everything of value and loaded it onto the backs of mules and camels, then set fire to their homes so the Chinese couldn't make use of them, so deep is their hatred of the Chinese. When the Russians left they took all their culture and the salons that used to sustain us. Life here hasn't been the same since."

"I've always been a great admirer of Russian hospitality," said Bonvalot. "When I was in Samarkand two years ago, General Karalkoff was a superb host, always providing me with everything I needed, giving excellent advice, providing inspiration when all hope was lost. It was he who proposed the idea of crossing the Pamirs in the middle of winter to reach India."

Uspensky's eyebrows shot up. "Did he? That wouldn't surprise me. We're always looking for ways to push the frontier forward, never resisting any opportunity to cock a snook at the British Empire. And now we have British India within our sights. But while we would never dream of conquering India, every Russian soldier worth his salt dreams of invading it. Well, my conquering days are over now. You're a brave man for attempting the impossible, Monsieur Bonvalot. You took a huge chance with your life."

"Without a doubt," said Bonvalot. "That was the closest I ever came to dying. There were times I cursed the cold, the hunger, the hostile natives, and my luck. Without the assistance of Lord Dufferin I doubt we would have made it out of the Chitral fortress alive."

Uspensky chuckled. "All you explorers share the same love of danger. Like our Prejevalsky. There's a bit of a wild streak in all of you. Where would we sedentary types be without your adventures? You give us the chance to experience life's thrills vicariously through your stories and legends. Still, it's not often that I have the pleasure of entertaining fellow Europeans, let alone a royal prince.

I keep some necessities for the occasional visitor, but it's almost impossible to replace the luxuries. I can never get enough soap or champagne to meet our basic needs, let alone those of an important guest. It seems the locals haven't acquired a taste for either."

"You're in luck, Colonel Uspensky," said Prince Henri. "I brought a crate of Dom Perignon with me. I would be honored to donate a few bottles in the interest of friendship between our two countries."

"That would be marvelous," said Uspensky, his eyes twinkling. "So tell me, gentlemen, where are you headed on your latest adventure?"

Bonvalot leaned forward. "I'm about to attempt something no other European has been able to accomplish, an overland journey from Paris to Tonkin by crossing through Tibet. Naturally, we plan to make a stopover in Lhasa."

The Russian drained the last of his brandy. "Lhasa! I don't wish to be the prophet of doom, but are you aware of the odds you're up against?"

Bonvalot smiled self-assuredly. "I've studied all the maps, consulted with all the experts. I believe we have a good chance of making it to Lhasa, especially if we find the route that Professor Foucaux spoke about, the one he called the 'southern road'. After we see Lhasa, I intend to veer east to Batang just like Fathers Huc and Gabet did nearly fifty years ago, and then we'll continue east to Yunnan where we plan to follow the Mekong River to Tonkin."

"Good heavens," said Uspensky, mentally calculating the distance. "You're talking about a journey of approximately six thousand miles. I hope you know what you're up against."

Prince Henri laughed. "What's life without some risk? I've had my share of dinner parties, costume parties, shooting parties; it's all a tedious bore. This time I've got the chance to prove my mettle. When I show those stuffed shirts at the Geographic Society a photograph of me and the Dalai Lama, I'll finally get the respect I deserve."

"I'll drink to that," said Uspensky, lifting his glass. "As we say in Russian, *za udachu,* good luck. You'll certainly need it. When the British catch wind of what you're up to, they won't like it one bit."

"I don't give a fig what the British think," said Prince Henri. "As far as I'm concerned, they're a bunch of lazy wastrels only capable of tiptoeing in during the dark of night and seizing our assets like Egypt and the Suez Canal."

Bonvalot smiled wanly. "His Highness has a reputation for being an outspoken Anglophobe. While I hold the British in much higher regard than Prince Henri, let's just say I don't intend on letting the British find out our destination is Lhasa. In my estimation, subterfuge will get you much further than brute force. But if push comes to shove, I'll shoot my way to Lhasa if that's what I have to do. I have a whole arsenal at my disposal. But that's where my resemblance to your Prejevalsky ends. I am, after all, a Frenchman. I know how to enjoy the finer things in life and the pleasures of polite company."

Uspensky leaned forward and smiled. "Speaking of polite company, perhaps the two of you could be of service to me."

"Really? How so?"

"I've got a bit of a problem on my hands," said Uspensky, scratching his beard. "You see, there's been a woman and her brother holed up in the compound for weeks now. The interesting thing is, they're countrymen of yours, and they've caused a bit of a diplomatic stir. I could certainly use your help in getting rid of them."

Bonvalot stared at the consul. "Did you say a Frenchwoman and her brother are staying here?"

"Indeed, it's a most peculiar situation," said Uspensky. "She came here with the radical idea of organizing a caravan to Tibet of all places. I tried talking her out of it but she won't listen to reason. It seems her husband went missing some time ago. The poor wretch refuses to give up looking for him. The tragic thing is, she hasn't made any inroads with the local guides. They won't work for a woman, much less a *kafir*, an unbeliever."

All at once Bonvalot remembered the lovely Madame Dancourt and her head of flaming hair, and all the pieces of the puzzle began to fall into place.

Henri puffed on his cigarette. "Sounds like a spiffing lady."

Uspensky chuckled. "And what a character she is. She has a head of flaming gold hair, and is about as stubborn and sharp-tongued as an Oriental merchant. Her brother, on the other hand, is her exact opposite, being of a more docile nature. Actually, my wife has grown quite fond of the girl. She reminds us of our own daughter who we lost to typhus several years ago. I admit I look forward to our daily chats with the spirited young Frenchwoman. The day she leaves will be a sad one indeed."

Bonvalot leaned forward. "What is this lady's name?"

"Camille Dancourt and her brother is François Raymond."

Bonvalot nodded knowingly. "I should have known. If anyone had the gumption to come out here on her own it was Camille Dancourt."

Colonel Uspensky peered at him. "Do you know this woman?"

"We met back in Paris. She begged me to take her along on my expedition but I refused outright. I never thought she'd be bold enough to defy common sense and travel out here on her own."

Uspensky shook his head. "Foolish girl! She got herself in quite a fix, indeed."

"It's that streak of stubbornness you pointed out," said Bonvalot. "Even her brother can't control her."

Uspensky sat back and sighed. "Well, since the two of you are here, the least you can do is try and talk some sense into her. I can arrange for the consulate to buy her a ticket back to Moscow if she agrees to vacate the premises."

"I can talk to her, but I can't promise you any results. She's got a mind of her own and won't listen to reason."

Uspensky smiled. "Then perhaps you should change tack. Offer to take her along and when she sees what she's up against, she'll naturally back down. As the Turkis say, It's easier to teach a camel to jump than reason with a fool. Come to dinner tomorrow night and we'll try to talk some sense into Madame Dancourt. I've already got the measure of her."

Bonvalot reluctantly agreed.

CHAPTER 11

The next evening, Bonvalot and Prince Henri arrived at Colonel Uspensky's house armed with a box of cigars and two bottles of Dom Perignon, which was no small sacrifice for the prince, who insisted on champagne with every meal. But knowing this would most likely be their last dinner party for many months, Henri was in an uncharacteristically generous mood. His Highness was also anxious to meet the mysterious flame-haired Frenchwoman who had captivated so many men while getting herself stranded in the Chinese hinterlands. It promised to be an interesting evening indeed.

When a servant brought them to the dining room, Bonvalot met Camille's gaze instantly. She sat in the glow of the candlelight, a delicate figure in green muslin with coils of coppery hair that blazed like fire. His heart lurched in his chest and his knees went weak. In that instant, all the angst and rashness of their first meeting melted into oblivion. Bonvalot tried to speak, but before he could say anything, Camille had turned to Madame Uspensky and was pretending to preoccupied with something she had said.

Bonvalot scanned the room. The only face he didn't recognize belonged to a bespectacled Catholic priest with a full beard and a long black frock.

Colonel Uspensky greeted his guests. "Oh, there you are. Welcome, welcome. Ladies and gentlemen, allow me to present His Royal Highness Prince Henri d'Orléans and his traveling companion, Monsieur Gabriel Bonvalot, both representing the French Geographical Society." The guests bowed in their honor. Uspensky continued, "Your Highness, allow me to present my wife, Olga, and our guests Father Constant Dedeken from the local mission, and Monsieur François Raymond and his sister Madame Camille Dancourt."

All eyes turned to Camille. She gleamed like an exquisite piece of jade in her green muslin dress that was propped up by several layers of petticoats and a bustle that resembled a Turki camel saddle. She stood with the erect bearing of a Chinese soldier, but beneath her coiled ringlets of reddish-gold hair, Bonvalot was certain he detected a faint trembling. Her brother, on the other hand, shook his fellow countrymen's hands with as much vigor as he could muster despite his gaunt appearance, a result, no doubt, of the many weeks of arduous travel he had endured.

"It's an honor to meet you, your Highness," said François. "My sister and I were surprised to hear that a member of the Royal Family would be joining us for dinner tonight. We never expected to meet two of our own countrymen out here in the Chinese hinterlands. It's quite an honor."

"As a matter of fact, the honor is all mine," said Price Henri, kissing Camille's hand with great ceremony. "I never expected to meet up with such delightful company."

To Bonvalot's horror, Camille's face flushed, prompting him to place himself squarely between her and the dissolute prince.

"Well, well, well," said Bonvalot, lifting Camille's chin to meet her eyes. "Fancy meeting you here of all places."

"No one is more surprised than I am, Monsieur Bonvalot," she said. "After you turned down my generous offer, I had no choice but to travel out here on my own, with the help of François, of course."

"Naturally," said Bonvalot. "You have a very devoted brother. But what experience does François have in organizing an expedition to Tibet? Can a little lady such as yourself make it all the way to Tibet without proper guides?"

Camille's shoulders dropped. "I have grave doubts about my ability to organize an expedition; none of the local guides will work for a woman. The truth is, I'm afraid, we're dangerously out of our league. And now François is too ill to travel any further. I didn't count on having so many obstacles. I can only imagine what my husband must be going through, wherever he is."

Bonvalot felt a lump in his throat. He was quite certain that Armand Dancourt was dead, but the only way Camille would accept that was with tangible proof. Apparently she was wiling to risk her life to find that proof. But how far would she go? Bonvalot decided to change tack.

"Judging by your brother's appearance, I see how hard the journey has been on him." Gazing intently in her eyes, he added, "Perhaps it's time the two of you returned home. If your brother falls seriously ill in China, there are no proper hospitals, no Western doctors. I give you my word as a gentleman that I will do everything possible to find your husband."

Camille shook her head. "There's nothing for me to go back to. My only choice is to go to Tibet and find out what happened to my husband. François is equally committed to helping me because he loves me. Perhaps you've never known a love like that, Monsieur Bonvalot, the selfless, giving kind of love."

Bonvalot sighed. "Please be reasonable, Madame Dancourt. Isn't your brother's suffering reason enough to stop this folly?"

Overhearing their conversation, François laid a protective arm on Camille's shoulder.

"Monsieur Bonvalot, Camille knows I would do anything to help her find her husband."

"That's all well and good, but you can't be of much help if you fall gravely ill. Without a male relative, Camille's life would be in grave danger. With all due respect, Monsieur Raymond, I hope you realize the seriousness of your situation."

Colonel Uspensky cleared his throat. "Gentlemen, let's leave serious talk for later—after we've had a chance to imbibe a few libations. Monsieur Bonvalot, there's someone I would like for you to meet. I believe the two of you have much in common. Allow me to present Father Dedeken, the founder of our local parish here in Kuldja. And what's more, Father Dedeken is fluent in Russian, Mongolian, and Chinese, isn't that remarkable?"

Bonvalot's eyebrows shot up. "That is astounding. It is a pleasure to make your acquaintance, Father."

Dedeken shook the explorer's hand with great warmth.

"Likewise, Monsieur Bonvalot. I've read so much about you."

As the guests took their places around a formal dining table, Colonel Uspensky rang a dinner bell. Soon, a troupe of turbaned Turki servants brought out the most delicious Russian cuisine they had seen since Moscow: blinis, caviar, borscht, and Beef à la

Stroganov, all served on elegant Chinese serving platters. As they dined, Colonel Uspensky regaled his guests with stories about his years in Central Asia, delighting them with tales of Mandarins and court intrigue, even a tale or two about the scoundrel Yakub Beg, the legendary Tajik warrior who crowned himself king of the ill-fated kingdom of Kashgaria. Everyone laughed and drank copious amounts of champagne, the pleasant company and good food even having a salubrious effect on François, whose face regained some of its lost color.

Father Dedeken turned out to be a fascinating dinner companion, displaying an extraordinary knowledge of Chinese culture and society. To Bonvalot's surprise, Father Dedeken knew a great deal about his own travels through Central Asia.

"You should know, Monsieur Bonvalot, that I'm a great admirer of yours," said Father Dedeken, stroking his beard. "I've read every article about you in the bulletin of the Geographical Society. We men of the cloth are not immune to adventure, but we resign ourselves to experiencing it vicariously, through the exploits of explorers like you."

Bonvalot blushed. "Thank you, Father, but I'm most anxious to hear how you learned Chinese. That is an extraordinary achievement."

"Spoken Chinese is based on tones," said Dedeken. "Which for a tone deaf person like myself is like conducting a symphony orchestra with ear plugs."

Bonvalot smiled. The missionary's intelligent, laughing eyes looked twice their size behind a pair of thick spectacles, and his beard was so thick, it clung to his face like a hairy mop. Indeed, Bonvalot had never met anyone quite like this globe-trotting, polyglot priest. He was certain this meeting was more than simply fortuitous; he saw it as divine remuneration for being forced to take along an insufferable, feckless princeling on the greatest journey of his life. Perhaps the gods of exploration were smiling down on him after all.

"Tell me, Father, are you always this witty?" said Bonvalot, taking a sip of his wine.

"As a priest, I have taken a vow of humility," said Father Dedeken, his eyes twinkling behind his thick spectacles. "But one vow I could never make was to curb my adventurous spirit. I came to China eight years ago because I was attracted to the East. I spent my first three years in Kansou where I studied hard to perfect my Chinese while I evangelized to the locals in my spare time. Those years were the toughest; we lost many wonderful colleagues to the ravages of typhus. Later, my superiors offered me the opportunity to start the mission here in Kuldja to spread the gospel to the entire Ili Province. I learned a lot during these last eight years, but soon I'll be forced to return to Antwerp. My parents aren't getting any younger."

Prince Henri scowled. "I have no patience for the Chinese. They call us Europeans foreign devils, the sons of harlots and pigs."

"How horrible," said Camille, covering her mouth in shock.

Father Dedeken turned to Prince Henri. "Your Highness is making a grave mistake by judging the Chinese according to our European standards. Their culture views such things like life, death, colors, and even numbers in a completely different manner. For instance, it would be unthinkable for a Chinese bride to wear white on her wedding day as white is associated with death. They have a great respect for scholars and elders, but wouldn't hesitate to eat a live animal, something no educated European would even consider. And though they love to keep dogs as pets, they savor the taste of dog meat. It's quite shocking, actually."

"It sounds brutal to eat a beloved companion," said Camille. Her brother nodded in agreement.

"Tell me, Father, how did you adjust to life in China?" said François Raymond.

"It wasn't easy, to tell you the truth," said Father Dedeken. "Most of my colleagues either resigned their posts or suffered health problems or nervous breakdowns. Learning Chinese requires enormous dedication and hours of study. We lost many a good man. It's a miracle I lasted as long as I did."

"Father, just how good is your Chinese?" said Prince Henri.

Dedeken smiled mischievously. "According to my Chinese servant Bartholomeus, I'm almost as fluent as Confucius himself, though he claims I'm not half as witty nor half as rotund."

Colonel Uspensky turned to Father Dedeken. "Father, Monsieur Bonvalot and Prince Henri have set a very lofty goal for themselves. They are about to be the first living Europeans in

Lhasa since the days of Fathers Huc and Gabet more than fifty years ago."

Father Dedeken's eyes widened. "That's quite an ambitious plan. I wish you gentlemen success, but I hope you realize the odds you're facing. The mandarins in Lhasa forbid the Tibetans from aiding foreigners in any manner whatever. Convincing a Tibetan to sell you food or horses is nearly impossible. The punishment for assisting travelers is mutilation and death."

"How horrible," said Camille, blanching. "Don't they believe in our Christian doctrine of loving the stranger?"

"Madame Dancourt," said Father Dedeken. "Tibet is a devout Buddhist country with no knowledge of Christianity whatever. They cling to their beliefs with the tenacity of a mastiff. Converting them has proven all but impossible, more difficult than converting a Mohammedan. The Tibetans adhere loyally to their Dalai Lama and Panchen Lama as they believe they are different aspects of the Buddha himself. It's a strange and wondrous country, yet rarely have any outsiders managed to reach Lhasa. And I doubt that anyone will ever successfully convert the Tibetans to Christianity."

"We're not going to Tibet to convert them," said Bonvalot. "Only to study their geography and culture. I heard a strange story back in Paris from a Professor Foucaux about a prophecy concerning the reincarnation of a Tibetan goddess. He asked me to investigate this prophecy bring him back any evidence that it has been fulfilled. Luckily for me, the public has an insatiable desire for any information at all about Tibet. I hope to bring back photographs, biological samples, artifacts, and maybe even the Dalai Lama himself. At this point, anything's possible."

"From you I would expect nothing less, Monsieur Bonvalot," said Camille. Turning to Prince Henri, she added, "If I may be so bold, your Highness, I think your plan is extraordinary. I admire explorers who risk their lives to discover new worlds and enlighten the rest of us with their findings."

"For me exploration is as natural as breathing," said Prince Henri. "I never desired the life of a dilettante. My spirit seeks novelty and adventure, the call of the open road. I pity those who do not travel."

"How I do admire you hardy explorers," said Camille, beaming from ear to ear. "Putting your lives in grave danger when man's natural inclination is to seek the comforts of home and hearth."

"That is because they do not have the soul of a traveler," said Prince Henri, moving his seat closer to hers. "This is something one must be born with. Traveling for me is almost as much a spiritual journey as a physical one, where part of the quest is becoming one with nature. My life's quest is to penetrate to the very depths of men's souls."

Hearing this, Bonvalot rolled his eyes.

Camille blushed. "If I may say so, Your Highness seems like a deeply spiritual person."

"The deepest journeys are those of the heart," said Henri as he stared intently into Camille's eyes. "Or shall I say, the meeting of two hearts."

Bonvalot felt his blood beginning to boil. He had the unmistakable urge to grab Henri by the shoulders and fling him out of the nearest window. He was so agitated, he could barely sit still.

"Is that true Monsieur Bonvalot?" said Madame Uspensky, interrupting his thoughts. "Can explorers really penetrate to the depths of men's souls?"

Bonvalot shot an icy glare at Henri. "Madame Uspensky, I concern myself with the physical world and leave matters of the spiritual world to men like Father Dedeken. As for His Highness the prince, I believe he has much more experience peering into the eyes of a charging rhino than the darker recesses of men's souls."

Father Dedeken laughed. "Well, good luck to you both. And the next time we meet, I hope to hear all about your adventure in Tibet."

Just then, a thought occurred to Bonvalot.

"I have a better idea, Father. Why don't you come with us?"

Father Dedeken's jaw dropped.

Colonel Uspensky cupped his hand around his ear. "Pardon me, Monsieur Bonvalot, what did you say? I don't think I heard you correctly."

"I just invited Father Dedeken to join us on our expedition to Tibet," said Bonvalot. "Seeing as he's an expert in Chinese, he'd make a splendid addition to my team. I could use a man with his experience. Please consider it, Father. I can't promise you a thousand converts to the faith, but I can promise you the adventure of a lifetime."

Dedeken shook his head. "Thank you for your kind offer, but I must decline. I recently returned from an arduous journey on behalf of my mission and couldn't possibly undertake another. Not to mention I would need permission from my Superiors in Brussels. I could not undertake such an arduous journey without their blessing."

Prince Henri persisted. "Father, the more I think about it, the more I see how much we could use you. If it's permission you need, I will send an urgent telegram to your superiors in Brussels or even to the Vatican if necessary."

"I'm humbled by your offer," said Father Dedeken. "But my answer is still no. I don't see how a bumbling, near-sighted Catholic priest could be of use to a group of rugged explorers when I can barely make it up the stairs without tripping."

For the rest of the dinner, Bonvalot seethed by all the attention Henri was lavishing on Camille. A gentle touch of his hand against her shoulder, the casual way he brushed a stray lock of hair from her face, the flirtatious smiles they exchanged that felt like a stabbing pain in Bonvalot's heart. Later, as the men retreated to the drawing room for brandy and cigars, Bonvalot motioned to Camille and François that he wanted to speak with them alone.

"Listen, Madame Dancourt," he began. "I've had a change of heart. After much consideration, I've decided to allow you to join my expedition after all. I feel it's not only my duty, but an honor to assist you in any way I can."

Camille's face brightened instantly. "Really? I'm surprised, Monsieur Bonvalot. I can't imagine what has caused this change of heart. But no matter, I'm very grateful to you."

"I believe meeting you again tonight was providential in many ways," said Bonvalot. "Since we first met in Paris, I've thought a great deal about you. Besides, I'm not the sort of man that could leave a lady stranded in Central Asia. But before you accept my offer, I have certain conditions you must agree to."

"And what are those?" said François.

"First of all, you must agree to abide by my rules. The first being that I'm the leader on this expedition. Second, neither of you may stray away from the caravan at any time, under any circumstances. And third, that you agree to perform certain tasks, such as guard duty, except the little lady, of course. Is that clear?"

"Perfectly clear," said Camille. "We accept your terms whole-heartedly."

Bonvalot smiled. "Good. I can see we'll get along fine."

"There's just one thing, Monsieur Bonvalot," she said.

"What's that?"

"Must you keep referring to me as the little lady?"

Bonvalot was speechless.

After Bonvalot had recovered somewhat, he returned to Prince Henri in the drawing room. The latter had seen him talking to Camille and asked him what they had spoken about.

"I told her she and her brother could join our caravan."

Henri's eyebrows shot up. "Are you serious? Isn't that highy *irregular?*"

"Of course it is," said Bonvalot. "But I couldn't leave them stranded out here in the middle of nowhere."

Henri took a long drag of his cigarette. "Either they've got the Mad Hatter's disease or you've got it. I feel I should warn you, I grown rather fond of the young lady and I hope you don't have any designs on her. She's a proper bit of frock."

Bonvalot swallowed his whiskey in one gulp. "With all due respect, Your Highness, she's off limits to you as well. I promised your father I'd keep you out of trouble."

Prince Henri, laughed derisively, flicking his ashes into an antique Chinese vase. "We'll see about that."

The next morning, Bonvalot was anxious to speak to Camille again. After a hasty purchase at the bazaar, he returned to Colonel Uspensky's house and knocked on the door. He waited on pins and needles while a servant went to fetch her. When Camille entered the drawing room, Bonvalot tossed what appeared to be a dead sheep at her feet.

Camille took a step backwards. "What in Heaven's name is this?" she said, pointing at the lifeless carcass.

"A sheepskin coat I bought for you. Try it on."

Reluctantly, Camille picked it up. "It smells awful, like a dead carcass. Do you expect me to wear this hideous thing?"

"Your life may depend on that hideous thing," said Bonvalot. "It's your best protection against the cold. You don't expect to cross the Chang Tang in a taffeta dress, do you?"

"It wasn't taffeta; it was *muslin,* but I'd hardly expect you to know that."

Bonvalot scratched his nose. "And you'll also need some thick woolen socks, a pair of hob-nailed boots—"

"A pair of *what*?"

"Hob-nailed boots. We'll be crossing over glaciers and icy mountain passes under the most hazardous of condition. That is, if you still intend to go through with this foolish plan of searching for your husband in Tibet. I'll be expecting you to keep up with the rest of the men. But if you're having second thoughts...it's not too late to back down."

Camille forced her arm into the sleeve. "I have no intention of backing down."

Bonvalot raised his eyebrows. "I see. Well, since that's settled, you'll need to carry an ice axe and learn how to load and shoot a carbine. It could mean the difference between life and death."

Camille stared open-mouthed as Bonvalot turned to leave.

"But I have no doubt you'll be a fast learner," he said, glancing back over his shoulder.

CHAPTER 12

The next item on the agenda was to purchase sturdy horses and to organize the caravan.

After breakfast, they headed to the bazaar. In Asia, there's never any lack of loafers and men with no discernable occupation who are available for hire. Many of them claim to have skills and assorted talents that can never be verified until it's too late. The trick is to interrogate them and see where their story falls apart. The ones who hold up under questioning are hired on the spot. As Bonvalot and Rachmed made their way past a display of melons they found a sharp-eyed man named Abdullah, a Turkish-speaking Taranchi, who was squatting on the ground selling squirrels in makeshift cages. Rachmed approached the squirrel dealer and explained that they were organizing a caravan headed to Lob Nor and needed some guides.

"Look no further than Abdullah your servant," said the squirrel dealer, poking his finger at one of the squirrels. "I'm the best man for the job. I can guide you there in my sleep. I had the honor of accompanying the great Prejevalsky on his last trip to the Lob Nor."

"So you knew Prejevalsky?"

"Better than his own mother," said Abdullah. "He carried himself like a Pasha, but he was the best marksman I ever saw. The ground trembled where he stood."

"How many languages do you speak?" said Bonvalot.

"One of noble birth, your servant Abdullah speaks Turkish, Russian, Chinese and Mongolian better than Genghis Khan."

"What about Tibetan?" said Bonvalot.

"On my mother's honor I speak Tibetan as good as the Dalai Lama himself. I once worked for a Tibetan lama who taught me everything I know."

"Have you ever traveled to the Tsaidam?" said Bonvalot.

"I may have on one or two occasions," said Abdullah, his eyes turning suspicious. "But if you want my professional opinion, you should avoid it like the plague. It's a lifeless salt marsh with no animals, no birds, no trees, only pillars of salt left over from the days of the Prophet Ibrahim. It's a place of misery and death."

"Are you brave enough to attempt another crossing of the Tsaidam?" said Bonvalot, squinting at the candidate.

"One of noble birth, if you live to be one hundred and twenty you will never find a man braver and humbler than your servant Abdullah."

"Brave enough to travel all the way to Batang?"

"*Batang?*" said Abdullah, his eyes widening. "Abdullah is brave, not stupid. You will need a miracle to reach Batang. Does one of your noble rank have a Chinese passport?"

"No."

"What about a felt tent?"

"No."

"An official escort?"

"No."

"Then how do you expect to reach Batang? On a magic carpet?"

After securing the services of Abdullah (with the help of a generous down-payment) and a dozen other Taranchis, Kirghiz, and Siberian Mongols, Bonvalot and Rachmed headed out to the livestock market to barter for fifteen more horses and twenty more camels, enough to last for the next leg of the journey across the Tian Shan mountains to Korla, a Silk Road oasis town on the northern fringes of the Taklamakan Desert. After observing all the varieties of horses, they selected the wiry Kirghiz variety, known for their stamina and endurance during long marches.

Next they headed to the livestock market where they inquired about hiring a suitable camel driver. Each time they asked they were pointed in the direction of Imatch, an elderly, bow-legged Chinese Kirghiz who had a reputation for being more comfortable with camels than with people, and was blessed with the ability to speak the camels' own language.

Imatch was so comical-looking, he looked like a Chinese circus attraction. He had a short, squat frame and enormous ears that stuck out like fans. His face was so wrinkled, it resembled a piece of ancient Chinese parchment, and his hands and face were so dirty, they looked like they were formed from clay. But no one doubted Imatch's skill as a camel driver. When it was feeding time, all he had to do to call them home was stand at the edge of the field in his long sheepskin coat and kalpak, his traditional Kirghiz cap, and call out to the grazing camels. Sure enough, when they heard his voice, the camels would come bounding across the grassy steppe like puppy dogs.

Imatch's only failing was his coarse tongue, which could rattle off a pungent stew of colorful phrases strong enough to cause the birds to drop from the sky. His tirades came as a byproduct of a violent temper, but other than that, Imatch was a valuable if somewhat eccentric member of the team.

All that remained was to clear the way for Father Dedeken to join the expedition. As promised, Prince Henri had sent numerous telegrams to Brussels requesting permission from his superiors to allow him to accompany the famed French explorer on his newest expedition. When the telegram finally came releasing him from his duties at the mission, no one was more shocked than Father Dedeken. With a gleam in his eyes, Father Dedeken packed his bags and hugged his fellow brothers goodbye. He was even more elated when his Chinese servant, Bartholomeus, a convert to the faith, agreed to accompany him. Bartholomeus was a perfect blending of East and West with his expert command of French and his penchant for dressing like a European. They had no way of knowing that his expert knowledge of Chinese habits and customs would prove invaluable during their many run-ins with the Chinese Ambans.

The next morning, when it was time to make the final preparations, a group of half a dozen Kirghiz wearing white hats atop their weather-beaten faces came riding into camp. These were the new caravaneers Bonvalot had hired, and by all appearances, they were well-equipped. The bedrolls they had attached to their pack saddles testified to their nomadic way of life, and their expert knowledge of the terrain would prove to be invaluable. Also on the field were Bonvalot, Father Dedeken, and Prince Henri, who had changed into warm coats, riding breeches and boots, while towering above the crowd was Rachmed. As caravanbashi, or caravan leader, he was the picture of confidence in his full Uzbek garb which consisted of a black sheepskin cap, a caftan of coarse grey wool, trousers, and tall boots of untanned leather.

The last item on the agenda was to visit the Governor of the Ili Province and request his formal permission to travel in Chinese territory. This step was strictly a formality, but since Bonvalot lacked a Chinese passport, it was a vital necessity. Together with Father Dedeken and Bartholomeus, they set out for the Governor's house.

Garbed in the manner of Chinese Ambans with a loose blue silk jacket, tunic, and a round porkpie hat, the Governor received Bonvalot and his companions in his private room where they engaged in a long conversation, exchanging pleasantries and drinking the ceremonial three cups of tea.

Servants brought in platters of grapes and delicious melons and peaches for the guests. Using tact, diplomacy, a bottle of French cognac, and a sack of silver ingots, Bonvalot did his part to guarantee the meeting went along splendidly. Finally, after an exotic-tasting dessert of pudding and spices, the Governor presented Bonvalot with the necessary documents, and even offered to supply his caravan with two mounted Chinese guides. Bonvalot was overjoyed. The meeting had gone even better than he expected.

The travelers stood up and bowed deeply, thanking his Excellency for his kindness and consideration. Later, as they made their way back to the inn through the busy streets of Kuldja, Bonvalot wondered if all the Chinese mandarins would be as cordial and generous as the Governor of the Ili Province. He had no way of knowing that even as they were sipping tea, the governor had dispatched a runner to Korla to warn the Hakim of Bonvalot's impending arrival.

CHAPTER 13

When it was time to load the camels, all hands were needed. The job of loading temperamental beasts with heavy burdens required tact and skill; it was, in fact, a job that every caravaneer dreaded. Keeping a team of moody camels pacified required no small amount of finesse, especially if one wished to avoid unnecessary injury.

First, the animal was made to kneel on the ground while the caravaneers stuffed grass in its mouth. Next, two men, one on each side, secured the bundles against the animal's sides with heavy ropes, careful to distribute the weight evenly between the two humps. This part of the job involved a lot of guesswork and much trial and error. If the load was too heavy, the animal would balk, causing unnecessary delays. If it refused to stand, the men would have to open up the packages and take out excess items including cookware, shovels, pick axes, ammunition, tents, even Prince Henri's cases of goose liver pâté, caviar, and Dom Perignon, and redistribute them to some other unfortunate beast.

Sometimes Imatch and Niaz worked together as a team. Other times it was Niaz and Abdullah, and still other times it was Rachmed and Niaz. And when the others were busy trading insults, throwing sand in each other's faces, or dueling with swords, the responsibility fell on Bonvalot and Father Dedeken's shoulders. But after several hours of hard work and heavy lifting, the job was finally complete, the animals were fed and watered, and the men were ready to go.

Hovering on the fringes, Bonvalot spied a hooded figure who appeared to be a Buddhist monk of sorts. Sidling up to Rachmed, he asked about the stranger's identity. Looking up from the horse's shoe he was checking, Rachmed peered at the silent loner.

"Oh, him? That's an old Mongolian lama who asked to travel with us as far as the Tsaidam."

"What do the men say about him?"

"They say he's a holy man, so I couldn't refuse to take him. Mostly they just leave him alone."

"There's something odd about him. Keep an eye on him."

Rachmed nodded and continued checking his horse's shoes.

When Camille at last joined them on the field, she had wisely substituted her muslin dress for a pair of baggy Russian trousers and top-boots. Her reddish gold hair was twisted and coiled on top of her head, and in her arms, she carried her new sheepskin coat, albeit reluctantly. When Prince Henri spied her lithe shape ensconced in a pair of khaki trousers, he dropped his trooper saddle and whistled. This, in turn, alerted Rachmed, who did a double take when he spotted the memsahib ensconced between a pair of gruff-looking camel drivers,

"Bonvalot, who is this woman?" said Rachmed, scratching his unwashed head under his sheepskin cap.

"Oh, this is Camille Dancourt. She's coming with us."

Rachmed looked stunned. "What did you say?"

"I said she's coming with us," said Bonvalot. "As in, she is joining our expedition."

"But you have a policy of never taking memsahibs on expedition. This is highly irregular."

"I didn't have the heart to refuse her," said Bonvalot. "She and her brother were stranded out here. She claims her husband is missing in Tibet and will do anything possible to search for him. Please do me the favor of welcoming Madame Dancourt and making her feel at home."

Rachmed composed himself and sauntered over to Camille, towering over her like Goliath in his sheepskin cap and coat.

"Welcome, memsahib. I am your servant Rachmed. Allow me to help you mount your camel. If you will be so kind, please give me your foot."

Trembling, Camille lifted her foot and in a flash Rachmed hoisted her atop the camel's back where she settled in a camel saddle between its humps, her hair losing some of its delicate coiffure in the process. And then, almost as an afterthought, Rachmed kicked the camel's side, and the enormous beast hoisted herself to a standing position, the violent lurch throwing her forward as it rose on its hind legs, and just as abruptly she was propelled backward as it heaved up on its forelegs. Camille screamed and grabbed the saddle horn for dear life, at which point the caravan burst into laughter. Even Rachmed had to struggle mightily to stifle a grin.

Camille's face reddened. "Why didn't you tell me he was going to stand up? I almost toppled over!"

"Begging a thousand pardons memsahib," said Rachmed. "With the help of Allah it shall not happen again."

"It better not," she said with great indignation as she adjusted herself into a more comfortable position.

"Is something the matter, Madame Dancourt?" said Bonvalot, striding toward her. "A little camel trouble? It's not too late for you to back out. I'm sure Madame and Monsieur Uspensky would be glad to have you back while we go off in search of your husband."

Camille stiffened. "As much as you'd like for me to quit, Monsieur Bonvalot, I refuse to do so. If *you* can manage to ride a camel, so can I. I'm not some shy, retiring person who can't handle a simple beast of burden."

"I'm glad to know you plan on showing the camel who's boss," said Bonvalot, grinning. "As for me, I'll be riding my trusty mare, Jupiter. We arranged for you to ride a camel as that is the most suitable arrangement for a lady. If your brother has no objections, I have also assigned him to a camel." Bonvalot looked around. "Just a moment, I don't see your brother. Where is he?"

Camille took a deep breath. "François will not be joining us."

"Come again?" said Bonvalot.

"I *said* he's not coming with us. He came down with a bout of dysentery and the Russian doctor said he would ruin his health if he travelled to Tibet. He said it was inadvisable."

"Really? And did that same Russian doctor say it was advisable for *you* to travel to Tibet?"

"I don't recall asking him, Monsieur Bonvalot," said Camille, glowering. "Besides, it's none of his business since what I do is my own affair."

"Well it is my business since this is my caravan," said Bonvalot. "Your brother's absence has created a considerable problem since it means you are now traveling unchaperoned.

Which means I shall have to assume full responsibility for your safety."

"I'm sure it will only be for a short while, Monsieur Bonvalot, as I have great confidence we will find my husband. Then I shall no longer be *your* responsibility."

"You mean *if* we find your husband," said Bonvalot, patting her camel's flank. "You do realize that finding your husband on the Tibetan Chang Tang will be like finding a needle in a haystack."

"I have great confidence in your abilities," said Camille, tying a kerchief around her hair. "That's why I hired you."

"Let's be clear about one thing," said Bonvalot. "There are no guarantees. But I give you my solemn word as a gentleman that I will do everything in my power to find your husband, but I can't promise you a miracle."

Before Camille could respond, someone called out to them and the two looked up to see Prince Henri strolling toward them, dressed in a smart tweed suit.

"Ah, here comes his Highness now, dressed for adventure," said Bonvalot.

Henri gazed at Camille admiringly. "Well, well, now there's a rational costume if I've ever seen one. Madame Dancourt, allow me to offer my assistance on anything you may require during this expedition. I have my own private store of Dom Perignon, as well as a library, dishes, carpets, crates of goose liver pâté and caviar. Consider it all yours."

"Thank you, your Highness," said Camille, blushing. "That's very kind of you."

"You'll soon get used to Henri," said Bonvalot. "He's something of a bon vivant. He knows how to appreciate the finer things in life. Isn't that true, Henri?"

"Indeed, I consider myself a connoisseur," said Henri. "And not just food, but *all* the finer things of life. Music, wine, race-horses, beautiful..."

"Let's leave it at that, shall we?" interrupted Bonvalot. "I think we'd better get on with things."

"*À bientôt, Madame*," said Henri, bowing and returning to his horse.

Without another word, Bonvalot strode back to his horse to make his final preparations. As he fastened his saddle, Rachmed could hear him muttering under his breath, and wondered if the unspoken rivalry between the two sahibs would lead to drawn swords.

After fastening his saddlebag, Bonvalot strapped on a goatskin full of water. He made sure to add a change of clothes and a sheepskin blanket. Likewise, Prince Henri and Father Dedeken also saddled their horses and attached goatskins filled with water, as well as saddlebags containing all their most important supplies. As safety was of paramount importance, Bonvalot instructed Prince Henri and Father Dedeken to keep a loaded carbine in the bucket of their trooper saddles at all times.

"Chances are there won't be any emergencies that will require needing a loaded carbine," he said. "But if something happens, you'll need it in a split second. Your life may depend on it. Well, I guess that's all there is. The weather looks good so, with any luck we should have several days of clear skies. Henri, I know you've been anxious to get on the road, but now that you've seen firsthand what a difficult job it is to organize a caravan, I hope you appreciate all the hard work that went into it. Imagine how distressing it would be to arrive in Lhasa only to discover you've forgotten your camera."

"I leave all petty matters to my valet," said Henri, searching through his saddlebag for a pair of riding gloves. "And please, no more lectures. Packing is best left to the coolies. Isn't that why we have that Rachmed fellow? He's speaks the local language and has been an enormous help. I daresay he's so good I may be forced to give him a raise before long."

Bonvalot glared at Henri but this was no time to argue. There was still much left to do before they could leave. He rode his horse down the line of camels, checking to make sure everything was tight and secure and that nothing had been overlooked. Loaded on the camels' backs were several months' worth of food, fodder, tools, tents, surveying equipment, rifles, ammunition, and bedding.

Unexpectedly, as Prince Henri reached for his riding crop, his horse whinnied and reared, creating a great ruckus and startling the entire caravan. The animal flailed his forelegs and shook his head defiantly, trying to free himself from his master. Prince Henri struggled to remain in the saddle, but lost control as the horse continued his rearing, finally losing the battle when the horse flung him to the ground where the chastened prince landed on his back, groaning in pain.

Once free, the horse galloped away, leaving the prince shaken, distraught, and in a fit of pique. Henri picked himself up and shook an angry fist at the wayward beast, cursing and swearing, but the horse was gone. The beleaguered animal galloped across the barren steppe as if he were possessed by a demon, carrying Henri's belongings with him.

As he stood watching his horse disappear, Henri cupped his hands around his mouth and yelled, "*Come back, Charlemagne! Come back!*" But the angry beast kept galloping away.

Taking out his spyglass, Bonvalot watched the horse disappear in a cloud of dust. He said to Rachmed. "What the devil happened?" What could have scared that jittery beast?"

Rachmed shook his head. "Perhaps it was a snake…"

Bonvalot yelled for his camel driver, "Imatch, get over here now!"

The bow-legged Kirghiz dropped what he was doing and hobbled over to his employer.

"Yes, sahib?" said Imatch, squinting his sunken eyes in the glare of the sun.

Bonvalot pointed to the dot on the horizon. "Did you see that crazy animal? What could have caused him to bolt like that?"

Imatch motioned in Prince Henri's direction. "Begging a thousand pardons, sahib, but I believe it was the prince's fault."

"What do you mean?" said Bonvalot.

"Last night I saw the prince beating his horse after he'd been drinking," said Imatch. "I tried to stop him but he pushed me away. I dared not interfere anymore lest he shoot me."

Bonvalot stared in shock. "Why didn't you tell me this before? How could you keep something like that from me? Every time Prince Henri drinks he turns into an enraged bully and takes it out on anyone he can. From now on, you must tell me everything that goes on regarding the animals. Especially after his Highness has been drinking. Do you understand? Now I've got to figure out how to get the animal back."

"I can try, sahib," said Imatch, glancing nervously at the prince, who was taking swigs from his flask. "But you know how moody those horses can be. It may take a little while to coax him back. I will ride out there with some sugar in my hand and try to lure him in."

"Very good," said Bonvalot. "Do whatever it takes. I paid an exorbitant price for that horse. We need him back with all the equipment strapped on his back. It's quite urgent."

Imatch left and Bonvalot walked over to where Prince Henri was nursing a sprained leg.

"Are you alright? It looks like you took quite a bruising there."

"My leg hurts bad," said Henri, rubbing his backside. "As soon as I get my hands on that monster I'm going to beat the tar out of him."

"There'll be no more of that," said Bonvalot, grasping Henri by the shoulder. "That's a way to ruin a good horse. The blighter's almost as hot-tempered as you are. Probably has royal blood lines, too. Can you remember what you had packed in your saddlebag?"

"Well, there was my shaving kit, my mirror, my comb, my cigarettes, my billfold, my writing kit, my compass, my thermometer, and one more thing."

"What's that?"

"My camera."

Bonvalot blanched. "Was that our only camera?"

"I believe it was," said Prince Henri, taking another swig from his flask. "And now it's gone."

Bonvalot threw his hat to the ground. "Bloody hell!"

CHAPTER 14

Two hours later, they spotted Imatch heading back to camp across the dusty steppe, a smile planted across his craggy face. He was leading Prince Henri's horse by its reins while his camel followed close behind, wailing like an abandoned pet.

Prince Henri grumbled as he took out his pocket watch. "Well, it's about time." He ground out his cigarette and ran toward them, chastising his belligerent horse with an upraised fist and loud oaths.

"Don't you dare hit that horse again," yelled Bonvalot. "And don't let me catch you drinking spirits during the day."

"I'll do as I please," said Henri, grabbing the wayward beast out of Imatch's grasp.

Bonvalot shook his head in disgust. He hoped this escapade would be the worst setback to occur on the journey, but he knew from hard-won experience that it was probably just a harbinger of more mishaps and disasters to come.

At last the caravan started out. Following the two mounted Chinese guides provided by the Governor of the Ili Province, they headed southeast in a line of camels, horses, donkeys, and sheep that spread across the steppe like a fleet of sailing ships. There were twenty camels in all, fifteen horses, fifteen men, and various sheep and donkeys, while in front, the dusty plain stretched as far as the eye could see, like an earthen sea that pitched and rolled, occasionally giving way to low brown hills with steep ridges and rounded crests. Further in the distance they saw a ghostly chain of snow-capped mountains, the Tian Shan, hovering like celestial pyramids bathed in a purple-blue haze.

It was harvest time in the Ili valley and the countryside was still green; the forests that cloaked the foothills perfumed the air with a rich piney scent and a fragrant sea of lavender blanketed the plains. Camille knew that traveling thousands of miles on the back of the camel would be no easy task, and it took a great deal of effort before she got used to the rocking and swaying motion of the animal. Each time the camel stumbled on a rock she would shriek, causing the men to stop what they were doing and glance in her direction, alarmed that she had taken a spill. Once she had recovered from her fright she would smile sheepishly and pretend as if nothing happened, while the men pretended they hadn't noticed. Luckily, she was young, quick, and agile, and kept herself from tumbling to the ground on numerous occasions by clinging to the saddle horn for dear life. At no time would she admit to Bonvalot that she needed help, or felt any sort of fear or trepidation about what lay ahead. She was determined to prove she was just as capable as any of the men.

Meanwhile, Bonvalot kept a wary eye on the Mongolian lama, who rode beside the camels on his mule in silent mediation. Something about the holy man unnerved Bonvalot, but he couldn't quite put his finger on it. With his face obscured by his hood, and the constant spinning of his prayer wheel, Bonvalot feared the lama was another hallucination, and he vowed that as soon as they reached Korla, he would send the old lama away.

Before sunset they made camp. Their cook was Tong-Kia, a Chinese Kirghiz who Father Dedeken had managed to convert to Christianity. His method for cooking was as ancient as the desert sands. He would dig a hole in the ground and turn it into a makeshift oven by adding fuel and lighting it. Over the fire he suspended a blackened pot into which he threw a freshly-butchered lamb, rice, spices, and vegetables. That night, and almost every subsequent night, they feasted on *palao*, a dish native to the Mohammedans of Central Asia, that became their staple food.

Rachmed as caravan leader, or caravanbashi, formed a tight circle with the caravan men as they ate side by side around the fire, laughing and joking in their native tongue. Off to the side, the Mongolian lama hovered in the shadows, keeping to himself as he spun his prayer wheel and meditated in low, mournful tones.

Seeing Camille all by herself, Bonvalot scooped up some *palao* and brought it to the young lady along with a loaf of round Turki bread.

"Care for some supper, Madame Dancourt?" he said, trying to sound friendly. "It's quite tasty, but I should warn you, you'll need the stomach of a Mongol to digest it."

Camille accepted the food. "Thank you Monsieur Bonvalot. It seems I may have misjudged you."

Bonvalot wrinkled his forehead. "How so?"

"Since I met you in Paris, I took you to be an ambitious, single-minded individual who cared only about success and glory and nothing else. In your eyes I was a liability, a burden, if you will. My goal now is to prove how wrong you were."

Bonvalot was taken aback.

"Indeed I believe you have misjudged me," he said. "What you call single-mindedness I call concern for safety. To a certain extent I am ambitious, I admit, but I never let ambition get in the way of common sense. I put the lives of my men above medals and glory."

"I didn't mean—"

"Didn't mean what?"

"I didn't mean to say you were uncaring."

Bonvalot's eyes twinkled. "Once you get to know me better, I think you'll find me as warm-hearted as any other big game hunter or rugged explorer. And now, if you'll excuse me, I have some important matters to discuss with my men."

Camille stared as Bonvalot doffed the brim of his hat and sauntered over to join Father Dedeken and Rachmed. He sat with his back to her, although he would occasionally crane his neck to sneak a glance at her over his shoulder.

Seizing the opportunity, Prince Henri took his own plate and plopped himself down next to Camille. Exploiting her solitary state, he launched into a lengthy monologue about his hunting exploits, his thoroughbred race horses, his winning streaks in Monte Carlo, his stories becoming more convoluted as the meal wore on, his hands becoming more daring with every swig of brandy from his flask.

From the corner of his eye, Bonvalot watched Henri's overtures with mounting disgust, occasionally muttering phrases like 'princely poltroon' and 'underbred booby' under his breath.

As Camille's discomfort became apparent, Bonvalot had to restrain himself from kicking the shameless womanizer in the shins several times. When Prince Henri edged a little too close to the lady, he decided to put a stop to it. He got up and strolled over to the Prince like an arrow hitting its mark.

"I think you've had enough to drink today, your Highness," said Bonvalot, seizing the flask of brandy from Henri's hand.

"What's this?" said Prince Henri, his face reddening. "I'll ask you to mind your own business. I don't need you or anyone else telling me what to do."

"I'm ordering you to behave like a gentleman."

Henri's eyes blazed. "You insufferable—"

Camille stood up abruptly. "That's enough, gentlemen. It's been a long day and I'm feeling rather tired. If you'll excuse me, I shall be heading to my tent."

They watched as Camille returned her bowl to Tong-Kia, and retired to her tent. Prince Henri scowled at Bonvalot, then stalked off to smoke in peace.

Bonvalot grabbed his carbine and headed across the steppe to clear his head. But even out in the wilderness he found no peace. He was haunted by the thought of Henri stealing Camille's attention and possibly her affection that his jaw clenched in anger. He lifted his carbine and took aim at a distant target. Luckily, the blast cleared his head. After a few clean shots, his temper cooled and he was able to stroll back to camp renewed.

Since the weather was clear, the men decided to sleep under the stars instead of pitching their tents. First they laid a piece of oilcloth on the ground over which they placed a sheepskin, then topped it off with their own blankets. Without exception, everyone was exhausted and fell asleep as soon as the sun set.

Before snuffing out the hurricane lamp, Bonvalot glanced over at Camille's tent and worried about her safety. He feared the sudden appearance of bandits in the night who wouldn't hesitate to slit a man's throat for a shotgun or a piece of meat. Or a slave. Quietly, he snuck out of bed, grabbed his carbine, and slid it under his makeshift pillow, then slipped back into his sleeping-sack, closed his eyes, and fell into a deep but troubled sleep.

CHAPTER 15

Korla, Chinese Turkestan
October, 1889

After navigating through the snow-covered passes of the Tian Shan Mountains, they made their way down the final pass, then wended through a rocky gorge that led to a grassy steppe. Soon the landscape grew drier and more desolate until they found themselves entering the desert.

Almost at once the air changed from warm and moist to hot and dry, vegetation became sparser, and the terrain transformed into a maze of undulating sand dunes in fiery shades of orange, yellow, sepia, and bronze, like waves in a vast golden sea of sand. After several days of trekking across the desert, they finally arrived through the gates of Korla, the last Silk Road oasis on the outskirts of the Taklamakan Desert.

Korla was like a window to the past. The town was divided into two sections, one Chinese and one Turki, and consisted of a colorful bazaar, a sepia-colored fortress with crenellated walls and a pagoda-style watchtower, a Chinese-style mosque, and rows of mud-bricked hovels sprawled along the shores of the Konchi-Darya.

Bonvalot dismounted his horse and stood on the dusty road marveling at how little of this ancient town must have changed in the last six hundred years. Nearby, the bazaar teemed with life. Turbaned traders were bargaining in Turki and Pushtu for brightly-colored fabrics and carpets, while veiled women floated on the edges like silent, drifting shadows. Men in sheepskin caps with round faces and Chinese eyes sat in alleyways smoking long pipes, while others engaged in a brisk trade from rickety donkey carts filled with caged geese, ducks, melons, apples, figs, grapes, and apricots. The smell of baking bread mixed with the odor of sweat, dust, and hot wool that drifted over from the crowded marketplace.

The weary travelers lodged in a caravanserai owned by a prominent Mohammedan merchant. After Camille dismounted, a female servant led her to the women's quarters while the men began the task of unloading the camels. After their arduous journey over mountains, rivers, and deserts, everyone was greatly in need of a proper bath and a few days of rest.

While in Korla, Bonvalot's main order of business was to make his final preparations for the journey to Tibet. Given the complexity of organizing such a lengthy expedition, he had little time to rest. Luckily, their host was an agreeable sort who lavished his guests with stories and legends while lavishly them tea, honeyed cakes, crusty naan bread, and hot palaos.

Once everyone was settled, Bonvalot decided it was time to expel the suspicious lama from the caravan. Deciding the matter should be handled with tact, he summoned Abdullah and explained the situation to him.

Abdullah found Bonvalot sitting on a carpet drinking tea.

"Yes, one of noble birth?"

"Abdullah, I'm entrusting you with a very important job. I want you to find the Mongolian lama and tell him that he must leave the caravan. Order him to find other accommodations at once."

"Sahib, this matter sounds very serious, indeed," said Abdullah. "I was not prepared for such a large increase in my duties. Therefore, I must request a corresponding increase in my salary."

"You're asking me for more money?"

"It's the custom in these parts when you ask a servant to take on additional burdens that you show him favor with a small token of your appreciation."

Bonvalot frowned, dug out a coin from his money belt, and threw it at the erstwhile squirrel dealer.

"May Allah the all merciful shower you with His blessings," said Abdullah. He then bowed and retreated. A little while later, Abdullah returned, looking as if he'd seen a ghost.

"Sahib, I regret to tell you I was unable to carry out your request," said Abdullah, sweating profusely.

"Why is that?" said Bonvalot, setting down his tea cup.

"The job you gave me is far too dangerous for a simple squirrel dealer."

"Too dangerous? I hired you because you claimed to be the best. You said you accompanied the great Prejevalsky to the Lob Nor and Prejevalsky wasn't in the habit of hiring poltroons."

"I know what I said but this is different," said Abdullah. "The lama is crazy. He's a demon. When he spoke to me he filled me with such terror, I feared for my life. I turned and ran as fast as I could. That's why I'm keeping the coin you gave me although my mission was unsuccessful. I must be compensated for my trouble. Indeed, that is no ordinary lama. I'm warning you, sahib, don't trust him. He may put a curse on you."

Bonvalot slammed his fist on the carpet. "Do you think I'm afraid of your stupid curses and black magic? I don't have time for that nonsense. Now get out of here." He dismissed Abdullah with a wave of his hand.

Reaching for his revolver, Bonvalot made sure it was loaded then shoved it back into his holster as he tiptoed out of the inn.

Outside, darkness had settled over Korla. Dogs barked in the distance and crickets chirped. Stars twinkled in the night sky and the moon cast a warm glow over the mud-bricked hovels. Guided by a faint glow from the stables, Bonvalot made his way over to the barn, his hand hovering over his revolver.

Entering silently, Bonvalot walked past the stalls peering inside each one. His heart pounded as he scanned the barn like a hawk in search of prey.

He spied the lama sitting on a bed of hay. He was spinning his prayer wheel and chanting a Buddhist prayer in a dull monotone. And though his face was shrouded by his hood and his back was turned to Bonvalot, his menacing presence filled the room.

"Turn around," ordered Bonvalot. "I've been hearing reports about you from my men. I don't know who you are but you're not coming with us any more. I'm ordering you to stay in Korla and find another caravan."

Unexpectedly, the lama spun around and pulled down his hood. Bonvalot recoiled and took a step backwards. The lama's face was a mask of death. His skin had a yellow pallor and was badly cracked. His bloodshot eyes glared like red orbs and his hair was a tangled mess that seemed to be falling out in patches. There was hardly any flesh on his bones. His body was so raw from lice bites, he looked half dead. That's when Bonvalot knew for certain the old Mongolian lama was none other than Prejevalsky. The hallucination had already taken on a fixed form.

"You..." said Bonvalot, removing his revolver. "I warned you to stay away. Now get out of here before I shoot you."

A devilish laugh escaped Prejevalsky's mouth. "I told you I would guide you to Lhasa and I intend to do precisely that. Together you and I will reach the Forbidden City. If you think you can make it without me, you're sadly mistaken. Without me, you're nothing. If you try to send me away, I guarantee that your expedition will end in failure."

Bonvalot cocked the revolver and pointed it at Prejevalsky's head. "Get out, now."

"I'm not going anywhere," said Prejevalsky "You need me."

"I don't need you because you're not real. You don't exist."

"Oh, I exist. You see me don't you? This is my last chance to reach Lhasa. My soul won't rest until I've seen the Dalai Lama."

"Your soul is damned," said Bonvalot, pointing the revolver at his adversary's head. "You're not coming to Tibet. I can guarantee that."

Prejevalsky locked eyes with his rival. "If you don't want any harm to come to the woman, you'll take me with you. If you do, I can guarantee you'll reach Lhasa. But if you try to shoot me or send me away, the woman will die. And I will make sure you never reach Lhasa."

Bonvalot stared at Prejevalsky's ghastly countenance and blinked his eyes. His finger hovered over the trigger, sweat poured down his face in rivulets, his heart thumped wildly, and his breathing came in heavy gasps.

"And you'll die also," added Prejevalsky. "Now make your decision."

"I can kill you right now and be finished with you."

"No you can't," said Prejevalsky. "You can't kill me with a gun. Your only choice is to take me with you. If you refuse, the woman will never wake up in the morning."

Bonvalot stared into Prejevalsky's sunken eyes and saw a vision of Camille's dead body slumped under her sheepskin blanket. When he pulled aside the blanket all that remained was a skeleton dressed in baggy Russian pants and a crumpled shirtwaist. Her reddish gold hair lay strewn across the pillow like lifeless straw matted with blood. Her eye sockets were covered with flies. Revolting desert flies.

Bonvalot uncocked the revolver and placed it back in his holster.

"Wise choice," said the demonic lama, turning his back on Bonvalot and taking up his prayer wheel. "You're a smart man Monsieur Bonvalot. A very smart man."

CHAPTER 16

Korla, Chinese Turkestan
October, 1889

Panicked and out of breath, Bartholomeus raced back to the inn. Dodging servant girls with platters of tea and sweetmeats, he made his way to the guest quarters where he found Father Dedeken seated on a raised carpet, reading his Bible and helping himself to bowls of figs, grapes, and apricots.

"Master, there may be trouble ahead," said Bartholomeus, struggling to catch his breath. "Big trouble."

"What are you talking about?" said Dedeken, gazing at his Chinese servant over the tops of his spectacles.

"I was wandering through the bazaar when I heard some Chinese people saying that the Hakim, the Mohammedan chief of the town, was planning to order us all back to Kuldja."

"He what?" said Dedeken, closing his Bible. "Are you sure?"

"Indeed," nodded Bartholomeus. "They may arrest us if we refuse to comply. Please warn Monsieur Bonvalot to expect a visit from a group of Chinese mandarins. They will surely demand his traveling papers and cause him a great deal of trouble."

Several hours later, Bonvalot and Rachmed returned from the bazaar with two wagons full of supplies. In addition, they rented an additional twenty camels for the next stage of the journey and hired a new caravaneer, a man by the name of Parpa, a broad-shouldered, boastful man with a long black beard and a swaggering nature. He was rumored to have worked for the Englishman Carey when he attempted to break into the Forbidden Kingdom. Parpa had an interesting history, he was a native of Ferghana and arrived in Korla in the company of the infamous Yakub Beg, the Tajik adventurer who proclaimed himself King of Kashgaria. Bonvalot was hoping that Parpa would be able to help guide them across the Altyn Tagh Mountains.

When they arrived, Father Dedeken pulled Bonvalot and Rachmed aside to warn them about the rumor Bartholomeus had heard in the bazaar. Bonvalot waved it off as a bunch of nonsense.

"I refuse to get worked up over a silly bazaar rumor," said Bonvalot, checking off the supplies in a notebook.

"This could be serious," said Father Dedeken. "Ambans or Hakims rarely go against the orders of Peking. They will demand your Chinese passport and cause you a great deal of trouble if you refuse to obey."

"I have a general pass from the Governor of Kuldja right here in my pocket. That's the only passport I need."

Rachmed dropped a burlap bag on the ground. "If they want to give us trouble, let them. I believe that if a man is compelled to fight, he should exclaim "Allah Akbar!" and die with a sword in his hand. Any other way is pure cowardice."

"Please sheath your sword my dear Uzbek friend," said Bonvalot. "There will be no fighting on my watch. I prepared a bag of silver ingots for precisely such a confrontation. Leave it to me."

After the supplies were stored away, Rachmed and Parpa left to get the horses shod, and to prepare new saddles for the camels. Nothing more was said about the Hakim's visit that night.

The next day, when Bonvalot, Parpa, and Rachmed returned from the saddle-maker, they found the servants of the Hakim pacing around the caravanserai, waiting for them. When Bonvalot approached them, they bowed respectfully and announced the imminent arrival of their master. Wasting no time, Bonvalot and his men dropped their saddles and dashed off to find Father Dedeken and Bartholomeus, who would act as interpreters.

A short while later, a great commotion arose from outside as the Hakim and his entourage of mandarins rattled down the road in two-wheeled, canopied carriages. They stopped at the door of the caravanserai and the officials stepped out with great pomp and ceremony, causing the neighbors and passersby to drop what they were doing and watch with curiosity.

The Hakim, a stern-faced man with hooded eyes, hawkish cheeks, and a long black moustache, was wearing a Mohammedan-style tunic over a set of trousers, while on his head he sported a round Chinese headdress with a long pigtail hanging down his back. Bartholomeus whispered to Bonvalot that the pigtail symbolized that the Hakim, although a Mohammedan, was a vassal of the Chinese Empire. Indeed, the entire prefecture of Karachar was a vassal state of China and subject to the laws of Peking.

As the Hakim and his entourage entered the inn, Bonvalot and the caravan men greeted them by bowing low, in accordance with his rank. They led the visitors to the sitting room and offered them white felt seats, which they unrolled with great honor. Bonvalot was on his guard, expecting an interrogation of sorts, but before the meeting started, the Hakim's servants entered bearing porcelain tea pots which they passed to all those present.

After they had drunk the ceremonial three cups of tea, the Hakim cleared his throat and began speaking Chinese. Sitting on either side of Bonvalot, Father Dedeken and Bartholomeus translated his Chinese into French. From her vantage point in the women's section, Camille sat with the innkeeper's wife with creases of anxiety on her face. From across the room Bonvalot caught her eye and gave her a reassuring nod, which caused her to smile and nod in return.

The Hakim started by inquiring after the visitors' health, and congratulating them on having made a safe journey thus far. While he spoke, more servants entered and placed bowls of dried fruits, melons, and almonds in front of Bonvalot and his men, in accordance with the custom of Turkestan.

Bonvalot thanked the Hakim for his hospitality and glanced in the corner where Rachmed, Parpa, and Abdullah sat huddled together, eyeing the Hakim and his mandarins with suspicion.

When the Hakim spoke next, his voice grew more somber. He explained that the standard procedure in the Chinese Empire was to require all visitors to produce their traveling papers, no exceptions. Expecting this, Bonvalot handed over the general pass which he had received from the Governor of the Ili Province. He stated that he was taking the prince hunting in the Tsaidam Basin, and had received permission from the Governor and hoped to receive the same treatment from the mandarins in Korla.

The Hakim eyed the document, a curious letter with red Chinese characters. "Indeed, we understand the Governor of the Ili Province has authorized your journey. However, here in Korla we require that all travelers who enter China obtain a passport issued by the Imperial court in Peking, which explains the nature of their visit and contains all the necessary stamps and approvals. I see that in your case, this has not been done."

Bonvalot frowned. He did not wish to explain to the Hakim that applying for a Chinese Passport from Peking was the last thing in the world he wanted to do since by doing so he would have to hand over his full itinerary to the authorities, who would use the information to track him down and stop him. Bonvalot's only option now was evasion. And if that failed, his next option was to point a gun at the Hakim's head.

"Indeed," replied Bonvalot, settling comfortably in his seat. "Your custom is a good one since one can never be too careful when it comes to strangers. However, with regard to me and my men, the pass from the Governor of Ili clearly states that a member of my party, the fair-haired young gentleman to my right, is allied to the Kings of the West. Even the Russian Tsar trusted us enough to facilitate our passage through his territory. We sincerely hope the Emperor of China and his ministers will be equally obliging and not delay us unnecessarily."

The Hakim sat back and scratched his cheek.

"If you wish," continued Bonvalot. "You may keep the general pass, which contains the Governor's signature."

The Hakim gave a sly half-smile and said, "Very well. I will keep the pass in my possession until I reach a final decision on whether or not to grant you my approval."

"Thank you, Excellency. I hope we didn't take too much of your time."

The entire assembly rose and bowed. As soon as the Hakim and his entourage left, Bonvalot began to pace around the room, jingling the coins in his money belt as he muttered under his breath. Rachmed emitted a low whistle and rolled his eyes.

"It sounds like the old story to me," said Rachmed. "You'll see, those pork eaters will be back, and when they do, they'll torture us with their increasing demands. It's far from over. It'll get much worse, you'll see."

Bonvalot poured himself another glass of tea and added a shot of brandy. Prince Henri reclined on the carpet and blew out a stream of smoke from his cigarette.

"I think you handled him quite well, Bonvalot," said Henri. "Our Hakim friend doesn't want to start a war with the West. Rachmed, be a good fellow and fetch me another glass of sherry, will you? We'll just have to make these chieftains understand that I'm a prince and deserve to be treated with proper respect."

Rachmed fumed as he poured Henri a glass of sherry, then he slammed it down on the table.

"The only thing these petty tyrants understand is force," said Bonvalot. "We can't afford to show them any weakness."

"Then it will certainly come to war if we refuse to comply with their demands," said Rachmed.

"They can go to hell the whole lot of them," said Prince Henri. "I have no patience for petty bureaucrats and their puny laws. If they try to push us around I'll send a telegram to my father. He'll have it out with the Chinese Ambassador and that Hakim will be sent into exile."

Bartholomeus stepped forward. "Excuse me for interrupting, but if you make the Hakim look bad, he will only make things worse for you, prince or not. These men are like hard jade. They do not bend. You must try to soften him up."

"I'm not worried about a bunch of bumbling bureaucrats," said Bonvalot downing the last of his tea. "If I have to shoot my way out of Korla, I will. But just in case, I think we should pack up and be ready to sneak out of here by tomorrow latest."

Camille strolled over from the ladies' section.

"Monsieur Bonvalot," she said. "There's no need to cause a diplomatic tussle. I suggest we negotiate with this man. Every official has his price. But if you try to evade their laws, you'll make it worse for the rest of us. Maybe you can afford to play the role of swashbuckler, but I came here for a very serious purpose. I don't want to end up in jail."

"Madame, do you want to find your husband or not?"

"Of *course* I want to find my husband," she said, indignantly.

"Then let me handle the matter," said Bonvalot. "I promised to take you to Tibet but I never said it would be easy. You knew the risks beforehand. For every mile we go, the stakes get higher. Right now we're playing a high stakes poker game, winner takes all."

"Except that in this game of poker, all the cards are written in Chinese," said Henri. "The only policy these barbarians understand is the *lex talionis*, the law of retaliation: an eye for an eye, a tooth for a tooth. The only way we can win is with a show of greater force."

"How is that possible when they have a whole garrison at their disposal with soldiers and guns?" said Camille.

"You have nothing to fear from those soldiers," said Bonvalot. "My spies tell me they are all opium addicts, disorganized and untrained. Rachmed can beat a whole garrison of them."

The men burst into laughter.

"So what do we do now?" said Camille.

Prince Henri sauntered up to Camille and brushed her cheek.

"We could open up a bottle of Dom Perignon and go for a camel ride through the streets of Korla, would you find that suitably romantic Madame Dancourt?"

"That's enough," said Bonvalot, pulling Henri away from Camille. "We've got more pressing matters at hand."

All at once, the Mongolian lama emerged from a dark corner of the room. By now his appearance was horrifying, with skin that was bruised and cracked, matted hair, and sores on every part of his body. Everyone in the room froze as the devilish monk made his way across the room and stood directly in front of Bonvalot. He pushed back his hood, revealing a ghastly form that caused Camille to gasp in horror and take several steps backward.

With a gravelly voice, the lama said, "The Hakim will be back tomorrow. If you want to get out of here, you must do exactly as I say."

CHAPTER 17

Early the next morning, Rachmed salaamed as Camille emerged from the women's quarters, drawn by the smell of black Arab coffee and fried naan bread. "Good morning, memsahib."

"Good morning, Rachmed," she said, looking around. "Where is Monsieur Bonvalot?"

"He went to the saddle-maker with Abdullah to hasten the sewing of the new camel saddles. We cannot leave for Lob Nor without them. Come and have some hot naan and coffee."

"Only if I don't have to see that vile creature again. He gave me such a fright, I couldn't sleep the entire night."

"Don't worry memsahib. He sleeps in the barn with the animals. He won't bother you or anyone else."

Father Dedeken looked up from his Bible. "By his ghastly appearance, I suspect he's suffering from some sort of spiritual malady as well. My seminary training did not prepare me for matters of the occult."

Just then, Prince Henri entered the room in an agitated state.

"Rachmed, where the devil is my shaving kit?" he said, rummaging through his saddlebag with a look of exasperation. "Why is everything so messy and disorganized?"

Rachmed's face darkened. "I did not touch your shaving kit, Your Highness. Are you suggesting I took it?"

Prince Henri kicked the saddlebag. "It's your job to prepare my things! What kind of valet are you? I have half a mind to dock your wages."

Rachmed's face turned crimson. He balled his hands into fists and shook them with rage. "I am not your valet. I am the caravanbashi, the leader of the caravan."

Henri shook his head. "It's so hard to get good help. I suppose I shall have to speak to Monsieur Bonvalot when he returns."

Rachmed threw up his hands and stormed out of the inn.

Camille looked perplexed. "Really Your Highness, I think you insulted the man. You can't speak to the natives here like you do in Paris or London. They're not used to being treated like servants. It hurts their pride."

"Indeed," said Father Dedeken. "Rachmed comes from a proud race of Turkish Uzbeks. Without his extraordinary knowledge and guidance, we wouldn't last five minutes out there."

"The qualities of a good servant are meekness and servility, not pride," said Henri. "Something about him has always bothered me. I intend to get rid of him as soon as possible."

"Your Highness, you don't understand. Rachmed wasn't hired to be your servant. He and Monsieur Bonvalot have been traveling companions for years. If you want my advice, you should treat him with more respect. Some day he might even save your life."

Prince Henri laughed as if that was the funniest thing he had ever heard.

Later that afternoon, Bonvalot and Father Dedeken were ready when the Hakim returned. They greeted the entourage at the door with the same obsequious bowing, the same ceremonial three cups of tea, but this time, no pleasantries were exchanged. Before they even finished their third cup of tea, the Hakim ordered Bonvalot to see the Governor of Karachar before continuing on his journey.

Bonvalot took out a sack of silver ingots and slid it across the table. "Perhaps this gift of friendship will enable me to bypass all this needless bureaucracy."

The Hakim shook his head and pushed the money away. "I cannot accept a bribe under these conditions. I am ordering you to visit the Governor of Karachar immediately."

"That's impossible," said Bonvalot. "Who is this governor that I should go out of my way to visit him? If he wants to speak to me, let him come here."

The Hakim's face turned to stone. "Your papers are of no value, Monsieur Bonvalot. Furthermore, I have a warrant here for your arrest."

The Hakim held up an official Chinese document written with bold strokes. Each character contained ominous overtones, as if the scribe had slashed his quill across the scroll in fury.

Bonvalot and Rachmed exchanged a worried glance. Father Dedeken adjusted his spectacles and asked to read the document up close. The Hakim obliged by handing it over to Dedeken, who studied it with Bartholomeus, their bespectacled eyes scanning the scroll like two nodding donkeys.

Bonvalot neck grew hot. "Where is the general pass I gave you yesterday? I demand you return it at once."

The Hakim's voice turned menacing. "It is at Karachar."

Without thinking twice, Bonvalot snatched the warrant out of Father Dedeken's hand and stuffed it in his pocket.

"Then I shall keep the warrant until you return my pass. I don't believe a word you say. Now go. Please leave these premises at once."

The Hakim blanched. He turned to his mandarins, but they were similarly alarmed. This was a serious breach of protocol that could result in the whole lot of them being thrown into prison. Now frantic, the Hakim begged Bonvalot to return the document, emphasizing the severity of the punishment he would face by making a cutting gesture across his throat. Behind him, the mandarins nodded gravely.

Bonvalot was unmoved.

"You'll get the warrant back as soon as I get my pass back," said Bonvalot. "I believe I asked you to leave."

"But Monsieur Bonvalot," said the Hakim. "I told you I do not have your pass."

"Then I refuse to return your warrant," said Bonvalot, pointing to the door. "Now get out and don't come back until you bring my pass."

Crestfallen, the Hakim and his entourage rose and started for the door. A few minutes later, one of the mandarins returned bearing the missing pass. Bonvalot snatched it out of his hand and stuffed it in his pocket.

"I will return your warrant tomorrow *after* I've had a chance to photograph it," said Bonvalot, crossing his arms. "Now go."

Dejected, the mandarin left at once.

After Prince Henri had photographed the Chinese warrant, Father Dedeken sat down to translate it for Bonvalot:

"I, Han, fulfilling the duties of prefect of the district of Karachar, have received the following order from Governor Wei: 'At the present time, a prince of royal blood from the kingdom of France, Hengli (Henri), is traveling without a Chinese passport and on his own initiative, and is presently making his way toward Lob Nor. Wherever the French prince is found, I order the local authorities to stop him and turn him back. As a result of this order, I am dispatching two agents to gather information and will proceed at once to Korla and will act in concert with the Mussulman chiefs of this locality in order to inspect the country. If the French prince is found, he must be arrested and prevented from penetrating further and turned back. The agents must not be guilty of negligence or delay under pain of the severest penalty. This order is valid and in force. The eighth day of the ninth moon of the fifteenth year of Kouang-Sin."

"Well that's great," said Bonvalot, tossing the warrant down in disgust.

"Do they think I'm going to turn around because of some silly Chinese gibberish?" said Prince Henri, puffing nervously on his cigarette.

"I warned you not to anger the Hakim," said Bartholomeus. "Now look what's happened. The Hakim made it worse. I predict big trouble ahead."

"I expected as much," said Bonvalot. "You can't trust those Chinese mandarins even if you lay out the red carpet for them. They're lying, deceitful scoundrels."

"Bonvalot-sahib," said Rachmed. "You still have one more option. You can do what the old lama told you."

"Yes I know," said Bonvalot, rubbing his forehead with the heel of his hand. "I'll attend to that matter today. I suppose we'll have a showdown of sorts because I have no intention of backing down."

"Be careful what you vow," said Father Dedeken. "We're vastly outnumbered."

The next day, the Hakim and the mandarins arrived in a cavalcade of carriages and horses that drew uneasy glances from the neighbors' windows. This time, when they entered the inn there was less bowing and their faces were strained. The Hakim strode into the guest quarters and got straight to the point. Fixing his eyes on Bonvalot, he demanded the return of the warrant.

Without hesitating, Bonvalot handed the document to him and watched with amusement as the beleaguered bureaucrat snatched it with shaky, sweaty hands. Glancing in the corner, Bonvalot caught sight of Abdullah and Parpa stifling a laugh.

The Hakim clenched his jaws and glared at Bonvalot.

"I've had enough of your games, Monsieur Bonvalot. I came here to warn you that you are forbidden from continuing further into Chinese territory. I order you to stop now and turn around."

"I have no intention of stopping," said Bonvalot. "Tomorrow we leave for Lob Nor and nothing can stop us. I am taking the prince on a hunting expedition and no one, not you, not the Governor of Karachar, and not even the Emperor of China can stop us. As soon as we're ready to leave, we'll load up our camels and be off. If you make any attempt to stop us by force, there will be bloodshed, and the blood will be on your hands. Need I remind you that Prince Henri is a prince of royal blood. If anyone touches a hair on his head there will be serious repercussions."

The Hakim looked like he was about to explode. His face turned a deep crimson and his eyebrows twitched. A stir broke out among the mandarins, each one whispering in the ears of his colleagues as the translations flew back and forth.

"We are not evil men," continued Bonvalot. "We are not here to cause trouble. We have done you no harm and we expect the same protection you provide to the other caravans. I have nothing further to say on the subject."

The Hakim scratched his chin and switched tactics. This time, he switched from Chinese to his native Turkish dialect, which he infused with great emotion.

"Please be reasonable Monsieur Bonvalot. I'm caught in the middle between you and my superiors. I mean no harm to you or to His Highness. I can see you're not bad people, but what do you expect me to do? If I go against my orders they will bring a heavy punishment down on my head. I'm like a nut caught between two heavy stones. I swear by Allah my life is at stake."

The Hakim was panic-stricken, but Bonvalot was stone-faced.

"Then at least do me one small favor," continued the Hakim. "I will travel to Karachar tonight to speak to my superior. Let me take a man from your party with me. Let him explain the matter to the Governor. He can do a much better job than I can, and with the help of Allah, the matter will be arranged in your favor."

Bonvalot was not about to fall for such a simple trick.

"I'm sorry Excellency, but what you ask is impossible. I don't recognize your sub-prefecture and sending one of my men there would be a waste of time since even if your superior tries to stop us, we would leave regardless."

"I'm warning you, Bonvalot," said the Hakim, narrowing his eyes. "Do not try to escape. There will be serious repercussions."

"And I'm warning you that if you try to stop us, I shall send a photograph of the warrant to our Pasha in France and there will be even more trouble."

The Hakim blanched. He turned to his chiefs and shouted something in a voice so furious, that the entire party of mandarins rose from their seats and left.

As they stood by the window watching the Hakim's carriages disappear down the street, Prince Henri turned to Bonvalot and said, "Do you think it worked?"

"Do I think what worked?" said Bonvalot, pouring himself a glass of brandy.

"Your little ruse, the ploy the old lama told you about."

"Oh that, we're just getting started, my friend," said Bonvalot. "Rachmed, take Parpa and go to the saddle-maker at once. Pick up the remaining saddles and come back quickly. The rest of you load your rifles. We will leave tomorrow no matter what."

The next day as expected, the Hakim and his entourage returned to the inn with great fanfare and commotion. This time, no one bowed and the Hakim's face looked drawn and haggard.

"Monsieur Bonvalot, you have tried my patience enough," said the Hakim. "I order you to take your caravan and return from wherever you came. You have no permission to venture any further into Chinese territory."

"I refuse," said Bonvalot.

"Then I shall have to resort to force," said the Hakim.

At this pronouncement, Bonvalot and his men burst out laughing.

The Hakim's jaw clenched; his face turned a deep shade of purple. He glared at Bonvalot with a look of pure rage. Before he could speak, another member of the Hakim's entourage pushed his way forward. This man was the Russian Aqsaqal, the head of the Russian subjects in Korla. In a voice full of terror, the Aqsaqal related how the Chinese authorities had threatened to put his neck in chains and drag him to Karachar if he assisted Bonvalot's party in any way.

"While I pity your dilemma," said Bonvalot. "Your tale of woe does not compel me to change my travel plans. My answer is still no."

But something about the Russian Aqsaqal's eyes bothered Bonvalot. He had the look of an indentured slave. His servility unnerved Bonvalot. He knew they had to flee Korla at once.

After the Hakim and his entourage left, Bonvalot called all the caravan men to the courtyard for a strategy meeting. When the men were seated in a semi-circle, Bonvalot laid out his plan.

"I've received reports that a contingent of soldiers from Karachar is on their way to Korla to reinforce the garrison, which we know from observation to be manned by poorly-trained soldiers who fritter away the hours in an opium-induced state. Therefore, time is running short. I want each and every one of you to finish your preparations at once. Abdullah, please purchase another ten sheep for the journey. Tonight we will eat an early dinner, sleep until midnight, and then load the animals as quietly as possible. If all goes as planned, we'll head out at dawn. Under no circumstances should you speak to any of the locals, especially the servants. Have I made myself perfectly clear?" The men nodded solemnly. "Good. I have one final question. If the Hakim decides to detain us by force, how do you intend to respond?"

Each man held up a defiant fist.

"Good," said Bonvalot. "If anyone tries to attack you, give him a show of strength he'll never forget it. Now let's get going."

That night, under a bright yellow moon, while dogs yelped and donkeys brayed, the caravan men roused themselves from their slumber and crept outside to load the camels. By daybreak, all the horses were saddled and the men kept their rifles slung over their shoulders in case of a surprise attack. Following the advice of the lama, Bonvalot dashed off a letter to the Governor in Karachar stating their intention to go hunting in Lob Nor where they expected to remain until the necessary documents arrived from Peking.

Bonvalot sent a copy of the letter to the Hakim, but to his chagrin, news of their impending departure was leaked to the townspeople who showed up en masse in the courtyard to see them off, when their true intentions were really to ransack their supplies.

Thinking quickly, Rachmed, Abdullah, and Parpa picked up sticks to drive off the scoundrels, but not before they managed to pick a few pockets.

"Bonvalot-sahib, we must go quick before the soldiers arrive," said Rachmed, putting down his stick after driving off the last villager.

"Do you think it worked?" said Bonvalot.

"By the will of Allah I am sure it worked," said Rachmed. "Indeed, you were very wise in your dealings with the Hakim."

"How so?"

"By writing the letter you allowed him to save face," said Rachmed. "And what's more, I am certain the Hakim was secretly hoping for this solution. But being a good Chinese subject, he could not say so openly."

"So where does that leave us?"

"We load our carbines and make haste."

After Bonvalot distributed bags of silver and gifts to the Innkeeper, he and Rachmed leapt into the saddle. Riding to the front of the caravan, Rachmed raised his hand to his beard and proclaimed, "Allahu Akhbar!' and the caravan started up again.

The men on horseback rode in front while the camels followed behind single file, nose to tail, swinging their necks and swaying their bodies as they trudged down the dusty streets of Korla. As they progressed, they caught sight of the unveiled faces of the women observing them from darkened windows while the men stood along the rooftops watching the caravan wend its way to the outskirts of the city. Running alongside them, barefoot children called out *'salaam'* to the sahibs, and squealed with delight when Bonvalot and Prince Henri answered *'salaam'* in turn.

They followed the crenellated city walls of Korla and made their way out to the open desert. Meanwhile, Rachmed trotted ahead to the city's gate, keeping a lookout for any sign of trouble from the garrison. Luck was on their side; the only activity he could detect was a plume of black smoke curling up from the fort's watchtower against the turquoise blue sky. When the camels finally caught up with Rachmed, he breathed a sigh of relief. But they did not have long to rejoice. Several hours later, as they made their way south over the Taklamakan Desert, they glanced over their shoulders and saw a telltale cloud of dust rising from the direction of Korla.

PART 2

CHAPTER 18

Taklamakan Desert
November, 1889

A dozen of the Hakim's horsemen were gaining on the caravan. Bonvalot grabbed his spy glass. Twisting the ring, he focused on the cloud of dust and saw the Hakim and a military escort galloping steadily toward them. There was an occasional staccato burst of gunfire followed by terrifying yells as the horsemen pounded their way across the desert.

Bonvalot ordered Imatch to lead the camels southward while he, Father Dedeken, Prince Henri, Rachmed, and Abdullah would wait behind to stave off the Hakim's men. He instructed Father Dedeken to take his carbine and camouflage himself behind a mound of rocks several dozen feet away and wait for the signal to fire. Adding to their distress, they heard the camels plodding southward, the tinkling of their bells growing fainter with the passing minutes until they were no longer audible. Once the camels were out of earshot, all they heard was stamping hooves, and the whoops and hollers of the approaching soldiers.

Creases of anxiety appeared on Bonvalot's forehead as he pulled Rachmed aside to talk strategy. Seconds later, Rachmed removed his black sheepskin cap, dismounted his horse and disappeared behind a sand dune.

As the Hakim's soldiers got closer, Bonvalot ordered the men to unlatch their safeties and keep their rifles pointed skyward. Soon, the soldiers halted several dozen feet away. Bonvalot watched their dark, sullen faces and menacing jezail rifles with growing anxiety. This was their last chance to evade arrest.

The Hakim trotted forward until he was facing Bonvalot.

"So, we meet again Bonvalot-sahib. It was very discourteous of you to leave without saying a proper goodbye."

"I do not like to overstay my welcome," said Bonvalot.

"I hear you gave a nice present to your host," said the Hakim, showing a set of gold teeth in a forced smile.

"We stayed a little longer than I anticipated. I felt it was only proper that I compensate him for his trouble."

"I have come to execute the warrant for your arrest issued by the Governor of Karachar," said the Hakim, his smile now completely vanished.

"With all due respect," said Bonvalot. "I told the governor we intended to go hunting at Lob Nor. When my travelling papers arrive from Peking, you may send a messenger to deliver them. But I refuse to return to Korla under any circumstances."

"These soldiers are under orders to not return without you."

"Then I deeply regret they have come this way for nothing," said Bonvalot without flinching.

Slithering along the dunes like a desert snake, Rachmed crept up behind one of the mounted mandarins. With a knife clenched between his teeth, Rachmed pulled the mandarin off his horse and dragged him several feet away. The mandarin screamed and struggled, but Rachmed held him firmly in a choke hold as he pressed the knife against the man's ribs.

"If you attempt to stop us, this man will die," said Bonvalot. "And his blood will be upon your hands. Once we are safely on the other side of the Konchi-Darya River, we will send him back on a donkey with enough food and water for two days."

The soldiers stared with cold, hardened eyes. They held the reins of their horses with their left hands and held their jezail rifles with their right hands, pointing skyward. They did not attempt to rescue the hostage.

By now, Rachmed was pressing the knife against the terrified man's throat.

Seeing the mandarin's helpless plight, the Hakim's eyes bulged from his head.

"I order you to release that man at once!" he said.

Bonvalot shook his head. "Not until after we are safely on the other side of the river."

"I could order my men to shoot you now," said the Hakim.

"And I have a sniper hidden behind a pile of rocks with a carbine pointed directly at your head," said Bonvalot. "If you give the order, you will be the first to drop dead. You must decide if detaining me is worth getting your head blown off."

The Hakim's face turned purple. "I demand you compensate me the same way you compensated the Innkeeper. It's not the custom in these parts to go behind the backs of the local mandarins."

"Of what good is the money of kafirs?" said Bonvalot. "It is as unclean as the meat we eat. Normally I would throw some coins in the sand since that is the only way our money can be made clean, but since you have showed us such gracious hospitality, I will reward you properly."

Bonvalot tossed a sack of coins at the Hakim, causing the man to bristle. He threw the sack to the sand and raised a defiant fist.

"Cursed infidels!" he yelled, then he ordered his men back to Korla.

With a defiant cry, the soldiers turned and galloped back toward Korla. Bonvalot watched as the horsemen grew smaller and smaller until they disappeared in a cloud of dust. Rachmed removed the knife from the mandarin's throat whereupon the stricken man fell to the sand, unconscious. Picking him up, Rachmed laid the hostage across his horse and climbed back in the saddle just as Father Dedeken returned from his hiding place.

"By Jove you did it!" said Dedeken, wiping the sweat off his forehead. "For a minute I though we were finished. As we used to say back in seminary, *finita la commedia*."

"Prince Henri, how did you enjoy this impromptu lesson in Chinese diplomacy?" said Bonvalot, grinning.

"I rather enjoyed it although it was a little too close for comfort," said Prince Henri. "And I must offer my compliments to Rachmed for a job well done. Taking that soldier hostage was dash cunning of you."

"It is worth remembering your Highness," said Rachmed, grinning beneath his sheepskin cap. "Never to try the patience of an angry Uzbek, especially not in the desert."

Leaving Prince Henri speechless, Rachmed called out, "Allahu Akhbar!" and took off at a canter across the desert without once looking back over his shoulder.

CHAPTER 19

For several days the camels marched single file over the golden sands of the Taklamakan Desert. Every now and then signs of life would appear: tamarisk trees, desert shrubs, distant herds of wild donkeys, but they saw no evidence of human life. Indeed, in the Turki language, Taklamakan meant 'you can get into it, but you can never get out.' After hours of endless trekking, they stopped to rest at an oasis.

The guides gave a signal to halt and all at once the camels sank to the ground with an unmistakable sigh of relief. Prince Henri dismounted, called for a groom to unsaddle his horse, and set about unpacking his camera to capture the unspoken beauty of the wilderness. Hoping for some fresh game, Rachmed and Father Dedeken galloped off in search of wildlife, while Bonvalot decided it was time to teach Camille some of the basics of survival.

"Madame Dancourt, I think it's time you learned the basics of wilderness survival. Do you care to join me?"

"I would love nothing better," she said.

Grabbing her by the hand, Bonvalot led her through the maze of kneeling camels until they reached a shady spot under a clump of tamarisk trees. Extracting his compass, he held it lovingly in his hands.

"A compass is an explorer's lifeline," said Bonvalot, sitting close enough to catch the rosy scent of her skin. "But when conditions are difficult, a traveler must be able to find his way to safety by any means possible, with or without a compass. If you ever get lost or separated, you can always locate true north by looking at the stars. First you locate the North Star—which is also called Polaris—by scanning the night sky for the Little Dipper. The North Star is the last star in the handle of the Little Dipper.

From there you draw an imaginary line to the ground. That point is true north, and if you can spot a landmark at that point, you can use it to guide yourself. Is that clear?"

"That sounds extraordinary," said Camille. "Yes, I believe I've got it."

"Good, you're a quick learner," said Bonvalot, squeezing her hand. He launched into an advanced discussion of course plotting and direction finding, teaching her everything she should know if she should ever get lost or separated. When he was done, Camille was overwhelmed.

"Monsieur Bonvalot, thank you for taking me along. You took a tremendous risk on my behalf. I'm very grateful to you."

Bonvalot's voice turned serious. "I feel I should warn you, the journey will soon become much more dangerous. When we reach the Tibetan high plain, we will be traveling at high altitudes where the air is so thin even the hardiest men suffer from mountain sickness, and the temperature drops to well below freezing. When I saw you're your determination back in Kuldja, I decided to give you a chance, but soon you may wish you had never come along."

"I appreciate the warning, but I'm well aware of the danger. And please forgive me for misjudging you before. I realize now how hot-headed I behaved back in Paris. I'm not proud of myself."

Bonvalot grinned. "There's no need to apologize. If I had to count every time I behaved foolishly I would need Imatch's abacus. When it comes to acting foolish and hot-headed, I have much more experience than you."

Camille blushed. "I guess that makes us even. And I hope we can be friends now. Tell me something about yourself, I feel as though I hardly know you. What drew you to this life of exploration?"

"I never wanted to do anything else," he said. "A newspaper reporter once said I have a *passion for the planet*. I love discovering new places, new cultures, new animals, all the mysteries of our world. I'm drawn to anything foreign and exotic— what they call the unknowable. And lastly, I've always been more at home in the saddle than in a cozy chair by the fire. Or maybe it was because I never had the patience for an ordinary life. Curiously enough, my life started out very ordinary. My father was a mounted tax collector, but I didn't have the heart to follow in his footsteps. Instead, I dreamed about seeing the world and I followed my dream. I discovered out in the wilderness that the eye sees more clearly and the heart feels more deeply. It's only out here that I began to understand the mysteries of our universe. Does that answer your question, Madame Dancourt?"

"Indeed, you've lived an extraordinary life," she said. "Perhaps in my own small way I share your love of adventure. But for a girl born to a stiff-necked banker and a social-climbing mother, the only way I could see the world was by marrying a naval officer. As it turned out, our married life was very brief. Armand became obsessed with mapping Central Asia. Perhaps I was a bit naïve when I married him; his sister told me he wasn't the marrying kind. And now I find myself risking my life to find out what it was that drew him to this exotic and mysterious land. It's actually rather comical to think that a banker's daughter from Lyon may be the first European woman to reach Lhasa."

Bonvalot laughed. "Stranger things have been known to occur. But if I can dissolve any of your worries, I have high hopes for a successful outcome for this expedition."

"And what entails a successful outcome?" said Camille.

"It wouldn't hurt to find gold statues, precious jewels, antique curiosities," said Bonvalot. "Or rare manuscripts or works of art. But I think the most successful outcome would be to meet the Dalai Lama himself. For that we'll need a lot of help from the gods of exploration."

"Or your impressive arsenal," said Camille. "Which you are no doubt anxious to put to good use. But more than anything, I'm amazed by how closely the men have bonded. The way they work in teams is remarkable."

"And I've noticed how some of the men have more than a sisterly affection for you," said Bonvalot.

"I assume you mean Henri," she said. "He doesn't bother me. He's just a spoiled, petulant child."

"A spoiled, petulant child who's likely to get himself killed with his rash behavior." He scanned the horizon. "I think we'd better get back on the road, Madame Dancourt. We've got a long stretch ahead of us and very little daylight left."

Rising, Bonvalot took Camille's hand and led her silently back to the caravan.

They continued south across the windswept desert for hundreds of miles, the men on horseback riding ahead to scout the way, while the chain of camels brought up the rear. For hundreds of miles they marched over gritty yellow sand and past sparse desert foliage, while the wind whipped them without mercy.

Soon they entered the vicinity of Lob Nor, a dry, desert region that was almost entirely devoid of life. The sparse, barren wilderness, exactly how Father Dedeken imagined the Biblical city of Sodom must have looked.

All of a sudden, they spotted a tall peak rising from the mist.

"Sahib, look!" said Abdullah, pointing at the strange formation on the horizon. "There it is! The Altyn Tagh, the golden mountain. You can spot it through the clouds. It looks exactly how I remembered it when I traveled this way with Prejevalsky years ago. Beyond this mountain lies the country of eternal snow."

Bonvalot whipped out his field glasses. "Ah yes, there it is. The Altyn Tagh Mountains, the natural border between Chinese Turkestan and Tibet."

The caravan men stared reverently at the magnificent golden mountains hovering in the distance. It's highest peak, the Altyn Shan, rose to 19,000 feet and was the object of many local legends and myths. Sitting astride his horse, Bonvalot took a deep breath as he calculated the distance to reach the mountains, and what it would entail to scale such an enormous obstacle. And then, without warning, the clouds thickened and the vast wall of mountains vanished like a mirage.

CHAPTER 20

Qarkilik, Chinese Turkestan
November, 1889

The desert of Lob Nor gradually gave way to the oasis of Qarkilik, a village containing mud-bricked hovels, well-irrigated tamarisk and poplar woods, and fields of peach and apricot trees bounded by hedges. To everyone's relief, the villagers greeted the travelers with melons, peaches, grapes, and freshly-baked bread, a welcome relief from the heat and monotony of the desert.

Bonvalot decided to make camp just outside Qarkilik, and immediately set about planning their attack on the Altyn Tagh Mountains. Proper planning was essential. They would require an enormous supply of food, experienced guides, and the sturdiest animals that could withstand the privations of the Chang Tang once they reached Tibet. Bonvalot made a careful list of all the supplies they needed, but progress was slow as his own body was weakening from fatigue.

The first order of business was to get some much-needed rest.

After traveling through the desert for more than a month, most of the men were exhausted, filthy, and sported scruffy-looking beards and sunburned skin that made them look like wizened old men of the desert. Even the hardiest of them was forced to admit they were desperately in need of a bath, with sand penetrating their clothes, boots, hair, and every nook and cranny of their bodies.

Camille especially was a wreck after spending so many weeks on the back of a camel. She asked Bonvalot to arrange for the villagers to bring her a tub of hot water to her tent along with some soap he had brought from Kuldja. When the servants lugged a basin to her tent, she sat down in the water and scrubbed herself with a loofah to remove the dirt that clung to her like a second skin. When she was finished, she dried herself off and put on a clean set of clothes before collapsing in her sleeping-sack, the very idea of venturing into Tibet as impossible to imagine as climbing the Great Pyramid of Giza.

Tired from the difficult journey, Imatch the camel driver reminded Rachmed that he intended to return to Korla as soon as possible. When Bonvalot had first hired him, Imatch only agreed to travel as far as Qarkilik, but now that they were so close to Tibet, Bonvalot was afraid of losing not only Imatch, but also his servant Niaz. He decided to use every tactic in his book including bribery and cunning, to convince the two camel drivers to continue to remain with them, but he knew the price would be very steep. What he didn't know was that the two camel drivers would soon pay an even higher price.

Bonvalot's next order of business was to replenish their much-needed supplies. From the local inhabitants, he ordered 2,000 pounds of bread baked in small loaves. He also purchased rice, flour, tea, dried fruit, thirty live sheep, rope, horseshoes, nails, and for the animals, barley and corn. For all the caravaneers he ordered a *pelisse*, a heavy sheepskin coat, leather trousers, leather gloves, stockings, and a new pair of felt boots—cold weather clothes to withstand the freezing temperatures of the Chang Tang. Bonvalot was leaving nothing to chance.

All the while Bonvalot kept his true goal, namely Tibet, a closely-guarded secret. All he told the caravan men and the local villagers was that he was taking the prince on a hunting expedition to the Tsaidam. To this effect, his next step was to find adequate guides. From the local villagers, Bonvalot selected two who seemed most able to guide them through the passes of the Altyn Tagh. One was called Timur, an older shepherd who occasionally dabbled in gold-mining. When Bonvalot questioned him, he showed no fear of traversing the Tibetan high plain. He claimed to have explored it himself on numerous occasion. Timur also possessed natural curiosity, a propensity for hard work, and a good facility with horses and camels, which made him a splendid addition to the team.

The other guide he hired was Isa, a young man of around twenty whose chief skill was skinning and cooking animals. He worked quickly, and had no qualms about performing other domestic duties such as splitting logs, fetching water, and washing dishes. But Isa also had his share of bad habits, which included occasionally dabbling in hashish, but he more than made up for his occasional stupor with his usefulness and good character.

With those duties taken care of, Bonvalot set out to discover the location of the 'southern road' that Professor Foucaux had spoken about. But each time he brought up the subject with his new guides, they were evasive, claiming to have never heard of it. In the end, Bonvalot decided to discover the route on his own, relying on the crude map Professor Foucaux had given him.

Meanwhile, when his previous caravan men from Korla and Lob Nor discovered that Bonvalot intended to cross the Altyn Tagh Mountains to reach the Tsaidam instead of taking the safer route through the desert, they used every tactic to persuade him to change his mind. Later, when they learned that Bonvalot intended to search for Bokalik, there was almost a revolt in the camp as the guides deemed it a suicide mission. Of all the caravan men, Abdullah was by far the most vocal. He tried every trick in his arsenal to persuade Bonvalot to return to Korla. With each passing day, his anxiety grew greater since it would soon be too late to return across the Taklamakan Desert.

When Abdullah reached his breaking point, he decided to confront Bonvalot. He found the Frenchman sitting at the edge of camp, wrapping the bread and stuffing it into burlap bags for the long journey ahead. Sidling up to his employer, Abdullah tried an old Mahommedan trick that entailed veering into the realm of fantasy.

"Sahib, I feel it is my duty to warn you," he said, keeping his voice low so the others would not hear. "On the other side of the Altyn Tagh Mountains is Tibet, the land of eternal snow. If you venture into this land you will meet with some of the most ferocious beasts imaginable, big, scaly, green monsters with wings and spiked tails, enormous fire-breathing dragons that are taller than the highest minaret with eyes the size of melons. These dragons will chase you to exhaustion and eat you if you are not careful. If you manage to escape, you will have to contend with the vicious brigands that roam the Chang Tang freely, heartless bandits who won't hesitate to chop off a man's head with their enormous curved swords. Tibet is a very dangerous place, sahib, please be reasonable and turn around."

"Is this another one of your Arabian fantasies, Abdullah?" said Bonvalot, not bothering to look up as he secured the burlap bag with a bit of rope. "Nothing you can say will make me change my mind. I intend to reach the Tsaidam by the 'southern road' and my mind is made up. Now, if you don't mind, I must get back to work. Please go back and fix the horse's shoes. Enough joking for one day."

Abdullah leaned in closer. "One of noble birth, truly I have misjudged you. If I live as long as the Prophet Adam I will never understand how a reasonable, learned man such as yourself would wish to cross the Altyn Tagh. Like the others, I thought you were only boasting, which is natural for men in our position. All of us guides brag about our accomplishments in order to get work. Naturally, I assumed that once you had reached the Lob Nor your sense of self-preservation would override your ambition and compel you to turn around."

Bonvalot sat back and eyed the erstwhile squirrel dealer.

"Why Abdullah, do I detect *fear* in your voice? Is our brave Taranchi adventurer *afraid* to cross the Altyn Tagh Mountains?"

"Afraid? Me?" said Abdullah, his voice rising a few notches. "Nothing could be further from the truth. But please listen to reason. I have more experience than you in these matters since I accompanied the great Prejevalsky back in his day. I feel it is my duty to warn you about the dangers that await us. Look at how low the mercury dips at night. When you climb to the Roof of the World, the mercury will drop so low it freezes inside the thermometer, rendering it useless. I swear this is true since I have seen it before. Listen to me, One of noble birth, it is too close to winter to venture into Tibet. Please give up this foolish plan up."

"Abdullah my sly little friend, I don't remember asking you your opinion on the matter. I only inquired if you knew the location of the 'southern road.' At this point, nothing short of a catastrophe could convince me to turn around. Do you understand?"

"I am trying to save your life," said Abdullah. "Don't blame me when it's too late."

"Thank you from the bottom of my heart but please go back to fixing the horses' shoes."

Abdullah let out a loud sigh and trudged off, grumbling under his breath. Bonvalot returning to filling another sack of bread, but inside, a grain of doubt had begun to germinate.

And now, even nature seemed to be turning against them.

That night, a blizzard tore through Qarkńlik, sending temperatures plummeting to well below freezing. Bonvalot collapsed in pain as his rheumatism flared up, causing his joints to swell and his chest to throb, forcing him back to the safety of his sleeping sack. Taking turns, Rachmed, Father Dedeken, and Tong-Kia watched over Bonvalot. Even Camille stopped by his tent to bring him food, hoping to revive his flagging spirits.

After many cups of steaming hot tea and mutton soup, Bonvalot regained some of his lost strength, but his recovery was slow, and he was left with a lingering ache in his joints that reminded him of his own mortality. For the first time in his life, Bonvalot worried about defeat.

"Bonvalot-sahib," said Rachmed, bending over his stricken companion. "Are you going to make it this time?"

"Yes, I just need a little more rest," whispered Bonvalot. "I know I can do it. Just give me a few more days."

Rachmed shook his head. "Why do you do this to me every time? Before we met my hair was shiny and black and now, because of these foolhardy expeditions, my hair is turning grey and I lost several desirable marriage prospects. Now, I am a worthless old bachelor."

Bonvalot tried to laugh but ended up grimacing from pain instead.

"Rachmed, you know you were never meant for a domestic life. What kind of husband would you have made anyway? You were born with the spirit of adventure; you live for the road. I couldn't chase you away with a stick and you know it."

"That's because I was born a *saya*," said Rachmed, drawing out the last word with great seriousness, as if it were a curse.

"A *what*?"

"A *saya*. A man who is doomed to wander the land forever. Like the wind, we are cursed to blow from one end of the earth to the other, never knowing a proper home. You see, while our mothers were pregnant, they traveled through the desert on the backs of camels, always straining their eyes to see what lay beyond the horizon. When they gave birth, their children arrived with that same searching eye, always seeking out new horizons. All our lives we live like vagabonds, with just a rifle and a knapsack and only Allah knows where our road will end. I am quite certain that you are also a *saya*."

Bonvalot smiled. "Then it is good that we have found each other."

"Speaking of which," continued Rachmed, "if we don't get out of here, we may never leave. The path you have chosen is a long and dangerous one, and these cursed camels cannot travel very fast. Time does not stop because you are sick."

Father Dedeken stuck his head inside Bonvalot's tent.

"A large group of men just rode into camp," said Dedeken, his brow creased with worry. "They say it's the local chief from Lob Nor accompanied by a number of villagers from Khotan and Lob Nor who are looking for you. What should I tell them?"

Bonvalot winced as he pushed himself to a sitting position. "Tell them to wait outside. I'll get dressed and greet them shortly. Rachmed, hand me my sheepskin coat and grab my holster from over there."

Outside, the ground was covered with a thick layer of frost. Their breath hung in the air like tiny icicles as the cold seeped into their bones. The temperature hovered at ten degrees Fahrenheit, which alarmed the locals because of its severity. Bonvalot stifled a cough as he wrapped his *pelisse* tighter around himself. His legs felt weak and his chest ached as he crunched over the snow-covered gravel in his hob-nailed boots. A visit by officials was never good news. He found the Lobi Chief standing near the campfire surrounded by a throng of angry-looking villagers; their loud grumbling drowned out the howling wind.

Bonvalot and Rachmed pushed their way through the crowd. With Rachmed interpreting, Bonvalot addressed the Lobi Chief, but the latter's belligerence descended into rough talk, which sent the conversation down an ominous path.

"Greetings to you, Chief," said Bonvalot, trying to disguise his weakened state by standing as erect as possible with his hands on his hips. "Are you looking for me?"

"You are the one they call Bonvalot no doubt," said the chief, bowing half-way. Noting the older man's scanty goatee, hardened features, and swaggering posture, Bonvalot sensed trouble. His body braced against the wind as silence descended over the crowd.

"Indeed I am. What can I do for you?"

The chief's face froze. "I have brought a message for you. I've come to tell you the Council refuses to supply you with the donkeys and guides that you requested. The weather it too cold and we believe it's no longer safe to conduct a mountaineering expedition under such harsh conditions. I cannot allow you to risk the lives of my men no matter how much you agreed to pay them. I have therefore cancelled all the agreements you made up to now."

Bonvalot folded his arms over his chest. "With all due respect, Chief, that's impossible. We have no intention of canceling this expedition. We've helped the people of Lob Nor and Qarkilik by spending a fortune in gold and silver buying all our food, supplies, and sheepskin coats at exorbitant prices. Every man we hired will be paid handsomely and travels of his own free will. You have no right to come here and cancel everything because of a little cold weather."

The Lobi Chief was taken aback. "Did you not hear me? I said I've *already cancelled* your contracts. Your expedition is finished."

Rachmed's eyes blazed with fury. "What kind of nonsense talk is this? Only yesterday your people promised to supply us with all our needs and now you come along and cancel everything? Have we given you any reason to doubt our ability to pay? Or are you trying to blackmail us?"

Before the chief could respond, Father Dedeken and Bartholomeus raced across the frigid ground. They pulled Bonvalot aside and explained the real reason for the sudden turn of events.

"We know what caused this sudden reversal of fortune," said Father Dedeken. "Yesterday two agents arrived from Korla who prohibited the Lobis from assisting us in any way. Essentially, the

Mandarins blackmailed them, leaving them with no choice but to obey."

"Damn!" said Bonvalot under his breath. "What can we do now? How do we get around this obstacle?"

"Simple," said Rachmed, motioning toward the chief. "We hold their leader hostage until they have no choice but to help us."

Bonvalot chuckled at the suggestion. "I should have known you'd come up with your own unique strategy."

Rachmed removed his revolver with the stealth of a Chinese pickpocket and slipped it into his pocket.

By now, the Lobi Chief had lost his patience; his face had contorted into a gruesome mask resembling a Chinese demon.

"How dare you call it blackmail!" he screamed. "Even if you offered to pay double for our donkeys, we wouldn't sell you a three-legged mule! I forbid any man from Lob Nor to accompany you on this reckless expedition or to offer you any assistance. My word is final. We are brave fighters and you don't scare us in the least."

Rachmed whipped the revolver out of his pocket and aimed it at the Lobi Chief's head. "This says you will help us."

Rachmed grabbed the startled chief by the throat and dragged him away from the protection of his tribesmen. With his right hand pointing the gun at the chief's head, he used his left hand to squeeze his neck. "Do you care to try my patience?"

The Lobi Chief gurgled and turned colors. His hands flailed and his eyes bulged, but Rachmed tightened his grip until he was almost suffocating the captive chieftain. The villagers gasped as they watched their leader's disgrace at the hands of foreigners, their venom rising to fever pitch.

"*Now* are you going to help us?" said Rachmed in a menacing voice. Though he was speaking to the chief, he was directing his veiled threat at the crowd of stone-faced villagers.

At this point, Bonvalot pulled out his own revolver and addressed the crowd.

"Listen to me," said Bonvalot. "We will hold your chief captive until you supply us with five horses, eighteen donkeys, and experienced guides. Do you understand?"

The proposal was met with silence. The villagers' eyes were fixed on their chief who was by now kneeling on the ground with

Rachmed's revolver aimed at his temple. His face was a contorted mess; he was sputtering out incomprehensible orders as he struggled to free himself from Rachmed's grip.

Bonvalot cocked his gun. "You have two minutes to decide."

CHAPTER 21

Several of the Lobi men broke away from the crowd and advanced toward Bonvalot, their eyes full of murderous intent. When one of them pulled a knife, a bolt of energy shot through Bonvalot's veins. He aimed his revolver and fired, sending the knife flying out of the attacker's hand. The mob gasped as the men turned and fled. The bloodied knife came to rest on the ground, but no one else was brave enough to challenge Bonvalot.

Meanwhile, Prince Henri and Father Dedeken held their carbines primed and ready as they moved on either side of Bonvalot and Rachmed, providing cover as they kept their weapons pointed at the agitated crowd.

"Stand back!" yelled Bonvalot. "One false move and your chief will feel the cold wind between his ears."

Hearing this, the chief wailed and flailed his arms. Rachmed threw him to the ground and ordered him to stay quiet, which had the effect of silencing the crowd.

Several villagers pushed their way through the throng until they were twenty feet away from Bonvalot. They raised their hands in surrender and offered to mediate a compromise. Incensed, their women emitted piercing screams from the rooftops that reverberated through the desert, sending shivers up everyone's spine.

That was when Timur sprang into action. His years of solitary wanderings through the desert following his flocks and singing his desert songs had instilled in him a deeper understanding of human nature. He picked up a hot cup of tea with sugar and strode to the front where he offered it to the downtrodden chief, who grabbed it with quivering hands as he brought it to his lips. Seeing this act of kindness, the village women soon fell silent.

Gaining confidence, Timur addressed the Chief. "Please reconsider your decision. You have everything to gain and nothing to lose by helping these strangers. I have every reason to believe they are serious when they say they will not release you until you agree to cooperate."

The disgraced Chief eyed Timur with suspicious eyes and scowled at the mere suggestion of cooperating. But after careful consideration, he motioned for his advisors to approach him.

Bonvalot watched the interaction with guarded optimism. Keeping his revolver pointed at the angry villagers, he whispered to Dedeken, "I had a feeling today was going to be memorable. My joints were so sore I could barely get out of bed. If only we'd gotten out of here before the agents from Korla arrived with the bad news, then everything would have been smooth sailing."

Father Dedeken smiled knowingly. "Monsieur Bonvalot, prophecy is best understood by hindsight, so we should not trust too much in our foresight. At times like these it is important to count your blessings and remember those less fortunate than you."

"Oh? And who are they?"

"People with empty cartridges in their revolvers."

After conferring with his advisors the Chief managed to recover part of his dignity. He signaled to Rachmed that he wished to stand and the latter was only too happy to oblige.

"Having given the matter much thought" said the Chief, brushing sand and debris off his tunic. "I've reached my final decision. I've decided to cooperate with these strangers and provide them with all they require. Therefore, I order each and every one of you to supply them with the horses, mules, and guides they require."

A wave of relief washed over Bonvalot. Rachmed broke into a wide grin and Prince Henri lifted his carbine over his head and gave a holler of delight.

"But," added the Chief. "I am only granting the guides permission to travel as far as the Tsaidam. Not one mile further. Once they reach the Tsaidam, they must turn around and return home at once. No exceptions."

Bonvalot smiled and shook the Chief's hand. The whole crowd cheered. Watching the proceedings from her tent, Camille clutched her sheepskin coat as her apprehension gave way to relief. She realized her hands had been clenching the small revolver Rachmed had given her for protection. The thought of using it caused all the blood to drain from her head. With the danger over, she collapsed on her bedroll and fell into a deep slumber.

As a precaution, Bonvalot held the Lobi chief in custody until the horses and mules arrived the next morning. With so much at stake, he could not afford to let the chief slip away into the night, taking with him their only chance of reaching Tibet. When at last the precious cargo arrived the next day, the chief took his leave. He mounted his horse, saluted Bonvalot, and rode back to Lob Nor.

Quiet at last descended over the camp, but not for long. Seeing the calamity that had befallen the Lobi Chief for refusing to assist Bonvalot, Imatch decided to abandon the expedition. Although he had initially agreed to travel as far as Qarkilik, Bonvalot had pressured him to remain with the caravan until they reached Bokalik, but the idea did not sit well with Imatch. The ill-tempered camel driver flew into a rage, screaming and cursing his servant Niaz under the pretext that they never should have accepted the job in the first place. Niaz took great offense at the accusation, which resulted in a shouting match that reverberated across the desert sands until the camels could be seen lifting their heads and pricking their ears at the vicious tirade.

"I should have never listened to you," screamed Imatch. "Now they've got me in a hole from which I can never escape. And it's all your fault."

"My fault?" retorted Niaz. "How is it my fault when you haven't even paid me my wages yet? At least pay me what you owe me so I can leave this place and go back to Turpan. Look at me, I don't even have the proper clothes for traveling to Bokalik. If they force me to go, I'll probably die from the cold."

"Do I look like an idiot to you?" shouted Imatch, his brutal side in full display, just as the camel merchants had warned them back in Korla. "If I pay you now you'll just take my money and run away, you lazy good for nothing!"

"And you're the meanest man in all of China," said Niaz. "I curse the day I started working for you. You've brought nothing but tragedy on my family. You're nothing but a worthless, filthy liar."

Imatch lunged at Niaz's throat. In an instant the two were rolling around in the dirt, beating, scratching, and cursing each other. Seeing the melee unfolding, Rachmed, Timur, and Abdullah sprang into action. Rachmed twisted Imatch's arms behind his back and ordered him to stay quiet, but old Imatch would not be silent. Out of desperation, Bonvalot offered to give him some silver ingots so he could pay Niaz the money he owed him.

"Don't trust the snake!" seethed Niaz. "And don't believe a word he tells you. It's always the same old story, he'll smile to your face then hoard all the money and pay me nothing. He's been stealing my wages for years. He's a half-empty bottle of vinegar! An evil spirit!"

"You shameless foreign devil lover!" screamed Imatch, his face now a deep shade of purple.

"You arrogant old fool! Your conscience was eaten by a dog!" said Niaz, whose breathing was rapid as sweat dripped down his forehead.

By now Imatch looked like he was about to explode. His wrinkles were the size of canyons as he let out a tirade of vile curses that shot through poor Niaz like arrows. Imatch tried to break free, but Rachmed and Timur kept a firm grip on the old camel driver, preventing him from acting out the dictates of his evil temper.

To compensate poor Niaz for his trouble, Bonvalot paid him a few silver ingots to hold him over until pay day, but he worried that this vicious outburst might be the harbinger of more bad luck on the horizon. The men were growing more agitated by the day, and the locals were growing more suspicious of their motives. Soon, the weather would turn colder, robbing them of their last chance to make a break. Despite his ill health, Bonvalot knew they had to leave now, before more shooting or fighting broke out that could sabotage the entire expedition.

After sunset, the men wrapped themselves in their sheepskin coats and huddled in their tents drinking tea and eating palao from a communal bowl while Camille ate alone in her tent. After a great deal of planning and strategizing, Bonvalot called the caravan men outside for a meeting.

By now it was the middle of November and nighttime temperatures were well below freezing. Bracing themselves against the cold, the men assembled around the campfire while Bonvalot took his place at the center. Without much fanfare he announced that early the next morning they would push off for the Tsaidam where the prince intended to go hunting. Hearing this, the caravan men nodded. The Tsaidam was a huge swampy marshland covered with salt beds and reeds where herds of wild camels were known to run free, making it the perfect hunting ground for sportsmen. Seeing the fair-haired French prince with his vast array of hunting rifles and ammunition made perfect sense to them.

But Bonvalot had no intention of heading to the Tsaidam. He knew that to keep the men in his employ he had to use subterfuge. If he revealed that his true goal was Lhasa, they would revolt outright, forcing him to abandon the expedition and give up his dream of reaching Lhasa. But before he dismissed the men, Bonvalot added a simple caveat, that instead of reaching the Tsaidam via the normal route to the east, they would take a more direct route through Bokalik, using the so-called 'southern road,' which entailed scaling the Altyn Tagh Mountains.

At this pronouncement, the caravan men raised an outcry. They argued that climbing the Altyn Tagh this late in the season was impossible, almost suicide. No one had ever accomplished this feat before, much less an entire caravan. They reminded Bonvalot that previous explorers like Prejevalsky and Carey had encountered numerous problems when they attempted to scale the Altyn Tagh Mountains with horses and donkeys, much less camels. With furious voices, they argued that the plan was pure foolishness, and might result in getting them all killed.

Bonvalot held up his hands to quiet them.

"I've heard your concerns," he said. "But with all due respect, Mr. Carey was nothing more than an English civil servant on holiday. Not long ago I crossed the Pamir Mountains in the middle of winter when all the experts said it was impossible. What was Carey's big accomplishment? He threw on a knapsack and set out without consulting a single expert. That was his one big mistake. Not that I'm diminishing his accomplishments, but I have the experience it takes to go much further."

The caravan men shook their heads and raised loud objections. Bonvalot scanned their faces in the glow of the campfire but held his ground.

"I have good reason to believe we can make it," he said. "I suspect that several of you are familiar with the 'southern road' of which I spoke. Carey mentioned it as well as an *unfreezing lake*. I heard a rumor that not too long ago a caravan containing some European men was ambushed somewhere in the vicinity of Bokalik," said Bonvalot. "I have a very pressing reason to go there. The woman who is traveling with us believes that one of those men may have been her missing husband."

Timur shook his head. "Sahib, I am very sorry but it is out of the question. We cannot go with you to Bokalik. This plan of yours will never work. You cannot drive temperamental camels across steep, frozen passes. It is much too dangerous, even for men with nailed boots and ice axes."

"And besides," added Parpa. "We cannot help you find Bokalik. It's location is a mystery even to us. And you cannot rely on the people who live on the other side of the mountains as they are suspicious and untrustworthy. They will refuse to speak to us or help us in any way. And you better believe they will try to rob us, maybe even try to kill us. On the other side of the mountains live the *Chukpas*, bloodthirsty brigands who will not hesitate to slit our throats and steal everything."

Everyone nodded in agreement.

Bonvalot swallowed hard. Given such strong objections, he was certain a less-experienced traveler would have given up in discouragement. But he was not in that class. He had learned from hard-won experience that the only way to succeed was by taking enormous risks, and never shying away from danger. There was no objection the caravan men could raise that would convince him to give up his dream. If they reached a stalemate, he would stand his ground and refuse to pay them until they agreed to join him.

Later, as Bonvalot retired to his tent, a gravelly voice boomed in the darkness: "Remember Monsieur Bonvalot, we made a bargain back in Korla. I am leading this expedition to Tibet. You cannot make it without me."

Bonvalot groped in the darkness for his hurricane lamp.

"Who are you?"

"I think you know…"

Prejevalsky?

In a flash, an unseen attacker jumped on Bonvalot and tried to strangle him. Bonvalot struggled to free himself, but his attacker had a power that was beyond human. He tried to scream but all that came out was a helpless gurgle. As his attacker tightened his grip, Bonvalot saw his whole life flashing before his eyes, but he refused to give in. He thrashed about, kicked, and resisted his attacker, but slowly he was losing the battle.

Finally, an idea came to him. In the darkness, Bonvalot fumbled for his knife and when he grabbed it, he plunged it into his attacker's back. A terrifying roar filled the tent. Writhing in pain, the stranger staggered backward, trying desperately to extricate himself from the knife. Bonvalot gasped for breath and watched in horror as his rival turned and fled. When he looked outside the tent, there wasn't the faintest trace of footprints on the fresh-fallen snow.

CHAPTER 22

That night, Bonvalot barely slept. He tossed and turned and took a few swigs of brandy to help him relax, but he was too agitated to fall asleep. Of all his hallucinations, this one had been the worst. He still felt the painful bruises on his neck. In the darkness of his tent he worried that his failure to control these disturbing visions would jeopardize his greatest chance for success. When the night passed without further incident, Bonvalot was convinced they were gone for good.

Rising early the next morning, the caravan men ate a quick breakfast and then loaded up the camels. When it was time to go, Rachmed helped Camille mount her camel and he gave her a goatskin of water and an extra sheepskin blanket for warmth. It was the seventeenth of November and dangerously close to winter. They had only the smallest chance to make it across the Atyn Tagh Mountains, but Bonvalot was consumed with his chance for success and was ready to risk everything to attain it.

As he mounted his horse, Rachmed noticed the dark circles under Bonvalot's eyes and shook his head. "Bonvalot-sahib, I don't think you slept well last night."

"My nerves kept me up all night, not to mention the pain from my rheumatism. I'll need a flask of brandy to keep the blood flowing in its proper channels, then I should be fine."

Rachmed grinned. "Fear not, as long as your horse follows mine, you can sleep the first leg of the journey, like a Tatar soldier after a night of drinking too much *kumis*."

"Just promise me one thing," said Bonvalot. "If something should happen to me, take the woman to the nearest French or

British embassy. Guard her with your life. You know where I keep my gold."

"That is your rheumatism speaking, Bonvalot-sahib," said Rachmed. "Nothing of the sort is going to happen. When you escaped the fortress of Chitral, you extended your life by a hundred years at the least. Once you're back in the saddle, you'll be like your old self."

"If I could just get my muscles to agree with you I'd be fine," said Bonvalot. "Right now they've got the upper hand."

They headed out under a bright sky with a great display of fanfare from the local villagers to mark their departure. The village chiefs escorted the caravan to the edge of the desert and showed them where they could find a stream for a last drink of fresh water before the journey ahead. The elders wished them a safe, successful journey with Allah's guidance and protection. Bonvalot shook their hands warmly and thanked them for their hospitality, adding that he hoped that henceforth they would regard him as their friend.

When Bonvalot gazed up at the Altyn Tagh Mountains, he remembered Abdullah's warning, that once they crossed these peaks they would be in the land of eternal ice and snow, and prayed that Providence would guide them.

That night they pitched their tents under the starry, moonlit sky. The animals grazed and rested while the men cleaned their guns and repaired their tools. Everyone seemed to be in good spirits, that is, except for Imatch, who had pitched his tent apart far away from the others and could be seen sulking while Niaz his servant did most of the work.

When Bonvalot asked Niaz what was wrong with Imatch, he said, "Truly sahib, I do not know. I've never seen him this bad. All he does is grumble and complain of being humbugged."

"Humbugged?"

"He thinks you tricked him into making this journey."

Bonvalot furrowed his brow as he stared at the ill-tempered Chinese Kirghiz, who was making a terrible racket banging out the dents of a pot with a hammer.

"Just look at that scowl on his face," added Niaz. "He looks like a dog whose owner pulls him on a leash until he bares his teeth and growls."

"Leave that old grouch to sulk by himself," said Bonvalot. "Come and sit with us. You're not obligated to sit by Imatch's fire. I'm waiting for the day his camels grow tired of his foul moods and spit in his face."

Niaz laughed. "As you wish, sahib. I will come and sit by your fire."

"Tell me something," said Bonvalot. "When did you start working for Imatch?"

"When I was a little boy my father sold me to him," said the young camel driver. "This is the only life I've ever known. I haven't seen my mother in so long I can barely remember her face. My only dream is to one day buy my freedom and start a new life as my own boss. I want to own my own herd of camels."

"That's a fine dream," said Bonvalot. "And I hope you achieve it some day."

Bonvalot watched Niaz talking and laughing with the other caravan men. When Tong-Kia placed a bowl of palao and a cup of sweet tea before him, his eyes lit up and he ate with a hearty appetite. He listened to the stories of the older caravan men with delight. Bonvalot was grateful he'd been able to ease the young camel driver's torment even for a short while.

That night, as they lay in their tents huddled under their sheepskins, the temperature plummeted to five degrees below zero. Everyone wondered what mysteries lay beyond the great wall of mountains that blocked their path. No one was willing to admit they were scared.

"Tomorrow morning we start our attack on the Altyn Tagh," said Bonvalot before snuffing out the hurricane lamp. "And then there's no turning back."

CHAPTER 23

Altyn Tagh Mountains
November, 1889

The next day they reached the first pass. Advancing single file with the horsemen in the lead, the camels marched through a natural tunnel carved out of rock with sheer walls that rose over two hundred feet in height. Over their heads, huge stalactites carved out of solid rock dangled precariously, as if they were suspended by a thread.

"Quiet everyone," whispered Rachmed. "The slightest noise can send those rock formations crashing down on our heads."

The caravan progressed and after several hours, the temperature plummeted inside the tunnel until it became an ice palace of sorts with frost-covered walls and icicles hanging down from the roof like glittering chandeliers. The men shivered in their sheepskin coats, wondering if they would ever feel the warmth of the sun on their faces again. The ground beneath them turned into a solid sheet of ice that gleamed like a mirror. Fearing that the camels would slide on the icy surface, Rachmed ordered the men to throw down sand to keep them from losing their grip. The trick worked splendidly and the camels, donkeys, sheep, and horses passed through the ice cave without an incident. But no sooner were they out of danger than they came to an even greater hazard.

They found themselves facing an impossible obstacle, a passageway filled with large rocks and boulders that resembled a natural staircase because of the way the boulders had lodged against each other. Bonvalot dismounted his horse and studied the situation. Joining him were Rachmed, Abdullah, Timur, and Isa, who stared at the rock-strewn passageway in shock.

"What the devil do we do now?" said Bonvalot, running his hand through his hair. "Rachmed, how do you propose we get an entire caravan over a sea of boulders?"

"Even if we wanted to double back, the ravine is too narrow for the camels to turn around," said Abdullah, shaking his head. "We're in a real fix."

"The only way we can get through this pass is by hammering our way out," said Rachmed.

"Do you mind repeating that?" said Bonvalot.

Rachmed lifted his pickaxe and pointed it at the boulders.

"I said, we must hammer our way out. Like this." Rachmed lifted up a stone and threw it against a second, causing the latter to split into smaller stones. "Did you see that?"

"Yes, but it'll take hours to hammer our way out," said Timur. "And by that time the camels will be exhausted, not to mention the men. We've already lost so many valuable daylight hours, and I don't recommend spending even one night in this God-forsaken ravine."

"Do you have a better plan?" said Rachmed.

Timur shrugged his shoulders. "I warned you not to come this way."

"Well, until you have a better plan for getting us out of here, hold your tongue," said Rachmed.

"Keep your turban on, I was just giving you my best advice," said Timur.

"When I want your advice I'll ask for it," said Rachmed, now at his boiling point.

"Hold it men, hold it," said Bonvalot. "Stop cackling like a bunch of hens. We're not in any danger of getting stuck here. If we have to work all day, we will. Unpack your pickaxes and get to work. I want us out of the ravine before dark."

For the next several hours the men hammered at the rocks with their iron pickaxes until the boulders, rocks, and stones were reduced to shards small enough for the camels to walk over. By late afternoon, the clanging of metal ceased. They had finally reached the summit of the pass and were out of the claustrophobic ravine. Basking in the warmth of the sun, the men clapped each other on the back.

They made camp on a grassy patch of scrubland beside a stream that had not frozen. No sooner had they dismounted when the men spied a herd of eight Himalayan blue sheep with long, curved horns gazing at them from the crest of a nearby hill. The thought of fresh meat taunted the caravan man, and they thanked Allah for providing this unexpected bounty.

Seizing the opportunity, Prince Henri grabbed his hunting rifle, aimed at the sheep and fired off a few shots. All at once, the herd scattered across the rocky terrain.

"Damn, I missed!" said Henri. "But I'm not giving up just yet."

Henri ran off in pursuit of his game as the men clapped and cheered, their mouths watering at the thought of fresh roasted game. Bonvalot and Rachmed watched the prince climb up the rocky gorge with apprehension, but it was too late to stop him. Soon the caravan men were hard at work making fires, unloading the camels, and pitching the tents. The minutes stretched into hours and the prince never returned. By sunset the prince was nowhere to be found. Grim-faced, Rachmed scanned the nearby hills for any sign of Henri but he was gone. He was lost without a trace.

Panicked, the caravan men raced across the rocky hills shouting Prince Henri's name. They fanned out across the nearby mountainsides hollering at the top of their lungs, shooting their rifles dozens of times as they searched for the missing prince. But each time they returned to camp, they were crestfallen, wringing their hands in desperation, wondering what disaster could have befallen the gallant prince. Bonvalot was beside himself, fearing the worst.

"What the devil happened to him?" said Bonvalot, reloading his Winchester. "What will I tell his father? How can I ever return to France?"

"One of noble birth, we must search for him," said Abdullah. "His Highness may be trapped somewhere."

"Abdullah is right," said Father Dedeken. "We can't wait any longer. We must send a search party out before the wolves and leopards get to him, and before the temperature drops below freezing."

"I will lead the search party," said Rachmed. "It's my fault for letting the young prince go in the first place."

"It's not your fault," said Bonvalot. "I'm responsible for him. Rachmed, you stay here and guard Camille and the supplies. Meanwhile, I'll take some men and head out in the direction the prince was last seen climbing. Perhaps he fell off a cliff and is too wounded to save himself. Abdullah, Timur, Isa and Mahmud, come with me. Bring some hurricane lamps, rope, and your ice axes. Let's go."

Bonvalot and the others climbed the rocky walls of the gorge surrounding the camp. They moved around the sharp ridgeline, then headed up the rough terrain that led to a nearby hill. For the next several hours, Bonvalot and the others called out Henri's name and fired occasional shots in the air to locate him.

Two hours later, back in camp, Rachmed, Camille and Father Dedeken heard the sound of gunfire and shouts—Prince Henri was alive!

A short while later, the search party scrambled down from the hills carrying the wayward prince with his arms splayed across their shoulders looking worse for the wear. They set him down by the fire and Bonvalot recounted the whole story.

After running off in pursuit of the game, Prince Henri had reached the crest of the hill only to find the mysterious Himalayan blue sheep gone. By now, night had fallen and he was hopelessly lost. Making his way across the steep, rocky terrain, he followed the glow of a distant campfire until he descended into a rocky gorge thinking it would only be a short walk back to camp. Somewhere along the way he lost his footing, slid down a steep ridge, and landed on a rocky ledge that was hundreds of feet above a rock-filled gorge, trapped and with no way to climb up or down.

When Henri ran out of ammunition, his plight seemed hopeless.

Luckily, Bonvalot traced the sound of gunfire until he found the stranded prince perched helplessly on the ledge. After securing a rope around a sturdy boulder, Bonvalot tied the end of the rope around his waist and lowered himself down to the ledge. The search party threw down a second rope which he tied around the prince's waist and then whistled for the men to pull them up, one at a time. Everyone agreed it had been a close call for all parties involved, as they might have ended up wandering aimlessly among the endless maze of hills.

As Henri sat by the fire wrapped in a sheepskin blanket, he nursed his wounded ego with a flask of brandy.

"Bonvalot, I owe you my life," he said.

"You don't owe me anything," said Bonvalot. "Next time be more careful before you run off like that."

"It wasn't my fault those sheep bolted, causing me to lose my way in the dark. It was bad luck."

"It was stupidity," said Bonvalot. "I expect you to be more responsible in the future and not risk the lives of my men going out and searching for you."

"They risked their own lives," said Henri. "I'm not responsible for them."

"Let's get one thing straight," said Bonvalot. "Out here in the wilderness we're all responsible for each other. One wrong move can get us all killed."

"I've had enough of your lectures," said Henri, hotly. "If I wanted long-winded speeches I would have gone to Oxford University."

Inside, Bonvalot seethed with anger, but before he could respond, Camille arrived with the medicine kit. She sat down next to Henri and began to patch up his cuts and bruises while the young prince winced in pain.

"There, there," she said. "It'll only sting for a second."

"I'll leave you in good hands now," said Bonvalot, turning to leave. "And Henri, I expect you to behave like a gentleman."

He made his way across camp to where the caravan men were huddled around their fire.

"Timur, I want to talk to you," said Bonvalot.

"About what?" said Timur.

"Get over here now."

Reluctantly Timur picked himself up and went over to Bonvalot.

"Yes, sahib?"

"While we were out scouting, I noticed there were tracks of men and donkeys. It looks like a caravan passed this way not too long ago heading south. What can you tell me about it?"

Timur exhaled a long breath. "About a month ago I heard there was a party of fourteen men who went on a shooting expedition near Bokalik," said Timur. "But I don't know what became of them."

Bonvalot's eyebrows shot up. "Why didn't you tell me this before? Can you find this place called Bokalik?"

Timur shrugged. "I'm not sure, sahib. I haven't traveled this way in many years. Nothing is familiar."

Bonvalot bit his lip. He knew Timur was an experienced gold miner who had probably visited the gold mines near Bokalik many times. He was sure the hired men from Qarkilik were hiding something, and their evasiveness only strengthened his resolve to find the truth. Once and for all he was going to break the stalemate.

The next morning he called the caravan men to a meeting. Crossing his arms in front of him, Bonvalot addressed the guides with a firm voice and unflinching eyes.

"I have good reason to believe that some of you have traveled to Bokalik. I will pay a handsome reward to any one who can guide me there. Come now, speak up."

Parpa raised his hand. "Sahib, I once heard about a 'southern road' that leads to the Kizil-Sou River and to Bokalik, but it will be difficult to find it without a proper map. I believe Timur knows the way better than anyone else. He's the most-experienced guide."

Timur shook his head. "I don't recommend we go near that area. It's very dangerous. It's known to be the hunting ground of the Chukpas, fierce brigands who rob and maraud anyone they can. I've heard stories about unsuspecting travelers who went there and never returned."

Bonvalot scanned the faces of the men. They were creased with anxiety and fatigue; their clothing was in tatters; their boots were wearing thin. Still, he was not about to give up. He would simply change tactics.

"I have good reason to travel to Bokalik," said Bonvalot. "And I will pay a fortune to any man who can guide me there."

"One of noble birth, please listen to reason," said Abdullah. "We should veer east and head to the Tsaidam where you will find good hunting ground for the prince. I will show you where to find the best wild camels and bears to shoot. But don't go to Bokalik.

There is nothing worth shooting there except the carcasses of dead animals."

"I'm afraid not," said Bonvalot, shaking his head. "We're heading *south*, not east. Well, Timur? Will you cooperate or not?"

Timur shrugged his shoulders. "Do I have a choice?"

"I don't like this one bit," said Abdullah. "We're doomed; I can feel it in my bones."

"So it's settled," said Bonvalot. "Parpa and Timur will team up as guides. Everyone else will follow them. Anyone who quits now will not get paid and will return home in disgrace. Do I have your full cooperation?"

The men groaned their consent.

"Good," said Bonvalot. "First thing tomorrow morning we head south toward Bokalik."

Bonvalot retreated to his tent but before he snuffed out the hurricane lamp, he peered through the tent flaps at the uneasy figures of the caravan men as they arranged their bedrolls by the fire. Something in their eyes worried him. He reached for his revolver and made sure it was loaded.

CHAPTER 24

The next day the terrain became even more hazardous.

The caravan progressed through a maze of rocks and boulders that led to the summit of the mountains. The ground was so steep, the animals grunted and groaned with each painful step. Only once did they lose a camel, when the exhausted beast lost its footing and slid down the side of the mountain, howling and screaming, until it fell into an unnatural heap at the bottom.

The men looked on in horror, wondering if the wounded animal would attempt to stand up, but she was in too much pain and never regained the use of her legs. In the end they were forced to shoot her.

After that incident, a wave of gloom spread among the caravan men.

After hours of exhausting climbing, they dragged themselves to the summit of the pass. The air was so thin at that altitude, their breathing became labored and blood trickled from their noses. As they struggled to catch their breath, they marveled at the extraordinary view spread out in front of them. For miles and miles they saw nothing but enormous, snow-capped mountains of rock and ice that glittered under the sun's rays like frozen pyramids, each one higher than the last.

When they finally crested the summit, Rachmed had to carry an exhausted-looking Camille with her arm across his shoulders.

"Memsahib was feeling faint, so I helped her up," he said, setting her gently on the ground.

Bonvalot kneeled down beside her. "Are you feeling alright, Madame Dancourt? Is the altitude getting to you?"

Camille took a deep breath. "I'm somewhat out of breath, but I'll be fine. Just a little dizzy is all. I feel as though we've reached the heavens."

Bonvalot smiled. "Welcome to the Roof of the World. For the remainder of the journey we'll be traveling at these altitudes. Have you ever seen anything as beautiful as this sight?"

"It's mesmerizing," she said, gazing out over the mountains.

"Now you know why I love doing what I do. It's only out here where you start to feel truly alive. Wait a minute while I get an altitude reading."

Bonvalot instructed Tong-Kia to start a fire and bring a pot of ice to boil. He inserted a thermometer into the boiling water and noted the temperature, then he pulled out a notepad and made some calculations.

"According to my reading we're at 17,000 feet. It may take you a while to get acclimated. You can expect to experience nausea, headaches, nosebleeds, dizziness, and a little vomiting. That's normal. But if you start to feel faint, let someone know. I'm quite certain that if your husband knew you would risk your life to find him, he never would have come to Tibet in the first place. Certainly not as part of a surveying party."

"Monsieur Bonvalot, I don't think he came here just to survey Tibet," said Camille.

"What do you mean?"

"I think he came here to find gold. Armand had dreams of striking it rich."

"That's a plausible story. Now it all starts to make sense. I expect we'll find out soon enough what sort of man your husband was, now if you'll excuse me, I must confer with my men."

Bonvalot headed to his guides, who were resting on the slope.

"Timur, Isa, Parpa, come here," he said, staring at the wide, sweeping vista in front of him. "You know these mountains better than anyone. Can you get a fix on our position?"

"Yes, sahib," said Timur, pointing southward. "If we descend by this path here, we should end up on a plateau at 13,000 feet of elevation over there. And if we keep descending, we should reach the Amban Ashkan Pass which turns southeast toward Bokalik. That's all I can tell you until we find a native who can guide us to the 'southern road.'"

"Splendid," said Bonvalot. "Can the camels make such an arduous journey?"

"I don't think so," said Timur. "The camels will give us a great deal of trouble since they are useless at high altitudes."

"And when the temperature drops to twenty or thirty degrees below zero, they quickly lose their tolerance," added Parpa. "My advice is to switch to yaks as soon as possible since yaks are better suited to extreme cold and high altitudes."

"Parpa is right," added Isa. "The camels will not last long under these conditions. And neither will the rest of us unless we get to lower ground. Some of the men are already showing the first signs of mountain sickness."

Prince Henri staggered over to Bonvalot. "Well? Are we there? Have we made it to Tibet?"

"Technically yes," said Bonvalot. "But we still have a long road ahead of us. How does it feel to be standing at 17,000 feet?"

"I feel like I'm on top of the world," said Prince Henri. He began to stagger and sway until he collapsed on the ground.

"Get the prince back on his horse," said Bonvalot. "We have to get him to lower ground before he passes out."

With much tugging, the men pulled Henri back on his horse and began the long trek down from the summit. After several hours of descending down a steep, rocky path, they reached a frozen valley surrounded on all sides by tall hills. The valley was like a barren ice-field, with no vegetation, no wildlife, no fresh water, and no sign of brushwood; there was nothing to burn for heat even as the temperature continued plummeting to thirty degrees below zero.

As they made camp that night, they had their first inkling of what conditions would be like on the Chang Tang where they would be forced to melt ice for water and burn yak dung for heat. The harshness of the environment had a deleterious effect on the men's spirits, causing them to become disheartened. They grew listless and despondent, their eyes stinging from the cold, their lips chapped and bleeding, and their hands too frozen to perform much work. Most of them complained of migraines, nausea, and nosebleeds; some were vomiting, all symptoms of a creeping mountain sickness. It was a scourge that would afflict them for the rest of their journey through Tibet.

As they huddled together in their sheepskin coats, bracing themselves against the fierce winds, Bonvalot heard the caravan men complaining in voices that betrayed raw fear, "What's to become of us?" They wailed and moaned. "What will happen to our families if we die up here? There's no hope. We are all doomed."

The next day, the men loaded up the camels and continued their silent march southward, fighting relentless gusts of wind and the miserable conditions. After several hours they descended to a grassy plain that was surrounded by snow-covered mountains with jutting ridges and rocky cliffs. To their relief, the plain was 2,600 feet lower than their previous day's camp and gradually their symptoms of mountain sickness abated. They also found that the plain contained brush for fire and a stream of fresh water.

According to the calendar, it was the first of December, and everywhere they looked they saw unmistakable signs that they had reached Tibet. They found herds of wild Tibetan antelopes and gazelles, and caught glimpses of Himalayan blue sheep, wild partridges, and even the occasional *kiang*, a wild Tibetan donkey.

That night as they lay in their tents listening to the crackling of the fire, they heard the animals growling and bleating in fear. Something was lurking out in the darkness.

Taking his revolver, Bonvalot slipped on his boots and went out to investigate. Crouched behind a tent, he scanned the animals in the light of the moon and saw a sight that took his breath away.

In the cover of darkness, a Himalayan snow leopard came stalking down from a rocky ledge. Bonvalot stared in awe at the enormous cat, marveling at her sleek mottled grey fur and elegant form; he dared not move or utter a sound. And then, in a flash, the cat lunged at one of the sheep, clamping her teeth on its throat. With the prey locked in the grip of her jaws, the leopard gave it a forceful swipe of its paw, sending it toppling on its side. After several minutes, the sheep lay completely still.

Bonvalot watched with fascination as the leopard dragged the carcass back up a rocky ledge from whence it had come. Showing enormous strength, the leopard climbed farther up the steep ridgeline, her long tail sweeping the air as she skirted a rocky promontory. Prince Henri joined him behind the tent, watching the rare sight with fascination.

"That's the cat of my dreams," said Henri, the smell of alcohol apparent on his breath. "I must shoot it." He lifted his carbine to his shoulder and took aim.

Bonvalot pushed the barrel upwards. "Are you mad? You're in no condition to aim. If you miss, you'll give the leopard time to charge at us."

"Leave me alone," said Henri, lining the leopard again in his sights. "I'm an expert marksman and this is the chance of a lifetime."

He pulled the trigger and the blast of gunfire caused the leopard to drop the sheep and run for cover behind a rock.

"Now look what you've done," said Bonvalot. "We've lost her."

"Dammit!" said Henri, his eyes blazing with fury. "You cost me a rare leopard skin for my collection."

"And you almost cost us our lives," said Bonvalot. "Now I've got to find the damn thing and shoot it before it can do more damage."

He crept out and took cover behind a boulder. In the distance, they heard the animal's ominous growling, sending a shiver up their spine. Bonvalot kept his eyes peeled on the telltale phosphorescent glow in the darkness. He cocked his carbine and lay in wait as time stood still. Suddenly, a flash of white and grey fur shot down the mountain and dived toward the animals.

A bolt of energy surged through Bonvalot's veins. He jerked his rifle to his shoulder, sighted the leopard's chest, and squeezed the trigger. "I've got her now!"

A burst of gunfire ruptured the night air. The caravan men came running from their tents, waving their rifles, shrieking with fright. Bonvalot watched as the bullet hit its mark. The leopard growled and screeched in pain as blood squirted from a jagged wound on her chest. She stumbled over the rocky terrain for a minute before collapsing into a lifeless heap.

"There," said Bonvalot, beaming with pride. "That's how it's done. Now you've got your pelt."

Inside, Bonvalot's heart was beating furiously. His first encounter with a snow leopard in the desolate Tibetan wilderness had almost been his last.

CHAPTER 25

Chang Tang, Tibet
December, 1889

For nineteen straight days, they did not encounter a single human being as they marched across the cold, windswept Chang Tang.

Lying at 15,000 feet above sea level, the Tibetan high plain was a vast white amphitheater of snow, rock, and ice against a backdrop of mountains so high, the Tibetans believed their summits were the abodes of the gods. Guided by Bonvalot's compass, the caravan navigated southward across the frozen tundra, searching in vain for the mysterious 'southern road' that Professor Foucaux had spoken about. Now that they were deep inside Tibet the caravan men were driven by a single imperative: survival.

After traveling for what seemed like an eternity, their luck changed.

Several hours earlier, Rachmed had galloped ahead to conduct a scouting mission. Now they spotted him galloping toward them, waving his hands and hollering at the top of his lungs. By the sound of his voice, they sensed he had struck gold.

"A caravan!" shouted Rachmed, trotting toward them. "Look! Over there!"

Bonvalot lifted his field glasses and focused on a spot on the horizon. Sure enough, several miles ahead he saw a chain of camels heading in their direction.

"They must be Kalmyk pilgrims," said Rachmed.

When the caravan men heard the news, their hearts soared.

From her camel, Camille called out, "Who are they?"

"Kalmyks are Mongolians who adhere to the Tibetan form of Buddhism," said Bonvalot. "Which means they are followers of the Dalai Lama. The Kalmyks probably know these roads better than anyone else, even better than the Tibetans themselves. Surely they can lead us to this mysterious 'southern road.'"

As he was fluent in Mongolian, Father Dedeken offered to ride out to the Kalmyks and speak to them. Bonvalot agreed, but told Rachmed to accompany him. And so, the two fearless adventurers galloped over the ice-covered desert hoping to glean any scrap of information they could about plotting their course to Lhasa.

Several hours later Rachmed and Dedeken returned with a strange story that left them with a terrible sense of foreboding. Father Dedeken and Rachmed discovered that the caravan belonged to an important lama who was revered as a king among his people. Because of his noble rank, Rachmed and Dedeken suspected he was returning from Lhasa. They approached the caravan in a friendly manner, waving and calling out greetings in Mongolian, and even won an audience with the lama himself, who was riding in a royal litter. When the lama pulled aside the curtain, they marveled at his magnificent appearance.

The lama had a broad Mongolian face, world-weary eyes, and a long grey beard that led to an embroidered silk tunic. The caravan itself appeared to be of a royal stature, with twenty-one camels laden with finely carved trunks, each one covered with expensive fabrics. Aside from the lama's litter, there was another one carrying another important passenger, but they were unable to determine who it was.

"It was very strange," said Father Dedeken, stroking his beard as he recalled their encounter. "No matter how many times we asked, the lama refused to admit he was returning from Lhasa. He claimed to be traveling from the Tsaidam, and then asked me the strangest question point blank: 'Are you traveling with a party of Russians?' I looked at the lama as if he'd just fallen from the moon and shook my head. 'Absolutely not!' I said. 'I am traveling with a party of Frenchmen.' Without flinching, the lama uttered a veiled threat, 'We have intelligence that a party of Russians is traveling in the area who intend to infiltrate the holy city of Lhasa without permission. If you are these men, I suggest you stop now and turn around.'

"Naturally," continued Father Dedeken. "I was shocked by the lama's impudence, so I repeated what I had told him previously, 'I told you we are *not* Russian. Our caravan belongs to a party of Frenchmen among whom is a prince of royal blood. They have no intention of entering Lhasa.'"

"Hearing this, the muscles in the lama's face appeared to relax, but by the way he narrowed his eyes I gathered he thought I was suspicious. And then, to my surprise, he said, 'So why are the Frenchmen traveling here?' I was afraid to respond lest I entangle myself further in my lie so I merely shrugged my shoulders and said, 'They came here to hunt.' To which the lama shook his head, lowered his veil, and ordered the caravan to proceed, leaving Rachmed and myself on the side of the road as if we were a pair of dead mules. As the lama's caravan passed, one of his servants whispered that the lama was so holy, he was regarded as a 'living Buddha,' which I took to mean that had visited the holy city of Lhasa. And so, taken together, all the clues suggest that the caravan was traveling by the 'southern road,' and if we follow their tracks, we are sure to arrive at our proper destination."

Bonvalot was encouraged by this report, but he knew the time had come to tell the caravan men the truth about where they were really heading. He also knew that by telling them the truth, there was a good chance they would desert.

The next morning, they discovered to their chagrin that during the night, two of the men from Lob Nor had stolen two horses and deserted. Dismayed, the remaining caravan men loaded up the camels and started out again, following the tracks the lama's caravan had left behind. But the constant threat of wind and snow worried the men. The harsh elements would eventually erase the tracks, leaving them without any marks to guide them. A quick test of the thermometer showed that they were at an altitude of 16,400 feet, 700 feet higher than Mont Blanc, the highest mountain in the Alps. As expected, the men began to experience migraines brought on by the altitude, which no remedy could alleviate. Occasionally, someone would vomit and collapse in anguish, only to be hoisted on the back of a camel by the ever-vigilant Rachmed.

From their present position, Bonvalot calculated the distance to Lhasa to be a two month trek, during which time, they would not descend below 13,000 feet and the temperature would not rise above thirty degrees below zero. The hardships would undoubtedly bring the men to the verge of collapse. With each passing day, Bonvalot realized that he could no longer keep his true destination a secret. He had no choice but to tell the men the truth.

That night after they made camp, Bonvalot called all the caravan men to a meeting. They sat in a semi-circle around the fire while he stood facing them, bracing himself against the howling wind.

Looking into their rough, weather-beaten faces, Bonvalot addressed them in a stern voice.

"I've heard rumors that some of you know the roads better than you've been letting on. Tell me the truth, which one of you has traveled this way before?"

The men refused to answer.

"Come now," said Bonvalot. "Don't give me the silent treatment. What about you, Mahmud? You're an experienced hunter. Do you know where the road leads?"

"No, sahib," said Mahmud. "I swear I've never been this way before. Ask Timur, he has traveled more than me."

Timur shook his head and pointed to Parpa. "It's Parpa you should ask. He knows the road that leads to the Amban-Ashkan pass. He told me he came here once before with two Europeans."

"Is that so?" said Bonvalot. "Why didn't you tell me before? Where did you take these Europeans?"

"We went to Bokalik," said Parpa. "They came here to search for the gold mine, but they abandoned me for another caravan, and I never heard from them again. While I was traveling back home, I found out by accident that directly after the pass lies a road that leads south to Tibet. It's possible that this is the 'southern road' you seek."

Hearing this, Rachmed handed Parpa a cup of tea with a lump of sugar in it and urged him to continue.

"At the time I was also looking for gold, so I didn't think much about it. Later, when I climbed the pass, I stumbled into a caravan returning from Lhasa, so I followed their tracks a short distance and saw that they led southward. That's how I found out about the secret route, but I have never traveled there myself."

Bonvalot's heart leapt. "Very good, Parpa. Excellent information. So if I'm understanding you correctly, what you're saying is that once we cross the pass, the road leads directly south to Lhasa."

"Yes, sahib" said Parpa. "But I see no reason to take this road if you intend to take the prince hunting in the Tsaidam. It will only take you further away from your goal and none of us has experience traveling this way. There may be robbers stationed along the way, waiting to ambush us."

Bonvalot took a deep breath. "There's something I must tell you. I didn't organize this caravan to take the prince hunting in the Tsaidam. Our intention is to reach Lhasa. We intend to be the first Europeans to reach the Forbidden City."

There was a sharp intake of breath among the caravan men. Creases of anxiety appeared on their foreheads as the full weight of Bonvalot's words sank in. Their shock soon gave way to raw fear as they envisioned the privations they would suffer if they became lost or trapped in this frozen wasteland at the height of winter.

The men huddled together talking in hushed voices until Abdullah signaled that he wished to speak.

"One of noble birth," said Abdullah. "It appears there has been a grave misunderstanding. I am only a simple squirrel dealer from Kuldja. I have no experience guiding caravans to Lhasa, and neither do any of the others. And what is more worrying, none of us have permission to travel in Tibet. Surely the Amban's soldiers will detain us and give us a great deal of trouble. The Tibetans punish any traveler caught infiltrating their forbidden city.

"But you told me you traveled with the great Prejevalsky," said Bonvalot, raising an eyebrow. "And you spoke Tibetan like a native."

"While I did meet the great Prejevalsky once," said Abdullah, shame-facedly. "It was my *brother-in-law* who traveled with him to Lob Nor. I see this has all been a terrible mistake. One of us should tell the prince that he will not be able to reach Lhasa and he must give the order to turn around at once.

Bonvalot struck a match to light a cigarette.

"Nobody's turning around," he said. "We're going to Lhasa and you men are going to guide us."

"Sahib, you are putting our lives in great danger," said Mahmud, his voice displaying panic. "Our wives and children need us. Don't you see, once we are spotted by the soldiers, they will turn their matchlocks on us and no one will ever hear from us again."

"Every man who stays with me will receive double pay," said Bonvalot. "I'm prepared to reward you well for your efforts. And as for the soldiers, I have a full arsenal at my disposal. But don't be so glum; our situation is not so bad as you would believe. The camels have weathered the journey well so far, we have more than enough provisions to reach Lhasa, we have plenty of ammunition, the tents are in good shape, and all of you appear to be healthy. With so much going for us, there's no reason not to travel to Lhasa."

"There's one very good reason not to travel to Lhasa," said Isa.

"And what is that?" said Bonvalot, losing patience.

"They will kill us if we dare enter their holy city."

CHAPTER 26

Bonvalot's announcement threw the caravan men into a funk that lasted for several days. Once the news spread to Imatch that their true goal was Lhasa, the camel driver flew into a rage that echoed across the barren hills. He cursed, abused, and berated his poor servant Niaz, and made a racket by throwing pots and pans on the ground. When poor Niaz could not take his abuse any more, he fled to Father Dedeken's tent to complain about his master's cruelty.

"Help me please," said Niaz. "Imatch is an evil, wicked man. For the past two weeks he has made my life miserable and now he's absolutely impossible. He swears at me, insults me, reproaches me for every crumb of bread I eat. Please stop him before he kills me."

Worried about the young camel driver, Father Dedeken and Rachmed headed over to Imatch's tent to pacify him as Niaz followed close behind.

When they approached the foul-mouthed camel driver, they expected to be showered with a torrent of insults. Instead, Imatch turned into a paragon of charm and diplomacy, offering them bowls of Chinese noodles and chopsticks. With extreme delicacy, Imatch inquired about their health and listened with interest to everything they said. After they had finished eating, Imatch's face turned grave.

"Tell me the truth," said Imatch, the creases around his eyes deepening. "Where are we going?"

"I haven't the foggiest idea," said Father Dedeken.

When Imatch turned to Rachmed the latter only shrugged his shoulders.

In an instant, Imatch turned vicious.

"You lying Devil from the West!" he growled. "Do you expect me to believe that educated men who can read, write, and consult charts and instruments can't tell me where we're going? Do you think that old Imatch is that stupid? Are you lying to me even after I have served you so faithfully?"

"As they say in Tashkent, better the devil you know than the devil you don't," said Rachmed.

Imatch shook an angry fist. "You foreign devils tricked me! You are dragging me to my death. All I can do now is pray to Allah that he spare my life from this band of wicked men!"

Imatch lashed out at poor Niaz, hitting him on the head with his fists and screaming insults and curses. "You stupid dog! Don't you know how to saddle a donkey properly? And why do you leave your cups everywhere? Do you have less sense than a mule? And those saddles, why the devil did you put them there anyway?"

When he could no longer take Imatch's abuse, Niaz escaped to Bonvalot's side of the camp with tears in his eyes as he repeated his sad lament, "I'm lost, I'm finished, my life is over. There is no hope."

Taking pity on the young man, Rachmed sheltered Niaz in his tent, but he worried that the poor servant's spirit had been broken by years of Imatch's relentless abuse. By the time the last hurricane lamp had been extinguished for the night, the trouble with the caravan men wasn't finished. If anything, it was just starting.

CHAPTER 27

Amban Ashkan Pass, Tibet
December, 1889

It was a cold unlike anything they had ever experienced.

Bonvalot halted his horse and tried to take a deep breath, but found it was impossible. At an altitude of 18,000 feet, he had to gasp for each breath. There were shooting pains in his head and his lungs felt as if they were going to burst. Next to him, Prince Henri slid off his horse and vomited on the side of the road. The others were struggling with lethargy and dizziness, and to make matters worse, a huge storm was heading their way. As they coaxed the camels over the pass, a torrent of flurries and hail turned their world white. Like icy knives, the sleet tore at their faces and whipped their bodies. The wind picked up and nearly pushed them over the edge.

The cold seeped into their sheepskin coats, leather leggings, felt boots, flannel underclothing, and settled into their bones. They made distressingly slow progress. Bonvalot worried that Camille was in danger of frostbite. He grabbed an extra sheepskin blanket and wrapped her in it; she carried on without complaint.

By now Prince Henri was a shadow of his former self. He had lost much wait and his skin was sallow under his sheepskin cap.

"We have to get out of here," he yelled over the squall. "We can't hold up much longer."

Bonvalot strained to be heard above the storm. "Our only chance is to make our way down to the lake on the other side."

At this point, turning around was impossible. With the constant blinding snowfall, the path was blocked on either end.

They had reached a point of no return. Their only hope was to keep moving forward. But with the constant blinding sleet, it was a pointless task. The caravan men complained of fatigue and shortness of breath; they spent hours chopping huge chunks of ice with their pickaxes and shoveling away the debris. Underneath their sheepskin coats, their clothes were wet from perspiration. The wind made it so cold the tears froze on their eyelashes before they could roll down their faces. There was no grass for the animals to graze on and no water to drink. And much worse than that, they were slowly freezing to death.

The previous evening, two camels, a horse, and a mule had died from exposure. The loss of life was incalculable, but Bonvalot refused to admit defeat.

"Sahib, we must get to lower ground or we'll die from the cold and altitude," yelled Abdullah over the howling wind. "The young memsahib is in danger of freezing to death. She cannot last much longer."

Bonvalot's head was spinning. They were navigating across a frozen white world with no path in sight, no hope of escape. All around they were surrounded by steep ridges and dangerous cliffs that gave way to a blackened abyss. One wrong move could send them tumbling to their deaths. Bivouacking at this altitude was also impossible. The wind could blow them off a sheer cliff or into a crevasse where there would be no chance of rescue.

Several minutes later they were infused with hope.

Several yards away they spied a curious object, an obo: heaps of stones upon which prayers are inscribed. This particular obo had a line of colorful prayer flags that bore the ubiquitous Buddhist prayer *Om mane padme hum* (Hail jewel in the lotus). A short distance away they spotted another one, and another one. Bonvalot decided the safest course of action would be to follow the trail of obos until they had crested the summit, then course their way down to the plain below.

As the camels neared the summit their movements became more plodding, their breathing more laborious; foam appeared at their mouths as they struggled under the burdensome weight of their loads.

After what seemed like an eternity, they finally reached the summit, which resembled a gorge between two steep, snow-covered mountains. They rejoiced, thinking the worst of their ordeal was over. But that was not to be the case.

Out of the blue they heard a noise like thunder followed by a rushing sound. Looking up, the men scanned the mountainside, their eyes wide with fright. Then, without warning, someone screamed, "Avalanche!"

Bonvalot looked up in horror. A massive chunk of snow had broken loose and was careening down the mountain toward them.

CHAPTER 28

Someone screamed 'run' and then panic broke out among the caravan men. They beat their animals to make them move faster, out of the way of the impending avalanche.

Kicking his horse's side, Bonvalot galloped past the line of animals until he reached Camille. Grabbing her, he raced with her to safety, then he galloped back to help the caravan men lead the animals out of the path of the oncoming snow.

Sensing danger, the animals plodded as quickly as they could, the horses leading the way followed by the donkeys, mules, and sheep. Some of the smaller animals were too weak to make it across the snow drifts. Left with no choice, Rachmed lassoed a sheep and pulled it to safety. Now in a state of panic, the animals hastened across the pass. No sooner had they made it to the other side when an enormous cloud of snow-dust followed by a massive white mound come crashing down where they had been standing only moments before. The avalanche fell with such force it drowned out all noise and the swirling snow drifts blinded them.

When the air cleared, they saw to their horror that the force of the avalanche sent the snow plummeting downward, toppling over the side of the cliff where it fell into a blackened abyss. The men stared at the near-fatal catastrophe in shock.

"Praise Allah, we are saved," said Rachmed, struggling to catch his breath.

Prince Henri stared over the side of the precipice, his face ashen and his hair blown wildly about his face. "That was dash close for comfort. One minute more and we would be at the bottom of the ravine."

"It was a miracle," said Father Dedeken. "Not one man or beast was hurt. If I hadn't seen it for myself I never would have believed it."

Placing Camille back on her camel Bonvalot said, "Are you alright?

"Yes, thank goodness," she said. "That was a close call."

"We must descend to the lake as quickly as possible. The fresh water and game may infuse the men with more hope."

Bonvalot mounted his horse and rode off in search of the path that led down to the lake. They eventually found it several miles south, and for the rest of the day, they made steady progress. By the time they reached the 'unfreezing lake,' the caravan men were spooked by the near-fatal disaster and were complaining about their aches and pains nonstop.

After pitching the tents, the men from Lob Nor and Qarkilik told Bonvalot they decided to quit the expedition and return home. The abrupt manner in which they announced their imminent departure left Bonvalot with no choice but to agree to pay them and release them.

That night as Bonvalot sat brooding in his tent nursing a migraine with a flask of brandy and a cigarette, he hoped the situation would improve. But unbeknownst to him, the caravan men were already planning to revolt.

CHAPTER 29

Early the next morning, the caravan men spoke little as they sat beside the fire drinking tea and eating hardtack. Though distant, their eyes seemed to be watching Bonvalot's every move. After breakfast, they loaded up the camels and continued their southward march over a frozen river. About halfway across, they made a horrifying discovery.

Emerging through the ice were the humps of five dead camels. Dismounting, the men slid across the glistening surface to get a better look. What they saw filled them with sheer terror.

The camels were frozen solid. Their fur was covered with tiny icicles and fresh-fallen snow; the baggage was still attached to their backs with ropes, as if they had only recently been loaded. One of the men shrieked as he pointed to another macabre figure protruding through the ice. It was the caravan driver, frozen in suspended animation with his arms reaching through the ice, his face a white mask of death.

The men gaped at the scene for several minutes. From her perch on her camel, Camille called out, "What's wrong? What is it?"

Bonvalot slid over the ice toward her. "Sorry for the delay Madame Dancourt, but there's been a terrible accident. A passing caravan slipped through the ice and froze in the icy water. We counted five camels and one rider that may have been part of the Kalmyk caravan we passed not too long ago. Most likely they got careless and forgot to test the ice before venturing out. They simply fell in and froze to death."

Camille's face blanched. "How awful! May I go closer and have a look?"

"No, don't go anywhere near it," said Bonvalot. "The men are quite disturbed by the sight. They're quaking with fear."

"Oh dear," she said. "Those poor wretches. I feel terrible for them."

"Not half as terrible as they feel, I'm afraid," said Bonvalot. "They say it's a bad omen, especially after what happened yesterday with the avalanche. They think we're doomed."

"So why are we standing here on the ice?" she said, gripping the saddle horn for dear life. "Let's get moving!"

"Don't worry, at ten degrees below zero the ice is frozen solid. We'll proceed as soon as the men compose themselves. I've never seen them this upset. But I promise you that as soon as we reach Bokalik, I will make inquiries about your husband. Until then, please be patient."

Camille shivered in her sheepskin coat. After all the privations they had suffered during the past few weeks, she knew the chances of finding her husband in this cruel environment were slim. She clutched the saddle horn for dear life and prayed no similar fate would befall them.

After crossing the frozen river, they continued marching over a monotonous stretch of desert plain, braving sandy winds that cut into their skin and stung their eyes. They burrowed deeper into their sheepskin coats and pulled down their caps as they coaxed the camels to keep moving forward, following what remained of the tracks from the previous caravans, knowing it was only a question of time before the wind and snow erased them forever.

By the time they made camp, the men's spirits were crushed. They sat around the campfire with their backs to the wind, lamenting their migraines and the relentless nausea and dizziness that made even the simplest of tasks impossible. Each man dreaded the idea of venturing further into Tibet without the proper guides or high-altitude yaks that could guarantee their safe passage. One by one the men cursed their fate.

As he sat gazing into the fire, Abdullah reminisced about his home back in Kuldja, how his greatest pleasure had been to sit by the fire cracking pistachio nuts as his children gathered around him listening to his stories. He wondered if little Aziz with his big black eyes and round cheeks was paying attention in the madrassa. He worried that his wife would not be able to keep her eyes on the older boys, who were already starting to hang around the alleyways with the opium dealers. He had given up on them, but the thought that little Aziz would tag along after his older brothers gave Abdullah no end of agony.

Meanwhile, with his dark beard and brooding eyes, Parpa also turned pensive. As the fire crackled in the dark, cold night, he approached Bonvalot and asked for a large sum of money in advance, which he intended to send back to his family with the men from Lob Nor. Something in Parpa's eyes caught Bonvalot off guard. Without hesitating he gave Parpa the coins, hoping they would keep him quiet. But later as he sat in his tent writing in his journal, Rachmed stuck his head in with a worried look.

"Bonvalot-sahib, something is going on with the caravan men," said Rachmed in hushed tones. "I can feel it in my bones."

"What do you mean?" said Bonvalot, setting down his pen.

"They're acting strange, as if they're planning to revolt. During the night they may try to steal our horses and desert us."

Father Dedeken, who was sitting nearby, laid down his Bible. Prince Henri stopped polishing his rifle.

"What the devil are you talking about?" said Prince Henri.

"They've got a mutinous look in their eyes," said Rachmed. "I overheard talk some of them talking, and when they saw me coming they went mute. Ordinarily I wouldn't think twice about it, but this time it seemed serious since Parpa asked for a large sum of money. I never trusted that fiend. They may try to get their hands on your gold and leave us here to die."

"We must keep watch the entire night," said Bonvalot. "Make sure your rifle is loaded and your money belt secure. I'll sleep with one eye open and both ears peeled."

All night long Rachmed guarded the camp through the flaps in his tent. Wrapped in his sheepskin coat, he loaded his Winchester and kept watch over their precious horses, the crates of ammunition, the valuable instruments. About an hour after midnight, he heard a strange rustling sound over near Bonvalot's tent. Picking up his rifle, Rachmed crept out into the freezing cold to investigate.

As he approached the tent, Rachmed detected a strange shadow crouching down by the entrance. Cocking his gun, he pointed it at the man's back and said, "Get up now before I shoot."

Sure enough, it was Parpa. Terrified, the guilty man stood up with his hands raised.

"Did you take me for a fool?" said Rachmed. "What have you got there?" Rachmed ripped a sack of money out of the quivering man's hands. "You bloody thief! I should shoot you on the spot."

"Please, don't shoot!" said Parpa, terrified. "I was only trying to save myself. I have a wife and children."

"You double-crossing little scoundrel," said Rachmed. "You're nothing but a damned deserter! And now that the men from Lob Nor are leaving, we need you more than ever. And to top it off, you're also a thief!"

"Why should I trust you?" said Parpa. "How do I know you'll pay me? How do I know you won't steal my wages?"

"Because you saw the Frenchman pay the Lobi men all the money he owed them. He's a man of his word but you're nothing more than a thief. We don't like thieves, liars—and deserters!" At which point Rachmed rammed his rifle into Parpa's chest.

"Don't shoot!" cried Parpa. "If I was going to run away, I would have already. You would never be able to stop me."

"Just try me," said Rachmed. "I can run circles around you. If I had to chase you through the desert to shoot you, I would do it without giving it a second thought. Care to try me?"

Parpa shook his head.

"Good," said Rachmed. "At least you have some common sense. Now if you continue to serve us well, I'll make sure they reward you, but if you try to steal from us or desert one more time, I give you my word I'll hunt you down and shoot you in the back. Do I make myself clear?"

Before Parpa had a chance to answer, the other caravaneers raced to Rachmed's side in a panic.

"Look!" screamed Parpa, pointing to the other side of camp. "The Lobi men are stealing your horses. Go quick!"

Rachmed and the others dashed over to save their horses. But by then, the Lobis had already saddled the best horses and were leading them out of camp. Rachmed fired several shots in the air and screamed, "Stop or I'll shoot!"

CHAPTER 30

Freezing, the Lobi men turned and raised their hands.

"Don't shoot!" they cried, dropping to their knees.

"I'll shoot the head off the first man who tries to run away," said Rachmed. "And I'll hunt down any man who escapes and shoot him in the back like the coward he is. Now, move away from the horses and return everything you stole."

Mortified, the Lobi men inched away from the horses and returned the money, the saddles, and all the equipment they had pilfered. Rachmed kept guard over the deserters the entire night. Before dismissing them the next day, he ordered them to first help load the camels for the day's journey ahead. When they had finished, he gave them bundles of food, tools, and several mules before dismissing them.

With only fourteen caravan men left, they continued marching southward over the frozen desert through blinding sandstorms and freezing winds. After several hours, they caught sight of two sheepskin-clad hunters on donkeys who appeared to be heading back from Bokalik. Bonvalot's heart raced. When he questioned them, he learned they were indeed from Lob Nor and had spent the past year in Bokalik mining for gold and hunting. Bonvalot presented the hunters with gifts and then showed them the picture of Armand Dancourt. He asked them point blank if they had seen the man in the photograph. The hunters nodded right away, saying they were sure they recognized him, but they did not know where he was since he had left Bokalik many months before in a caravan that was heading south toward Lhasa.

Hearing this, Camille's face drained of color. She met Bonvalot's gaze but he was stone-faced. When Bonvalot asked the hunters to point out the way to Lhasa, they merely shrugged their shoulders and continued on their way. For the rest of the day Camille was anxious and withdrawn while Bonvalot worried that she was losing hope.

Later that day they had a near disaster.

Hoping for some fresh game, Prince Henri and Father Dedeken went hunting on horseback, intending to shoot a wild yak for their dinner. Several miles from camp they spotted one and took aim, but something went terribly wrong. Even after the prince had fired eight Martini bullets into the enormous beast, he refused to die. Angry and furious, the yak ran for miles, forcing the two hunters to chase after him. When they finally caught up with the yak, their energy was completely depleted; they were short of breath and near collapse. Hunting game, they learned, was a dangerous sport at 15,000 feet that required an enormous amount of energy. When they were ready to return to camp, they got so hopelessly lost they ended up wandering among the barren hills for hours until they nearly died from exhaustion.

When the pair failed to return for several hours, Bonvalot panicked and sent a search party out looking for them with hurricane lamps. It took several hours and many gunshots Father Dedeken and Prince Henri found their way back to camp. After that experience, which cost them many valuable rounds of ammunition and almost cost the lives of two men, Bonvalot forbade all movement away from camp.

That night, Rachmed came to Bonvalot and gave him devastating news: Niaz had fallen ill. The poor camel driver lay in his tent delirious and coughing up blood, signs that he had a serious case of mountain sickness. Camille attempted to brew some tea to relieve his suffering, but found it took two hours to boil the water. Desperate, she grabbed Bonvalot's Army Railway Medical Companion and retrieved a bottle of Cockle's pills, which she fed to the stricken camel driver with some melted snow. She hoped it would at least alleviate his suffering.

Bonvalot watched as she spoon-fed the medicine to Niaz.

"I'm quite impressed how you handled that," he said. "You wouldn't happen to be a trained nurse by any chance?"

"Not exactly, Monsieur Bonvalot. But as the oldest of five siblings I was often required to look after them. I suppose it's in my nature."

"We're certainly better off for having you with us."

"Honestly, I never thought I'd live to hear you say that," she said, grinning.

"You've shown tremendous courage and steadfastness, Madame Dancourt. I'm even impressed by the way you handle Henri. You seem to have tamed him."

Camille laughed. "Well, I occasionally let him win at baccarat, but when he reaches for the whiskey, I head for the hills. The truth is, since that episode with the yak, he's lost a lot of strength. He's almost too weak to keep in the saddle. Truly I fear for his safety."

Bonvalot's face turned solemn. "Yes, his Highness almost got himself killed that time. I've got to watch him more carefully. He's completely irresponsible."

Three days later, the horse that Prince Henri had ridden in pursuit of the wild yak died of exhaustion. This was Prince Henri's favorite horse, and he took it the loss very hard. The second horse, which belonged to Father Dedeken, suffered permanent lung damage and never fully recovered. Overcome with grief, Prince Henri, stumbled through camp in a state of drunkenness, kicking everything in his path, screaming in agony.

"*Mon Dieu*, why?" cried the grief-stricken prince, taking a swig of brandy, and wiping his mouth on his sleeve. "Why did You take my horse? Why did You bring me here to die?"

Henri dropped to his knees and fell forward on his face, his arms and legs splayed sideways.

Bonvalot came running out of his tent. When he saw the intoxicated prince he said, "What the devil happened here?"

"He collapsed from too much drink," said Rachmed, joining him. "He's behaving like a Mongol warrior who misses his horse more than his wife."

"Well, that was a damn foolish thing he did chasing after that wild yak," said Bonvalot. "He could have died out there. Help me drag the little miscreant back to his tent before he freezes to death."

They grabbed Prince Henri's legs and dragged him back to his tent, dumping him in his sleeping-sack.

"Let him sleep it off," said Bonvalot, closing the tent flap.

"He'll be even worse tomorrow when he wakes up and sees the dead body of his horse," said Rachmed. "It will be too much for him to bear. He'll scream and carry on like a spoiled little princeling."

"He *is* a spoiled princeling," said Bonvalot, wryly. "And he's more trouble than he's worth. But somehow I think the little rapscallion is starting to grow on me."

The next morning, Prince Henri sat by the fire with swollen, red eyes, nursing a migraine with a cigarette and a cup of coffee. When Camille tried to console him, he just shrugged his shoulders and demanded that Bonvalot return his missing bottles of whiskey.

"You've had enough spirits," said Bonvalot. "Too much alcohol at high altitude makes the brain fuzzy and the reflexes slow. A man dies much quicker from exposure if he's drunk, so please try to remain sober for the remainder of this expedition."

"I have no intention of remaining sober," said Prince Henri. "I can't live without my Charlemagne. I want to drink myself to death."

"Drinking away your sorrows won't bring Charlemagne back, said Father Dedeken. "All of us should learn from this terrible experience and never repeat it. The high altitudes and freezing temperatures are a serious threat to our lives."

"And another thing you can do is quit smoking," said Bonvalot, pulling the cigarette out of Henri's mouth and stomping on it. "At this altitude it's just as intoxicating as liquor and creates more bile than *Le Figaro*. From now on, only the hunters from Qarkilik will do the hunting. The rest of us will conserve our energy as much as possible. So until there's fresh meat, just nibble on some hardtack and drink tea."

"What I drink is no one's business but my own," said Prince Henri. "I resent being watched over by a nanny goat."

"You should be ashamed of your drunken behavior, falling over the baggage like a sailor on shore leave, losing at baccarat every night to the caravan men. You must have squandered hundreds of rubles by now. It's a miracle you didn't stumble into a crevasse during one of your nightly jaunts."

"Go easy on the lad," said Father Dedeken. "The prince has suffered an enormous blow no less tragic than the loss of his kingdom. Perhaps he needs some spirits to soothe his pain."

Father Dedeken's servant, Bartholomeus, who was observing the scene, added, "The Chinese have a saying: A small hole not mended in time will become a big hole much more difficult to mend. Prince Henri has a big hole in his heart with the loss of his horse."

"If it was just a little spirits I wouldn't complain," said Bonvalot. "But spirits in large quantities depletes a man of his stamina and vigor. I promised his father I would get him back to Paris in one piece."

"Oh, go on and give it to him," said Camille. "The cold is frightful. I don't know how any of us can bear it much longer. We need the spirits to keep our courage up."

"Very well," said Bonvalot. "Henri can have one bottle of brandy. I will decide how to dispense the rest. I may need it to bribe the Tibetan officials when we get closer to Lhasa."

Just then Abdullah came running from the other side of camp.

"One of noble birth, we must get out of here quick. A terrible storm is approaching. If we sit here much longer waiting for fuel and water, the animals will perish."

"Very well," said Bonvalot. "Tell the men to start loading the camels. We'll leave as soon as they're ready."

"Forward then," said Father Dedeken. "We must keep moving and rely on Providence to watch over us, and if we're destined to die here on the Chang Tang, let us not die as cowards and poltroons, but as heroes!"

Hearing this, Prince Henri buried his head in his fur cap and sobbed.

After escaping the full brunt of the storm, they continued marching. By the next day they had climbed to an altitude of 18,000 feet. To their amazement, they found dry grass and sparse bushes for the animals to graze on as well as ice to melt for tea. For the time being, their misery was alleviated, but the men complained of cracked nails, skin ulcers, migraines, and joint pain. From time to time one of the men would collapse on the ground, groaning like an animal waiting to be slaughtered. Camille tried to soothe them by bandaging their wounds and feeding them Cockle's pills dissolved in melted ice, but she was powerless against the effects of mountain sickness. Unless they got to lower ground, they would all succumb sooner or later.

Later, Bonvalot, Rachmed, and Abdullah set out from camp to do a bit of exploring. They had not gone far when they made a ghastly discovery. In a cleft between two ridges were the bodies of five camels from a previous caravan complete with saddles, blankets, and luggage. Nearby was a collapsed tent, almost completely covered with snow, and inside Timur made a frightening discovery: *frozen in suspended animation lay the body of a European man.* His face locked in a horrifying grimace, his chin resting on his chest, and his waxen hands still clutching his rifle.

The men stared in horror at the lifeless body as the wind howled in their ears. After the initial shock had abated somewhat, Bonvalot said to Rachmed, "Oh my goodness, this man may be the husband of the memsahib. I'm going to ride back to camp and fetch Camille. Stay here with Abdullah and guard the body. If I'm not back in an hour, fire some shots with your rifle."

"Be careful out there," said Rachmed.

Without another word Bonvalot mounted his horse and galloped back to camp. When he got back he told Camille they had discovered the remains of a failed caravan along with the body of a dead explorer. He asked her to come with him and see if she could identify the body. With great trepidation, Camille climbed into the saddle behind Bonvalot and together they rode back to the doomed caravan.

When they brought Camille to the corpse her face blanched.

"Is this man your husband?" said Bonvalot.

Camille shook her head. "No, I've never seen this man before."

"Please be certain, Madame Dancourt. See if you can identify his clothes, his boots, perhaps the color of his hair—"

"No, no, I'm sure this is not my husband," she said, turning away. "Please, I can't bear to look anymore…"

Camille buried her head in Bonvalot's chest and burst into sobs. Meanwhile, Rachmed picked up a blanket and covered the dead man.

"I know this is hard for you," said Bonvalot. "But we had to be certain."

"Do you know what happened to this man?" she said. "What may have caused his death?"

"We believe the caravan was caught in a storm and he simply froze to death. A less likely scenario is that his guides ran away with the horses and left him here to die."

"How horrible," she said.

"One of the hazards of being an explorer," he said.

Without another word they returned to camp.

Later that night no one had any desire to eat. Although Tong-Kia had prepared a dish of yak meat, the food was undercooked from the high altitude, and almost everyone was suffering from some degree of mountain sickness. It was clear that Niaz's condition was deteriorating; his moans echoed throughout the camp and his face had gone pallid. He had lost a tremendous amount of weight and could not longer feed himself. The men sat around the fire, staring at the flames like lost souls, their hopes for surviving waning as the fire grew smaller and smaller.

Rachmed sat next to Bonvalot and produced a piece of paper.

"I found this letter in the dead man's pocket," said Rachmed.

Bonvalot grabbed the yellowed paper and unfolded it. Apparently the dead man had been English according to his letter.

Dearest Delia,

Well at last we have made it to the area known by the natives as Bokalik. The night we arrived it began to rain and at 11pm when all were asleep it turned to snow. We slept unconsciously until the weight of the snow brought down our tents and nearly suffocated us. Then there was the dreadful ordeal of having to crawl out in to the blizzard and try to erect our tents again—as the poles were mostly broken this was an impossibility and several men had to walk about all night.

Of course everything in the tent became wet and it was impossible to dry anything as it continued to pour all the next day and the camp was running in slush and water—one got soaked every time one left the tent. However with a tin of biscuits and tea made from melted snow, I managed to survive the day. All of us agreed that it was the worst day that any of us had ever spent. It finished off one of the coolies who was suffering from dysentery and had been lingering for the last six weeks. Poor fellow, we buried him yesterday.

The Frenchman who was travelling with us left to join a native caravan that was heading south toward Lhasa. I think the blighter's got some idea about meeting the Dalai Lama. Abdul said the Frenchman was planning to go there disguised as a Buddhist pilgrim. Given the dangers of such a journey, I expect we won't hear from him again. Please give my love to the children.

Your loving husband,
Charles Edward Hughes

"Good heavens," said Bonvalot. "He must have written this just before he died. And he states that a Frenchman left the caravan and headed south toward Lhasa."

"Could this Frenchman be the memsahib's husband?" said Rachmed.

"It is possible," said Bonvalot. "I suppose we shall have to follow his trail to find out what happened to him. In any case, I don't suppose Mr. Charles Edward Hughes had the slightest notion this letter would be his last goodbye."

Just then a voice called out to him from across the camp.

Bonvalot looked up to see Father Dedeken heading toward them. He had just left Niaz's tent and was certain the end was near.

Father Dedeken struggled to catch his breath in the thin air.

"I'm sorry to have to tell you this but we must descend to lower ground at once if there's any chance of saving Niaz's life. If we remain at this altitude not only are we sure to lose him, but we risk losing more men from mountain sickness."

"I'm afraid that's impossible," said Bonvalot. "According to my charts it will take months or weeks until we reach lower ground. Our only option right now is to keep the patient as dry and comfortable as possible. He's young, he may pull through."

But both men suspected the worst.

That night, a blizzard tore through camp, sending the temperature plummeting down to thirty degrees below zero. All night long the men huddled under their sheepskin blankets fearing they would either freeze to death or simply never awaken. The fire died down and with it, their last remaining source of heat. Misery spread quickly throughout the camp. Shivering in their tents, the men wondered if this reckless journey to Tibet would end in disaster.

The next morning when they awoke they made a chilling discovery: all the horses had fled during the night. They simply broke free and ran away in the storm, desperately searching for food. Bonvalot was furious that Prince Henri, who was supposed to be on guard duty, had failed to report the missing horses. If they did not retrieve them quickly, the entire expedition would end in disaster and their chances of surviving would be diminished.

Four caravan men stepped forward and offered to go out in search of the horses, but when they returned several hours later, they were empty-handed and suffering from exposure. Left with no choice, Timur and Rachmed volunteered to go next. Armed only with a sack of food, a goatskin of water, and rifles slung across their backs, they headed out in the squall, promising to return shortly with the missing animals, but by sunset, there was no sign of them.

Hours passed. As darkness descended over the camp the men wrung their hands and paced around their tents, making small talk to pass the time. After what seemed like an eternity, they caught sight of a lone figure staggering through the blizzard toward camp. Someone shouted that it was Timur.

Seeing their companion half frozen to death put them in a state of panic. Horrified, they raced to his side and brought Timur to his tent, but when they brushed aside the snow from his face, they gasped in horror: Timur was more dead than alive. His face was blue and covered with frozen tears; icicles hung down from his beard and his limbs were frozen stiff. Without a moment to lose, they rubbed his limbs with snow, hoping to restore vitality, but Timur only moaned in agony.

Bonvalot turned to Isa. "Run! Get some naphtha! Quick!"

Isa dashed off and returned with a tin of naphtha that they usually used for cooking. They rubbed it all over Timur's arms, legs, hands, and feet, hoping to restore vitality. Moments later, Timur cried out in pain and a wave of relief washed over the men. If Timur could feel his limbs, he was out of danger.

"Praise be to Allah," moaned Abdullah. "That is a good cry. It means we have a good chance of saving his hands and toes. When it comes to frostbite, pain is a good sign. Our friend's guiding days may not be over yet."

After several more minutes of vigorous rubbing, color and feeling returned to Timur's hands.

"You're a lucky man," said Bonvalot, although Timur's face was still a wretched sight. "If not for the spirits, you might have lost your hands."

Timur broke down and sobbed. "I'm sorry, sahib," he said, cradling his injured hands. "I've failed you and I've failed Rachmed. I can never forgive myself for letting everyone down."

"You did your best," said Bonvalot. "Just rest now."

"But Rachmed..." said Timur. "He's gone. The last time I saw him he was heading toward a distant mountain. He cannot last much longer out there. How can the rust of us survive without him?"

Bonvalot's heart lurched in his chest. He grabbed his rifle and raced out into the storm, firing indiscriminate shots in the air as he screamed Rachmed's name over and over. But all he heard was the howling wind as the blizzard raged on. Panicked, he ran back to the tent and ordered the men to keep the fires burning as long as possible, but the situation seemed dire. They were lost on the Chang Tang in the middle of a snowstorm with a dwindling food supply and only two days' worth of yak dung for the fire while temperatures hovered at thirty degrees below zero. And to make matters worse: Rachmed was hopelessly lost.

CHAPTER 31

Bonvalot couldn't sleep the entire night. He sat in his tent with his head buried in his hands fretting over his missing companion while the blizzard raged outside like a howling demon. From time to time Bonvalot would fire shots in the air as he yelled out Rachmed's name, but the wind drowned out his voice, making it impossible to carry through the storm. The caravan men sat in their tents mourning their missing companion, fearing they would never find his body to give him a proper burial.

Occasionally, one of the men would stick his head out of his tent and cry out like a madman that he had heard Rachmed calling to him through the storm, but each time they strained their ears to listen for his voice, all they heard was the wind taunting them.

For her part, Camille kept a vigil over Niaz, using their few precious supplies to prolong his life, but time was running out. She did not know how much longer he would survive in his weakened condition. His face had turned gray, he was mumbling incoherently, and his pulse was racing. He did not look long for the world.

Sometime during the early hours of the morning she fell asleep. In her dreams, she saw her husband dressed in his wedding suit, but when she reached out to touch him, he shook his head and told her they should veer west if they wanted to stay alive. If the caravan continued heading south, they would perish. When she woke up, her heart was beating wildly and she was sweating. Her husband's face lingered in her memory for several minutes, then faded. She was left with an overwhelming feeling of dread.

She crawled out of her sleeping sack and peered outside. The blizzard was still pounding with a full force. In the distance, she heard the animals crying and bleating for food. If the animals died, she knew the men would follow soon thereafter. Their animals were their only hope of survival.

Under the present conditions, she didn't know how much longer they could last. Sitting back, she took stock of their situation: they were trapped in a frozen white hell with no discernable landmarks, no help for possibly hundreds of miles, nothing for the animals to eat, and no way to communicate with the outside world. She no longer believed her husband was alive. All she wanted now was to get out of Tibet alive, but even that seemed impossible.

Soon she heard signs of life as Bonvalot and others began crawling out of their tents to assess the situation. They scanned the horizon in their sheepskin coats and felt boots searching for any sign of life, but their situation was unchanged. It was bleak at best, beyond hope at worst. There was no sign of Rachmed anywhere. They knew it was impossible for anyone, even a formidable giant like Rachmed, to survive for three days on the frozen Chang Tang with no shelter, no warmth, no fire, no protection from the cold, and no food. The landscape was so white, there were no landmarks to navigate by. Downhearted, Bonvalot ordered Tong-Kia to melt more snow for tea but he knew it would do little to lift the men's waning hopes.

Pulling on her sheepskin hat and coat, Camille traipsed through the snow to Bonvalot's tent.

"Any news?" she said, trying to sound hopeful.

Bonvalot tried to put on a brave face.

"Nothing, I'm afraid."

"Perhaps we should send a search party out looking for him," she said. "Even if there's only a slim chance that Rachmed is alive, we've got to help him in any way possible."

"Unfortunately, I can't allow it," said Bonvalot. "It's too risky. I can't take the chance of losing more men. Niaz is deathly ill and Timur may have gotten himself a case of frostbite. The temperature is too cold and the storm is too dangerous. I'm afraid the indomitable Rachmed is on his own."

"But we can't just leave him to the elements," she said. "How can he possibly survive all by himself?"

"Rachmed is an experienced tracker. If anyone can find their way out of a storm it's him. I appreciate your concern, but sending another man out in that blizzard is out of the question."

"Really Monsieur Bonvalot I must object," said Camille. "What if it was *you* who was lost out there? Wouldn't you expect some help? Some compassion?"

"I would expect the second in command to display some common sense," he said. "Which entails doing what's in the best interest of the majority of the survivors. Rachmed is a professional guide with many years of experience. He knew the risks he was taking when he agreed to accompany me to Tibet. This is not the first time he's risked his life. He's quite adept out in the wilderness."

"That seems very callous...."

"Madame Dancourt, it would be more callous to leave us dangerously short-handed. So many men have already quit the expedition. I need every hand I can get."

"But this is Rachmed, your companion," she said, her voice rising in anger. "I thought I had the measure of you, Monsieur Bonvalot, but I believe I was mistaken. Can you not see you're your own ambition? Is the success of your expedition worth more than the life of your friend?" Bonvalot turned to her and froze. "There are others to consider here, people whose lives are hanging in the balance. I suggest you stop for a minute and consider them for a change. Consider that Rachmed's life may be just as important as your own."

Bonvalot stared at her, his eyes wide with shock. Mortified, Camille turned and fled back to her tent.

Later, when Bonvalot went to check on Timur, he breathed a sigh of relief. Although Timur's face and hands showed signs of frostbite, he was able to move them and color had returned to his face. For now it looked as though Timur would keep his hands. Nevertheless Niaz's condition had gotten worse during the night. The skin on his face and lips had a bluish tinge and he was coughing up blood. He was delirious and mumbling incoherently; there was little they could do for him. Descending to a lower altitude was all but impossible.

The day passed slowly while the men waited for any sign of Rachmed. Several times Bonvalot took his field glasses and hiked to a nearby hill where he kept a lookout for his missing companion, but there was no movement anywhere on the horizon. Although the cold air inflamed his lungs, his hands and feet went numb from the cold, and the skin on his lips and hands cracked and bled, Bonvalot refused to give up. He kept a constant vigil for his formidable Uzbek caravan leader, hoping and praying for his safe return.

As a precaution, Bonvalot hung a hurricane lamp on a pole hoping it would guide his missing companion home, but he did not labor under the delusion that Rachmed could still be alive after spending so many days exposed to the elements. Rachmed's empty bedroll was a constant reminder that even an indomitable giant was not impervious to the elements, or even to death.

Out of desperation, Parpa offered to go out and search for Rachmed. He could not believe it was possible they could simply abandon him to so cruel a fate. Parpa decided he was willing to take the risk, and begged for the chance to go out.

Unequivocally, Bonvalot refused, citing the danger and the poor visibility, but after some prodding, he finally relented. All at once, Parpa dressed in a double layer of sheepskin, saddled one of the strongest camels, and rode off in search of Rachmed.

Hours ticked by with no sign of Parpa. While he was gone, Niaz's groans grew louder and the men's desperation grew more obvious. Occasionally they would fire a gun or call out Parpa's name through the storm, but their frantic calls were only met by the howling wind; their little caravan seemed to be the only sign of life on the forbidding Chang Tang.

Finally, after waiting for hours on end, a miracle happened.

Through the snowstorm, they caught sight of Parpa on his camel riding back to camp. Behind him they made out the figures of the missing horses being led back to camp by a rope.

Everyone cried out with joy. They greeted Parpa like a returning hero and helped him alight from his camel. Then they brought him to his tent and made him sit down with a cup of hot tea. They fed the starving horses with what little remained of the grain and thanked their lucky stars for their good fortune, but the men still fretted over the greatest loss of all, that of their missing companion Rachmed.

And then, just as they had given up all hope, a black speck appeared on the horizon.

"Look!" cried Abdullah, pointing with incredulity. "Over there! Something is moving!"

Bonvalot grabbed his field glasses and focused them with sweaty, trembling hands.

"Good Lord! I can't believe it. It's Rachmed, he's alive!"

The caravan men jumped for joy. They ran out into the snowstorm to greet their fearless companion who was stumbling across the frozen Chang Tang in a state of delirium. When they got close they saw how close to death Rachmed had come: icicles dangled from his beard and ice covered every inch of his body. Rachmed was near collapse, but he had made it back alive.

They dragged Rachmed into his tent and began the process of reviving him. They rubbed snow on his skin and used naphtha to bring the color and circulation back to his limbs. Overjoyed, Tong-Kia brought a cup of tea and held it to Rachmed's bluish lips. To their surprise, for all his brute strength, Rachmed was a compliant patient. He mumbled a word of thanks as the color slowly returned to his limbs. In the end, everyone agreed that it was a miracle that Rachmed had not succumbed to the elements. He had been missing for thirty hours during which time he was subjected to the full brunt of the storm with nothing to eat and no shelter for protection. A few minutes more and he would have died from exposure.

When Rachmed was finally able to speak he told them about his ordeal, how he managed to keep on his feet for thirty hours, fighting the cold by keeping in constant motion for fear his feet and legs would freeze. He navigated by the stars and the positions of the mountains and never gave up hope. When his feet became soaked with sweat, he tore the lining from his clothes and wrapped it around them to keep them warm and dry. Later, when the pieces of cloth grew saturated with sweat, he placed them under his armpits to dry. By repeating this process over and over, he saved his feet from frostbite. By Rachmed's skill and resourcefulness, he managed to save his own life.

The next day the caravaneers ate a hearty breakfast and loaded up the camels. It was time to get moving again. For the next several days, they headed south through a maze of snow-covered mountains and bleak valleys. The cold was so intense and relentless that Imatch came close to his breaking point. He was in such a foul mood that when he went to fetch Niaz, who was strapped to the back of a camel to prevent him from falling off, he loosened the ropes before first making the camel kneel down, causing his poor camel driver to fall to the ground in agony.

Seeing this act of unrestrained cruelty was the last straw for Bonvalot. His face turned red and his hands shook with rage as he drew his revolver and pointed it at Imatch's head.

"You heartless bastard I should shoot you right now."

Imatch slunk at the sight of the gun, his eyes bulging.

"Don't you dare kill me you foreign devil!" screamed Imatch.

"I've had enough of your cruelty," said Bonvalot, unlatching the safety on his revolver.

In a split second, Abdullah and Timur lunged at Bonvalot, gripping his arms and restraining him with all their might while they struggled to remove the revolver from his grip. Two shots rang out into the night sky, causing Camille to scream in horror. After more struggling, Timur finally wrestled the gun away from Bonvalot.

"Give me back my gun!" yelled Bonvalot.

"No sahib, you cannot kill a man!" cried Abdullah, struggling to keep his grip on Bonvalot.

"Let me go," said Bonvalot, struggling to free himself. "I'm going to kill that heartless bastard if it's the last thing I do."

"No, sahib!" yelled Timur, "That is murder!"

Bonvalot writhed in a fury. His breathing came in gasps and his face turned a deep shade of crimson. They had never seen Bonvalot so angry before.

"Get that scoundrel out of my sight before I shoot him!" said Bonvalot.

"One of noble birth, I cannot release you until you promise not to shoot Imatch," said Abdullah.

Bonvalot continued his tirade but Abdullah and Timur swore they would not release him until his ire had sufficiently cooled. After several minutes, Bonvalot's breathing returned to normal and he no longer seemed as agitated as before, but they still wouldn't release him until he agreed to not shoot Imatch. After Bonvalot relented, they brought a flask of brandy to his lips, but it took several swigs before Bonvalot's nerves had sufficiently calmed down. Meanwhile, Imatch was nowhere to be found. He ran to the far side of camp and kept out of sight for the remainder of the night.

Once peace was restored, the caravan men dragged Niaz's unconscious body into a tent and kept vigil over him. Everyone feared the poor camel driver would not last the night.

CHAPTER 32

At midnight, Timur came to Bonvalot's tent with terrible news: Niaz the camel driver was dead. Bonvalot set down his flask of whisky and followed Timur to Niaz's tent where he found Father Dedeken, Bartholomeus, and Rachmed sitting beside him.

When Bonvalot saw the poor camel driver's face his heart sank. Niaz was unrecognizable, but upon closer inspection he saw the young man was still breathing, if only faintly. With no other hope, they prayed for the patient's recovery, but feared the end was near.

They spent the night huddled in their tents existing on hardtack and melted snow, muttering that even if Prince Henri could track and shoot an antelope, they would never be able to cook it at such a high altitude. Out of desperation, Prince Henri opened his last can of goose liver pâté which he offered to share with the others, but no one had the heart to eat. As long as Niaz's life hung in the balance, they would not touch any food. As the night dragged on, they shivered in their tents until they fell into an exhausted, troubled sleep.

The next morning, Rachmed came to Bonvalot's tent with tears in his eyes.

"It's all over," he whispered. "Poor Niaz is gone."

Bonvalot felt a lump in his throat. "Poor boy. He lived such a miserable life but at least now he's at peace. How can we go on without him?"

"And what's worse, there's no water to wash the body," said Rachmed. "And no clean garments to dress him. How can we give him a decent Muslim burial?"

"Don't worry about that," said Bonvalot. "If you do your best, Allah will forgive you. Just roll him up in a piece of white felt and bury him as best you can. That will suffice for the poor, brave Niaz."

"How shall we dig him a grave?" said Rachmed. "The ground is frozen solid. Surely the wild beasts will get to his body…"

"Just cover his body with rocks."

Later, when they went to collect Niaz's body, they found him situated outside Imatch's tent wrapped in his sheepskin coat. Under a steady snowfall, the men wrapped their fallen companion in a long piece of felt, then took their pickaxes and with every last ounce of energy, they went to work breaking the hard ground. When they failed to make progress, they used hatchets to hack at the frozen earth. But all their efforts proved useless. They only managed to dig a shallow grave for poor Niaz.

Rachmed then remembered to turn the dead man's head toward Mecca and he wailed that all their efforts had been in vain. When he questioned Bonvalot as to the proper direction, the latter took out his compass and pointed west, whereupon the men picked up Niaz's body and gently turned him in the proper direction, just as a mother might reposition her sleeping infant. Each man said a few words over their faithful camel driver after which Father Dedeken recited some suitable prayers. By the end of the funeral, everyone was sobbing over the body of the forthright and honest Niaz, and it was a long time before they were able to get back on the road.

For the next two days, the trail climbed to altitudes so high it took Tong-Kia three hours to boil a pot of water for tea and cooking meat was all but impossible. But no one had much appetite anyway. Severe mountain sickness had gripped everyone. In their weakened state, their frustration and anxiety had reached a breaking point. They lashed out at Imatch for abusing Niaz and for taking advantage of his sweet, gentle nature. They accused Imatch of selfishly exploiting Niaz's kindness and decency to satisfy his own greedy impulses. It took the combined efforts of Bonvalot, Father Dedeken, and Rachmed to keep the caravan men from venting their anger out on Imatch.

It was precisely at this moment that disaster struck.

Restless by nature, Prince Henri would occasionally sneak out of camp on his own. He wandered off without a rifle to do a bit of exploring and it was during this particular jaunt that he stumbled upon a herd of wild yaks. As the young prince stood gaping, the monstrous-sized beasts lifted their heads and took him for a threat. A jolt of raw fear shot through the prince's veins as it dawned on him that a rampaging yak with long, pointy horns could do a tremendous amount of damage. When he saw that one of the beasts was eyeing him suspiciously, he cursed his stupidity.

Backing up slowly, Prince Henri tried to escape, but every movement on his part agitated the ferocious yak. His heart raced as the animal took a step closer and sniffed the air. Sweat pouring out of his temples, Henri inched his body backwards ever so slowly, but to his horror, the animal came even closer. With fear coursing through his veins, Henri took one more step backwards, and then another, trying to will himself invisible, but the yak only grew more aggressive. And then, to Henri's horror, the beast snorted, stomped at the ground, and charged.

The young prince fled across the frozen tundra. Breaking into a run, the yak chased the prince with malicious intent. Stumbling, Henri collapsed on the icy gravel and cut his hand as his glove flew away. To his horror, the yak continued its menacing advance, snorting with anger as he barreled all of his 2,000 pounds in the prince's direction.

Terrified, Henri picked himself up and ran for dear life. With the animal's hoof beats echoing in his ears, he raced with every last ounce of strength in the direction of camp, screaming at the top of his lungs as blood dripped from his wounded hand.

Glancing over his shoulder, his worse fears were realized when he saw the woolly black monster careening toward him, getting closer with each hoof beat. Running now for dear life, Henri headed toward a nearby rocky ridge. Breathless and near collapse, he climbed up to safety and hid behind a large boulder. Crouching down, he struggled to catch his breath, but at that altitude it was all but impossible. Pain seared his lungs as he cradled his injured hand, his breathing now coming in hoarse gasps.

When at last he peered around the boulder, he caught sight of the ferocious yak running in confused patterns back in the direction of the herd. For the moment, the danger had passed.

Breathing a sigh of relief, Prince Henri picked himself up, climbed back down the ridge, and then stumbled back to camp.

When Henri arrived, he was near collapse. He couldn't speak and he couldn't tell anyone what had happened. Alarmed, Father Dedeken and Bonvalot carried him to his tent and wrapped him in a sheepskin blanket and brought a shot of brandy to his lips to revive him. They asked him what had happened but the prince could only shake his head as he gasped for air; he was too weak and too out of breath to speak. Henri merely clutched his chest in pain and groaned with each excruciating breath.

Seeing the young prince's distress, Bonvalot and Father Dedeken exchanged a worried look. They were certain something terrible had happened but had no idea what. After what seemed like an eternity, Prince Henri finally managed to speak.

"Thank God I made it," gasped the prince. "I'm l-lucky to be al-live. I almost got k-killed." He clutched his chest in pain and winced. "A y-yak chased me, tried to k-kill me. I forgot my gun."

"Good heavens," said Bonvalot. "How could you be so careless? Didn't I warn you about wandering away from camp without your rifle? You could have been killed."

"I d-didn't know there would be so many y-yaks," said Henri, his teeth chattering from the cold. "The d-damn thing nearly gored me to d-death."

Bonvalot shook his head. "You damned fool! You took a huge risk with your life. Well, I intend to put a stop to it once and for all."

Prince Henri's face twisted with rage. "I'm sick of your damn lectures. I can take care of m-myself. I refuse to be treated like a baby!"

Bonvalot lashed out in fury. "You agreed to abide by my rules. I'm responsible for your life. I'm responsible for *everyone* on this expedition. I've already lost one man and I'll be damned if I lose another. No more wandering outside of camp without permission from me."

Henri glared at Bonvalot and took another swig of brandy. For now, his life was saved, but all that physical exertion at high altitude had permanently damaged his lungs.

For the next several days, they headed across several enormous glaciers that seemed to stretch on forever. There was no water to be had, no grass for the animals. No sign of any life. The men's boots crunched over the frozen gravel as the miserable camels and horses pecked aimlessly over solid sheets of ice for any morsel to eat. Steadying themselves with poles and tying themselves with ropes, the men negotiated their way across the vast whiteness, aware that one misstep could send them plunging through a crevasse to their deaths. In that vast frozen world, the hardy explorers wondered if they would ever see trees, flowers, or even grass again. Even the sight of a cat or a house was impossible to imagine. Bracing themselves against the freezing winds, they continued marching until they reached an abandoned camp where they decided to stop and rest.

The next day, their luck worsened.

They awoke to a raging blizzard that dwarfed anything they had ever experienced. The storm tore across the frozen wilderness with a fury that bordered on savagery. The roar of the wind was more deafening than a freight train; it blew so hard, it battered the canvas of the tents like the sails of a ship. Throughout the night they heard the agonizing cries of the animals who had no shelter to protect them from the onslaught. Exhausted and weak from hunger, Bonvalot fell into a deep, but troubled sleep.

When he awoke the next morning, something had gone horribly wrong: his tent was gone. He found himself buried under a mound of snow. There was so little air, he almost suffocated to death. During the night the storm had ripped the tent out by its pegs and blew it away. Alarmed, he clawed his way through the snow and gulped in the fresh air. When he looked around, he was overcome with terror: every single tent was gone. They had all blown away during the night. Every man, including Camille, was buried under layers of snow.

Now frantic, Bonvalot dug like a madman, searching for his missing companions. Grabbing any tool he could find, he dug and shoveled through dense layers of snow until he finally managed to expose them one by one. When he saw their faces his heart sank. The men were as still as corpses, their faces colorless, their bodies motionless.

With his heart pounding in fear, Bonvalot shook the men and rubbed their faces, calling out their names in desperation. It seemed the worst had happened: his men were dead and he was trapped on the Roof of the World with no hope of escape.

He began to search frantically for Camille. When he finally found her, he stared at her lifeless body and sobbed. Her skin was chalky white, her lips an unnatural shade of blue. He pressed his lips against hers and breathed into her lungs. To his tremendous relief, he felt a warm current coming from her nostrils. He rubbed her limbs and face, calling out her name in desperation. Slowly but surely her eyelids fluttered and her face began to twitch. Bonvalot lifted her to a sitting position and wrapped a sheepskins around her for warmth.

"Wh-what happened?" said Camille, opening her eyes.

"The storm blew everything away. Took away our tents, destroyed our camp."

"Are we both alive?"

"Yes, thank God," he said. "We're both very much alive as are the others. Thank heaven I found you in time."

"Monsieur Bonvalot, I don't think I can go on any more. I haven't got the strength."

"Of course you do" he said. "You're going to be fine." He brushed the snow out of her hair and rubbed her hands for warmth. "You've got the courage and strength of several men," he said.

"Monsieur Bonvalot," she said. "I've been meaning to tell you something. About the other day—"

"Don't speak now," he said. "Just stay warm. Concentrate on staying alive. We'll have plenty of time to talk later."

"Don't leave me…"

"I'm not going anywhere."

He kissed her forehead and stayed with her until she was well enough to stand. As the caravan men began to take stock of their ruined camp, they began to frantically search for their missing tents. After an hour, they recovered them a quarter of a mile away, blown away like leaves by the violent winds.

Later, they made a grim discovery. The storm had left a camel, two horses, and a mule dead. With their situation becoming increasingly uncertain, few of the men believed they would be able to survive the Chang Tang for much longer. They had already buried Niaz and feared losing more men. Every day more animals succumbed to the privations of the journey and the survivors were nearing the point of collapse. As much as he hated to admit it, Bonvalot saw their situation as increasingly desperate. Their animals were their lifeline. If all the animals died they would be dead too within a matter of days.

CHAPTER 33

Chang Tang, Tibet
January, 1890

By the beginning of January, the men were convinced the expedition was doomed. Blinded by a raging blizzard, they had lost all trace of the pilgrims' tracks and were reduced to navigating solely by compass. For several days they wandered southward in an almost trance-like state, meandering through a maze of hills and valleys, traversing frozen lakes and glaciers in a never-ending quest to reach the forbidden city. In all the time, the temperature never climbed above thirty degrees below zero, and on one particularly frigid morning they awoke to find the mercury had frozen in the thermometer. At some point during the night the temperature had dropped to forty degrees below zero. The men stared in horror at the useless thermometer, scarcely believing their eyes.

Nevertheless, they continued traveling as remaining in one place meant certain death. Veering eastward, they passed enormous herds of yaks. The men looked at the animals with wide eyes; they were starving but no one had the strength to hunt a yak and drag its carcass back to camp. Gazing southward, they prayed for salvation, but all they saw before them was a labyrinth of ice-covered peaks glistening under the golden rays of the sun. Somewhere beyond this amphitheater of snowy mountains lay Lhasa. As they stared at this foreboding obstacle, the caravan men demanded to know how Bonvalot planned on crossing it. They were at their wits end. They pointed at the mountains and argued that the further south they traveled, the colder it got and the higher the mountains appeared.

Turning around Bonvalot pointed at the enormous mountain ranges they had already scaled and told them they had managed to cross them though they looked just as impassible. But his answer only made the men to shake their heads in frustration; nevertheless, they pressed on.

By now, the animals were near the limits of their endurance. The camels, horses, and donkeys had gone for days without food and water, so when they reached a narrow valley that contained an enormous sparkling lake, their hearts soared.

Marching with renewed fervor, the men led the animals to this unexpected oasis amidst the barren hills, scarcely believing their good fortune. Everyone grew excited at the thought of drinking fresh water, and as they neared the water's edge, even the animals showed signs of elation: the camels growled and the horses whinnied, but as soon as they drank the water, they spit it out in disgust. The water was pure brine, completely undrinkable.

The riverbank was covered with a layer of salt nearly a foot thick, the sight of which caused the men to sink to the ground in agony. Even the poor camels could not partake of the salty water. As soon as they plunged their noses in, they withdrew them, coughing, spitting, and growling to the disgust of the men.

The caravan men cursed their luck, kicking the sand and raising their hands to the heavens.

While they bemoaned their fate, one of the men wandered off to explore the area and soon he called out to the others. When they looked up, he was holding up a strange object. It turned out to be a curious-looking wooden saddle ornamented with metal plates and covered with a cushion. They had never seen anything like it. They had no doubt it was a camel saddle, but it looked like something from the days of Genghis Khan.

"I swear by my life this saddle is Tibetan," said Parpa. "Look at its curious markings. Strange dragons and Buddhist symbols. This is unlike any saddle I have ever seen before."

The others nodded in agreement.

"This is good sign," said Timur, rubbing his gloved hands together. "It means there are people out there. Tibetan people. Maybe they will help us."

Rachmed was doubtful as he looked around at the desolate landscape. "It is said that where you find saddles you will find people, so perhaps it won't be long now before we stumble upon an inn with a fireplace and hot food."

Imatch, who was admiring the exquisite detail of the saddle, smiled his toothless smile and said, "Sahib, this means we are saved! I am sure that in a week's time we will find tents."

Bonvalot shook his head. "Men cannot live at this altitude for long. We must descend at least another three thousand feet before we will find tents. It may take another two weeks before we find any Tibetans."

"You devil from the west," hissed Imatch, his face contorting into a derisive scowl. "You are a prophet of doom. If we have to wander in this hellish land for another two weeks we will die and I predict you will be the first to go."

Rachmed pulled aside the irate camel driver and ordered him to lead the camels back to camp. They watched the bow-legged Imatch hobble over the hard snow toward the camels. He had a bad case of frostbite on his feet and seemed it be in a lot of pain. They winced as Imatch grabbed the camels' halters and plodded back to camp, muttering and cursing under his breath the entire way.

"If it was up to me I'd fire that wretch immediately," said Prince Henri, struggling to light a cigarette with his freezing hands. He took a few puffs, coughed loudly, and then spit up blood. The others looked on in dismay.

Bonvalot grabbed the cigarette out of the prince's mouth and stomped on it. "No more cigarettes for you, your Highness. Your lungs are badly damaged from that yak incident. You must preserve your hcalth."

"I'll smoke if I want to," countered Henri, his hacking growing louder as he coughed up more blood.

Bonvalot's face grew hot with anger. "Do you want to end up like Niaz?"

Henri glared at Bonvalot, who stalked away in anger. Rachmed, who was overcome with pity for the young prince, said, "Your Highness, perhaps its time you returned to your tent. The salty air will only inflame your lungs."

Later that evening, Father Dedeken made a dreadful discovery. His beloved horse was dying. He found the poor animal hanging its head, breathing heavily, and suffering from a nasal discharge. He stroked his horse's muzzle, cognizant that the animal was doomed and probably would not last the night.

After a while, the horse grew so weak he fell to the ground. Devastated, Father Dedeken forced back tears as he turned and walked to camp. He collapsed by the fire and buried his head between his knees. But to his surprise, the noble beast would not give up so easily. After exerting a supreme effort, the valiant horse rose to his feet and walked on shaky legs back to his master. Seeing the loyalty of his brave horse broke Dedeken's heart. He caressed his beloved companion's neck, calling him by name as the stricken animal responded with a plaintive whinny. The horse lifted his head to look at his master one last time then collapsed on the ground, dead.

Later that night, two more horses and a camel died after they came upon a source of fresh water and drank too quickly. Watching the animals die such a miserable death caused the caravan men to wail with misery, thinking they would be next.

It was at this point that Imatch reached the end of his rope.

After watching the needless deaths of the horses, he approached Bonvalot and tried to convince him to turn around. He pointed out that the camels were limping after marching over the stony ground, and the salt from the desert had saturated their wounds, causing huge, bleeding ulcers and unimaginable pain. He said that once the animals were dead, they would die shortly thereafter.

"Sahib, I beg you to please turn around," wailed Imatch, his eyes wide with fright. "We cannot last much longer in this freezing cold. Please be reasonable."

"I'm sorry, that's impossible," said Bonvalot. "We're not going back. Any man who tries to leave will be shot. That's a warning."

A shadow fell across the camel driver's face. "Sahib, we are down to nine camels out of forty. The six horses we have left won't last much longer. When our horses die, we'll die as well."

"True, but stopping now will only hasten our deaths," said Bonvalot. "We must keep moving forward."

Imatch gritted his teeth. "When was the last time you looked at the calendar? Soon it will be the Chinese New Year. How can we celebrate it properly in this cursed place? Look at how thin the animals are; they look like skeletons. What will become of us?"

"Have no fear, Imatch, I will provide a feast," said Rachmed. He slung a rifle over his shoulder and headed out to hunt. A short while later he returned with a wide grin on his face. Behind him, he was dragging a hefty Tibetan antelope, which Timur and Tongkia butchered and cooked. But because of the high altitude, it took hours for the meat to soften. Luckily, no one complained since the high altitude had robbed most of them of their appetite. In the end, everyone nibbled on partially-cooked meat, grateful for the chance to relieve their hunger and stop their bodies from wasting away.

Bonvalot noted with alarm that Camille seemed to be growing despondent. Since they had found the body of the English explorer, she had become more sullen, more withdrawn. Unable to quell the worry in his chest, Bonvalot brought some hot stew and a cup of tea to Camille's tent, but the sight of her ashen face made him stop short. He set the food aside and rushed to her side.

"Camille, what happened to you?"

He laid two fingers on her pulse and felt her forehead. She was not feverish, but her heart was beating rapidly and she was flushed. Beneath her sheepskin coat her body was wasting away. He asked her how she was feeling and she admitted that she was suffering from nausea, dizziness, and headaches: mountain sickness. Bonvalot worried that if they did not descend to lower ground, Camille would end up like Niaz. He knew that if something terrible happened to the flame-haired beauty, the caravan men would never forgive him. They would curse their fate and give up all hope.

"Listen to me, Camille. You must eat."

"I'm not hungry."

"That's an order. You've lost too much weight and you're getting weak. You must keep up your strength. Do you want me to call Father Dedeken?"

She smiled weakly. "I'm not ready for my last rites yet. I just want to sleep."

"No, you must stay awake and eat."

"I'm too tired…"

Bonvalot shook her. "Camille, this is serious. I'm ordering you to eat at once."

Reluctantly, Camille picked up the spoon and brought a morsel of food to her mouth. She took a bite and chewed it carefully before swallowing it, and then took a sip of tea.

"Very good," he said. "Keep it up until the bowl is empty."

"I'm not hungry any more."

"Don't stop. I want you to finish the bowl"

"Very well." Camille took another bite of food and then another until the bowl was mostly empty.

"I feel better," she said. "I hope I haven't been too much trouble."

"You'll cause me a great deal of trouble if you get sick. The men are deeply worried about you."

Tears welled up in the corner of her eyes. "Monsieur Bonvalot..."

"Yes?"

"I don't think we're going to find my husband."

"Don't lose hope, my dear. It's not over yet. There's still a chance we may find him. What matters now is that you get well."

"I'm sure there's no chance," she said. "The situation seems hopeless. No one can survive out there for long."

Bonvalot hesitated for a minute. "There's something I must show you." He pulled out the letter he found on the body of Charles Edwards Hughes and gave it to Camille, who had a good enough command of English to read it. When she had finished, she looked at him questioningly.

"What does this mean? Is it possible the Frenchman he was referring to was my husband?"

"Yes, it's possible. It's definitely worth investigating. With any luck, we may meet a passing caravan that may be able to provide us with some more information. I haven't given up searching yet. As soon as we meet up with some people, I will continue making inquiries. I must run now, but I'll send Father Dedeken along later to check on you. Is that alright?"

Camille's voice broke. "Monsieur Bonvalot, about the other day..."

"Don't mention it, it's already been forgotten."

"I was stupid."

"No my dear, you were a gallant, brave soul."

As Bonvalot turned to leave, he looked back over his shoulder and saw the color returning to Camille's face. She was sitting up straighter and sipping her tea. He smiled at her and closed the tent flap behind him.

CHAPTER 34

By the middle of January it was bitterly cold on the Chang Tang. The westerly winds besieged them without cease as the temperature plummeted to forty degrees below zero. After climbing steadily for several days, they reached an altitude of 18,000 feet and were so exhausted that they had no choice but to make camp. Though dizzy and nauseous from the lack of oxygen, they braced themselves against the wind as they pounded the tent pegs into the frozen ground. The men helped Camille into her tent and set about making a fire with the yak dung they had acquired along the way.

When Bonvalot surveyed the area, he saw that the camp lay at the foot of an enormous peak that rose over 26,000 feet in height and was situated on the highest massif he had ever seen. They were at the middle of a labyrinth of white mountains with icy peaks that formed the last remaining barrier that separated them from Lhasa.

To their astonishment, the area was littered with the bones of dead animals for which they dubbed the area 'Camp Bones' as a reminder that death was always present.

By now Prince Henri was perilously thin; his face was blotchy from the violent winds and his hands were raw. Father Dedeken tried to hide his gaunt appearance behind his matted beard, and his servant Bartholomeus had lost so much weight he was almost skeletal.

By now they had resigned themselves to following the compass south until they reached Lake Namtso, which they knew was situated north of Lhasa. Bonvalot believed he could find the famous landmark solely by using the stars and his compass to guide them.

The next day they made a startling discovery. The found the first signs of human life. They descended to a valley that contained a great variety of animals including yaks, goas, koulanes, arkars, and even the chamois, the Himalayan goat-antelope, a sight that cheered the men since they believed it signaled they were approaching the Indian frontier. After stopping to rest for a while, they continued over a pass that cut through a chain of white-capped mountains and led to a sheltered gorge. Here they found horse droppings and the remnants of a stone fireplace that contained ashes. Clinging to a nearby rock they found a fragment of skin from a partridge that still had feathers attached.

After examining the feathers, Timur and Abdullah declared them to be fresh, not more than a few days old at most. A short while later, an argument broke out among the men as to how long it would take until they met the mysterious Tibetans. Some said a few days, others said a few weeks, still others said a month. They placed bets on how long it would take and even Bonvalot and Prince Henri participated.

The next day, after going on a scouting mission, Rachmed and Timur ran back to the camp, breathless.

"We found men!" shouted Rachmed, pointing south. "Over there, look!"

"Yes," said Timur, struggling to catch his breath. "I saw them. They're grazing flocks of yaks and sheep. Huge flocks. There is plenty of meat for everyone."

The caravan continued south in the direction where Timur and Rachmed had spotted the men, but they were overtaken by a sudden snow squall that blinded them. They braced themselves against the wind and snow when all at once the sky cleared. There in front of them they were shocked to see a large herd of wild yaks roaming the mountainsides, feeding so quietly they had mistaken them for domesticated animals. They scanned the hillsides, certain that the Tibetans were watching them from unseen locations. As a precaution, they urged Imatch to remove the bells from his camels to maintain secrecy. In a region as inhospitable as Tibet, they argued the wisest approach was to not attract unnecessary attention. Given the precariousness of their situation, even Bonvalot was forced to agree.

CHAPTER 35

Two weeks later they descended to 14,200 feet but the cold and wind were still intense. Nevertheless, the change in altitude did wonders to lighten the men's moods and alleviate their mountain sickness. As soon as they filled their lungs with pure, crisp air, they become more sure-footed and their appetites returned. While the camels grazed in a grassy field, several of the caravan men hiked to a nearby ridge to see if they could spot any black yak hair tents. Everyone agreed it was time to end their solitary existence on the Chang Tang. But there was nothing in sight.

A little while later, as Bonvalot, Father Dedeken, and Prince Henri sat in a tent sipping tea, one of the men came running up with a startling announcement: a man was approaching.

They jumped up and headed outside. Sure enough, a man was heading their way, the first human they had seen in seventy-two days. By the stranger's exotic manner of dress, they were certain he was a Tibetan. Abdullah smiled gleefully as he whispered into Bonvalot's ear, "Sahib, get ready to open your purse and pay a handsome reward to whoever won the bet." Bonvalot shot him a sideways glance and nodded. No doubt, the winner would be swimming in silver ingots that night.

They called out to the Tibetan and, speaking in Mongolian, invited him over for a cup of tea. To their relief, the Tibetan smiled and provided the appropriate response in Mongolian. Unable to restrain their natural, childlike curiosity, the men crowded around the guest, eager to hear what he would say, but Bonvalot shooed them away before they could crush him. The Tibetan took a seat by the fire and Tong-Kia brought him a cup of sweetened tea, which he drank with pleasure.

Bonvalot studied the Tibetan with fascination. He was extraordinary-looking; proud, dignified, and tied to the earth in a physical and spiritual sense, the Tibetan regarded them with equal curiosity with deep-set eyes that were as black as onyx against his earthen face. He wore a sheepskin tunic with a pleated skirt that contained a large pouch where he kept his snuffbox and a curious-looking prayer wheel that appeared to be carved from the polished horn of a goa. By the way he caressed it, they assumed the prayer wheel was his most prized possession. He was somewhat old, short, with a face that was heavily-lined and bronzed from the sun. His hair was braided into long plaits that were fastened with rings made from animal bones. His cheeks were hollow from hunger and his nose was large and flat above a toothless mouth. There was no sign of hair anywhere on his face, and it was obvious from his sunken cheeks that he was malnourished and possibly sick; with quivering hands, the Tibetan removed a tiny snuff box carved out of horn from his pocket, and shook out the red tobacco powder which he snuffed up his nose.

The Tibetan inquired about their journey. He looked genuinely curious as he spun the prayer wheel with reverence. Replying in Mongolian, the men related that they came from the north, and that most of their horses and camels had died during the journey. They asked the Tibetan if he would sell them butter, horses, and sheep, as they desperately needed all three to survive.

Hearing this, the Tibetan smiled his toothless grin and invited the strangers to visit his tent, which he explained was situated westward behind a large ridge.

Bonvalot demurred. He explained that they were in a hurry to reach Lhasa and didn't have time to visit his camp. At this, the Tibetan grew impatient; he grabbed Bonvalot by the arm and pointed west with his other hand. He shook an admonishing finger in Bonvalot's face and insisted that they head west and not south.

"You...head...west...Lhasa," said the Tibetan in Mongolian, his black eyes gleaming under the harsh sun. "South no good. You never go south."

Bonvalot glanced at Rachmed. They knew the Tibetan was lying. He was using friendship as a means to divert their attention and dissuade them from heading south toward Lhasa. The only question was, how far would the Tibetans go to force them to veer away from their goal?

"We are sorry," said Rachmed in Mongolian. "But we cannot head west since we are heading south to Lhasa."

The Tibetan changed tack. He clasped his hands reverently and inquired if the visitors intended to offer prayers to the Dalai Lama.

"Yes," said Abdullah. "When we reach Lhasa we intend to visit His Holiness the Dalai Lama."

Hearing this, a toothless grin spread across the Tibetan's face. But his urgings became more forceful. He stood up and pulled on Abdullah's cloak, insisting that everyone come to his camp, promising to give them provisions as well as fodder for their animals. With urgent gestures and forced generosity, the Tibetan invited Bonvalot's party, implying that if they did not come, there would be trouble.

A sickening bile rose in Bonvalot's throat. He sensed deception. In all likelihood, if they accepted his offer they would find themselves surrounded, overpowered, and in all probability would not survive the night.

Bonvalot shook his head forcefully. "No, we cannot come with you. I am very sorry."

In an instant, the Tibetan's grin turned into a scowl. His friendly demeanor turned menacing, but before he could issue any threats, they heard the distinct tinkling of bells and stamping of hooves coming from one of the surrounding hills. Looking up, they saw a flock of sheep heading toward them, driven by several men on horseback with lances strapped to their backs and swords hitched to their sides.

Bonvalot's hand hovered near his revolver. Rachmed unslung his rifle and signaled to the rest to be on guard.

One of the horsemen trotted up to them and eyed them suspiciously. He was much younger than the first man, and his manner was more brusque, but his features were finer, with a long ruddy face, wide cheek bones, an ample mouth, and a short nose.

The new man leaned on his lance and regarded them like a curiosity. Around his waist he carried a sword whose sheath was made of wood and iron plates, similar to the camel saddle they had found near the salty lake. The newcomer also carried a gun that looked Oriental in design; it was short and square, firing by means of an ancient fuse.

The young man dismounted and launched into a conversation with the older Tibetan. They eyed the caravan's supplies greedily, which consisted of a large number of chests and burlap bags. They strode up to them casually to get a better look, even going to far as to kneel beside the chests and attempt to open them by force, but before they could take their recklessness further, Rachmed drew his revolver and pointed it at the young man's head.

"Don't even think about it," said Rachmed.

The Tibetans drew back and eyed the gun's six chambers with fascination. Peering beyond the giant Uzbek, they caught sight of Camille, who was peering at them from the entrance of her tent. Fascinated, they took a step toward her, but when the caravan men aimed their carbines at their heads, they drew back, realizing they were vastly outnumbered.

The young man looked at them insolently and said, "You men from Bomba? From Calacata?"

Rachmed shook his head. He motioned to Bonvalot, Prince Henri and Father Dedeken and said, "No, these men are not from Calcutta or Bombay. They are from the West."

Before the Tibetan could reply, the sheep arrived accompanied by two young boys dressed in filthy rags and sheepskin coats. In the distance a feminine figure on horseback also drew nearer. She was smaller than the men and clad entirely in sheepskin down to her heels; she partially hid her face behind long, black braids that were adorned with coral and turquoise beads. She stared at the caravan with mild curiosity; they noted how she handled her horse with expert precision.

Using a lasso of sorts, the boys caught one of the rams by its horns and dragged it in front of Bonvalot, who immediately shook his head. He said the animal was too frail, unsuitable to eat with meat that would be stringy and tough. Hearing this, the Tibetans roared with laughter, amused that people from the West could recognize a good sheep from a bad one. They released the sickly ram and selected several fat ones instead, which they presented to Bonvalot for his approval.

This time Bonvalot nodded and counted out silver ingots which he weighed with Chinese scales. The older Tibetan accepted the silver, which he scratched vigorously, searching for signs of lead. Meanwhile, another Tibetan checked the accuracy of the scale. Bonvalot offered to buy more animals, including horses, if they would return the following day. The Tibetans agreed but before they left, they walked around inspecting the tents, the texture of their Western clothing, and the leather of their English saddles.

Turning abruptly, the Tibetans pointed to their European weapons and asked if they would demonstrate how they fired. Rachmed aimed his Berdan rifle and shot at a distant rock, which amazed the Tibetans. Bonvalot wanted to ask the Tibetans more questions, but before he had the chance, they waved goodbye and rode away on his horse, whistling and swinging their lassos until they were out of sight.

"What an extraordinary encounter," said Father Dedeken. "It seems the Tibetans have been cut off from mankind since the time of the flood."

"I have an uneasy feeling about them," said Rachmed.

"I know what you mean," said Prince Henri.

Abdullah's face was solemn. "One of noble birth, I think we should get out of here quick. If the Chukpas decide to attack, we won't be able to defend ourselves."

"I've already thought of that," said Bonvalot. "I have a plan."

Bonvalot ordered the caravan men to pitch the tents in a triangular fashion in case the Tibetans attacked during the night, in which case they would have a lookout stationed in every direction. At the center he placed Camille's tent and all the remaining horses and camels. Before they retired for the night, the men oiled and loaded their weapons, then placed them under their sleeping sacks for safe-keeping. By now, there was a general feeling of despair among the men. The relentless cold, the fear of attack, combined with Imatch's deteriorating condition, put them in a state of misery.

Since the great blizzard, Imatch had gotten steadily worse.

His feet were so frostbitten, his big toes were in danger of dropping off. He suffered gravely from mountain sickness and his sores were so dreadful, they wondered how he managed to stay in the saddle. No one believed Imatch would live to see his native steppe again.

CHAPTER 36

The next morning as they sat drinking tea by the fire, Rachmed speculated that if they only had a few more strong men, they could creep up on the Tibetan camp, seize their horses, and ride them all the way to Lhasa without stopping.

"But the way things stand now, that plan would never work," said Rachmed, his face drooping. "With Imatch in danger of losing his feet, Abdullah limping, and Parpa so weak he can barely stand, we're condemned to march only in short stages. Time is running short and our chances of reaching Lhasa grow slimmer with each passing day."

"That is foolish talk," said Isa. "How can we attack the Tibetans when we are so weak ourselves? At the rate we're going, it will take weeks to reach Lhasa, let alone make it back to Lob Nor, if we even make it that far."

"I know I'll never see my family in China again," said Bartholomeus. "Sooner or later the soldiers will come for us and when they do, we won't be able to defend ourselves. I think we are all doomed to die among these heathens."

"Indeed, we're in a great deal of trouble," said Abdullah. "We are running short of our most basic supplies, we have no Chinese passport, no letter from Peking, no guide, and no proper maps. They may throw us in jail and toss away the key."

"It seems even Allah has forgotten us," said Timur, dejectedly.

Father Dedeken closed his Bible. "Nonsense. We're not alone. Where is your faith? It says in Psalm 50: 'Call on me in the day of trouble; I will deliver you, and you will honor me.' Now is not the time to lose our faith."

"A lot of good that will do us," said Prince Henri. "Look what happened to Charlemagne. He was the fastest, strongest horse yet he dropped dead from exhaustion, which will happen to all of us before long. I'm down to my last two tins of caviar and once they're gone, you may as well shoot me."

"Forget the luxuries," said Bonvalot. "What we need are horses. If the Tibetans keep refusing to sell us some, we'll have no choice but to steal them."

Everyone nodded in agreement.

Later, as they were loading up the camels, five Tibetan horsemen rode up to camp.

Isa was the first to spot them. He noticed suspicious clouds of dust on the horizon that turned into a party of lance-wielding horsemen with weather-beaten faces, sheepskin coats, leather breeches, and long black hair that was braided and studded with agate, turquoise, and copper rings. By the swift gait of their horses, the caravan men instinctively reached for their carbines.

"Here comes trouble," said Rachmed, his face set with worry.

After studying them through his spyglass, Bonvalot recognized the short one as the elderly man from the previous day. But the one who made the strongest impression was the tallest of the group. With his imposing stature, stern features, aquiline profile, shiny brown skin, and panther-lined robes, he carried himself like a chieftain.

The Tibetans halted and greeted the strangers by sticking out their tongues. Bonvalot and Prince Henri stiffened at the sight of it, but Father Dedeken explained that it was a Tibetan custom, one that meant no disrespect. The Tibetan horsemen dismounted and dropped several offerings at their feet: a small jar of foul-smelling milk, a pat of butter wrapped in animal skin, and a small bag of tsampa (roasted barley-meal), a Tibetan dietary staple.

The unexpected bounty left Bonvalot speechless. For several minutes the men stared at the presents without daring to approach them. For their part, the Tibetans studied the foreigners with fascination, as if they were an exotic circus attraction.

Rachmed reminded the Tibetans that they needed to buy horses. The older Tibetan shrugged and said all the horses had gone West and there were none to be had. The others nodded and stared at them sullenly. Rachmed inquired about the location of

Lake Namtso, which he knew was due north of Lhasa, but the Tibetans acted as if they hadn't heard the question.

Seeing a young Tibetan standing off to the side by himself, Bonvalot attempted to engage him in conversation. Using a combination of gestures and his rudimentary knowledge of Mongolian, Bonvalot gradually began to earn the young man's trust.

He explained that they were heading to Lhasa in order to pray with the Dalai Lama. Hearing this, the Tibetan threw down his cap and fell on his knees in reverence. He clasped his hands in prayer and turned in the direction of Lhasa, mumbling the Buddhist chant, *"Om mane padme hum"* (Hail, jewel in the lotus).

For the first time in months, Bonvalot's heart soared. This was the first clear sign they were heading in the right direction. He glanced at Rachmed, who beamed in return.

Bonvalot told the young Tibetan that inside the chests were presents for the Dalai Lama. Hearing this, a wide grin broke out on the young man's face.

Bonvalot offered the Tibetan some lumps of sugar, dried apricots, and a handful of raisins, which he ate with pure delight. Seizing the opportunity, Bonvalot knelt beside him and pointed southward.

"Is this the way to Lhasa?"

Before responding, the young man turned to see if his companions were watching. When he perceived that no one was paying attention, he nodded in the affirmative. Leaning in closer, Bonvalot whispered, "How many days to reach Lhasa?" at which point the Tibetan stuck his hand out and demanded more sugar. Then, motioning discreetly, the young Tibetan strode behind the tent, picked up a stick and traced a curved line in a southeasterly direction. At the end of the line he placed a smooth stone and called it "Lhasa."

His heart pounding, Bonvalot asked the Tibetan about the location of Lake Namtso. Hearing this, the Tibetan added another stone further up, and when Bonvalot mentioned "Ningling Tanla," the name of a prominent mountain range due south of Lake Namtso, the Tibetan responded by placing a stone just south of Lake Namtso, then he fell on his knees and prayed with great reverence.

When the Tibetan had finished, he stuck out his palm and demanded an apricot, which Bonvalot happily supplied. In gratitude, the Tibetan stuck out his tongue.

Bonvalot grinned and leaned in closer.

"How many days to reach Lake Namtso?" he said.

For the first time, sweat appeared on the young Tibetan's forehead. With fearful eyes he said, "Eight," at which point Bonvalot leaned in closer and repeated his initial question, "How many days to reach Lhasa?"

The Tibetan said, "Twelve," after which his whole body began to tremble with fright.

Bonvalot ran back to the tent and retrieved the picture of Armand Dancourt and, holding it in front of the Tibetan, asked him if he had ever seen the man before. The Tibetan stared at the picture and then shook his head vehemently.

"Tell me the truth," said Bonvalot, staring into the Tibetan's coal black eyes. "Have you seen this man before?"

With great reluctance, the Tibetan nodded. He said that he had seen the man many months before in a caravan that was heading south toward Lhasa. Bonvalot wanted to hug the young man.

By now, the Tibetan chief realized what was going on behind the tent. He stalked over to the young man, grabbed him by the arm, and jerked him away. He berated him with a torrent of bitter, angry words that caused the young man to hang his head in shame.

When he had finished the chieftain turned to Bonvalot and said, "You stop now. Englishman may not go Lhasa."

"Abdullah, tell this stubborn man in Tibetan that we are not English, but French," said Prince Henri. "Make sure he understands the difference."

Abdullah was at a loss for words. He himself was only minutely aware of the difference between Englishmen and Frenchmen, and since there was no word for *Frenchman* in Tibetan, he had to settle for the generic term for European, which also meant *Englishman*.

Hearing this, the Tibetan chief's face darkened. He shook his head and pointed north, ordering Bonvalot's caravan back the way they had come.

"You men go back home! No enter Lhasa!"

With a flash of insight, Bonvalot ordered Prince Henri to take out his camera and encourage the Tibetans to sit for a photograph. The Tibetans looked confused, but they watched with great interest as the golden-haired Westerner set up his photographic apparatus. When he was finished he sat the Tibetans down and ordered them to remain still. After he had taken several photographs, the Tibetans got up and rode off without another word.

Rachmed watched them leave with great apprehension.

"Bonvalot-sahib, I have a feeling they'll be back," said Rachmed. "In which case we must be ready to defend ourselves."

CHAPTER 37

The next day, the signs of malice from the Tibetans became more obvious.

As the caravan headed across a valley dotted with black yak hair tents, most of which contained fluttering prayer flags, none of the villagers came out to greet them. Bonvalot dispatched two men to approach the Tibetans and offer to purchase horses and sheep, but the Tibetans only stared at them with cold, tight-lipped faces. When they explained that Imatch was sick and needed proper care, they refused to render any aid, or even to sell them ointment for his feet.

After several such exchanges, each one ending in disappointment and frustration, the men grew fearful and anxious, especially after they discovered they were being watched. At one point Bonvalot took out his spyglass and spotted a group of three uniformed soldiers who had been observing them with keen interest from a cleft between two hills. After a while, the soldiers started toward them, causing the men to tremble with fright. Soon the soldiers galloped toward them across the plain, their fur caps and coats billowing in the breeze, their swords and matchlocks gleaming under the harsh sun.

The soldiers halted twenty feet away and showed the travelers their outstretched tongues.

Bonvalot responded with a friendly wave while keeping his free hand hovering near his revolver. He studied the Tibetans' swords with fascination, noting their exquisite scabbards, which were lined with silver and encrusted with precious stones, weapons more reminiscent of a medieval army than soldiers of the modern age.

Bonvalot held out a handful of silver and offered to purchase one of their horses. The soldier shook his head and pushed his hand away while the others looked on with disdain. The soldier who appeared to be their leader explained in Mongolian that if his officer found out they had sold a horse to a foreigner without permission, he would be severely punished. He demonstrated this by making a cutting gesture across his throat.

The leader eyed them suspiciously. "Where are you going?"

"We're heading to Lhasa," said Bonvalot.

"Foreigners may not go to Lhasa. Go back from where you came."

Without another word, the soldiers rode off with menacing looks.

That evening they feared an impending attack. They chose the most strategic location possible for their camp, an elevated plain far enough away from the hills to provide sufficient opportunity to defend themselves in case the Tibetans decided to raid them from the hills. After they had pitched their tents, they sat warming themselves by the fire when two Tibetan horsemen suddenly appeared.

When they got within sight, they recognized them from the previous day. Riding behind one of the Tibetans was a short, slight figure in a sheepskin coat and whose face was covered with a heavy shawl. The horsemen halted a dozen feet away and stuck out their tongues in greeting. The elder of the two said something in Mongolian which Father Dedeken translated for the benefit of Bonvalot.

"They say they have an urgent matter to discuss with the chief of the caravan."

"I don't like the looks of those buggers," said Prince Henri, polishing his rifle. "Tell them we refuse to speak to them unless they agree to sell us horses."

"Now, now, your Highness," said Bonvalot. "We don't wish to offend our visitors. Abdullah, tell them they may join me in my tent. Rachmed, come along to translate."

The Tibetans quickly dismounted and handed their reigns to one of the caravan men.

Bonvalot led the three Tibetans to his tent. Then, like a broken dam, a flurry of words burst forth. The Tibetans explained that the young woman who was riding with them had recently escaped from the Amban's soldiers, and was desperately trying to reach Lhasa.

When Bonvalot asked why the Amban had detained her, the Tibetans explained that the Amban was acting under orders from Peking to send the girl into exile in Khotan where she would face trial and certain punishment. When Bonvalot asked what she had done, the Tibetans demurred, explaining that they felt obligated to save the young lady's life, even at the risk of their own as she hailed from an important family. They begged Bonvalot to take her in his caravan and deliver her to her family who lived near the Nechung Monastery on the outskirts of Lhasa.

Bonvalot furrowed his brow. What the Tibetans were asking was highly irregular. If she was a prisoner, he would be breaking their laws by helping her. Still, if the young woman was in fear for her life, he felt almost obligated to help her in any way possible. He glanced at Father Dedeken and Rachmed, but the two looked equally perplexed.

"I admit your request is highly unusual," said Bonvalot. "As travelers, we are mere guests in your country. I wouldn't want to anger your rulers by breaking their laws."

When the Tibetans heard Abdullah's translation, they protested vehemently. The elder of the two explained that the young woman had done no wrong, that she belonged to an important and noble family, and that by ordering her out of Tibet it was like taking a bee out of the beehive. He ended by saying, "If you do me this one favor I promise to repay you by coming back as your horses and yaks in the next life."

"Thank you but that's not necessary," said Bonvalot. "We only came to your country to do a bit of hunting, we didn't plan on getting involved in an international incident. What you are asking us to do may cause us great harm."

"No harm will befall you for helping the girl," said the Tibetan. "The Amban's soldiers will never think of searching for her in a caravan of foreigners. The Oracle has prophesized that no harm will befall anyone who aids the golden bird who has been wrongfully caged. For your great kindness, may the Lord Buddha shower you with his blessings."

Bonvalot scratched his head. What the Tibetan was asking was sheer lunacy. They were asking him to harbor a fugitive when he himself had no passport to travel in Tibet. The implications were frightening.

"Please explain to me why you would entrust such an important task to a group of foreigners?"

The Tibetan spoke again, but this time his voice changed. He began to chant as if he had gone into a hypnotic trance. He closed his eyes and recited a mantra that sounded like a prayer from another world.

"Our Oracle predicted that during the year of the Iron-Tiger the Jade Emperor would capture the golden bird and send her into exile, but a small army with metal sticks would sweep down from the north and rescue her. Once free the golden bird would fly to the Potala Palace to perform the sacred duty of acting as tutor and maidservant to the Dalai Lama. The Oracle said that for this great service, good fortune would follow the foreigners all the days of their lives. But if the golden bird is captured by the mandarins, they will lose their heads."

The Tibetan continued, "When you told us you came from the north I took it as a sign the prophecy would be fulfilled. Otherwise, I never would have risked her life in this manner. For my crime I must run away and hide for the rest of my life. But, as the Buddha teaches, The fragrance of sandalwood and rosebay do not travel far, but the fragrance of virtue rises to the heavens. May the Buddha repay you in this life and the next for your great virtue in saving the life of the golden bird. And may Lord Buddha repay me in my next life as my present incarnation will no doubt be very short. As the Buddha says, It is better to live for one day as a tiger than to live for a thousand years as a sheep. For your great service we are prepared to pay you thirty ingots of silver."

"Keep your money," said Bonvalot. "I cannot accept it."

"You must or the prophecy will not be fulfilled," said the Tibetan.

"Very well," said Bonvalot "I'll grant your request, but not for the money. I'll help you bring the girl to Lhasa, but if for any reason we're stopped, she will have to make her own arrangements.

In my party is a royal prince whose life I've sworn to protect. Is that clear?"

Hearing this, the Tibetans fell to the ground and thanked Bonvalot for his great kindness.

When they arose, Father Dedeken said, "Tell us, sir, what is the girl's name?"

"She is called Pema, or lotus flower," said the Tibetan. "Her true identity may not be known by anyone outside this tent, not even by your closest servants. For this reason, we call her the golden bird."

"I'll bear that in mind," said Bonvalot. "Don't worry, your golden bird will be safe with me. You may go in peace now."

Bonvalot led the visitors back to their horses while Pema stayed behind beside the tent, looking like a forgotten stupa on a windswept hill.

The Tibetans mounted their horses and galloped away. All that remained behind was the forlorn figure of Pema wrapped in her sheepskin coat, silent except for the humming of her prayer wheel. Her eyes followed their every movement.

"Now that we've got her, what do we do with her?" said Bonvalot, regarding the Tibetan girl with curiosity.

"I suppose our Christian duty is to feed her," said Father Dedeken. "And give her a warm place to sleep."

When Rachmed explained the situation to the caravan men, some of them objected to the intruder; others raised their eyebrows and cast suspicious glances in her direction, but otherwise they accepted Pema's presence, albeit guardedly.

Later, Bonvalot sat Pema down by the fire and offered her a bowl of tsampa and tea. When she became more comfortable, he urged her remove her shawl.

Reluctantly, the girl pushed away the shawl and when they caught a glimpse of her face in the light of the campfire, the men gasped: Pema was the most exquisite creature they had ever seen. She was beautiful in a mystical sort of way, with skin like polished white jade, rose petal lips, and black, almond-shaped eyes. Her hair was braided into dozens of tiny plaits that were bounded by a single strand of coral beads suspended from a golden disk on her forehead; around her neck she wore multiple strands of coral and turquoise necklaces, and in her hands she held a prayer wheel that she clutched like a golden scepter. Pema had an almost regal presence about her, like a royal consort. Or a goddess.

When Pema realized the men were staring at her she raised an imperious eyebrow and scolded them in rapid Tibetan.

"Abdullah, what is she saying?" said Bonvalot.

"She says, 'Why is everybody staring at me?'"

"Tell her it's because we've never seen so much jewelry on a human head before," said Bonvalot.

Pointing to Father Dedeken's beard, she said something and then burst into laughter.

"Abdullah, what did she say now?" said Bonvalot.

"She said she has never seen a man who was half-human, half-monkey before. She once heard of a monkey-god, but she never saw one quite so hairy or dressed quite so shabbily."

"Very clever," said Father Dedeken. "Apparently, the Tibetan girl has never seen a European man before, which corroborates the historical nature of our expedition. By the time we reach Lhasa I'm sure she'll have numerous amusing stories to delight the ears of the Dalai Lama. I can only imagine what she thinks of my horn-rimmed spectacles."

"Perhaps she thinks you have an extra set of eyes," said Bonvalot. "Or a pair of horns." At which everyone laughed.

The sound of the commotion brought Camille out of her tent.

"What in heaven's name is going on?" she said, and when she spied Pema she added, "Who is this?"

"We have a new traveler in our party," said Bonvalot. "She's traveling to Lhasa. For now, she'll be sleeping in your tent."

"My tent?" said Camille. "Are you mad? Are you sure you can trust her?"

"Apparently even the Dalai Lama trusts her. She comes from a noble family and I agreed to take her as far as the outskirts of Lhasa, which is only a twelve-day march away."

"What is her name?"

"They call her Pema, which means lotus flower in Tibetan. She doesn't speak a word of French and you don't speak a word of Tibetan so the two of you should get along splendidly."

"She is extraordinary," said Prince Henri, studying the young woman's face with fascination. "She's positively ravishing, like an exquisite painting. What do you propose we do with her?"

"Nothing," said Bonvalot, swirling around to face the prince. "And the same goes for you. Those men entrusted me to transport her to Lhasa so as far as I'm concerned, she's a paying client. And I don't want any trouble. Understood?"

"On my word of honor I shall behave like a perfect gentleman," said Henri. "You have nothing to fear from me."

"I desperately want to believe that," said Bonvalot.

"I have no intention of compromising this beauty," said Henri. "Instead, I will worship her from afar, pay her the greatest respects with my undying affection. At the very least she should be a nice distraction from the bitter cold of the Chang Tang."

"You can forget about it old boy," said Bonvalot. "She's off limits to you. And to make sure of it, I'm putting you on guard duty as of right now."

"And what pray tell should I do if the soldiers come back?" said Henri. "Do you expect me to handle them all by myself?"

"Yes, and you'll do a fine job of it," said Bonvalot. "As long as your Martini-Enfield is loaded, you'll be in fine company. And don't forget to put more yak dung on the fire. It's going to be a very cold night."

Without taking his eyes off the beautiful Tibetan girl, Henri bundled up his sheepskin coat, grabbed his rifle, and headed out into the darkness.

CHAPTER 38

The next day the travelers rose early and, after a breakfast of tsampa and tea, continued their southward march across the bitterly cold Chang Tang. For her protection, they placed Pema on a camel and told her to conceal herself in a basket strapped to the camel's side in case of trouble. Stoically, the girl clutched the saddle horn and sat with the regal posture of a queen, her shawl draped across her face to obscure her identity. After progressing for several miles, they found themselves surrounded by thirty Tibetan soldiers, each one armed with a sword and a matchlock.

From out of a cloud of dust the soldiers appeared looking like an apparition of a medieval army with their chain mail armor, rounded metal helmets with ornamental peacock feathers, and bands of ammunition strung across their chests. On their feet they wore thick woolen stockings bound with leather, while their sure-footed Tibetan ponies were outfitted with silver-encrusted saddles over colorful Indian-style cloth.

Bonvalot whispered to Rachmed. "Make sure the Tibetan girl stays hidden. And tell the men to keep quiet. I want Abdullah to translate, but he must reveal nothing about our plans. We've got to stay one step ahead of our adversaries."

The Tibetan officers ordered the caravan to stop. Whistling, Imatch brought the camels to a halt. They groaned and stamped their hooves as they came to stop while one of the Tibetan officers rode forward and addressed the caravan in Mongolian.

"Where are you from?" said the gruff-faced Tibetan.

The caravan men watched silently from the backs of their camels, donkeys, and mules, their carbines resting on their shoulders. Pressing his heels against his horse's side, Bonvalot rode his horse forward until he was directly facing the officer.

Meanwhile, Abdullah joined him, bearing in mind that he should remain cagey at all times, which was one of his specialties.

"Greetings," said Bonvalot. "We have come from the north."

The Tibetan narrowed his steely eyes. "Are you *Palang*?"

"What?"

"*Palang*. Are you Palang?"

Abdullah whispered into Bonvalot's ear. "*Palang* means English or Russian. Never admit you are one of these. They are the sworn enemies of Tibet."

Bonvalot shook his head. "No, we are not *Palang*. We are French."

The Tibetan glowered at them. He glanced sideways at his fellow soldiers, who shrugged their shoulders in return and shook their heads. The Tibetan officer turned back to Bonvalot and spoke once more in a voice that betrayed mounting impatience.

"Then explain to me what the devil are you doing here," said the Tibetan. "Who gave you permission to travel here?"

Bonvalot held up his Winchester. "We came here to hunt game. We followed the herds south, but as you can see by our appearance, we're not very good hunters. We have so little food for our camels and horses that they are dying of hunger, and some of our men have died as well. We need more horses and we're prepared to pay you good money to supply us with some."

Bonvalot's words fell on deaf ears. The Tibetan soldiers just stared back in sullen silence.

It's now or never, thought Bonvalot. He inched forward and grabbed the bridle of the nearest Tibetan horse. He pulled the animal forward as he tried to shove a handful of silver into the soldier's hands. When the luckless soldier reached for the silver, his officer drew his sword and threatened to chop the soldier's head off. Bonvalot drew back in horror. The caravan cringed in fear, their faces contorting at the sight of this cruelty. No one dared utter a word.

"You lawbreakers came here without permission," yelled the Tibetan officer. "I order you to turn around at once. You may not go one step further."

Rachmed unslung his rifle and pushed his way forward. He pointed it menacingly at the soldiers.

"Keep your distance," said Rachmed. "We are armed and ready to defend ourselves. If you take one step further, we'll consider you as robbers and treat you accordingly."

The Tibetans eyed Rachmed, but did not respond. Their horses twitched their ears and stamped their hooves as the wind rustled their manes. Despite Rachmed's threats, the Tibetan soldiers remained impassive.

Rachmed whispered to Bonvalot. "Don't be intimidated by these toy soldiers. They're not as tough as they look. We can wait until nightfall and raid their villages and steal all the horses we need. That will teach these Tibetans how to treat foreigners."

"We're in no shape to raid their village," said Bonvalot, stifling a cough. "We're too weak from mountain sickness, and some of the men are so sick they can barely stay in the saddle. It's too risky and bound to fail."

Shivering in his sheepskin coat Bonvalot sized up their situation. At twenty degrees below zero, the Chang Tang was bitterly cold. The wind cut through the protective layers of their clothing and seeped into the marrow of their bones. Most of the caravan men had the standard symptoms of mountain sickness: headaches, dizziness, nausea, lack of appetite, and some were even coughing up blood. Imatch was weakening with each passing day. Without proper care he would not have the strength to keep traveling.

"Move aside," said Bonvalot, raising his voice. "Let us pass. We've done nothing wrong."

The Tibetan refused to back down. "If you are *Palang*, you must turn around and leave at once. If you are not, you may proceed, but you must show us your Chinese passport first."

"I already told you, we're not *Palang*," said Bonvalot. "We received permission from the Governor of the Ili Province to travel to Tibet. You've no cause to detain us."

"If I allow you to pass and you *are* indeed *Palang*, then I will be severely punished." The Tibetan demonstrated this by making a cutting gesture at his throat.

"At the risk of repeating myself," said Bonvalot, his face growing red from anger. "I told you we are not *Palang*. We came here from the west. We are Firinghis from Feringhistan. Now let us pass."

Bonvalot clucked his tongue to start up his horse, but the Tibetan raised his lance and made a threatening gesture.

"Don't move!" screamed the Tibetan. "I order you to remain here. If you attempt to go any further we will use force. That is a direct order."

"That's impossible," said Bonvalot. "There's nothing for us to eat here. Would you have us eat dirt and stones and watch us die of hunger? I'm in charge of this caravan and I intend to keep moving forward until we find good hunting ground. If you try to stop us, we are prepared to defend ourselves. Consider that a warning."

As the Tibetan soldiers glared, Bonvalot gave the signal to Imatch, who whistled and cracked his whip, starting up the camels again. Miraculously, as the animals marched forward, the Tibetan soldiers moved aside, allowing them to pass. One by one the growling camels marched past the gauntlet of soldiers until there was a comfortable distance between them. Bonvalot let out a deep breath; that had been a close call. When he turned around, he saw the raw fear on Camille's face as she clutched the revolver he had given her for safety. He winked at her and she smiled wanly in return. From her basket, Pema cautiously crawled out and took her place on her camel. For now they had secured a narrow victory, but it was only a question of time before the soldiers returned.

CHAPTER 39

That night a fight broke out among the caravan men.

Several of the men accused Rachmed of behaving in a rash and irresponsible manner with the Tibetan soldiers, putting all their lives in danger. The men argued that if they had known how dangerous the journey would be, they would never have consented to come along in the first place. Rachmed held his ground, arguing that a show of fierceness was the surest way to quell violence. Their best method of self-defense was to show their superior weapons and demonstrate that they were not afraid to use them.

"But we were outnumbered," argued Timur, bristling at Rachmed's suggestion. "An army is always strongest in their own territory. For all we know they could be watching us right now, planning an attack."

"If I had the slightest notion our lives were in danger, I would have shot the first man that threatened us, no questions asked," said Rachmed. "When a man is compelled to fight, he should cry out 'Allahu Akbar' and die with a sword in his hand."

"Fine talk from a man who imitates the unbelievers," said Timur. "You can't even read Arabic, and your Persian is worse than a Chinaman's."

Rachmed's eyes blazed and his jaw dropped. "As Allah is my witness you speak like a goat."

Timur clenched his jaw. "And as Allah is *my* witness you speak like a donkey."

Rachmed lunged for his sword, but since it was dark, pulled out his whip instead, which he cracked and slashed in Timur's direction.

"Allah knows I am a good Muslim," said Rachmed. "May He preserve me from accidents and disease, and allow me to live for one hundred and twenty years. On the other hand, I've seen you sneaking a taste of forbidden food."

Timur's face turned red. He picked up a camel stick and struck Rachmed on the head. Incensed, Rachmed seized Timur's camel saddle and tossed it into a pile of sand. This made Timur even more outraged. He cursed and swore as sweat poured down his face. Then, to Bonvalot's horror, he drew his knife and began to toy with it menacingly.

"I should cut your throat for your evil words," said Timur, grinning like a madman. "After all, it was you who brought us here to die like sheep. Perhaps it's time I taught you a lesson."

Alarmed, Bonvalot drew his revolver and shot a bullet into the night sky. The burst of gunfire startled the two combatants for a second before they lunged at each other's throats. In an instant, Rachmed and Timur were on the ground wrestling, beating, and clawing at each other with the ferocity of wildcats. When they got back to their feet they cursed and swore, launching into a colorful invective that called into question the reputations of each other's female relatives.

Bonvalot forced his way between the two rivals and used all his might to separate them.

"By the will of Allah the merciful, the compassionate, the ruler of the day of retribution," said Bonvalot. "I command you to make peace between two Muslim brothers." Bonvalot grabbed Rachmed and Timur's wrists like recalcitrant schoolboys and forced them to shake hands. When they refused he said, "If the two of you don't apologize, I will dock you a week's pay."

"Asalaam Alaikum," said Rachmed.

"Alaikum asalaam," responded Timur.

Shaking his head, Bonvalot returned to his seat by the fire. He knew that if he didn't get the men into their sleeping sacks, there would be a long night of endless skirmishes and retaliations. Picking up his flask, he took a long swig of whisky. In the distance, he saw Camille peeking at him from her tent.

He lowered his flask. "Come here. Sit down beside me."

She wrapped her sheepskin coat tighter and sat down next to him. The fire cast a warm glow over her auburn hair, causing it to sparkle like gold; her blue eyes gazed at him with great intensity as her mouth curved with pleasure.

"You handled that like an expert, Monsieur Bonvalot," she said. "Where did you learn to break up such fights?"

"I've been doing this for years," he said. "I only intervene when one hero fails to knock out the other, in which case I assist them by knocking them both out. By tomorrow, they will have forgotten the whole thing and someone else will start a whole new fight over some such nonsense."

She laughed and said, "I've seen how the men look up to you."

"Out here respect is earned. It doesn't come easy or cheap."

"Doesn't anything frighten you? There was that matter of the Tibetan soldiers today. That could have ended in disaster."

Bonvalot nodded gravely. "Liquor goes a long way in getting you through the rough patches, and when none is available, you rely on sheer nerve."

"Perhaps I should indulge more," she said. "It may help me overcome all my doubts and nagging fears about traveling through the wilds of Tibet in the company of a band of brutes."

Bonvalot laughed. "Is that what you think I am, a brute? Then Madame Dancourt, you have much to learn about me. Deep down I love the finer things in life: a symphony orchestra, walks along the Seine, a play by Molière, galloping across the steppe, gazing into a pair of lovely eyes in the moonlight. Although I may seem outwardly different than other men because I chose this life of adventure, inside I'm like everyone else. Truth be told, I don't regret it one bit. Out here in the wilderness, I'm living my dream. Just looking up at the heavens you feel closer to the stars, as if you can almost reach up and touch them."

"Indeed," said Camille, gazing up at the night sky. "It is extraordinary. I feel the unmistakable power of the mountains. I've never experienced anything like it before."

"Now you're beginning to understand," he said. "Nature and all her beauty and mystery have captivated my spirit."

"Tell me something, Monsieur Bonvalot. If those Tibetan soldiers had used force to stop you, would you have shot them?"

Bonvalot smiled. "In poker that's called a bluff. It's a trick of deception meant to make your weak hand appear stronger. You'll see as we go along that we'll be using lots of tricks like that to deceive these scoundrels. The art of bluffing is to make sure your opponent doesn't perceive you as a wild man, in which case he'll call your bluff, dooming you to failure."

"And what happens if we fail?" she said.

Bonvalot took a puff of his cigarette and blew out a long stream of smoke. "I have never considered that possibility."

The next day brought more unrelenting cold. Tong-Kia grumbled as he added dung to the fire but it never grew large enough to cook. After waiting for what seemed like an eternity for the water to boil, he passed around hot mugs of tea. They ate in silence, keeping their eyes on the horizon in case the soldiers should reappear.

As Bonvalot sat drinking tea by the fire, Abdullah approached him, his face showing grave concern.

"One of noble birth, I think we're in big trouble," said Abdullah. "The Tibetan girl is no ordinary noblewoman."

"What are you talking about?" said Bonvalot.

"I heard her speaking to one of the men. She's a Buddhist princess, the daughter of the Panchen Lama. The mandarins captured her and sent her into exile on orders of Peking. She holds much power with the people. If they catch us hiding her, we'll be arrested on the spot."

"What's this?" said Father Dedeken. "Did you say the Tibetan girl is the daughter of the Panchen Lama? That would make her a powerful figure indeed, one that Peking would wish to control or silence. It does not bode well for a party of foreigners to become entangled in local politics."

Bonvalot nodded. "This throws everything in a different light. No wonder those Tibetans insisting on stowing her aboard our caravan. It was very clever indeed."

"What do you intend to do about it?" said Rachmed.

"I don't have much choice," said Bonvalot. "I gave them my word I would protect her. I can't abandon her now."

"Did I hear someone say *princess*?" said Henri, sauntering over from his tent. "Of royal blood?"

"Royal in the sense that the Panchen Lama is second only to the Dalai Lama in importance," said Father Dedeken. "The Tibetans believe he is the reincarnation of Amitabha—"

"Don't tell me—the celestial Buddha," interrupted Bonvalot. "I've heard of this before. While I was in Paris I met a professor who told me about a certain prophecy concerning the reincarnation of the goddess Kali, the consort of the god Siva. Perhaps this Tibetan princess is connected to this prophecy."

Henri laughed derisively. "That's a load of rubbish. You can't believe that Buddhist nonsense."

"I don't know what to believe anymore."

They watched Pema and Camille sipping tea from the corner of their eyes. Pema was teaching Camille some basic words in Tibetan, while Camille taught her a little French. Camille was admiring Pema's coral and turquoise beads and the two seemed delighted by each other's company.

"This certainly adds a twist to our situation," said Bonvalot. "Almost as if our voyage to Tibet has been preordained by the gods. A Buddhist princess indeed."

Before they finished loading the camels, they spotted a delegation of Tibetan soldiers galloping across the plain. It was the same band of stern-faced soldiers from the previous day. Bonvalot's heart raced. He told Rachmed to hide Pema and make sure she kept out of sight, then he grabbed his carbine and sat down to await his visitors.

When the soldiers approached, the officer dismounted and marched toward them. Trembling, and with a voice that broke every now and then, the officer explained the delicate position he was in, how his superiors would punish him severely if they found out he had allowed a foreign caravan to travel freely in Chinese territory. He asked to speak directly to their leader but Bonvalot refused unless the Tibetan officer agreed to sell them some horses.

The Tibetan's face broke out in a cold sweat. He explained that he was forbidden from selling them horses, but he would sell them as many sheep as they wanted. He scanned the ragtag group of foreigners huddled beside the dwindling fire and remembered an old Chinese trick he had learned when he was a junior officer. It had something to do with breaking down the enemy by causing him to lose face. A cunning smile passed his lips.

Scrutinizing their faces, the officer's eye fell on Imatch. Scratching his aquiline nose, he strode up to the elderly Kirghiz camel driver and demanded to see his papers. As he spoke, the

Tibetan pulled out his own papers with their official Chinese seals and stamps testifying that his policing authority came from Peking, and displayed them with bureaucratic pride.

"You, sir," said the Tibetan officer. "You are a Chinese man. Every respectable Chinese man travels with his papers and would never dare leave town without first receiving permission from his mandarins. How dare you defy our laws. Who knows what kind of ancestors you had to behave in such an impudent fashion."

Imatch's eyes blazed with fury. He snatched his papers from his saddlebag, hobbled over to the Tibetan officer in a rage and shoved them under his nose.

"Here you are," said old Imatch. "Take a look at these. As you can see, my papers are in perfect order. And just look at these Chinese seals. Have you ever seen such fine documents as these? Yours, on the other hand, appear to be of inferior quality while mine show only the finest character. How dare you speak to me in such an insolent fashion. Have you ever seen seals as large as these?"

The Tibetan officer was dumbstruck. As he stared at the Chinese seals on Imatch's documents, his face turned a deep shade of purple. He grunted in displeasure and, without another word, stalked off in a huff to rejoin his soldiers.

Stifling a laugh, Bonvalot patted Imatch on the back.

"Well done my friend," said Bonvalot. "You handled that perfectly. Alright men, trouble's over for now. We'd better get back on the road before these scoundrels change their mind and put us all in shackles. I want to make Lake Namtso before the end of the week. Hurry up, there's no time to lose."

CHAPTER 40

During the next few days they marched in silence. The only sounds they heard were the howling wind, the soft shuffle of camel footpads on sand, and the tinkle of the camel bells. They made their way across the windswept steppe where the only vegetation was a carpet of grass spread along the base of some low hills, occasional patches of shrubs, and coarse sedge. Despite the barrenness of their surroundings, wildlife abounded. They spotted dozens of orongos, wild Tibetan antelopes with buff-colored coats, grey muzzles, and tall, ringed horns, and occasional sightings of cranes and pheasants as well as droppings of kiangs, wild Tibetan asses, and yaks. To the south and west they gazed at the snow-capped mountains of the Himalayas stretched across the horizon like a majestic rampart of purple and blue bathed in a luminescent haze of clouds. Somewhere beyond those mountains lay the forbidden city of Lhasa. It was the fuel that drove them forward.

After ascending a range of rocky hills, more signs of life appeared. They found a number of stupas, which the Tibetan called *chortens*, which were burial mounds topped by golden spires, some of which had colorful prayer flags fluttering in the wind. They also saw great herds of wild yaks grazing along grassy slopes and orongos peering at them with curious eyes. During this time, Princess Pema sat perched on her camel watching the landscape unfold like a low-flying bird. She resembled an Indian maharani with her golden headdress, flowing coral beads, and billowing silk robes. She rarely spoke and if she did, it was to chant her mystical mantras as she spun her prayer wheel. The men began to see their mission as spiritual or mystical in nature. It infused them with greater strength.

By now it was obvious that Prince Henri was infatuated with the exotic princess. He rode his horse alongside her, teaching her words in French, reciting poetry, searching for ways to make her laugh. Pema tried to remain stoic, but when Henri would do something comical, such as sing *The Barber of Seville* in a deep operatic baritone, she would burst into a girlish laughter, her headdress and coral beads tinkling as her head swayed back and forth. Whenever Henri would shoot some game, he would first present it to Pema, waiting for her approval before tossing it Timur for skinning. It was obvious to everyone that Henri had fallen in love with the exotic Tibetan beauty. Or perhaps it was a touch of mountain sickness that caused him to fall into the princess's spell,

Bonvalot did not approve of the young prince's antics.

"He's acting like a fool," said Bonvalot, trotting alongside Father Dedeken. "All I need now is for that nincompoop to overindulge in spirits and cause a scandal."

"Fear not," said Father Dedeken, ruffling his horse's mane. "I'll keep an eye on the boy. He's just young and impulsive, like a wild yak in springtime. I have no doubt you've been a good influence on him. When you took away his baccarat set he accepted it with the equanimity of a Catholic martyr. He has cut down on smoking and hardly swears anymore. He's like a new man."

Bonvalot gave Dedeken a doubtful look. "Are we talking about the same Henri? The boy is just as insufferable as when he demanded fresh linen at his private table. With his constant dalliances, no wonder he's the black sheep of his family."

"You may have a point," said Dedeken. "But if you look close enough, you'll see Henri has undergone significant changes no matter how slight. For instance, did you notice the way he insisted on serving Pema her supper on his very own china? Or how he pitched her tent close to the fire to keep her warm? Or brushed the sand off her coat? A few weeks ago that would have been unthinkable. And look at the way the princess rewards him with those coy looks of hers. It's like a comical Chinese opera."

"Yes, but I intend to keep Cupid's arrow firmly in his quiver," said Bonvalot. "But like you, I've also noticed the good effect this Tibetan princess has had on Henri. For the first time in his life, he has the chance of becoming less shallow. If this keeps up, I may decide to give the little blockhead his baccarat set back."

"Will wonders never cease," said Father Dedeken.

As the sun drifted lower on the horizon, they brought the camels to a halt and made camp. The caravan men went to work unloading the animals while Tong-Kia unloaded a burlap bag of yak dung which he had collected during the journey. He used the dung to start a fire and soon had a batch of palao cooking over the fire. Later, as the weary travelers sat eating, Henri cozied up to Pema and taught her more French while she taught the young prince her own enigmatic language.

Henri started by teaching her his name.

"Henri," he said, pointing to himself.

"Hengli" she repeated, but Henri shook his head.

"Hen-ri," he said. "Repeat after me, Hen-ri."

"Hengli," she said. Henri shook his head and tried again. This went on for several minutes, each time with little success until Henri decided to switch tack.

"Now try this," he said, then he pointed at her. "I love you," he said. "Now repeat that."

Pema attempted to repeat the phrase, but her mispronunciation caused Henri to burst out laughing.

"Delightful," he said, taking her hands in his own. "My God you are beautiful. You have utterly captivated me. Pema, you are the princess of my heart, princess of my soul, my goddess of love."

Camille, who had been watching these outward displays of affection clearly did not approve.

"Your Highness I think you are guilty of toying with this young girl's affections," she said. "Pema is an important Buddhist figure, the daughter of the Panchen Lama. I believe she deserves more respect and deference than that. What you're doing breaks all the rules of decorum."

Henri broke into laughter.

"I've had enough of that stuffy nonsense. That's why I prefer this life of exploration where I can toss aside decorum and live by my own rules."

"And what rules are those?"

"I make my own set of rules about what I do, where I go, and who I associate with and to hell with lawyers, wills, and newspaper reporters."

"I should warn you," said Camille. "The Buddhists have this thing called karma. If you do something that displeases their gods you may have to come back as a dog or a snake."

"Or a rat," added Bonvalot, who was sitting nearby. "A cigar-smoking, spirit-imbibing, French-speaking rat to be sure."

"Very funny," said Henri. "Make your silly jokes if you want but someday when I'm sitting on the throne of France I'll have the last laugh."

"So you think you can win the Royal Steeplechase, eh?" said Bonvalot. "How can you sit on the throne of France if you're being chased by a yak across the Chang Tang?"

Everyone burst out laughing.

Pema, who had been listening to this discussion, reached out and stroked Henri's blond hair, then she said something in Tibetan that made Abdullah laugh.

"Abdullah, what did she say?" said Henri.

"She says you have golden hair like goddess Jetsun Dolma, the goddess of success and prosperity. She thinks you are the reincarnation of her consort since you share her bizarre nature and gift for idle chatter. She called you her golden prince."

"You see?" said Henri, beaming. "Out here all the petty, unreasonable rules of society don't apply. I'm free to live my life on my own terms. And if I want to fall in love with a beguiling Tibetan Buddhist princess, so be it."

Pema stood up and began walking away, her beads swinging to and fro, her headdress tinkling like the camel bells. Henri jumped up and chased after her like a lovesick schoolboy. As she headed out for a walk, Henri never left her side.

"I think there's hope for the boy yet," said Bonvalot.

Camille nodded. "The princess seems as taken with him as he is with her."

"Abdullah," said Bonvalot. "You're supposed to be keeping an eye on Pema. Tell her she's forbidden from leaving camp by herself. Make sure she doesn't go too far."

"One of noble birth," said Abdullah. "I don't believe the princess is used to taking orders. Anyway, the prince is with her."

"Then keep an eye on the both of them. His Highness is not exactly known for using common sense."

Later, Henri took Pema horseback riding. For hours on end they could be seen galloping across the steppe like gallivanting schoolchildren, laughing and giggling, while Bonvalot used his spyglass to track their movements. When they got too far he sent Abdullah out on a camel to bring them back. While Bonvalot was glad Henri had found someone to pass the time with, he worried that the prince's antics could draw unwanted attention. But for now he had more pressing concerns. Imatch the camel driver was slowly dying.

The next day the led the camels through a valley filled with black yak hair tents where they hoped to find a doctor for Imatch. His situation was grave. Every day his limping got worse and his cries of pain grew more heart-wrenching. More than once the old camel driver had begged them to leave him behind, believing he was doomed to die in the land of eternal snow, but Bonvalot refused to abandon Imatch.

When they passed the tents, they called out to the Tibetans but the natives only stood and stared at the travelers with eyes full of suspicion, refusing to render them any assistance. They waited for the caravan to pass while their guard dogs barked and growled menacingly. During these forays into Tibetan encampments, Bonvalot kept Pema hidden in a basket lest one of the natives would notice her and accuse the travelers of kidnapping the daughter of the Panchen Lama.

They had no luck in finding help for Imatch.

By now, Imatch's condition was so dire he could only get around by crawling on his knees. His feet were so frostbitten, they had turned black and were shriveled to the point of being useless. He was in constant pain and the others watched helplessly as he cried out in agony. They feared his feet would drop off any day now, leaving poor Imatch a helpless cripple.

Parpa was also in poor shape. Twice during the journey he had stumbled and fallen on the frozen ground, forcing Bonvalot to send a man back with a camel to fetch him where he lay in misery. The privations of the journey had completely changed Parpa. His normal swaggering nature was gone, replaced by a timid, fearful side of him that reduced him to a pittance of his former self. Bonvalot worried that if they lost Imatch, Parpa would follow soon thereafter. Even Timur and Isa, two hardy hunters, were getting weaker. And Abdullah, the sharp-eyed Taranchi wasn't much better. He could only walk alongside the animals by gripping the camels' ropes for support, and he had long since given up carrying his own rifle for self-defense.

Their only hope was to acquire new horses by any means possible, even if it meant stealing them. Up to now Bonvalot's policy vis à vis the Tibetans had been one of gentle diplomacy, but after so many flagrant refusals to sell them horses, or assist their ill companions had pushed him over the edge. To save the lives of his men, Bonvalot decided to switch to more aggressive tactics.

CHAPTER 41

Desperate to obtain horses, Bonvalot and Rachmed saddled up the remaining horses and rode off across the steppe, determined they would not return until they had achieved their goal. Finally, after riding until they were exhausted and starving, they found what they were looking for. After crossing a valley that was sheltered by low hills and ridges, they spied three Tibetan nomads sitting around a yak dung fire cooking tsampa and chatting. Nearby, three horses grazed contentedly. Bonvalot and Rachmed exchanged a quick look. This was the chance they'd been waiting for.

Seizing the opportunity, Bonvalot dismounted and approached the nomads. After exchanging a few pleasantries, Bonvalot offered a handful of silver ingots for one of their horses. He explained with gestures that one of his men had fallen sick and needed a horse to survive. No matter how many times he begged and pleaded with the Tibetans, they only shrugged their shoulders and pretended not to understand. They turned away from Bonvalot and continued with their chatting, eating their tsampa as if his presence was a mere annoyance.

Growing hopeless, Bonvalot pushed the silver under the noses of the Tibetans but they refused to look at it. One of them shooed him away so they could continue with their meal in peace.

Bonvalot's jaw clenched. He felt a sudden urge to pummel the Tibetans to the ground. He took a few steps backwards, removed his revolver, and pointed it at their heads.

The Tibetans gasped and dropped their bowls of tsampa. Meanwhile, Rachmed had crept up to one of their ponies and seized it for himself. While Bonvalot kept the Tibetans at bay with his revolver, Rachmed mounted the pony and galloped back across the rock-strewn steppe toward the caravan. Wasting no time, Bonvalot fled to his horse, grabbed the reigns of Rachmed's horse, and raced after him.

Later, when they got to camp, they celebrated their victory. When they offered the horse to Parpa, tears welled up in his eyes. Only minutes before, Parpa had crumpled to the ground in exhaustion, begging the men to leave him there to die.

Renewed by this success, the caravan started up again. They continued climbing until they reached another pass beyond which they caught a glimpse of a majestic white peak that gleamed like a pyramid of snow and ice. Bonvalot's pulse quickened when he realized this was the mysterious Ningling Tanla beyond which lay the pristine blue waters of Lake Namtso.

Pulling out his maps, Bonvalot fought to keep his hands steady in the bitter cold as he studied them. According to the charts, Lake Namtso was situated in the middle of four ice-covered peaks, beyond which lay the city of Lhasa. Scarcely believing his luck, he held up his spyglass and counted the peaks—one, two, three, four. It was true! Bonvalot could scarcely believe his luck. Success, he was sure, was close at hand.

But there was no time to celebrate. Imatch had taken a turn for the worse. Sometime during the night his condition had deteriorated to the point where he was constantly moaning in pain and his sores smelled awful. Rachmed feared he would not last the night.

To their consternation, the wind picked up and was now pelting them with snow, ice, and sand, causing the men to cry out in pain. The blizzard turned the world white with swirling snow, blinding them. Bonvalot ordered them to set up camp. Rachmed whistled and the camels groaned and sank to their knees. By now, everyone was weak from hunger and cold, they barely had the energy to set up the tents. Bonvalot feared the worst, but he pressed them to bivouac nonetheless.

That night hardly anyone slept. The wind howled and battered their tents, drowning out their groans. They had only managed to collect a little yak dung during the day, so the fire dwindled to a few orange embers, taking away their only source of warmth.

The next morning, Imatch was so weak, he was ready to give up. From his dirty sheepskin bed, he sent for Parpa and Rachmed and dictated his last will and testament, forcing them to promise to repay various debts he owed from his unpaid salary, with the remainder to be sent to his family in Yarkand. Bonvalot knelt by Imatch's side and tried to cheer him up by telling him they would soon reach a village where they would surely get help, but Imatch shook his head. He said it was too late for him. When he pulled aside the sheepskin blanket, Bonvalot gasped and had to cover his nose and mouth. Imatch's legs had decayed to the point where the flesh was dropping off in patches, emitting a foul odor that smelled of death.

"Sahib, it's all over for me," groaned Imatch between labored breaths. "Forgive me if I am no longer able to serve you. Death has come for me. Look how it has already taken my legs."

"Don't despair," said Rachmed. "You've served us well. Allah will have mercy on you."

Imatch looked at the faces surrounding his death bed. "Timur, Isa, Abdullah, Parpa, Mahmud, Rachmed, thank you for everything. You've been so good to me. Now I must go. Allah has decided that my life will end here. Goodbye my brothers. I die with my eyelids open."

Imatch stretched himself out and drew his last breath.

The men blinked back tears as they mourned Imatch.

"Poor Imatch," said Bonvalot. "He was a true man of the steppe. With his last ounce of strength he was still putting yak dung on the fire and drinking his favorite tea. He followed us all the way from Kuldja into this unknown land with a pure, unsullied heart. Now he will rest here for all eternity."

"Goodbye you bad-tempered old camel driver," said Rachmed, tears welling in his eyes. "We'll miss your colorful outbursts."

"Imatch was the best camel driver in the world," wailed Timur. "Nobody knew camels better than him."

"As Allah is my witness that is the truth," said Abdullah. "Imatch's name was known far and wide."

"Poor Imatch," wailed Isa. "He will never see his native steppe again. It was the will of Allah that he die here in Tibet."

They took a piece of felt and wrapped Imatch's body, then they buried him in a natural hollow and covered his body with large stones to protect it from the wild animals. This time they remembered to place his head facing southwest in the

Mahommedan fashion while Rachmed recited the appropriate prayers.

For the rest of the day, the men slumped down by the fire, their hearts too heavy to go on. They braced themselves against the wind as they reminisced about home.

"What I wouldn't do for the taste of naan one last time before it's my turn to go," said Abdullah, his voice grim and resigned.

"Or the crunch of pistachios," added Parpa. "Or the taste of my mother's palao." Tears welled up in Parpa's eyes and then he broke down and cried. "I don't want my mama to cry over me. I don't want her to feel sadness because of me."

Rachmed patted him on the back. "You're still alive. You're going to see her again. I promise. Just think about old Imatch."

"He always shared his Chinese noodles with me," said Timur, poking a stick in the fire. "Now he will never eat them again. I can't believe he's gone. Without him the camels have lost their will to live too."

Everyone nodded in agreement. Although Imatch had been ill-tempered and brutish, losing him was a heavy blow.

The next day, they loaded up the camels hoping to reach Lake Namtso. The kneeling Bactrian camels groaned and squeaked as the caravan men lashed the tents, bedrolls, crates, trunks, and baskets onto their backs. They were certain the lake lay just beyond a stretch of nearby hills. The men desperately needed fresh water and pasture land for the animals, as well as the chance to revive their own flagging spirits. By now the remaining horses were so weak from hunger they could barely walk let alone carry a rider and the weight of a saddlebag. Two of their best horses were little more than skin and bones, so close to death that Rachmed and Prince Henri were forced to abandon them on the frozen ground to await their inevitable fate. And so, with two remaining horses, six camels, and several sheep, the men marched across the pass, determined to reach the lake before they suffered any more major losses.

When they reached the summit, Bonvalot whipped out his spyglass and gazed at the precious sight before him: the glistening blue waters of Lake Namtso. The Heavenly Lake. Bonvalot was so overcome with joy he could scarcely believe his eyes. After all these months his dream was about to come true. Soon they would be riding through the streets of Lhasa about to climb the steps to the Potala Palace. With his hands trembling with excitement, Bonvalot handed the spyglass to Father Dedeken who passed it down the line so that everyone could take a look at the precious sight. Just the sight of the blue water seemed to restore everyone's vigor.

When they reached Lake Namtso, the men ran across the shore crying out with joy. They knelt beside the water and dipped their hands in, washing the layers of dirt and grime that caked their faces and hands. They fell to the sand laughing like children and hugging each other. Rachmed helped Camille and Pema alight from their camels, and as soon as Pema's feet touched the soil, she prostrated herself on the ground, chanting her Buddhist prayers.

Bonvalot was relieved to see an abundance of wildlife grazing around the perimeter of the lake. Wasting no time, Rachmed selected a choice yak, loaded his carbine, and after two quick shots, the yak slumped to the ground. The men rejoiced. That night there would be a lavish feast with plenty of fresh meat.

Prince Henri unpacked his camera and took some photographs of the lake and of the strange rock formations that jutted up from the shore like obelisks. Meanwhile, the caravan men went to work unloading the camels and letting them wander off to graze. Their easy smiles sent a wave of relief over Bonvalot. They had reached Lake Namtso not a moment too soon.

"Imagine the headlines when we get back to Paris," said Prince Henri, resting along the shore. "I can see it now: *Prince Henri d'Orléans and Gabriel Bonvalot: the greatest explorers in the world.* We'll be the toast of Paris, London, and New York. No doubt we'll be awarded the gold medal of the Geographical Society for our efforts and we'll spend our lives basking in the public's adulation."

"I wish it were that easy," said Bonvalot. "They actually make us explorers work for a living, giving long-winded speeches to crowded lecture halls, writing jaw-dropping accounts of our daring exploits and then convincing an eager public to buy them. Oh, there will be the occasional naysayer who'll deny our great achievement, but if I know one thing for certain, it's that we are the first Europeans in the modern age to reach Lake Namtso. Not even the great Prejevalsky made it this far. We've set a new world record."

Prince Henri beamed. "This is sure to put me back in Papa's good graces."

Looking up, Bonvalot spied Camille sitting by herself on the beach. "If you'll excuse me, your Highness, I have some important business to attend." He strolled over to join Camille.

"Is this seat taken?" said Bonvalot, shielding his eyes against the sunlight.

Camille smiled. "Please have a seat."

He slumped into the sand and drew his hands around his knees. They stared out to the turquoise lake and to the snow-capped mountains behind it. The peaks were so high they looked like the back of a sleeping dragon; the water sparkled under the blazing sun.

"Welcome to the heart of Tibet," he said. "You know, there's an old Tibetan legend that says Lake Namtso is the daughter of the god Indra and the wife of Ningling Tanla, the great mountain range south of here. They say the goddess of the lake has a turquoise body, three eyes, two hands, and holds an aquarium in her right hand and a mirror in her left. She rides a blue dragon and is said to be quite charming."

"She sounds positively delightful," said Camille. "How did you learn so much about Tibetan culture?"

"I read up on it before I left Paris," said Bonvalot. "I wanted to know everything about this mysterious land before I left. I met an extraordinary man, a Professor Philippe Édouard Foucaux, considered the world's foremost Tibetologist. He told me about a certain prophecy concerning a reincarnated goddess, the earthly incarnation of Kali, the consort of the god Siva. The professor begged me to find any evidence of the fulfillment of this prophecy. I can't imagine how that can be possible in so vast a country."

"How strange," said Camille. "I would expect that only a Buddhist could do that."

"He was a bit eccentric, but he believed so strongly in this prophecy so I had no choice but to agree to help him. Still, one never knows what can happen. You know, I've been watching you these past few weeks. I've seen how you've cared for the men, how you stood up for Rachmed, how you've watched over Pema like a big sister. You're a remarkable woman, Camille. I just wanted to tell you that."

"Thank you, Monsieur Bonvalot. I'm flattered. I love how the men look up to you. I do believe they'd follow you anywhere."

"I wasn't entirely honest with them from the beginning," said Bonvalot. "I had to keep our destination secret. If I had told them from the beginning I was planning to reach Lhasa, they would have deserted months ago. But these men are experienced guides; they know the rigors of travel. They just want a good sahib to work for who will treat them well and pay a reasonable wage. The truth is, we couldn't make it very far without them. If we're so fortunate as to reach Lhasa, it will be in no small part be because of the courage and resourcefulness of these men."

"I think they're drawn to the mountains much the same way as you are," said Camille. "Out of this great passion for the planet, this innate love of exploration and adventure. Certainly not for the mere pursuit of monetary gain."

"Some do it for their livelihood, others because they were born wanderers. But the most remarkable thing about these men is their willingness to undergo any hardship, any danger for relatively small pay. They're about as rugged and hardy as any man you'll ever find."

Rachmed came strolling over. "Bonvalot-sahib, I think we should stay by the lake for several days to give the men and camels time to rest. A few days by the water will do everyone much good."

"I agree," said Bonvalot, glancing at the withered camels that grazed nearby. They would not be long for the world, being almost depleted by exhaustion. "We'll stay here for a few days to prepare for the next stage of the journey, then we'll go out and search for more horses. But stay on guard. It's only a question of time before the soldiers return for another chance to harass us, at which point we'll be forced to defend ourselves."

Looking up, Bonvalot spied some horsemen in the distance heading toward the Dam Pass, the main route that crosses through the Ningling Tanla range. He was certain the Amban's soldiers were planning to intercept the caravan before they reached the pass and force them to turn around, in which case Bonvalot was prepared to shoot his way to Lhasa.

CHAPTER 42

Lake Namtso, Tibet
February, 1890

The day spent at Lake Namtso was like a soothing balm to the men's spirits. After resting near the water's edge they went for a walk around the lake, taking measurement and jotting down landmarks. By their estimation, the lake lay at an altitude of 15,300 feet and was approximately forty miles long by eighteen miles wide. The lake was surrounded by an immense wall of ice-capped mountains bathed in a purple haze the largest of which Bonvalot knew was Ningling Tanla, an immense peak that presented a formidable challenge to the travelers, as the only way to reach Lhasa was by scaling it.

Upon further exploration they discovered a rocky ledge that contained a variety of obos, mounds of rocks decorated with colorful prayer flags, that fluttered in the breeze like the sails of forgotten ships. They also found curious stone altars containing the remnants of burnt incense, while on the lake's southern shore they discovered a lamasery hewn out of solid rock, but sadly there were no monks in the vicinity, and no signs of human life.

While the men pitched camp, Princess Pema stood at the water's edge tossing grains into the sky as she recited her prayers. As an extra measure of protection, she tied prayer-flags to the tops of each tent, and then rotated her prayer wheel while meditating in silent devotion. The caravan men watched her with awe, convinced she was a holy woman of sorts.

That night they feasted on freshly-slaughtered yak meat, celebrating their good fortune until the night sky was dotted with a thousand twinkling stars. The caravan men sat cross-legged near the fire gazing up at the heavens and the glowing moon. It seemed there was no other life in the universe save for them, their aloneness being magnified by the grandeur of the mountains and the vastness of the lake spread before them. There was no sound save for the gentle waves on the beach and the wind that echoed through the mountains. Flickers of the fire danced in the dark like a will-o'-the-wisp, casting deep shadows on the men's faces.

Bonvalot saw Timur gazing thoughtfully at the night sky and asked, "What are you looking at Timur? The moon?"

"No, I see the Bear," said Timur.

"What's so special about the Bear?"

"It makes me happy to see it," said Timur. "They say when the Bear hangs low in the sky there will be plenty of grass for the herds."

Rachmed, who had been listening to this exchange grunted his disapproval.

"Show me the Bear," said Rachmed.

Timur stretched his hand in the direction of Orion.

Rachmed howled with laughter. "That's not the Bear, you idiot. That's the Balance. How can the Balance have any effect on the grass? Everyone knows grass grows during the rainy season or after a snowy winter. What nonsense. You speak like a donkey."

"Rachmed, my brother," said Timur. "I am only repeating what my father taught me. It has been passed down from father to son since the time of the Prophet. My father was never wrong."

Rachmed shook his head. "Every good Mohammedan knows the constellations. I knew the difference between the Bear and the Balance since I was a schoolboy in Tashkent."

"But Rachmed, my brother," protested Timur. "If my father said so it must be true."

"Then tell me this," said Rachmed. "If that is indeed the Bear, then why are the Dogs standing nearby?"

Isa offered his own explanation. "Timur the shepherd can find his way back to Qarkilik just by following the Bear. Timur is not afraid of the Dogs. Don't you know? The dogs are kept at bay by the presence of Al-Jabhah, the mighty Lion who roars nearby."

And so went the conversation for the rest of the evening.

Meanwhile, down near the water's edge, Henri and Pema went for a stroll, gazing into each other's eyes, speaking the unspoken language of lovers. Pema taught Henri words in Tibetan, while he taught her French. When Henri had gotten a good grasp of Tibetan, the princess began to teach him all about the mystical aspects of her religion while Henri offered her his undying affection.

"Hengli, you are my Golden Prince," she said. "I cannot bear to live without you."

"I promise I will never leave your side."

"But some day you must return to the land of your ancestors," said Pema. "Tibet is not your home."

"I will find a way so that we can be together forever," said Henri. "Now that I've found you I refuse to let you go."

Watching her face in the light of the moon Henri felt for the first time in his life that he was completely absolved of all his sins. Inside the tortured, jumbled mass of his soul he was finally cleansed from all the wrongs he had committed. As improbable as it seemed, high up in the Tibetan Chang Tang Prince Henri d'Orléans had found perfect absolution in the form of a beguiling Tibetan princess. She had saved him.

He gathered her up in his arms and kissed her.

"Hengli, some day you will leave me," she said. "It is written."

"Nonsense, I promise you I will never desert you."

She gazed at him with beguiling eyes. "Do you love me?"

"I love you more than I've loved any other woman."

"Yet you will leave me."

"I'm right here. I'm not going anywhere."

"But it is written."

He put his finger to her lips. "Shh, don't talk about that now."

Pema threw her arms around Henri and drew him close.

"I always knew you would come for me," she said. "It was written long before we were born."

Later, Henri brought Pema into his tent and she taught him all the mystical aspects of her religion, joining with him in meditation as they pondered the mysteries of the universe, their bodies intertwining, becoming weightless and sleek, like a pair of geese as they sailed over the Himalayas, soaring over snow-capped peaks and down to lush green valleys and over rivers of rushing glacial water. Together they drank in the beauty of the Himalayas and felt the power and majesty of the heights; they breathed in the sanctified air, tasted the cool, sweet dew of the flowers, purified themselves with vows of love. Later, when they fell asleep it was to the gentle lapping of the waves against the shore and the soft tinkling of the camel bells. From that moment on, Henri and Pema became inseparable.

The next morning, Bonvalot awoke with an uneasy feeling. Peering through his tent flaps, he noticed that the mysterious horsemen had vanished. The lake was utterly quiet. The sun's rays danced on the water's surface and the wildlife grazed along the shores, but the eerie silence caused his heart to skip a beat. He decided they had to get out of there as quickly as possible. He was certain the Tibetans were planning an ambush. Forcing an arm into his sheepskin coat, he ran to Prince Henri's tent.

"Henri, get up, we're getting out of here," said Bonvalot.

"What?" said the prince, still groggy.

"Get dressed and pack your things. We've got to get moving. The soldiers are planning to attack us."

"But we just got here."

"Hurry up, tell the others to get ready to go."

Remembering that Parpa was still weak, he ran to check on him. When he saw that the brooding caravan guide was eating heartily and his cheeks had regained some of their color, he ordered the men to load the camels as quickly as possible. They had scarcely swallowed a breakfast of tea and tsampa when they were on the road again.

After loading up the camels they traveled another ten miles, crossing a river and then continuing over an icy glacier until they found themselves at the foot of the Ningling Tanla pass. There was no sign of movement, no sign of life, anywhere for miles. The unnatural silence unnerved Bonvalot; he was certain they were being watched, but they were too exhausted to march any further that day, so after riding off to conduct a quick survey of the area, Bonvalot ordered the men to set up camp.

While they were pitching the tents the silence was finally broken. The telltale stomping of horses' hooves filled the air. Looking up, they spied ten horsemen riding across the ice, some of whom were ordinary soldiers, others who appeared to be high-ranking mandarins. Bonvalot signaled his men to pick up their rifles and hold them ready.

Father Dedeken whispered to Bonvalot, "Do you see the officials with the silk robes and rounded helmets? Those are the mandarins. Their job is to enforce the laws of Peking, which in this case means keeping all foreigners out of Lhasa. No doubt the higher authorities sent them to give us trouble."

"How should I deal with these scoundrels?"

"Hold your ground. Show them firmness. Keep them spinning in bureaucratic circles. Treat them as if they're too lowly for you to speak to. In China, the only way to gain respect is by conveying a high opinion of yourself, which means putting on your best poker face."

"Luckily I'm a master of the poker face," said Bonvalot.

When the horsemen approached, one of the soldiers addressed them in Mongolian. Perking their ears, the caravan men drew closer, straining to comprehend the Tibetan's choppy pronunciation.

"Excuse me, sirs, but what are you doing here?" said the Tibetan soldier.

Rachmed stepped forward. "Greetings to you. We are hunters. We have come here to hunt. When we are finished, we shall leave of our own accord."

"On whose authority did you enter Chinese territory?"

"On our authority," said Rachmed. "We followed the herds south."

The soldier's face darkened and his voice became brusque.

"You entered Tibet without proper authorization. My orders are to stop you and turn you around."

"That's impossible," said Rachmed, folding his arms. "Since we intend to travel south to Lhasa."

The soldier clenched his jaw. "Foreigners may not enter holy city of Lhasa. You have no Chinese passport and no permission to enter Tibet. Go back and get passport from authorities in Peking. But leave here at once."

Prince Henri opened his mouth to speak, but Bonvalot pushed him and motioned for him to keep quiet.

"Excuse me, but I'm the leader of this expedition," said Bonvalot. "And I have no intention of turning around." Bonvalot retrieved his pass and held it up for the soldiers to see. "I received this pass from the Governor of the Ili province who said it was valid for travel in Tibet."

"He told you wrong. Let me see that," said the mandarin.

The mandarin dispatched an orderly to fetch the pass. One of the foot soldiers snatched it out of Bonvalot's hand and brought it back to the three mandarins, who passed the document back and forth until each one had read it top to bottom. After a few minutes, the mandarins shook their heads.

"This document—no good," said the mandarin. "Not valid Chinese passport."

"I already told you," said Bonvalot. "We are not going back. We intend to proceed directly to Lhasa and my advice to you is to keep a safe distance. We will fire on any soldier who dares to approach us. And from now on I will no longer speak to men of your rank. I will only speak to *your* chief."

The mandarins bristled. They sent three soldiers forward, and when they came too close, Bonvalot took out his whip and snapped it in their faces, scattering them.

An older mandarin with a stooped posture and a wizened face motioned that he wished to speak to Bonvalot. He rode forward and addressed Bonvalot in Chinese, which Father Dedeken dutifully translated.

"You gentlemen are foreigners," said the elderly mandarin. "Let me explain something to you. The ground on which you are standing is Chinese territory. Only travelers who hold a valid Chinese passport may enter Tibet. Since you do not have this permission, the officials in Lhasa have ordered us to stop you and turn you around. If you require horses or food, we can provide you with these, but only on condition you agree to go back from where you came. Otherwise we have orders to detain you."

"I already told you," said Bonvalot. "We refuse to be detained. After we have rested overnight, we shall proceed directly to Lhasa. Consider this a warning: we will shoot anyone who tries to stop us."

The elderly mandarin's eyes widened. He pulled his horse backwards and turned around. Left with no choice, the other mandarins also retreated some distance, giving Bonvalot and his men opportunity to finish pitching their tents. After an hour, a second group of horsemen returned, this one comprised several mandarins on horseback and soldiers marching on foot followed by a Buddhist lama dressed in saffron robes and a round red helmet. The delegation approached the camp and trotted to where Abdullah and Father Dedeken were standing with their rifles poised.

The mandarins halted their horses and an orderly dismounted and presented them with various presents including a package of butter, tsampa, and a bottle of European-made spirits.

After Father Dedeken thanked them for the gifts, one of the mandarins said, "We were sent by Lhasa to find out your identities and the nature of your visit. I wish to speak to your chief."

"I'm very sorry," said Father Dedeken in Chinese. "But our chief refuses to speak to men of your rank. He will only speak to *your* chief."

The mandarin bristled. "Apparently, you do not understand. We are emissaries of the Dalai Lama and the Amban of Lhasa, the highest authorities in all of Tibet."

"I'm only repeating what my chief told me," said Dedeken. "He will only speak to *your* chief."

"Nonsense. Show us your documents at once," said the mandarin. "We wish to know who we are speaking to and what business you have traveling in Tibet."

"I'll show you my documents as soon as you explain why your people have treated us so poorly," said Dedeken. "Explain why they refuse to sell us horses or provisions, refuse to help our sick men. We cannot accept such poor treatment."

"I am very sorry," said the mandarin. "But the Tibetan people do not trust foreigners."

"That's rubbish," said Father Dedeken. "There is no justification for such treatment. We offered your people good money to buy what we need, but they refused to negotiate with us in a civilized, friendly manner forcing us to resort to seizing what we need just to stay alive. If you continue to treat us like outlaws, we will be forced to act that way. Are you willing to take responsibility for that?"

A dark shadow fell across the mandarin's face. Meanwhile, the Tibetan lama shuffled forward. Dressed in saffron robes, he wore a perpetually grim expression on a his pock-marked face, as if the weight of the universe were riding on his stooped shoulders. The lama bowed deeply and expressed deep sorrow for the way they had been treated, and he assured them they would have no further reason to complain. He urged them to hand over their papers and to remain where they were as all their needs would soon be met.

Dedeken shook his head. "That's impossible. We can't remain at such a high altitude much longer. Some of the men are sick and need proper care. We must get them to lower ground where they can rest and recuperate. Would you have more of our men die of mountain sickness?"

"That is not the way of the Buddha of compassion," said the lama in his halting Chinese. "Lord Buddha teaches that we must show kindness to the wayfarer, but first papers must be in order so mandarin can conduct proper investigation. This is direct order from Lhasa. You must remain here until we receive further orders."

"If one of our men dies, I will hold you responsible," said Father Dedeken.

"Patience, please," said the lama. "I will help you in any way I can."

Without another word, the procession turned and left. Watching from his tent, Bonvalot saw the delegation ride back to the contingent in stoic silence, the mandarin's silk robes billowing in the breeze. He knew their troubles with the Tibetans were far from over.

That night as they sat around the fire discussing the events of the day, Tong-Kia muttered under his breath that they were doomed. The rancid smell of the Tibetan butter had put him in an especially foul mood as he stooped over the pot to cook a Tibetan version of palao, but found the smell too repulsive.

"Firinghi no good," said Tong-Kia, shaking an angry finger in Bonvalot's direction. "Fool mandarin no good. Make big trouble."

Ignoring the cook's ire, they concluded that the Tibetans had no finesse in handling a group of uncooperative foreigners, especially uncooperative *French* foreigners. Bonvalot was certain that if they could just stall them a little while longer, they would be able to buy enough time to make a break for Lhasa.

"I know we're close to the Forbidden City," said Bonvalot. "According to my Russian charts we're less than a hundred miles away, which means we've traveled further than any other European explorer in the modern age. All we need now is one more push and we'll get there. I believe this is why the mandarins are so nervous."

"Our mandarin friends have their own plans," said Father Dedeken. "They intend to hold us here against our will indefinitely and watch us slowly die from mountain sickness."

"Then those petty tyrants have a lot to learn," said Bonvalot, thrusting his pocket knife into the frozen ground. "As I have no intention of letting them win. I learned a valuable lesson by watching how you handled them. Every time they asked you a question, you countered it by asking them an even harder question. You're a very clever man, Father."

"Yes, but soon they will get wise to me," said Father Dedeken. "I learned that little trick from my years in Kansou. My superiors taught me that survival in the east meant acquiring an intricate knowledge of Chinese habits and customs. How do you think we managed to evangelize to the common people right under the noses of the local mandarins? It was by subterfuge and trickery."

Bonvalot poured himself another cup of tea. "I'm certain that this race to Lhasa will only be won by a greater show of force. I've come too far to be turned around now. I've brought an entire arsenal and I intend to use it. And let those Tibetan scoundrels try and stop us."

Everyone agreed that nothing short of an army could force them to turn around.

PART 3

CHAPTER 43

Dam Pass, Tibet
February, 1890

The next morning, one of the mandarins visited the camp to interrogate Bonvalot. The object of his visit, he explained, was to determine if they were indeed British or Russian subjects. He explained that their Oracle, who resided in the Nechung Temple near the Drepung lamasery, had gone into a trance, warning them of an impending Russian invasion. The mandarin, a thickset, jovial man with a pragmatic nature did his best to convince Bonvalot that by cooperating with the authorities they would be provided with all the horses and provisions they needed. But, he added, on no condition would they be permitted to travel to Lhasa. Rachmed did his best to explain to the mandarin that the leaders of the expedition were neither British nor Russian, but French, from a faraway country called *France,* but that explanation only resulted in confusing the mandarin further as he had never heard of a place called *France* and he refused to believe it was not a part of Russia. Finally, the mandarin ordered them to stay put until after he had had a chance to consult with his officials in Lhasa.

Stalling, Rachmed pretended not to understand the mandarin's Mongolian. He shook his head repeatedly and urged the mandarin to send an official with a better command of Mongolian. Hearing this, the mandarin lost all pretense of friendliness and galloped away in a rage.

Bonvalot's heart raced. He knew there would be trouble with the mandarins and decided to make a break for Lhasa. Wasting no time, he packed up his saddlebag and ordered the men to take down the tents and load up the baggage as quickly as possible. He told them to arm themselves to the teeth and to expect an attack. He told them to march like soldiers with their rifles against their shoulders, and to return fire in case the soldiers threatened their lives. He instructed Camille and Princess Pema to disguise themselves with sheepskin hats and to cover their faces with pashmina shawls. He was not taking any chances with their safety.

After they had traveled a short distance, they started up the Ningling Tanla Pass, marching across an ice-covered trail that snaked around enormous, snow-covered peaks. By Bonvalot's estimation, they were at most eighty miles from Lhasa. With his heart thumping, he took out his spyglass and scanned the hills. He was certain they were being watched.

About an hour later, a group of soldiers appeared in front of them. Leading the procession was a lama-officer who wore a yellow tunic under a saffron-colored robe and on his head he wore a rounded mandarin helmet. Seated on his horse he looked like a Roman officer about to lead a charge.

Bonvalot signaled the guides to stop the camels while the caravan men unlatched their safeties and kept their fingers hovering over their triggers.

"Good day, gentlemen," said the lama-officer, bowing slightly. "What a surprise to meet you here. Why are you running away so quick? Did you not enjoy our hospitality yesterday?"

"We made it perfectly clear that some of our men are sick," said Bonvalot. "If we remain at this high altitude they will get sicker and may die and it will be entirely your fault."

"Is it also my fault that you entered Chinese territory without a passport?" said the lama-officer.

Bonvalot felt his neck break out in a fine cold sweat.

He said, "You promised to help us, but all you did was interrogate us and try to stop us. I'm finished with your empty promises. I'm warning you, if so much as one of your soldiers tries to stop us, we'll shoot."

"Stop!" shouted the lama-officer. "Do not go any further. Beyond this pass you will find only a barren desert and bitter water. It is no place to take your sick companions. If you don't believe me, I will lend you my horse so you can ride across and see for yourself. I will stay here and guard your men."

Rachmed violently shook his head.

"No chance. I refuse to leave my men," said Bonvalot.

The lama scowled. "Then I urge you to reconsider this foolishness. Behind me is a force of a thousand soldiers commanded by an Amban who has traveled all the way from Lhasa to speak to you. Do not be disrespectful and leave. He's not as patient as I am."

"Then we'll just have to take our chances," said Bonvalot. He turned around and gave the order to proceed. To his shock, as the camels proceeded, the Tibetan soldiers moved aside like the parting of the Red Sea, allowing the caravan to pass. As the caravan marched through the line of stern-faced Tibetan soldiers, no one dared utter a word.

With Bonvalot and Rachmed riding in front, the caravan continued marching across the Dam Pass for several miles until they reached the banks of a frozen river. All around the ground seemed to be composed of pure ice, as if they were traversing over an enormous glacier. Peering across the frozen desert, Bonvalot noted the presence of black yak hair tents, domesticated yaks with pack saddles, and several white canvas tents. This, he presumed, was the Tibetan camp, whose nomadic residents stopped and stared at the foreigners with curiosity, but were too far away to make eye contact..

Teetering on the brink of exhaustion, Bonvalot decided to pitch camp for the night. No sooner had they erected two tents when the sound of footsteps echoed in their ears. Looking up, Bonvalot saw a column of troops led by the notorious Amban marching their way.

"Blast!" said Bonvalot, dropping the tent peg on the frozen ground.

CHAPTER 44

Prince Henri raced over to Bonvalot. "There's a welcoming party headed our way. What do you propose we do?"

"We do what all good Frenchmen do," said Bonvalot, smiling at the advancing soldiers. "We sit, we drink wine, we talk. And then we blast their brains out."

Riding at the head of the column was the Amban. Looking like a figure out of a medieval tapestry, he displayed the rigid posture and elaborate costume of a high-ranking official of the Qing Empire. When he approached, they could see that beneath his rounded helmet he had a surprisingly youthful face, with eyes that were both kind and intelligent. Bonvalot studied his adversary with keen interest.

At twenty-three, the Amban was old before his time. He had a broad forehead of bronzed skin, and a long turquoise earring that dangled from one ear. They soon learned that his good-natured demeanor belied his sharp mind and dictatorial temperament.

Dismounting, the Amban approached Bonvalot's party and greeted them with the h the assistance of an interpreter, a heavy-faced Tibetan with downcast eyes and a somber demeanor named Jamyang. Returning his greeting in Mongolian, Father Dedeken introduced Gabriel Bonvalot and Prince Henri d'Orléans as the leaders of an important French expedition that was heading south to Lhasa. The Amban nodded politely and requested an audience with the distinguished travelers that would be held the following day. In the meanwhile, he ordered them to remain in their camp overnight and promised to send over provisions for the men and the animals.

After the Amban and his entourage left, Bonvalot huddled with his companions around the fire to discuss strategy.

"What do you think, Father?" said Bonvalot. "How should I handle them?"

"Now it is a matter of negotiations," said Father Dedeken. "How you conduct yourself will determine the outcome. Tact and diplomacy are extremely important in Chinese culture. I can only assume that Tibetan culture follows the same general pattern. But above all, you must hold your ground. Never show weakness. This is key. Don't give them an inch. Let them find the middle way to deal with you. You have much more power than you realize."

"What about Lhasa?" said Prince Henri. "Do we still have a chance of making it?"

Dedeken's eyes twinkled. "That depends on how well we play the game of subterfuge. Perhaps with firmness and diplomacy we can earn their trust. In the worst-case scenario, we must convince them to allow us to veer east toward Batang rather than turning back toward Lob Nor. Above all, we must try to win them over and avoid blundering at all costs."

"How do we do that?" said Bonvalot.

"By instilling confidence in them," said Father Dedeken.

Bonvalot laughed ironically. "Without the Tibetans' help we're as good as dead and you talk about instilling *confidence?* Excuse me if I find that about as absurd as riding to Lhasa on a bicycle."

Father Dedeken laughed. "Have you seen yourself lately? When was last time you looked in a mirror? The first thing you can do to instill confidence is to shave your matted beard, wash your face from weeks of dirt, and change your filthy shirt. It pains me to have to tell you this, but you look worse than a Peking street beggar."

Alarmed, Bonvalot ran his hand through his beard, dislodging sand, twigs, and pebbles. He grabbed his saddlebag and pulled out a pocket mirror. The image that greeted him made his eyes widen with shock: his face was covered with grime, his cheeks and eyes were swollen from the cold, his lips were so chapped the skin was peeling off, and his hair and beard were so overgrown they gave him the appearance of a shipwrecked sailor. Bonvalot burst out laughing.

"You're right, Father. Not exactly an image to instill confidence. We must rectify that at once."

Prince Henri snatched the mirror out of Bonvalot's hand.

"*Mon Dieu.* I look worse than Edmond Dantes in the Chateau d'If."

"In short, gentlemen," said Father Dedeken. "We're all in need of some basic grooming, which means our first impression was a miserable failure. But all that can be rectified with a little soap, water, a comb, and a razor. I suggest we get started right away."

The next morning, bolstered by their renewed appearance, the men anxiously awaited for the Amban to appear. By midday a messenger on horseback rode over from the Tibetan camp announcing that the emissary from Lhasa would be arriving shortly with an entourage of various chiefs.

Wasting no time, Rachmed prepared a meeting room. He laid a clean piece of felt on the ground of the main tent, which was the only tent large enough to accommodate a medium-sized gathering. Tong-Kia went to work boiling ice for tea, and a short while later, Bonvalot peered across the frozen desert and spied the Amban's procession heading toward them.

"Our friends are coming," said Bonvalot dryly. "The party is about to start."

When the Tibetan officials arrived in camp, the Amban dismounted and approached Bonvalot with an escort of twenty chiefs of lesser rank all dressed in a similar fashion: rounded helmets and warm sheepskin coats over Chinese-style tunics. The Amban presented Bonvalot, Father Dedeken, and Prince Henri with white silk scarves, the standard Tibetan greeting, then he signaled for his orderly, who stepped forward and set down various presents at their feet: butter wrapped in animal skins, sacks of tsampa, and grain for the animals.

Bonvalot presented Prince Henri as a royal emissary and then invited the Amban into his tent. Following the Amban was an orderly who carried a small carpet for his master to sit on, after which came various other officials, each one taking his rightful place on either side of the Amban. Most interesting among these characters was an elderly, corpulent lama, whose hairless face resembled a wrinkled prune. Throughout the meeting, this lama would hold a rosary in his hand, which he counted repeatedly with an expression of worldly indifference. To the left of the lama was a Chinese mandarin dressed in a rich robes. This mandarin resembled a tortoise, with small eyes draped beneath heavy eyelids, a straight nose, thick lips, and a cunning, sarcastic nature that made Bonvalot wonder if he was the real power behind the throne.

The rest of the Amban's entourage crowded into the tent with the remainder spilling out through the door. This group consisted of lamas of inferior rank and their servants, both of which displayed features that had a distinct Mongolian cast about them, with snub noses, prominent cheek bones, and small eyes. These men did not strike Bonvalot as being of pure Tibetan blood. Their clothing was even more exotic, coming in various shades of yellow, green, red, and black, and headdress ranging from Chinese hats to half-turbans and monk hoods. With their peasant faces, medieval clothing, and curved swords, the entourage reminded Bonvalot of characters straight out of the Dumas play, *The Tour de Nesle Affair.*

The Amban's servants brought in porcelain cups of tea which they passed around to the assembly, but to the Amban they served his in a special cup made of solid green jade. After the tea-drinking ceremony was finished, the Amban cleared his throat and began to speak in Tibetan, which Jamyang translated into Mongolian for the benefit of Father Dedeken, who in turn translated it into French for the benefit of Bonvalot and Prince Henri.

"By now I'm sure you know the reason for my visit," said the Amban, eyeing them under his oversized helmet. "We have been ordered to stop you wherever we meet you and force you to turn around."

"Forgive me, Excellency, but that is impossible," said Bonvalot. "Although I understand your position, we cannot consider turning around."

"That is the law in Tibet," said the Amban. "You must turn around as going forward is forbidden."

"With all due respect," said Bonvalot. "We must continue moving forward as going back the way we came is impossible. We traveled here with the intention of seeing the holy city of Lhasa."

The Amban crossed his arms and shook his head. "That cannot be arranged. The lamas have forbidden any foreign foot from trampling the sacred ground of Lhasa. You will be detained here for forty-five days, after which you will be turned around."

"That's impossible," said Bonvalot. "We can't remain here for forty-five days. We only stopped here to rest and meet with you, but we are anxious to reach a milder climate."

"Will you or will you not go back?"

"No," said Bonvalot, shaking his head. "We would rather die than go back. Ask any one of my men. They would rather die right here than go through that fearful journey again."

"Then at least you must double back and return to Lake Namtso," said the Amban, to which his advisors nodded.

"That's also out of the question," said Bonvalot. "We must descend to lower ground immediately. Some of my men are sick from the high altitude. We believe that if we continue south past the Ningling Tanla range, we will find a camping ground that is lower in altitude and not quite so cold. We're slowly dying from the cold and hunger."

"If it's food you need, that is no problem," said the Amban. "We will supply you with all your needs, including yaks and donkeys for the journey. But you must turn around and go back."

"With all due respect, Excellency, I said no," said Bonvalot. "Absolutely not. I refuse to drag my men back to certain death. Please don't bring up that point again, since it's a waste of time. Instead of amassing an army to stop three Frenchmen who are traveling in your country peacefully, you should be preparing for the massive Russian invasion that's right behind us. According to my calculations, they've brought over one hundred soldiers, each one armed with a machine gun."

The Amban's jaw dropped. A loud stir broke out among his ministers, as they contemplated the possibility of a Russian attack.

Composing himself, the Amban said, "You have just confirmed what our Oracle predicted. He said that during the year of the Iron-Tiger the golden bird would be set free by a small army with powerful metal fire sticks who would sweep down from the north. Have you seen this golden bird?"

"Absolutely not," said Bonvalot. "We have not seen this golden bird and neither are we these Russians your Oracle spoke about. As I stated before, we are French citizens."

"If we find out that you are lying to us," said the Amban. "I'll have no choice but to detain you indefinitely. Our Oracle has never been mistaken in his predictions."

"I have no idea what you're talking about."

A dark shadow fell across the Amban's face. He considered himself a reasonable man yet these foreigners were behaving in an insufferable manner. According to the laws of Karma he knew all action led to suffering. He had seen this hundreds of times during his life. In his position, he had only resorted to extreme measures about a dozen or so times depending on the circumstances. He was confident that each time a prisoner was beaten, beheaded, or thrown into a lake the punishment had been justifiable. Naturally, if he could avoid ending a human life, he would choose the Middle Way. Still, he knew that *dukkha,* suffering, led to rebirth. It was almost a prerequisite. In this manner, he held the tools and the power to help the prisoners achieve a state of Nirvana and extinguish the fires that caused suffering.

The Amban's voice turned ominous. "I expect I don't have to tell you that the punishment for harboring a fugitive is very severe. Several weeks ago a Tibetan woman of dubious ancestry claiming to be the daughter of the Panchen Lama escaped by bribing her guards and climbing down a rope ladder. I have received reports that she was spotted riding in a caravan of foreigners."

Bonvalot locked eyes with the Amban. "I assure you, we don't have this golden bird you are speaking about and neither are we Russian. Please do not ask me this again. My young traveling partner here is a French prince of royal blood. He is allied to the kings of the West and if you attempt to imprison us, his father will wage war on your country."

The Amban narrowed his eyes. "I've received word from Peking to expect a visit from a Russian traveler named Pyltsov who was sent here by the White Pasha, along with another man named Roborovsky. Are you these men?"

Bonvalot shook his head. "No, Excellency. My name is Pierre Gabriel Édouard Bonvalot. I am a French citizen and my traveling companion here is His Highness, Prince Henri d'Orléans, a pretender to the throne. We were sent here by his father, Prince Robert, Duke of Chartres, to establish friendly relations with the officials in Lhasa. Indeed, if you will examine our visiting cards, which are written in Chinese characters on official red paper, you will see that our names do not resemble the Russian names you mentioned in the least."

Bonvalot handed over the visiting cards, which the Amban inspected. When he had finished, he passed them to the other mandarins, who examined them with great thoroughness. After the entire entourage had read the cards, the Amban returned them with a good-natured laugh.

"Perhaps there's been a misunderstanding," said the Amban. "Or some kind of miscommunication, but you must understand my position. Since it is my duty to stop and interrogate any party of Russians, I'm obligated to stop any foreigner who enters Tibet. Anyone found traveling without the necessary documents must turn around and retrace his steps. Since that law applies to you as well, I must therefore ask you to leave."

"I've already told you, that's impossible," said Bonvalot. "We would rather die by the sword than go back through the Chang Tang. The climate is too inhospitable. There's no food, no water, no shelter, and no pasture for our animals. The journey already cost us the lives of two men. I cannot risk any more lives because of Chinese inhospitality."

"I've already told you we will supply you with warm tents and food, whatever you need. But all foreigners must leave Tibet immediately."

Bonvalot took a deep breath. "Even if we were willing to go back, we could not, since we need fresh camels, which you don't have. So I'm repeating to you again: we will not go back."

The mandarins leaned over and whispered in the Amban's ear.

Speaking in a voice that betrayed mounting impatience, the Amban said, "If going back is impossible, then tell us where you wish to go."

"I must get to lower ground so my men can rest. Some of them are sick, exhausted, and near collapse. Our camels and horses are dying every day. If you force us to stay here, the rest of us will follow them shortly."

"After you rest at lower ground, where do you intend to go next?" said the Amban.

"Lhasa," said Bonvalot.

"That is impossible."

"Why is it impossible?"

"Because foreigners are not allowed to enter our Holy City."

"In that case, since you refuse to allow us permission to enter Lhasa, we would like to go to Batang where we intend to follow the Yangtze River to the sea."

The sly-looking Chinese mandarin leaned over and whispered something in the Amban's ear, to which the Amban nodded.

"Will you kindly explain the exact nature of your visit?" said the Amban.

"We came here on a shooting party. We also wish to learn all about Tibet so we can enlighten the people of France about your country. That is why we wish to visit your Potala Palace and meet with your Dalai Lama. There is a great hunger in the west for any information about this mysterious land. We come in friendship and peace."

The Amban asked point blank, "Do you swear before this esteemed audience that you are not Russian?"

"Yes, I swear it," said Bonvalot. "We are *not* Russian."

The Amban conferred with the mandarins in a low murmur. After a while, they shook their heads. Apparently, they were not convinced.

The Amban ordered a servant to fetch something and several minutes later the servant returned with a package wrapped in packing cloth. When he opened the package, the Amban produced a box which contained an official-looking document that he read aloud. Afterward, the Amban asked for details about their journey: which road they had taken, how many men they had in their party, the names of each man, and their nationalities.

Bonvalot answered each question, articulating with precision the proper name of each men and his city of residence, which the Amban carefully noted. When he had finished, the Amban lifted up the document and said, "As you can see, this is the document I received two months ago from Peking ordering me to stop a Russian General named Pevtsov of Petsokon (St. Petersburg) along with thirty of his men."

"At the risk of repeating myself, Excellency, I am not Pevtov or Pyltsov or Roborovsky. My name is Gabriel Bonvalot and I am French. His Highness Prince Henri d'Orléans and I have traveled here all the way from France. On my honor I swear we are not Russian. You must believe me."

The Amban frowned. "I see your names do not resemble Pevtsov in the least, but something is not adding up. We have received confirmed reports that Prejevalsky died many months ago and Pevtsov is now in charge of leading the expedition and is presently on his way to Lhasa. In addition, we received another report claiming that an additional party of Russians was seen traveling through the Tsaidam with the intention of making their way to Lhasa. Surely you must be this group of Russians?"

"No. We are not Russian."

"Then you must be *Pelin*?"

"No. We're not English either. As I stated before, we are French. We are from a country called France, which is neither English nor Russian."

The Amban lifted an imperious eyebrow. "Need I remind you that the English are the sworn enemies of my people and have killed many with their far-reaching guns. We forbid all Englishmen from entering Tibet under any circumstances."

Bonvalot's head was spinning from dizziness. His nausea and chest pains were returning with a vengeance after hours of questioning.

"I assure you, we are not English but French citizens," said Bonvalot, trying to keep his voice under control. "And we are traveling peacefully in your country. I believe the Chinese word for France is *Fagwo*."

"*Fagwo*" repeated the Amban, furrowing his brow. He turned to his ministers and said, "*Fagwo.*"

"*Fagwo,*" repeated the ministers, though they had never heard the word before.

"Exactly," said Bonvalot, smiling through his discomfort. "That is correct: *Fagwo*. We are Frenchmen."

"Please excuse our confusion," said Amban Wu. "Since I have never met anyone from the country of *Fagwo* before, I didn't recognize you as such. Permit me to withdraw so I may consult with my chiefs. When the messenger arrives from Lhasa, I will give you my answer."

Bonvalot sighed and rose to his feet to escort the Amban and his entourage back to their horses. He was exhausted from the meeting, which had lasted for several hours and had sorely tested Father Dedeken's knowledge of Mongolian. After the procession was gone, Bonvalot and Father Dedeken collapsed in their tent, barely able to chew the half-cooked meat and rice provided by Tong-Kia. Pessimistic by nature, their cook was convinced this ordeal would end in disaster, with all their heads on stakes.

CHAPTER 45

Days passed with no sign of the Amban or the messenger from Lhasa.

During that time the men moped around camp, cleaning their rifles, replenishing ammunition, repairing their saddles, or waiting for hours on end while the ice melted for a glass of tea. Parpa and Isa were confined to their tents, too debilitated from mountain sickness to get out of bed. Timur was suffering from a lack of hashish, and Abdullah was miserable to the point of being useless. He was convinced he would never see his little Aziz again and he saw no more point in living. Princess Pema stayed in her tent spinning her prayer wheel and meditating, terrified the Amban's soldiers would arrest her, while Rachmed and Mahmud took turns keeping the fires burning with their dwindling supply of yak dung, trying to keep everyone's spirits up.

But try as they might, the men succumbed to despair.

Of all the men, Prince Henri suffered the worst from their involuntary detainment. Worried that the Amban's soldiers would separate him from his newfound love, he fell into a rage. Returning to old ways, he paced around the camp like a caged tiger, a bottle of brandy in one hand, his beloved Martini-Enfield in the other, wheezing like an old man on account of his weakened lungs before collapsing on the ground in a ragged heap, at which point Rachmed would drag him back to his tent.

They survived on half-cooked meat and tsampa prepared by an increasingly bitter and hostile Tong-Kia, their fatigue and vexation growing in proportion to their waning hopes. Most of the time the travelers nursed their migraines with a dwindling supply of spirits. All the while, they were cognizant that their every movement was being observed by a pack of steely-eyed Tibetan guards armed with matchlocks and swords stationed at strategic intervals around the camp. They were also aware that the life of the golden bird, the beautiful Tibetan Buddhist princess, lay in their hands. If the Amban discovered her presence in their midst, she would be sent into exile and certain death, and they would probably lose their heads.

The end of February came, signaling the start of the Tibetan New Year. Soon, herds of yaks began to arrive from Lhasa bringing food and supplies for the upcoming festivities, including curious long trumpets that sounded like the singing of elephants, as well as strange masks resembling the skulls of the dead, colorful folk costumes, exotic musical instruments, and long strings of prayers flags that they piously attached to the roofs of their tents. Bonvalot and the others watched the goings-on with fascinated interest, enjoying how the Tibetans dropped everything in order to prepare for the upcoming festivities, which they discovered would last for five days.

Unexpectedly, Jamyang rode his horse over from the Tibetan camp to invite them to a special feast to be held in the Amban's tent. For the occasion, the interpreter had worn a red hood, and his normally staid demeanor was decidedly more festive. Even his downcast eyes had taken on a certain glow. With his slurred speech and unsteady gait they assumed Jamyang had been drinking, which he corroborated every time he opened his mouth and assaulted them with the rancid odor of *arak*.

"Come on, friendsh, don't be sh-shy," said Jamyang, beckoning them in his most insistent manner, his cheeks displaying an abnormally rosy glow. "Come to the feasht. The Amban wantsh to shee all of you."

"Thank you, but we're not in a particularly festive mood right now," said Bonvalot.

"Thish is our New Year," insisted Jamyang, his head swaying like a Chinese lantern. "It comes only onsh a year. The Amban prepared special feasht just for his guests. Come join us at once. *He won't take no for an answer.*"

All at once, Bonvalot suspected the invitation was more an order than a request. He gave Jamyang his word that they would attend the feast; then he watched the interpreter stumble back to his horse and attempt to mount after his foot got stuck in the stirrup. Two members of his entourage rushed over to rectify the situation by pushing the inebriated interpreter back into his saddle. Then they slapped the animal's rump and sent him on his way.

So the Amban was summoning them to his tent. It was not exactly what Bonvalot wanted to hear. He broke the news to Father Dedeken and Prince Henri, that the Amban was ordering them to appear for a meeting. Dutifully, they shaved for the occasion and called for their horses. Leaving Rachmed in charge, they rode across the ice to the Tibetan camp, which by now was brimming with activity. Everywhere they looked servants in festive clothing were tending to a multitude of tasks, tending fires, melting large pots of ice for water, butchering animals, and churning butter for tea. On the hillsides, the yaks that arrived from Lhasa were grazing contentedly, watched over by a group of shepherds.

The Tibetan tents reflected the festive mood in the camp. Lines of prayer flags fluttered from poles on their roofs like a fleet of tiny sailing ships, while at the center, a lone white tent stood, decorated with colorful Tibetan motifs. They learned this was the Amban's personal tent, where the feast would be held that evening. Guarding the Amban's tent were a number of stern-faced soldiers in medieval chain mail armor, feathered helmets, and matchlock rifles slung across their backs.

Just as they arrived, the Amban stepped out to greet them. He smiled at his visitors as if they were old friends he hadn't seen in years, which put them immediately on edge. He had dressed for the occasion in a voluptuous, fur-lined silk tunic with a ceremonial rounded hat, while from one ear a large silver earring dangled down to his shoulder.

Treating the travelers like honored guests instead of captives, the Amban led them into his tent, showing them their places at a low table while he took his place on a tiger skin cushion that was perched on a raised dais at the head of the table.

Looking around the tent, Bonvalot noted the presence of numerous butter lamps and Buddhist icons, including an altar which contained an image of the Buddha nestled inside a golden case. Just in front of it were seven copper cups, each containing a mixture of saffron and oil as well as various sticks of incense that burned inside porcelain teapots. On the steps leading up to the altar there were bizarre figures molded out of butter, the largest of which appeared to be a ram's head.

A short while later, servants appeared bringing trays of butter tea and sweetened cakes, which they passed around to the guests. Seizing the opportunity, Bonvalot stood up and wished the Amban a happy New Year.

Pleased, the Amban smiled and said, "*Tashi Delek*, Happy New Year to you. It is a good sign that we are spending New Year's together as it says, those who pass New Year's together are destined to become good friends."

"Thank you, Excellency," said Bonvalot. "And please understand that we harbor no ill feelings toward you. We understand that you're an honorable man, and we would be deeply honored if you considered us your friends."

The Amban's face brightened. For the next several hours he feted his guests with endless platters of food and cups of butter tea brought in by a revolving carousel of servants. But although the Amban's tone of voice and pleasant demeanor were designed to put his guests at ease, Bonvalot sensed the feast had been designed to disarm them, like a salute before an assault.

Addressing the Amban, Prince Henri said, "Your Excellency, I suppose you know we're anxious to get back on the road. How much longer must we wait until you hear back from your superiors?"

"There is nothing to worry about," said the Amban. "We will hear from them very soon. There is nothing at all for you to fear, we will supply you with all the food and supplies you require."

"Pardon me," said Bonvalot. "But would you define 'very soon'? I know from personal experience traveling all over the world that 'very soon' can mean vastly different things depending on the culture and the climate. In some places it could mean an hour, a day, or even a year."

While attempting to translate this, Jamyang choked on a piece of meat. He coughed so loudly that Bonvalot was forced to pound on his back numerous times to get him to quiet down. Nevertheless, the hacking continued for several minutes, during which time the Amban forgot the question.

Sensing this was all an elaborate ruse, Bonvalot repeated the question. This time, Jamyang burst into laughter, his body shaking so violently that tears rolled down his cheeks. Watching him, the mandarins also burst into laughter until they sounded like a pack of hyenas.

Bonvalot and Father Dedeken exchanged a worried glance. Bonvalot had assumed Jamyang's erratic behavior was on account of the alcohol he'd consumed, but now he thought otherwise. He wondered if this exhibition was meant to break down his defenses. When Jamyang finally got around to translating Bonvalot's question, the Amban also burst into laughter.

"Ha ha! Very funny," said the Amban, chuckling with delight. "My new friend is a funny man. That was a good question. I see you are no fool. Since we are friends, I shall make myself absolutely clear so there will be no misunderstandings between us. In this case, 'very soon' means approximately a week, since our chiefs will wish to consult with a high-ranking Chinese mandarin who lives a two-day journey from Lhasa. I apologize for the delay."

The Amban returned to his butter tea, leaving his guests to absorb the dreadful turn of events. Inside, Bonvalot was seething with rage. He looked at Father Dedeken, who also looked perplexed. His hands were trembling so much his butter tea spilled on the table, prompting a servant to quickly refill the cup. Then, to his horror, Dedeken sat back and began to breathe heavily. His face drained of color and his forehead broke out in a cold sweat. Bonvalot feared his Belgian companion would was going to faint.

Prince Henri whispered, "I don't care what these bastards say, we've got to get out of here. We can't go on like this. Perhaps it's time I sent a telegram to Paris. No doubt the Minister of Foreign Affairs will be useful to grease the bureaucratic wheels of these petty tyrants."

"How exactly will that be possible?" said Bonvalot, losing his temper. "Especially since the closest telegraph pole is hundreds of miles away over the Himalayas in Darjeeling? Not that these blockheads would have the slightest idea where Paris is anyway. The message would probably end up in Peking or Pune or Timbuktu. I'm convinced these bastards think we're Russian spies. No, your Highness, the Minister of Foreign Affairs is not going to get us out of this dilemma. The only ones who can save our lives is ourselves."

"And how do you propose to do that?" said Henri.

"Right now I haven't the foggiest idea," said Bonvalot.

"And what about Princess Pema? We can't just leave her behind," said Henri.

"We can bring her to Batang," said Bonvalot. "As we have no hope of reaching Lhasa. From there she can find her way to Lhasa."

"That will only put her in more danger," said Henri. "As the Amban may have spies in Batang. We must get her to Lhasa."

"Henri, your first responsibility is to save your own neck," said Father Dedeken. "Naturally, we'll do what we can for the girl, but your life comes first."

"None of that interests me anymore," said Henri. "All I care about now is saving the life of that girl," said Henri.

Bonvalot and Father Dedeken exchanged a surprised glance. Indeed, Henri was showing signs of a latent heroism that had come about in the most unexpected manner. But for now, Bonvalot still had the problem of their detainment.

"Pardon me, Excellency," said Bonvalot. "But I must object to the way in which you are forcing us to remain here. It's not the custom in our country to detain travelers against their will."

The room went silent as the translations sailed around the room.

"Please understand, my hands are tied," said the Amban. "I am merely a servant following orders."

Setting down his teacup, Bonvalot rose. "I think we've heard enough. It's late and my men are tired. I think it's time we retired to our tents."

Hearing this, the Amban hushed the audience. Lifting up two porcelain cups, he began to speak in an ominous tone.

"Let me share one final thought with you, Gabriel Bonvalot. Friendship is a beautiful thing, like two delicate porcelain cups. Seated side by side they look splendid, but if you smash them together they break into a thousand bits and pieces. Let's not have any more disagreements."

Bonvalot's stomach lurched in his chest. Father Dedeken and Prince Henri stared at the Amban's face in terror, which had turned rigid and expressionless as he set the teacups down.

Composing themselves they scrambled out of the tent, wasting no time to vacate the oppressive atmosphere. When they passed the Tibetan guards, they saluted and bowed respectfully, then all at once, a loud blaring of trumpets rang out. Peering at a nearby ridge, they saw a group of saffron-robed lamas blowing the elongated trumpets in long, deep, haunting wails that seemed to carry the listener over the highest Himalayan peaks. Nearby, another group of lamas was chanting rhythmically under a canopy of colorful prayer flags. The scene both haunted and mesmerized them.

The evening had been memorable, but it left Bonvalot feeling hopeless and despondent. They were trapped in a hostile country with no way to communicate with the outside world, and no way to escape. If they got sick and died, no one would be the wiser; the expedition would be written off as a dismal failure and their families would only be able to guess at their fate.

When they reached their tents, they collapsed on their bedrolls and fell into an exhausted sleep, the chanting of the lamas and the blowing of the trumpets still ringing in their ears.

CHAPTER 46

Bonvalot lit a cigarette and paced around the fire, lost in contemplation.

He did not know how to answer Camille's concerns. He knew they were slowly dying from mountain sickness, but he hadn't yet formulated a plan of escape. Getting past hundreds of armed Tibetan soldiers would take all the cleverness and subterfuge he could muster. And the thin air was robbing him of his ability to concentrate.

"Monsieur Bonvalot, please listen to me," said Camille, clutching her sheepskin coat tighter around her. "We're getting sicker by the day. The men are coughing without cease and complaining of painful headaches. We've got to get out of here before we succumb to pneumonia or mountain sickness. His Highness Prince Henri is coughing up blood; Parpa is too crippled to walk; Isa is delirious and too weak to work. Sooner or later they will discover Pema hiding among us, giving them every justification to imprison us. We can't continue like this. Pay those devils whatever ransom they ask for but we must get out of here."

Bonvalot whirled around. "Do you think it's as easy as that? Do you think I haven't thought of that before? If it was merely a question of money, I have plenty of gold. You don't understand, they're holding us hostage for a reason, because they don't know what else to do with us. They can't do anything without orders from Lhasa. The mandarins are nothing but useless middlemen afraid of their own shadow. We're caught in a bureaucratic trap, a *chinoiserie* of a uniquely Oriental design and the only way out of here is by using our own cunning."

"Then we must do something fast," she said. "The longer we wait, the harder it will be to save ourselves. If we don't leave within the next few days it may be too late."

Bonvalot stared at Camille's pleading eyes. He opened his mouth to speak but no words came out. He took a long swig of brandy to deaden the pain, then he wiped his mouth with the back of his hand and stared into the fire.

"Patience, my dear," said Father Dedeken, putting an arm around Camille. "Eventually the Tibetans will have to release us. The last thing these people want is a British or Russian invasion. They may be fools but they're not willing to wage war over a bunch of wastrels like us. Eventually they'll send us east to Batang, then we'll be on our way home."

"I disagree with you, Father," said Camille. "I think we're in grave danger. The Ambans intend to keep us here until we die."

She buried her face in Father Dedeken's sheepskin coat and sobbed. The kind-hearted missionary patted her on the back and tried to soothe her. "You'd better stop crying, my dear. Your tears will only freeze on your eyelashes, making it impossible to see."

Camille laughed. "How do you do it, Father? How do you keep your sense of humor while we're facing an impossible situation? You're a remarkable man indeed."

"It's because Father Dedeken sees everything through the lens of Greek mythology," said Bonvalot. "He sees your husband as the brave Odysseus gone for twenty years fighting wars, and you as Queen Penelope, the beautiful, faithful wife, pining for him."

"Is that so, Monsieur Bonvalot?" said Camille. "And what would that make you?"

"I am the Trojan Horse," said Bonvalot, holding up the brandy bottle. "The secret weapon that will get us into Lhasa."

In spite of themselves, everyone burst out laughing.

"That's a laugh," said Prince Henri, stumbling out of his tent in an obvious state of drunkenness. "I would call you Hades himself, Lord of the underworld, bringer of destruction. Why don't you admit your plan failed and we're all going to end up like those miserable camel drivers?"

Bonvalot shook his head in disgust. "I thought I told you to stop drinking."

"And I told you that what I do is none of your damn business."

"It is my business when it affects the lives of my men," said Bonvalot. "Your drinking has caused numerous accidents and near-disasters. And now with the Amban's soldiers breathing down our necks we must be even more careful. I don't need you making the situation worse with your drinking. You're acting like a bloody fool."

"I've had just about enough of you," said Henri, picking up a stick. "You've goaded me enough with your moral preachings. I challenge you to a duel."

"You're delirious. I don't want to hurt you."

"Fight, you bastard!" said Henri, swinging the club with menace. "Defend yourself you bloody poltroon."

"I suggest you put that club down and stop playing the royal bear cub, your Highness. If it's a duel you want, it's not even remotely fair."

"I consider it my duty to shut your mouth," said Henri, aiming the stick at Bonvalot's head.

"You're not serious, are you?"

"Try me."

"Then you leave me with no choice," said Bonvalot. He reached down and picked up a tent peg. Gripping it like a saber, he swung it around and struck the prince's club right out of his hand, sending it flying. The force of the jolt sent Henri staggering backward, swaying from the effects of the alcohol, then he burst out coughing. He fell to the ground and vomited, clutching his stomach in severe pain.

Camille and Princess Pema ran to his side.

"Hengli hurt," said Pema, cradling Henri with a look of distress. "It is the suffering of Samsara. He must learn the path to true liberation from the Wheel."

"Really Monsieur Bonvalot, this is shameful behavior," said Camille. "What about noblesse oblige?" She handed Prince Henri a handkerchief while she and Princess Pema tried to get him to a feet.

"I won't forget this," said Henri, erupting in a fit of coughing. "I'll make sure the Geographical Society hears about this. I'll make sure they throw you out."

"I was just trying to keep Henri from killing himself," said Bonvalot. "All this excitement at high altitude has a deleterious effect on his lungs and my patience."

Before Camille could respond, Rachmed raced toward them shouting that a group of Tibetan horsemen was heading their way. Camille spirited Pema back into the tent and closed the flap shut.

They watched the soldiers ride stiffly to camp, then dismount. Among the entourage was Jamyang the interpreter and two other soldiers who were bringing a spacious new tent. The caravan men watched in disbelief as they unfolded it and helped set it up.

To everyone's relief, the new shelter was a welcome respite from the terrible cold and wind, but before the soldiers returned to their camp, Jamyang left them with a foreboding message. He told Bonvalot that the messenger from Lhasa had still not arrived, but they were expecting him any day.

"I urge you to be patient," said Jamyang. "If you cause the Amban any trouble, he will have no choice but to force you to return the way you came. He commands a powerful army reinforced by hundreds of foot soldiers that have sworn to fight all the enemies of Buddhism. To win Lord Buddha's favor the commanders have already prostrated themselves before the Dalai Lama during his Great Prayer session while two columns of monks paraded through the town with a skull symbolizing evil from the West. The whole town of Lhasa has been fortified like an army encampment. You cannot possibly overtake such powerful magic with your meager forces."

"Listen to me, Monsieur Jamyang," said Bonvalot. "The young prince is very ill. We must evacuate him from this high ground as quickly as possible. He desperately wants to meet your Dalai Lama and sign a peace treaty between our two nations. I entreat you in the strongest possible manner to bring the prince a disguise that will allow him to ride into Lhasa so he can prostrate himself before his holiness and present him with gifts of honor from the people of France. Please do not fail us."

Jamyang nodded thoughtfully.

"I see you are men of honor. Perhaps something can be arranged," he said. "But first I must consult our Oracle."

"There's no time to consult your Oracle," said Bonvalot. "The prince is getting weaker by the day. There's no time to lose. Please help us. If you do, I will pay you in silver ingots." As he said this, Bonvalot jangled a sack of ingots attached to his belt. "Gifts for your Dalai Lama, of course."

"Of course, said Jamyang, smiling. "Very well, I will consider your request." Jamyang, bowed with great reverence. "You will hear from me soon."

Then, without another word, the interpreter mounted his horse and trotted back to the Tibetan camp.

"Do you think he will help us?" said Father Dedeken.

"I don't know," said Bonvalot.

"But tell me something," said Father Dedeken. "What kind of business is this sending a royal prince to Lhasa without an official escort? He might be attacked by a gang of robbers or killed at the point of a sword. It would be very irresponsible to send Henri out on his own."

"The disguise is not for Prince Henri," said Bonvalot.

Father Dedeken looked confused.

"I have a plan for getting one of us out of here," said Bonvalot. "But no one, especially not Jamyang, needs to know who that someone is."

Father Dedeken nodded when it finally dawned on him what Bonvalot was planning to do. The two men glanced over at Prince Henri, who was sitting by the fire clutching his chest as he flung a deck of cards one by one into the roaring flames.

That night after supper, Jamyang rode back to camp under cover of darkness, bringing with him a Buddhist pilgrim disguise which consisted of a grey peasant costume, a greasy sheepskin coat, leather boots, and fur caps.

Jamyang displayed the items with pride. "With this disguise your prince will soon be kneeling before the Dalai Lama. Tomorrow, the prince and a servant of his choice will pretend to go hunting in a distant, agreed-upon location. There they will find horses. They may ride all night and spend the following day in an isolated tent where he and his servant will change into their Tibetan disguises. Later, in the evening, they will ride into Lhasa where they will be met by a procession of lamas who will escort them to the Potala Palace to greet the Dalai Lama and sign the peace treaty, but they must leave Lhasa before dawn. The entire process must be kept as secret as possible in order not to antagonize the Chinese authorities. This is the best I can do."

"Splendid," said Bonvalot, beaming. "May the Buddha reward you for your efforts."

Jamyang bowed low and left as quietly as he had come. Later, Bonvalot and Father Dedeken sat strategizing in his tent.

"That settles it," said Bonvalot. "Tomorrow one of us is getting out of this hellhole."

After the caravan men had gone to sleep, Bonvalot explained to Prince Henri that he had formulated a plan to help Princess Pema reach Lhasa under the noses of the Amban's soldiers. Bonvalot, Prince Henri, and Princess Pema would rise before dawn with Pema disguised as a Mongolian servant. They would announce their intention to go hunting and saddle up three horses, making sure to pack the Buddhist pilgrim costume in Pema's saddle bag. Once they reached the isolated tent, Pema would change into the pilgrim costume and continue on to Lhasa while the two of them would return to camp, explaining that their Mongolian servant had run away with one of the horses.

"I cannot sanction this plan," said Henri, noticeably distressed. "It's far too risky. We have been entrusted with spiriting Pema safely to Lhasa and that's what I intend to do. And if that's not possible, I intend to marry this girl."

"Come now," said Bonvalot. "You can't be serious."

"I am serious," said Henri. "I finally meet a woman I'm not tongue-tied around, who doesn't care what I say or if I'm witty or not, or doesn't care if I act like a bloody fool. For the first time I don't have to worry that something I do will end up in the newspapers and cause a scandal. She's the woman I've been waiting for all my life."

"Be reasonable. Stop thinking about yourself for a change. She's the daughter of the Panchen Lama. You have to do what's right for her and her country no matter what your personal feelings are. She's an important figurehead among the Tibetans. She's a Buddhist princess for heaven's sake."

"Then why do you propose to send her out there to the wolves?" said Henri, his face reddening. "What if somebody recognizes her? She could be arrested and sent into exile for the second time."

"Have you got a better idea?" said Bonvalot.

"Yes, I do," said Henri. "We simply *demand* they permit us to ride to Lhasa. This involuntary detention has gone on long enough. It's an outrage. We must protest it in the strongest possible manner."

"Now you're talking foolish," said Bonvalot. "These people don't care about France. They've never heard of it for goodness sake. I'm sure they think we're a bunch of frauds. If we're going to get out of this mess, it will be by our wits alone."

"Permit me, your Highness, said Father Dedeken. "Outrage or not, we have no permission to travel in their country and they have every right to detain us. We are trespassers, after all. This may be our best chance to help the golden bird flee to Lhasa."

"So what you're saying is I should give up the love of my life?" said Henri.

"What I'm saying is, let Pema follow her rightful destiny, which is to assume her position as the Dalai Lama's personal maidservant and tutor. This is, as the Buddhists say, her karma. Perhaps it was your destiny to help her achieve her rightful place."

"Alright, I'll go through with your plan," said Henri. "But I believe you're both wrong, and I'm willing to wager five francs that this will all end in disaster."

The next morning, while it was still dark, Prince Henri, Bonvalot, and Princess Pema, dressed as a Mongolian servant, crept out of their tents. They saddled their horses in utter silence and just as they were about to mount, ten soldiers pounced on them.

"You there. Where do you think you're going?" said their chief, waving his matchlock in their faces.

"Oh, Good Morning," said Bonvalot, smiling. "It's such a beautiful day we decided to go out for a nice leisurely ride and do a bit of shooting."

"Do not try to run away," said the soldier chief. "We will follow you wherever you go. If you try to enter Lhasa without permission, they will slit our throats and feed us to the vultures."

"That would be a pity, indeed," said Bonvalot, mounting his horse. He gave the signal to Prince Henri and Pema, who also mounted their horses. "Well, what do you say gentlemen, shall we go then?"

Kicking his horse's flank, Bonvalot galloped away followed close behind by Prince Henri and Pema, leaving the Tibetan soldiers red-faced and fuming.

The runaways sped across the Tibetan desert, kicking up clouds of sand in their quest to reach the isolated tent where Pema would assume her new disguise. After they had gone several miles, they found the tent which, to their relief, was watched over by a lone lama who sat spinning his prayer wheel and meditating, waiting to receive the golden bird. Wasting no time, Pema jumped off her horse and ran inside to change into her pilgrim costume. As Henri watched her transform into a lowly Buddhist pilgrim his heart sank. from beautiful gold-decked princess to lowly pilgrim his heart sank.

"I can't leave you," said Henri.

"I must go, Hengli, it is my destiny," said Pema. "I was born for a noble and virtuous task. To achieve greatness one most often forgo one's own desires."

"Goodbye my love," said Henri.

"Goodbye Hengli," said Pema, looking at the prince with adoring eyes. "Goodbye forever."

Henri cupped her head in his hands and kissed her tenderly on the lips. "I will never forget you."

"I will never forget you, Hengli," said Pema. "The Oracle said we were together in our past lives and will be together in the future, but in this life we were only destined to meet in our present incarnation for a brief moment. This was our karma, our destiny."

"Then I shall wait for you," said Henri, gazing into her eyes. "As long as it takes and I shall have no other love before you."

"I have loved you before and I will love you again when the time comes," said Pema. "Go now Hengli before soldiers come. Save your own life."

"Godspeed my love," said Henri, kissing her forehead.

Pema caressed his cheek and looked lovingly in his eyes.

"May the Buddha bless you, Golden Prince."

He kissed her one last time, then he turned and ran outside to find Bonvalot scanning the horizon with his spyglass, sweat pouring from his forehead.

"We've got to get out of here quick," said Bonvalot. "The soldiers are coming. We can't let them find Pema. We must steer them away from here."

"I can't leave her behind," said Henri.

"You can't stay with her either," said Bonvalot. "It will only guarantee her capture. Don't worry, she's in good hands. The lama will get her safely to Lhasa. Soon she will be at the Dalai Lama's side assuming her rightful place in the Potala Palace. We helped her achieve her destiny, surely that should earn us some karmic favors. It's time to set the golden bird free."

"Bonvalot, I have to admit, you're not a bad sort after all."

After one final glimpse of Princess Pema standing in the opening of the tent, Henri jumped in the saddle and the two fugitives galloped away. Soon, a stampede of hoof beats rose from the frost-covered plain behind them. Glancing over his shoulder, Bonvalot caught sight of five Tibetan soldiers chasing after them, their faces full of terror at the consequences they would face for allowing three foreigners to escape through their fingers.

The soldiers soon gained on the runaways. They galloped swiftly beside them, yelling, shrieking, and waving their arms in an attempt to force them to stop and turn around.

Out of desperation, one of the Tibetans lunged at Prince Henri's reins, but the agile prince just pummeled him on the back and shoved him away. Kicking his horse's sides, Henri urged his mount to go faster, anything to lose the soldiers in his wake. Undeterred, the Tibetans galloped faster, refusing to allow a group of impudent foreigners to trample the holy city and cause their own painful deaths.

It was only after they heard the blast of gunfire and the sound of bullets whizzing past their ears that Prince Henri and Bonvalot saw the futility of going any further. There was no hope they would reach Lhasa through a hail of bullets. They brought their horses to a halt and delivered a parting shot at their Tibetan captors before trudging back to camp.

"Where is your Mongol servant?" said the chief soldier, eyeing them suspiciously.

"He ran off with one of our horses," said Bonvalot.

"You let him go?" said the soldier. "You should have punished him for stealing your horse."

"I didn't have the heart to," said Bonvalot. "I set him free."

"Strange foreigners," said the soldier, shaking his head. "But don't worry. Your servant won't get very far. We will find him and send him to prison. If he is found guilty, he will be sealed inside a sack, beaten with sticks, and then thrown into a river to drown."

"You murderers!" said Prince Henri, gesturing to the Tibetans with contempt. "Is that all you know how to do? Is human life so worthless to you? Does it give you great pleasure keeping your holy city out of reach of foreigners? Do you think a bunch of unarmed foreigners are going to steal your precious city? Are you that stupid? Or maybe your holy city is so filthy you can't bear the idea of foreigners seeing it for themselves? What's the matter with you numskulls anyway? Are you all just a bunch of damned bird brains."

But the Tibetan soldiers only shook their heads and repeated the same mantra over and over, "Foreigners may not enter Lhasa."

Feeling the effects of the strenuous exercise, Prince Henri clutched his chest in pain. "I don't know who the bigger fool is, me for thinking I could outrun those dolts, or them for thinking I'm a Russian mercenary."

Bonvalot patted him on the back. "Be grateful it worked. Soon, the daughter of the Panchen Lama will be riding into Lhasa to greet the Dalai Lama and it will be all because of you. You saved her life and helped fulfill her destiny. Perhaps all of this was prophesied years ago and we are the fulfillment of that prophecy."

"I care nothing about prophesies," said Henri. "I was in love with the girl and now I've lost her forever."

Bonvalot looked at him thoughtfully. "All that matters now is that she's safe. But you still owe me five francs."

CHAPTER 47

The messenger from Lhasa never arrived.

Watching the men deteriorate from their involuntary imprisonment drove Bonvalot to his breaking point. They had to break out of their prison or risk dying on the Roof of the World.

Leaving the prince to rest in his tent, Bonvalot selected five men, Father Dedeken, Rachmed, Timur, Abdullah, and Mahmud, and instructed them to load their weapons, then they set off across the field of ice to confront the Amban. Before he left, his eyes met Camille's, who was watching them from the entrance of her tent, her eyes wide with fear. She mouthed the words *good luck* and Bonvalot nodded in return. That was when he realized he was utterly and entirely infatuated with the spirited lady explorer.

When they reached the Amban's tent, they strode up to the guards and demanded to see him. When the Amban appeared, he hid his surprise behind a wide grin and an expression of utter joy at seeing them, another one of his chicaneries. The Amban, they discovered later, had no intention of helping them.

"How happy I am to see my friends," said the Amban, clapping his hands together. "Come inside. Let's have a cup of butter tea and talk."

As soon as they were inside, Bonvalot pushed the remaining guards out and closed the flap.

"We didn't come here for a friendly chat," said Bonvalot, thrusting the muzzle of his rifle into the Amban's chest. "Listen to me. You know perfectly well we're not Russian or English and the order from Peking has nothing to do with us. Since all you care about is hiding your precious Lhasa from the rest of the world, you can keep it. Two of our men are dead. The prince and others are suffering from mountain sickness, and our remaining animals are on the verge of dying. You've been holding us against our will for ten days now. Enough is enough. I came here to tell you we have every intention of getting out, even if it means we have to resort to force. The Russian expedition will be here any day and when they arrive, there will be much bloodshed, and the blood will be on your hands. Then you will have to give a full account to Peking."

The Amban's nose twitched. His jaw clenched as he stared at the impudent foreigners. Left with no choice, the Amban was finally forced to admit the truth.

"Yes, it's true I haven't been entirely honest with you," said the Amban. "But put yourself in my position. What was I to do? During our New Year's celebration, all government business shuts down. Everything is devoted solely to our religious ceremonies, so I was forced to stall for time. Eventually, the messenger will come, but I have no control over that. I'm just as much a victim of circumstances as you are."

Bonvalot pointed the rifle at the Amban's throat. "I'm tired of your pathetic excuses. We're getting out of this hellhole and you're going to help us. Understand?"

"Of course, of course," said the Amban. "I'll do everything in my power to help you. But you must have more patience. Two more days is all I ask. What's two days between friends?"

"You lying little wastrel," said Bonvalot. "What's two days? My men are dying as we speak. Some of them are wheezing, vomiting, coughing up blood. *We don't have two days.*"

The Amban pushed the muzzle away from his throat. "Gentlemen, now is not the time to lose our temper. I promise you that in two days' time you'll have everything you need. On that you have my word. I swear by the Lord Buddha."

Bonvalot stared at the Amban's ingratiating face without flinching. When he saw the futility of his position, he lowered his rifle. "How do I know I can trust you?"

"Because if I wasn't speaking the truth, you would already be marching back to Lake Namtso under armed escort."

Bonvalot looked at the others, but in their eyes he only saw doubt and worry. Left with no choice, he agreed to the Amban's terms and they returned to camp under a black cloud.

When they returned, Camille jumped up from her seat by the fire and raced toward them.

"What happened?" she said. "Are they going to let us go?"

Bonvalot sank down by the fire. "Two days. He said we could leave in two days."

She looked skeptical. "Do you believe him?"

"Of course not," he said. "It's just another one of his ruses."

"We can't wait another two days," she said. "Prince Henri is getting sicker by the minute. Isa and Parpa can barely stand. We must leave tomorrow. And what about my husband? Did you ask the Amban about him?"

"I didn't have a chance but Abdullah conducted his own investigation. He approached some Tibetan servants and inquired about a European man. He found out that a caravan with a European man passed this way many months ago. They said it was heading to a lamasery in a place called Sok."

"*Sok*? Where is that?"

"That's what I intend to find out."

Two days later, they were sitting in their tents playing cards when they heard the sound of bells ringing. Peering outside, they saw a procession of horses and yaks heading toward the Tibetan camp. Loaded on the backs of the yaks were folded-up tents, cooking utensils, and other provisions. Behind the animals was a veritable army of servants and soldiers marching in procession. When Bonvalot asked the Tibetan guards what the commotion was about, they said it was the vanguard of two important officials who were arriving from Lhasa, a high-ranking lama and the Grand Amban.

Within hours, the officials had summoned Bonvalot to a meeting in their tent. Taking Father Dedeken and Abdullah along, Bonvalot set out for the Tibetan camp, but this time they were led to a different tent, a larger and more ornate one than either of the previous ones. Inside the tent they found a raised dais on which the Ambans were holding court. Dozens of butter lamps were lit up and the fragrance of incense perfumed the air.

The first official that greeted them was the high-ranking lama. Although in his late fifties, the Grand Lama still retained the handsomeness of his youth, with fine, aristocratic features, a bronzed complexion, and lively black eyes. He wore a terra-cotta monk's robe over the top of his yellow silk caftan, and a rounded mandarin helmet. The only thing that marred his appearance was a long, braided goatee that bounced from his chin every time he spoke. It was this peculiar appendage that prompted Bonvalot to dub the lama 'Rat Tail.'

The other official was the Grand Amban, a bent, stooped, older man in his sixties who suffered from arthritis and overwork. He wore the official costume of the Empire of the Great Qing, which included a headdress that was so large and bulbous, Prince Henri referred to him as 'Balloon Head.' During all their exchanges with the various mandarins and Ambans, Bonvalot learned that Lhasa was a hotbed of intrigue, with each official mistrusting the other, and each one fearing the false accusations of his rival. With power so highly divided and coveted, it was no wonder that those who possessed it guarded it very jealously.

After a preliminary exchange of pleasantries, the Grand Amban explained that the Grand Lama had come in the name of the Dalai Lama, and he had come on behalf of Nomakan, a high-ranking official in Lhasa. The Grand Amban repeated the laws of his country, which stated that no foreigner was allowed to enter Tibet, and under no circumstances would they be given permission to enter Lhasa. In voices that were both solemn and threatening, the Grand Amban and the Grand Lama ordered Bonvalot's party to turn around and go back from where they came. Nevertheless, they added with utmost courtesy that they would supply the caravan with all the food and animals they needed to compete the journey.

Bonvalot shook his head. "Never. We refuse to go back the way we came. It's tantamount to suicide. Your mandarins have already detained us for fifteen days at an altitude that is causing great damage to my men. His Highness the Prince is ill as are several other members of my expedition. The only place I will agree to travel to is Batang. From there I calculate it will take us three months to reach the sea, but if you force us to return to the Ili Province, it will take us six months or more, which is completely out of the question."

The officials waited for the official translation of Bonvalot's speech, after which they conferred with each other in hushed tones.

Finally, the Grand Amban spoke: "We will take your point under consideration. Is there anything else you'd like to add?"

"No, Excellency, that's all for now," said Bonvalot. "The only thing I ask is that you take my request seriously. I'm responsible for the lives of my men, a duty I don't take lightly."

"Very well, you may return to your camp," said the Grand Amban. "We will send you our decision shortly."

Once more, Bonvalot, Father Dedeken, and Abdullah returned to camp. When they arrived, everyone demanded a full report, but there was no news. Bonvalot told them they would just have to sit and wait.

After two days with no response, the men grew lethargic and despondent. Prince Henri had completely lost his appetite. Listless and dispirited over the loss of Pema, and suffering from the effects of mountain sickness, he was confined to his bed with dizziness, shortness of breath, a nosebleed, and a persistent, hacking cough. Abdullah wailed every night about the fate of his beloved boy, Aziz, and Mahmud had taken to prostrating themselves in prayer several times a day, his clothes and face so covered in grime and dirt he looked as pitiful as a street beggar.

Parpa had weakened to the point he could scarcely leave his sheepskin bedroll, and the formerly robust Timur had shrunken to just a shadow of his former self. The normally stoic Isa was a walking skeleton, with cheekbones that stuck out and haunted eyes that had sunken into their sockets; his beard was now almost completely white. Everyone feared he would be the next to go.

Watching his men deteriorate spurred Bonvalot to action. He ordered that his horse be brought to him and he saluted his men before galloping off across the field of ice.

Returning to the Amban, Bonvalot demanded to move his caravan to lower ground since the prince's life was at stake.

"I'm very sorry but I cannot give you permission to leave the premises," said the Amban. "Please understand. We wish to foster good relations with the *Fagwo*. We look upon you as our brothers and friends, but until now, we had never heard of the *Fagwo*. The only countries we knew of were China, Russia, and England, so until we receive further information about the *Fagwo*, we cannot give you permission to travel to Batang. I am awaiting new orders from Lhasa, which should take at least another six days."

"Six days!" said Bonvalot, fuming. "We don't *have* six days. We're talking about the lives of my men. Have you no respect for human life or is this another one of your tricks? Are you trying to slowly kill us?"

The Amban's face darkened; his jaw set and his eyebrows narrowed. "There's no need for anger. I'm helping you as much as I can. Come back tomorrow. The Grand Amban will see you then."

Bonvalot stormed out of the Amban's tent, so filled with rage he kicked one of the altars, sending golden Buddhas and porcelain vases filled with incense crashing to the ground.

The next day, Bonvalot and Father Dedeken saddled the two remaining horses and rode back to the Tibetan camp, determined to not leave until they had received a favorable resolution to their dilemma.

The Amban escorted them to the Grand Amban's tent and explained their request to the dignitary, after which Father Dedeken added his own personal request.

"Excellency," said Father Dedeken. "If your Buddhist religion is indeed compassionate, you must bestow on us this great favor of saving the lives of our companions who may not be with us much longer. In the Catholic religion, of which I am a priest, it is our duty to do anything possible to save the lives of the sick. Please have mercy on us and extend us the same favor."

After listening to the translation, the Grand Amban grunted and rejected the request with a dismissive wave of his hand.

Burning with anger, Bonvalot pointed at the officials. "How dare you refuse us? You call yourselves great leaders, yet you refuse to take responsibility for such a small request? Now I see you for what you really are: two slaves dressed up in fancy clothes. You call us your friends, yet if this is how you treat your friends, then I pity your enemies. After numerous requests, you refuse to allow us to evacuate a place that is slowly freezing us to death. I've hat it with you. I've already decided to join the Russian expedition so the next time we meet, I will be armed to the teeth and prepared to face you cowards in battle."

When the Ambans heard the translation, their faces paled and their mouths dropped open. Bonvalot stared at them with disdain, keeping his hand hovering over his revolver.

After he had recovered somewhat, the Grand Amban said, "You've made your point. Go back to your camp and pack up your things. Tomorrow you may head to a lower camp where you will wait further orders."

Bonvalot stared defiantly at the Ambans and then stormed out of the tent.

CHAPTER 48

The next day, the Amban and a large entourage rode their horses over to their camp. They informed Bonvalot that they would supply him with five horses, thirty yaks, and sacks of flour, beans, and rice. As soon as they were ready to go, added the Amban, they would provide them with a guide who would lead them to a lower camp. As much as Bonvalot wanted to believe him, fear and doubt gnawed at him.

When Bonvalot told Prince Henri the news, color returned to the young man's face. He sat up in bed and asked for a cup of tea. Not long afterwards, Henri was almost back to his former self, demanding his fine porcelain, his Dom Perignon, and his last tin of caviar.

When the caravan men heard that they would soon be heading to lower ground, they rejoiced. They wasted no time packing up the baggage and loading it on the backs of the newly-supplied yaks. This procedure took a long time as loading yaks turned out to be far more dangerous and difficult than loading camels since yaks are by nature more violent, given to sudden kicks and jumps. But despite the hardship of switching to yaks, the caravan men made progress and Bonvalot could see relief etched on their lined faces. After enduring so many privations during the last few months, he hoped the next stage of the journey would signal the start of their long-awaited return home.

As soon as the tents were taken down and piled onto the backs of the yaks, the caravan started up again, following the Tibetan guides supplied by the Amban. After they had traveled about twelve miles over rough terrain, they stopped along the banks of a river that Bonvalot calculated to be seven hundred feet lower than the Dam Pass. Breathing in the fresh air, everyone felt immediate relief which soon gave way to shock and alarm when it dawned on them that further down the valley, several suspicious-looking tents had already been set up.

Upon further investigation, they discovered that one of the tents belonged to the Amban, and that he had arrived the previous day and was anxiously expecting them. All at once Bonvalot suspected foul play. His heart began pounding and he shook with anger. After they unloaded the yaks, they learned that the Amban had prepared a special feast in their honor. The idea of eating with the Amban sickened Bonvalot. Soon, a group of Tibetan guards with vaguely familiar faces was stationed around their camp, keeping an eye on their every move. Seeing their freedom descend into imprisonment sent a cloud of gloom spreading among the caravan men. Something fishy indeed was going on, indeed.

When they awoke the next day, the men were even more convinced that the Ambans had hoodwinked them. Every time Bonvalot or one of his emissaries attempted to speak to the Amban, he was turned away by the guards, who claimed his Excellency was attending to more important matters. Later, when the Grand Amban trotted into the Tibetan camp together with a huge escort that included the same servants, the same tents, the same equipment from the previous camp, they knew the Tibetans had no intention of ever setting them free. Bonvalot broke out in a cold sweat when he realized the Ambans had duped him.

Sitting in his tent with Rachmed, Prince Henri, and Father Dedeken, Bonvalot tried to make sense of the new situation.

"We're back to the same old story," said Bonvalot, peering through the tent flap at the circus-like cavalcade of the Grand Amban's entourage. "We're their prisoners once again."

"I for one would love to tell those contemptible bastards what I think of their hospitality," said Prince Henri, lighting a cigarette. "One well-placed insult would curl the Amban's toes right in his funny, little upturned boots. I would say: Sir, you have the manners of an overly excitable yak and the speaking habits of a deranged camel. I find your manner to be unctuous and possibly scandalous, and whatever standard you set for cleanliness, it's not one I care for. Your tea makes me gag as I don't recall butter being an acceptable ingredient in tea anywhere in polite society. And though it pains me to point out, your ears have all the charm of an elephant and your gait reminds me of an intoxicated penguin. I imagine it takes a rather shocking amount of fortitude, ignorance or bravery to look in the mirror every morning."

Bonvalot sighed. "That's all well and good Henri, but it doesn't solve our problem. It might end up making things worse."

"We must protest this treatment at once," said Father Dedeken. "We can't let them get away with this."

"Really? And who do we protest to?" said Henri with disgust. "Their superiors in Lhasa? Even if we wanted to, they refuse to let us go there."

"I can see how this is all going to end," said Rachmed. "No matter how many times we complain they will keep feeding us the same lies, the same excuses, the same runaround. If we want to get out of this place of torment we must resort to more drastic action."

"Such as?" said Bonvalot, peering at his fearless Uzbek companion.

Rachmed folded his arms across his chest. "We must outsmart our enemy. The only thing these devils respect is force. It's time we let our weapons do the talking."

"That's sounds like my old friend Rachmed," said Bonvalot, his eyes glowing with mischief.

"I have an idea," said Father Dedeken. "The Amban said we should receive a response from Lhasa by the fifteenth of March. For now we have plenty of food and fodder to hold us over. When the deadline comes and nothing happens, let's give our friends a fireworks display the likes of which they've never seen. Loud enough to be heard in Peking."

"I like what I'm hearing," said Bonvalot. "It's time we gave those blockheads a little French hospitality—a Bastille Day celebration they'll never forget."

When the appointed day came, Bonvalot paced around the camp like a caged tiger. Rachmed kept watch with the spyglass, but no sign came from the Tibetan camp. As always, they felt the peering eyes of the Tibetan guards watching over their every move. Finally, at midday, a messenger from the Tibetan camp arrived with an invitation for Bonvalot, Prince Henri, and Father Dedeken to dine with the three Ambans in their tent that evening. Was this the news they were desperately waiting for? In preparation for the meeting, Bonvalot brought along a silver watch and a few other gifts for the Ambans, hoping to seal their friendship and this alleged Franco-Tibetan alliance with a show of good will.

Dinner was a sumptuous affair with numerous strange and exotic dishes containing hard-to-get ingredients such as dates from India, peaches from Ladakh, jujubes from Batang, berries from Lanzhou, and edible seaweed and shellfish from the coast. During the meal, Bonvalot was expecting to hear some news about Lhasa, but not one word was mentioned. The servants poured cup after cup of butter tea and served steaming platters of fragrant food which the guests savored with chopsticks, but not once did anyone mention anything about the messenger from Lhasa.

Running out of patience, Prince Henri leaned over and whispered to Bonvalot, "This is obviously a delaying tactic. Say something before we miss our chance."

"What shall I tell them?" whispered Bonvalot.

"Tell them that if they don't release us we'll shoot their heads off."

"That's getting straight to the point," said Bonvalot.

Setting down his chopsticks, Bonvalot said, "Excellencies, we were hoping to hear some good news from Lhasa. Has the messenger arrived yet?"

The tent quieted down. After a few tense minutes, the Grand Amban cleared his throat and said, "As you know, we are your friends, and this is why our king has decided to allow you to cross Tibet to reach Batang. But since we must adhere to Chinese law, you must wait for your Chinese passports to arrive, which releases us from all responsibility toward you. We have sent for the documents, but so far they have not yet arrived. Believe me, if it was up to me, we would grant you all your wishes, but bureaucracy is a fact of life so we ask you to remain patient. Our ways are not like yours. We do not believe in hurrying business matters, but I assure you that the documents will be arriving any day now. In the meanwhile, we are under orders to detain you."

Bonvalot felt his neck growing hot with anger.

"That's interesting," he said. "You never mentioned anything about Chinese passports before. This certainly is news to us. It seems your story changes every day. One day it's just a matter of waiting for permission to continue to Batang. Another day you say we need a Chinese passport. Frankly, I'm a little tired of this rigmarole and I don't believe anything you say anymore. And now that I see you are no longer keeping your word, then I shall have to keep mine. By tomorrow noon we are leaving, and if the Chinese wish to interfere with us, that's our business and not yours. And since you call yourselves our friends, I ask you now, will you or will you not sell us thirty horses?"

Flabbergasted, the Ambans stared at Bonvalot.

Without waiting for a reply, Bonvalot stood up.

"Then I believe it's time to say goodnight, gentlemen."

As Bonvalot and his companions walked out, not a sound could be heard coming from inside the Amban's tent.

Later, after they returned to their tent, something began to trouble Bonvalot. He started pacing back and forth.

"What the devil's the matter?" said Prince Henri. "Why are you pacing like that?"

"Something he said keeps bothering me," said Bonvalot.

"What is it?" said Father Dedeken.

"It was the way they brought up the issue of the Chinese Passports again. They're always bringing up some roadblock or another to keep us at their mercy. And when we complain about the delays, they just urge us to have patience. Something is wrong here. Something is very wrong. They're lying to us. Everything they say is full of deception."

All of a sudden, Bonvalot stopped pacing.

"Force. That's it, *force*. I have to go back and show these scoundrels we mean business, even if it means resorting to force. These warlords only understand threats of violence."

"Let me do it," said Father Dedeken, standing up. "That way if I fail you can always say I acted alone. If I get arrested, I don't want to bring doom down on Prince Henri and Camille."

Bonvalot shook his head. "I can't let you risk yourself. I dragged you into this mess. The least I owe you is a safe exit. I have to do it."

Bonvalot reached for a box of ammunition, but Dedeken grabbed it out of his hand.

"Not this time," said Father Dedeken. "I've already decided I'm going to do it, and you can't talk me out of it."

Bonvalot stared into the spectacled eyes of Father Dedeken and slowly broke into a grin.

"I see the resolve in your eyes, Father," said Bonvalot. "Very well. Here's what you should do. March right back into the Amban's tent and demand thirty horses right away. If he hesitates in any way, or if he refuses to help outright, or if he brings up the issue of Chinese passports again, tell him we've already made up our minds to join the Russian expedition. If they wave you away, show them you mean business by shooting a few holes in the tent. Teach those devils a memorable lesson about French pride when we're pushed to our limits."

Father Dedeken laughed. "Does that include Belgian pride?"

"By Jove you've got it!"

After loading his revolver, Dedeken stealthily made his way back to the Tibetan camp.

CHAPTER 49

He rode across the field of ice with only one thought in mind: to gain their freedom. Father Dedeken dismounted, pushed past the guards, and marched in front of the Ambans.

"You bastards! We've had enough of your lies. I'm warning you, we intend to blast our way out of here and join the Russian expedition that's headed this way."

The Ambans were rattled. Their eyebrows rose in surprise and their faces dropped by several inches. They squirmed and fidgeted in their seats as the droning of the prayer wheels came to an abrupt end.

"There's no need for violence," said the Amban, after he had composed himself. "Remember, we are your friends."

"You are detaining us against our will. That's not exactly a show of friendship. Now we have decided to join our *other* friends, the Russians."

"You have invaded our territory," said the Amban, taken aback. "Therefore you must now subjugate yourselves to our laws. It is not our custom to rush business. We attend to all matters with great ceremony; we pray fervently and await signs from Lord Buddha as to how to proceed."

"The lives of our men are at stake," said Father Dedeken. "We don't have time to wait for heavenly signs. We are presently loading up our weapons and preparing to fight."

All at once, the Ambans relented. With eyes full of fear they offered to supply the caravan with horses, yaks, anything they needed for their journey, but this time Dedeken shook his head.

"I'm tired of your empty promises," he said, then he pointed his finger at them. "You have behaved treacherously with us. You've lied to us numerous occasions and now it's too late to work out a compromise. My French companions are fed up with your deceit and they're determined to join the Russians when they invade your holy city. The next time we meet, let it be on the battlefield."

To drive his point home, Dedeken withdrew his revolver and shot a few holes in the tent. The Ambans cried out in alarm but before they could speak, Dedeken turned and stormed out.

The threat threw the Ambans into a state of panic. Early the next morning they sent a messenger to Father Dedeken, inviting him to a special meeting in the Amban's tent. Before Dedeken left, Bonvalot instructed him to raise the stakes.

"Make them think they need *us* more than we need *them*," said Bonvalot, who chuckled as drank his tea.

When he entered the tent, the Amban rose and greeted him like an old friend, smiling and clasping his hands together as if they were long lost relatives; then he invited the missionary to sit down.

"I have good news to tell you," said the Amban, showing a mouthful of large teeth. "After giving the matter considerable thought, we've decided to allow you to leave your current camp and relocate to a place called Samda, which is warmer, and much lower in elevation. There you will find much grass, juniper trees, and even corn for your animals. You may set up camp there and wait for further instructions from Lhasa. Naturally, we will provide you with all the horses, yaks, and provisions you need to reach there, and we'll even accompany you, and provide guides who can show you a safe route to Batang, a route that not even the Chinese know about, so you can be assured they will not bother you. From there, you will be free to go as you please."

Father Dedeken shook his head. "I'm very sorry, Excellency, but it's too late for that. We've already made up our minds to join the Russian expedition. As we speak, my leader is preparing our arsenal. Perhaps I should warn you that Russia and France are closely aligned, and once General Pevtsov hears how treacherously you have dealt with us, there will be hell to pay. And all your diplomatic finesse and fancy words won't save your necks against men who are convinced you're nothing but a pack of liars. As it stands now, you need us more than we need you. Only we can get you out of this mess. One simple letter written by Prince Henri d'Orléans, who you are now holding captive, will guarantee that Pevtsov and his soldiers don't ransack your precious holy city. But after the way you have treated us, you don't deserve a letter written by his Highness. I suggest you think about that."

After Jamyang had finished translating, the Amban's jaw dropped. He tried to compose himself, but his face looked like bile was about to pour forth. Having made his point, Father Dedeken picked himself up and turned to leave, but the Amban recovered just in time to race over and grasp his arm. Like a thief who was caught red-handed, he confessed everything.

"Please come back," said the Amban. "Yes, I admit everything you said is true. We have not been entirely honest with you, but we had a valid reason for behaving as we did. While it's true our superiors in Lhasa knew you were not part of the Russian expedition, our scouts were convinced that during your stay in the Dam Pass, the Russians would arrive and make trouble for us. Left with no choice, we used this Franco-Tibetan alliance as a ruse to scare away the Russians. Peking warned us about a potential invasion. If you were in our position, you would have done no different."

Father Dedeken pulled his arm out of the Amban's grasp.

"You cunning little fox," he said with disgust. "You detained us against our will and risked our lives by keeping us prisoner at 16,000 feet so you could use Prince Henri as a political pawn. That is an outrage."

"Yes, yes, I admit it's true," said the Amban, turning colors. "But we always considered you as our friends. Please believe me. All I ask now is that you stay here with us a few days more so His Holiness, the Dalai Lama can send you some presents as a show of good faith. Do not leave in your state of anger and bring shame down on us."

"It's too late," said Dedeken making no attempt to hide his revulsion. "We've had enough of you. We're leaving tomorrow. Goodbye."

"Stop!" said the Amban. "Don't do anything hasty you might regret."

Dedeken turned to face him. "Our minds are made up. We're joining the Russians and we're prepared to meet you on the battlefield."

The Amban took several steps forward. Sweat was pouring down his forehead and he looked as if he was about to faint. Finally, resigning himself to his fate, he said, "Very well, I see your patience has been exhausted. The tongue is like a sharp knife that kills without drawing blood. You have my word. Tomorrow you may go."

Without another word, Father Dedeken turned and left.

The next day, the Grand Amban summoned Father Dedeken for a secret meeting in his tent. When Dedeken arrived, the Grand Amban was sitting together with the Grand Lama Nima Dorje and the Amban. As soon as he entered, they ordered everyone except Jamyang to leave.

Once they were alone, the Grand Amban spoke first. During his oration, the Amban and the Grand Lama shifted uncomfortably in their seats, spinning prayer wheels and counting rosaries, but the tension in the air was palpable.

"You men have proven yourselves to be brave and straight, always dealing honestly with us," said the Grand Amban. "We believe what you have told us, that you are heading to Batang and to China, and we have no reason to doubt you. Given all this, we swear our eternal friendship to you and all the people of *Fagwo*. As you know, the English are our sworn enemies. They are a source of constant aggravation on our southern borders. They have killed many of our people with their far-reaching guns. As a show of friendship, we would like for you to procure for us some good European guns so we can properly defend ourselves. We'll pay whatever you ask."

Father Dedeken's mind raced. He knew that if he refused the Grand Amban's request outright, he would accuse the Frenchmen of not behaving as friends, which would mean certain death. On the other hand, if Bonvalot complied, he risked creating an embarrassing diplomatic tussle with the English, especially since Prince Henri d'Orléans was directly involved. Once the story reached the papers, the French royal family would be the object of ridicule and public mud-slinging in every foreign capital in the world. The French Government would also suffer tremendous embarrassment in the press, not to mention the possibility of diplomatic sanctions at a time when they could ill afford it.

Father Dedeken attempted to appear philosophical. "That is a very interesting request, Excellency. I will discuss this matter with my companions and I give you my word as your friend that we will do whatever we can to assist you."

The Ambans looked pleased. They rose from their seats and bowed to Father Dedeken, who bowed in return.

When he rode back to camp, Dedeken found Bonvalot nervously cleaning his gun. The caravan men were shivering by the fire while Tong-Kia passed around bowls of palao made from rancid Tibetan butter and a recently-slaughtered sheep.

"Bonvalot, we have a slight problem."

"What happened?" said Bonvalot, looking up.

"They've changed their story. They say we're free to leave as long as we sell them some guns. I believe 'good Europeans guns' was the expression they used."

Bonvalot's brow creased. "That is an outrage. I don't have any guns to spare. I picked up a few spare Russian Berdan revolvers when we were in Moscow, but I don't have the luxury of handing them out like cigarettes. I should have known they wouldn't let us off easy." He sat back and let out a deep sigh. "Very well, I suppose you could give them one of our Smith and Wesson cavalry models and a few boxes of ammunition and a nice leather holster. They'll have to make do with that."

"And if they say it's not enough?"

"You can always say it was the *White Pasha's* personal weapon. They can have it with our compliments."

Father Dedeken roared with laughter.

After Father Dedeken had delivered the gun to the Ambans, they thanked him profusely and stated the caravan was free to leave in two days. Although inwardly hopeful, something in the Ambans' voices worried the Belgian missionary.

When the appointed day came, the men mounted their new dun-colored Tibetan ponies and marveled at how swift and sure-footed they were. These ponies, Bonvalot noted, were very similar to the species of horse Prejevalsky discovered on one of his earlier journeys to Tibet. When all the supplies were loaded on the yaks, the caravan headed out in a northeasterly direction, following the Tibetan guides provided by the Ambans through a labyrinth of mountains, valleys, and barren hills. The only vegetation to be found were some sparse grasses and short bushes that dotted the dreary landscape. Patches of snow carpeted the mountaintops and, aside from the occasional Buddhist pilgrim prostrating himself on the side of the road, there was no other sign of life.

Accompanying the caravan were the two Ambans dressed sumptuously in red and yellow silk, along with an escort of several hundred servants carrying signs, flags, guns, and spears, as well as two hundred and fifty yaks and two hundred horses. In addition, the Amban had supplied them with an assortment of yak drivers and servants, some whose only job was to walk behind the yaks and collect droppings for fire. According to the guides, the only way to reach Ta-Chien-lu, which was located along the secret tea route between Batang and Lhasa, entailed crossing eighty mountain passes, some of which were very steep and dangerous.

Left with no other choice, they started out.

After traveling several days, they reached an altitude of 18,000 feet at which point three of the surviving camels from Korla dropped dead. The next day, after descending to 15,700 feet in the middle of a blizzard, they reached a valley that was dotted with black yak hair tents where the Amban instructed them to set up camp. According to the Amban, this was to be their new camp until they received further instructions from Lhasa. But something about the situation didn't sit well with Bonvalot. At twenty degrees below zero, it was freezing cold and the westerly winds blew so violently it brought back painful memories of the Dam Pass.

"Something is wrong," said Bonvalot, feeling the blood draining from his face. "This can't be the right place."

"It's bloody cold," said Prince Henri, shivering under his sheepskin coat. "It's worse than before. Those double-crossers are trying to kill us."

"They've done it again," said Bonvalot, clenching his jaws. "Those bastards have hoodwinked us."

CHAPTER 50

Snatching Abdullah from his horse, Bonvalot marched through the squall, past the jumbled procession of yaks, crates, sacks of provisions, servants sitting astride ponies, and large assortment of minor officials until he found the Amban's palanquin, which was carried on the shoulders of eight bearers. Close at Bonvalot's heels were Father Dedeken and Rachmed.

Pulling aside the curtain, Bonvalot said, "Is this the *good* camp you told us about? The one that's supposed to be a *paradise?*" Bonvalot waited for Abdullah's translation, and then watched as the Amban's face betrayed his alarm.

"Yes," said the Amban. "This is the place. This is where they instructed us to await further orders from Lhasa. Is something the matter?"

"Let me make myself perfectly clear," said Bonvalot, pointing his finger at the Amban. "We are *not* waiting for anybody's orders. We're getting out of here, and I don't care what Lhasa says. I don't care what the Emperor of China says. I'm responsible for the lives of my men. We're through with your tricks, your deceptions, and your lies. This camp is just as bad as the Dam Pass and you brought us here so we would die."

"There's no need for that tone of voice," said the Amban, appearing hurt. "We will give you everything you need. You won't lack for anything, and soon the presents from Lhasa will arrive. But you cannot leave without a Chinese passport. I am ordering you to remain here until it arrives or there will be serious trouble."

Bonvalot grabbed the Amban by his collar and yanked him forward. He shook the Amban like a rag doll and screamed at the top of his lungs, "Keep your bloody presents. Keep your bloody Chinese passport. I'm taking my men out of here."

The Amban's face contorted as he struggled in Bonvalot's grip until several soldiers tore them apart.

"Control your anger," said the Amban, his eyes snapping. "Anger is a poison that is the main cause of Samsara, all the sufferings of this world. If this camp does not suit you, you may travel to another camp which is a three-day journey from here and is lower in elevation. But you must wait here another seven days so you can receive your presents and the orders from the Dalai Lama."

"You don't understand," said Bonvalot, fighting to contain his fury. "We don't have another seven days. My men are sick, vomiting, delirious. The prince is wheezing and coughing up blood. We have to get out now."

The Amban shrugged his shoulders. "I'm sorry, but that's not possible. If you learn anything from your stay in Tibet perhaps it is to control your temper. That is not the path to enlightenment."

Bonvalot was burning with anger. He was sweating and his heart was racing. He was so weak from mountain sickness that he could no longer tolerate the constant haranguing from the Ambans. He feared that if they didn't escape soon, they would never make it out of Tibet alive.

"Very well, I agree to your terms."

"There is only one little condition," said the Amban, smiling like a Cheshire cat.

"And what is that?" said Bonvalot.

"For reasons of secrecy, when you depart you may not travel on the high road between Lhasa and Batang. You must only use the back roads, the ones used by the tea smugglers that the Chinese authorities know nothing about. But fear not, these roads pose no danger to your caravan. Naturally, we will supply you with knowledgeable guides who will see you to the outskirts of Batang."

"Very well," said Bonvalot, fighting to contain his anger. "But we must leave right away. Tomorrow at the latest."

"I'm afraid that's not possible," said the Amban, settling back in his palanquin. "I received word that the messenger from Lhasa has already left. You will remain here until he arrives with the official orders. Do not attempt to sneak past the guards. I have ordered them to shoot anyone who leaves without permission."

Bonvalot was too weak and dizzy to continue arguing with the Amban. Shivering in the cold he nodded his assent, then he returned to his men, who were struggling against the blinding squall to pitch the tents. Parpa, Timur, and Isa demanded a full report of his conversation, if he had managed to extract any new promises from the Amban, but all Bonvalot could do was mumble a curt reply before collapsing in his sheepskin bedroll for the night, the howling wind and hail drowning out any more thoughts of escape.

The next day, Bonvalot and his crew huddled around a yak dung fire to await news of the messenger from Lhasa, but no one arrived. No messengers came with news and no more presents of food and fuel arrived. They paced aimlessly around the camp until nightfall, but still no word came. Another day came and went, and then another, their strength and patience ebbing with each passing day, their migraines and nausea returning with a vengeance. Some of the men were so debilitated from the cold and mountain sickness they were delirious. Finally, when he could take it no longer, Bonvalot sent for Rachmed and instructed him to send a warning to the Amban demanding that he fulfill all his promises.

"The Ambans are leading us like a camel with a hook through its nose," said Bonvalot. "I've reached the end of my rope. Tell that smiling devil that if the yaks are not loaded within half an hour, there will be hell to pay."

Rachmed nodded and said, "Khoub!" They waited patiently for half an hour, but instead of hearing any activity on the part of the Tibetans, there was only silence. Peering through the tent flaps, they spied the Amban's servants huddled around the fire, preparing dishes of tsampa and churning butter for tea, but no one came to help them load the yaks.

When Rachmed returned, Bonvalot asked him what happened.

"The Ambans listened, but pretended not to hear. They waved me away like a beggar."

Enraged, Bonvalot grabbed an empty bottle and flung it against a rock.

"Go back and tell those bastards that if the yaks are not loaded within fifteen minutes, we'll steal their animals and flee."

With a grunt, Rachmed stormed back to the Amban's tent and delivered the message. When he returned, Bonvalot pulled out a watch and waited the requisite number of minutes, but there was only silence. Nothing stirred in the Tibetan camp; all they heard was the sound of yaks growling in the distance and the faint tinkling of bells.

Bonvalot balled his fists. "I've had enough of this. I'm going to teach those conniving scoundrels a lesson they'll never forget. Rachmed, go back and tell the Amban that if the yaks are not loaded within five minutes, there'll be hell to pay. Make sure they understand the meaning of 'hell.' Strike terror into their callous little hearts."

Rachmed chuckled and left. When he returned several minutes later, they fixed their eyes on the watch, but when the requisite number of minutes passed and nothing happened, they knew the Amban had played them for fools.

Bonvalot gathered up Rachmed, Father Dedeken, and Prince Henri and told them to grab their rifles and a handful of cartridges. It was time to declare war.

"We are going to teach our Tibetan friends a lesson they'll never forget."

CHAPTER 51

Armed with their rifles, they stormed out of the tent and headed to a nearby hill where a herd of yaks was grazing contentedly. Lifting their rifles, they half-cocked the hammer and aimed at the unsuspecting beasts. Bonvalot gave the order, "Ready, aim. Fire!" All at once, the men squeezed their triggers.

A burst of gunfire rang out. Loud blasts exploded in their ears, and black smoke filled the air. Bonvalot and his companions fired round after round into the herd, the volley shattering the peace and quiet of the Tibetan camp. One by one the animals fell dead, their blood staining the barren earth like barrels of red paint. The barrage continued until the field was littered with bloody corpses while the Tibetans stood transfixed by the horror, howling with fright.

"Stop! Cease fire!" said Bonvalot, lowering his rifle to survey the damage. The field was covered with sickening red puddles of blood and the corpses of dead yaks and horses. The smell of gunpowder filled the air. "Let's bring down those tents now. Ready, aim. Fire!"

Aiming at the tops of the tents, the men let out another barrage of gunfire that tore vast holes in the tents, causing them to fall to the ground in lifeless heaps. From inside the tents, the Tibetans screamed and clamored to escape, but the tents were too heavy and they were too terrified to escape the destruction. The remaining animals stampeded through the camp, causing more destruction as they stumbled over butter churns, baskets, crates, and chairs in their haste to escape. The Tibetan servants and nomads also ran for their lives, resulting in more chaos and confusion. Fanning out over the perimeter of the camp, the men continued shooting and reloading, shooting and reloading, destroying the Amban's camp with every blast of their rifles.

When Bonvalot saw they had had enough, he said, "Stop! Cease fire!" The he stepped back and surveyed the damage.

Bonvalot was convinced the barrage had done the trick. The Tibetan camp was utterly destroyed. Slaughtered animals lay in sickening pools of blood, tents were collapsed into heaps, butter urns were toppled over, pots, pans, and prayer wheels were scattered everywhere, food was littered all over the ground, horses could be seen galloping away in the distance.

Soon, a loud wail arose from within the camp as various Ambans, lamas, chiefs, nomads, and servants came crawling out of their tents like wasps from a burning nest, shrieking as they pointed to the carnage in terror. The camp was thrown into state of pandemonium at the wanton display of firepower.

"I believe that got their attention," said Bonvalot.

"I say, did you see how my Lee-Enfield No. 8 handled that?" said Prince Henri, beaming like a proud father as he held up his rifle for their admiration. "But the recoil did give my shoulder a nasty bruise."

"Allahu Akhbar!" shouted Rachmed, shaking his fists at the panicked Tibetans.

When the screaming reached a crescendo, the conspirators returned to their tent to contemplate the matter over a bottle of champagne and a bowl of tsampa. Shortly afterwards, the Amban showed up with an entourage of panicked soldiers ready to agree to all their terms. As far as the Amban was concerned, the entire matter had been a grave misunderstanding and they were free to leave at once.

"We shan't keep you here any longer," said the Amban, breathing heavily. "It is the wish of the living Buddha that we part as friends so that the alliance between Tibet and the people of *Fagwo* may continue for many long years."

"As you wish," said Bonvalot, stifling a grin. "And do you swear by the Lord Buddha that you will not detain us any longer? And that this is not another one of your tricks?"

"Yes, yes, I give you my word that we have no intention of deceiving you," said the Amban, nodding profusely. "You may go."

At this pronouncement, the men cheered and hugged each other like shipwrecked men rescued after months at sea. At last they were free to go home. The ordeal was finally over. Bonvalot paid the Amban for the loss of his animals, then made sure to extract a promise from his former jailer (while he was still in shock) that he would provide them with adequate guides and horses for the journey to Batang. Naturally, the Amban agreed to all his demands without hesitation. He was, after all, a reasonable man.

And so, the caravan men packed up their belongings one last time. Their next stop was Batang. With a lump in his throat, Bonvalot knew he would never reach Lhasa or see the Dalai Lama. The Forbidden City with all its magic and mystery would remain a fabulous legend. After giving the matter considerable thought, he came to the conclusion that Tibet was better off sealed away from the rest of the world. Some dreams were too lofty, too unattainable to be realized, like the mythical city of El Dorado, the Garden of the Hesperides, or Avalon. But as long as they existed in the hearts of men, their power and mystique lived on.

After loading the yaks, they bid a final farewell to their Tibetan hosts, who presented them with a number of gifts: Tibetan costumes, animal skins, necklaces with precious stones, prayer wheels, perfumed wood, even packets of prayers. It was a veritable treasure trove of Tibetan artifacts that greatly added to their collection. In addition, the Amban gave them a hefty supply of butter, tea, rice, beans, and tsampa for the remainder of the journey.

"Please understand, it wasn't easy for me to act as an intermediary between you and my chiefs in Lhasa," said the Amban. "It was like trying to make peace between a tiger and a monkey. But I am pleased it has all come to a good end, and you are leaving as friends. Promise me one thing, that you will never forget your friends in Tibet."

"Indeed, Excellency," said Bonvalot. "I will remember this journey for the rest of my life. Although I regret we will not be able to see your Potala Palace and meet your Dalai Lama, I can honestly say I believe our mission in Tibet is done. I have traveled further than any other explorer in the modern age. I have seen sights that no other man from the West has seen. And now, I would like to present you with a few gifts as well: a Russian revolver, several watches, some pocket knives, scissors, gold coins and silver rubles. Consider them as gifts of friendship from the people of *Fagwo* to the people of Tibet."

The Amban bowed and graciously accepted the gifts.

"Now that you are leaving for Batang, allow me to introduce to you the lama who will be acting as your official guide and escort. He will present you to the numerous tribes you will meet along the way and protect you from harm."

A short lama of about twenty-five stepped forward who the Amban introduced as Lobsang. Dressed in the typical saffron robes of Buddhist monks, Lobsang had a jolly face and round cheeks that belied his physical strength and quick-thinking mind. The Amban added that he had chosen Lobsang for this task because he had acquired an expert knowledge of the secret road to Batang, having once worked as a tea smuggler during his youth before devoting his life to Lord Buddha.

Then the Amban's voice changed, assuming a more paternalistic tone. "And please allow me to give you a final word of advice. Along the way you will meet some very wild tribes whose ways are rough and uncultivated since they have always lived apart from civilization. As long as you are patient with them, they will not give you any trouble. The worst ones live right near Batang, so once you reach that district, be on your guard. Not too long ago a European man was killed there."

Hearing this, Bonvalot perked up. He motioned to Camille to retrieve her husband's photograph.

"I have a question for you, Excellency," said Bonvalot, handing the photograph to the Amban. "This woman has traveled with us all this way to search for her missing husband. Is it possible that the man who was killed might in fact be her husband? Please take a look at this photograph and see if it bears any resemblance to the man in question."

The Amban studied the photograph together with his monks and lamas, but after several minutes, they shook their heads and handed back the picture.

"We are sorry, but this picture does not resemble the man who was killed. For our part, we will pray that the woman recovers her husband, and that your journey will be safe and prosperous."

"Thank you, Excellency," said Bonvalot, shaking the Amban's hand. "And please forgive us if we had to resort to extreme measures. In the end you helped us greatly and I will forever be in your debt."

The Amban smiled as he placed a white silk scarf around Bonvalot's neck. "The Buddha says no matter how hard a man's past, he can always begin again. You have a great soul, a wise soul; you must learn to conquer your anger to avoid *Samsara*. I pray that one day you will seek enlightenment. Go and may the Buddha light your way."

The Amban laid his hand on Bonvalot's head. Behind him, rows of lamas and lesser chiefs bowed and prostrated themselves on the ground. Bonvalot bowed as well, but he was too moved by this outpouring of respect to speak.

But before he left, Bonvalot had some important work to do.

It was time to dismiss the men from Korla and Lob Nor who were to travel north via the road to Tsaidam on yaks and horses supplied by their Tibetan hosts. Bonvalot turned to Parpa, Isa, Timur, Mahmud, and the rest of the men who had followed him from Sinkiang Province and thanked them for their extraordinary courage and loyalty. The men cried and hugged their leader goodbye, showing tremendous affection.

"We will never forget you, sahib," said Timur. "You will live forever in our memories as a man of extraordinary courage and bravery."

Bonvalot lavished them with sacks of coins and various trinkets and gifts, after which they salaamed with a show of great respect and then took their leave.

After saying a final goodbye to their Tibetan hosts, Bonvalot and his remaining companions mounted their new Tibetan horses and started up again, this time heading eastward on the secret road to Batang. Behind them, the beautiful snow-covered peak of Ningling Tanla glimmered in the golden hue of sunlight. As they marched over the dusty, rock-strewn path, Bonvalot wondered where his next adventure would take him. By his calculations, it was already April of 1890 and the world was anxiously awaiting of his expedition. He was anxious to take his rightful place in front of the grand auditorium of the Sorbonne and tell the world all about the wonders of Tibet.

CHAPTER 52

Expertly guided by Lobsang, the caravan headed northeast for several days, climbing over rocky mountain passes and across rushing rivers until they reached a steep gorge that traced the route of the Ourtchou River. After following the river's path for several miles, they looked up to see a curious sight hovering over the left bank.

Suspended like a birdcage above a rushing stream was a tiny white cottage built into the side of a craggy cliff. According to Lobsang, the cottage belonged to a hermit lama who had taken a vow of silence, cutting himself off from all humanity for the rest of his life. Scattered on the ground below the cottage lay hundreds of written prayers left by various pilgrims as well as by the nomads who lived in the black tents down in a nearby valley.

Bonvalot took out his spyglass and examined the curious dwelling. Its walls were chalk white, and it contained only a tiny white door and a small window to let in the light. It was so small, Bonvalot was certain the cottage could only fit one person, and even then, just barely. But the little dwelling was bathed in natural sunlight that gave it a cheerful appearance. Despite the loneliness of such an existence, Bonvalot did not pity the poor hermit for deciding to seal himself off from the rest of the world. In fact, he respected him for dedicating himself to perfecting his soul.

Camille came up alongside Bonvalot and asked if she could have a better look at the hermit's dwelling through his spyglass. When she saw it up close, she laughed.

"How does that poor hermit eat?" she asked Lobsang. "There's no room in that tiny hut to store let alone cook food. And I doubt hermits are in the habit of hunting game."

"Do not fear, memsahib," said Lobsang. "The hermit does not starve. Although he sits suspended between heaven and earth, the villagers supply him with all his earthly needs. Whenever he gets hungry, or requires something, he goes down to those tents and prays outside. Out of pity, the villagers give him bowls of food or fill his empty coffers with coins, so he can obtain what he needs. In this manner, the hermit lives through his prayers and has no fear of ever going hungry."

"I would like to meet this hermit," said Camille. "Is that possible? Perhaps he can pray for me."

"He won't speak to you directly," said Lobsang. "But if you climb up the mountain and put a silver rupee under his door, he will certainly pray for you."

Camille looked at Bonvalot. "Monsieur Bonvalot, I would very much like to ask that hermit to pray for my husband. It's the very least I can do."

"Of course you can go," said Bonvalot. "But don't go by yourself. Take Lobsang and Rachmed. I'll halt the yaks here by the river so they can graze for awhile."

Accompanied by Rachmed and Lobsang, Camille gingerly climbed up the mountainside until they were just outside the hermit's door. Tucked in her pocket was her husband's photograph. After she pushed a silver rupee under the door she slid her husband's photograph and requested that the hermit pray for him.

To their surprise, they heard a voice from behind the cottage door. The hermit spoke for several minutes, speaking in a language Camille could not fathom, but its singsong rhythm filled her heart with hope. When the hermit was finished, he slid the photograph back underneath the door.

"What did he say?" said Camille.

"He said the man in the photograph passed this way many months ago," said Lobsang. "He was in a caravan that was headed to the Sok Lamasery."

"How does he know?"

"He saw them from his balcony. When some of the men from the caravan climbed up the mountain and gave him alms, the lama said he prayed for the man in the picture. He said the man did not look well."

Camille was stunned. She clutched her husband's photograph and thanked the hermit for his help. "How wonderful and dreadful at the same time," she said. "We're so close to finding my husband; I feel his presence everywhere."

Without another word, they climbed back down the mountain and made their way over to Bonvalot, who was reclining by the river's edge.

"What did the hermit say?" said Bonvalot, standing up.

"Monsieur Bonvalot, you're not going to believe this, the lama claimed my husband passed this way several months ago. He was heading to the Sok Lamasery and he appeared to be ill."

Bonvalot's eyes widened. "What an extraordinary coincidence. So the rumor we heard was true. Armand Dancourt was making his way to Sok, but why? There's no gold in these mountains. If he came here to prospect for gold he would have headed in the opposite direction. Well, in any case, we should be reaching the village of Sok in about a week's time."

After the caravan started up again, they continued for the next few days across several mountain passes lined with limestone obos on which pilgrims had deposited small stones with prayers. They descended down to a valley, crossed over rivers, and lumbered across a large steppe where antelopes grazed freely. Continuing onward, they climbed another mountain pass at 16,500 feet and camped at the bottom along the banks of a river.

The next day, after crossing a final harrowing pass, they faced the ultimate test: a descent that was so steep, the path fell in an almost vertical drop to the valley below. With hearts beating wildly in their chests, they led the animals down the mountain road; the yaks and horses dragging their rear hooves together as they held onto the terrain for dear life, or sometimes by squatting on their hind legs as they eased themselves inch by inch down the sloping terrain. Two yaks, that were not so fortunate, plunged to their deaths over the side of a precipice, landing in a lifeless heap on the valley floor below. Once everyone had made their way safely down the mountainside, they were worn out and exhausted, but the sight that greeted their eyes instantly revived them.

Nestled over seven layers of a mountainside sat a lamasery whose white walls gleamed like mother-of-pearl. There were numerous *chortens* with golden spires adding to the mystery and exoticism of this sealed-off world, each part of the *chorten* showing another path to Enlightenment. There were dozens of buildings in all, each with a red-tiled roof and glassless, wood-framed windows. According to Lobsang, this was the Sok Lamasery, a citadel of Buddhism that was over two hundred years old.

Terraced over several hills, the lamasery resembled a medieval palace of sorts. For several minutes, they stood staring at the extraordinary sight, breathing in the scent of juniper and pine, listening to the distant blowing of trumpets. If Lobsang had not urged them to keep moving, they might have stayed there forever, lost in meditation.

"Bonvalot-sahib," said Lobsang. "I will go ahead and inform the lamasery that you will be arriving shortly. They will prepare rooms for your men to spend the night."

They watched the sprightly lama climb the long, winding staircase that rose up the mountainside to the lamasery's iron gate, and disappear inside.

Gazing at the various buildings that comprised the lamasery, they saw to their amazement that the structures were built directly into the sides of steep slopes such that the roof of one building acted as the courtyard for the next building higher up. Light entered the structures by means of doors, windows, and galleries. After a few moments they began to see monks with shorn heads and saffron robes appearing from the doorways, walking up and down the terraces, or sitting cross-legged in the sunshine. They seemed to be watching the strangers with the curiosity of cats peering from a window.

A short while later, Lobsang returned, telling the travelers the Chief Lama was waiting to receive them. With a great sigh, they began to climb the steps, unsure of what mysteries awaited them in the cloistered world of the lamasery.

CHAPTER 53

Sok Lamasery, Tibet
April 1890.

After passing through the lamasery's metal gates they entered into a courtyard where a large group of saffron-robed monks was waiting to greet them. From somewhere in the distance, a gong sounded, marking their entrance. The monks' wide smiles and welcoming eyes put them instantly at ease. According to Lobsang, this building was meant for important people traveling to and from Lhasa and even had a special chamber for the Dalai Lama himself. Several monks showed the travelers to their rooms, which contained only wooden slats for the floors, small burning fireplaces, and beds made of straw.

No sooner had Bonvalot settled into his room when a high-ranking lama and an entourage paid him a visit. They presented the weary travelers with a meal of rice, mutton, tsampa, and butter tea, and told them that after they feasted they would be permitted an audience with Tashi Thubten, the Chief Lama. Bonvalot bowed and graciously accepted the food. Together with his men, they sat down by the fire and feasted.

Later, the monks led Bonvalot, Lobsang, Father Dedeken, Prince Henri, and Camille Dancourt past a courtyard lined with large prayer cylinders, which the monks would spin every time they passed, colorful prayer flags, and yaks' tails, down a dark corridor lit by butter lamps, and through a multi-colored door that opened to a chamber that was lit up by hundreds of butter lamps that shone from every nook and cranny of the ceremonial room. When his eyes had adjusted to the light, Bonvalot saw that it was decorated with murals of the Buddha's life as well as altars containing golden statues of the Buddha as well as burning sticks of fragrant incense. The air was heavy from the acrid scent of burning butter and incense. As they entered the temple a service was being held; rows of monks in saffron robes sat cross-legged chanting prayers while, from a darkened corner, the clashing of cymbals rang out, followed by the beating of drums and the blowing of trumpets and conch shells. When the music and chanting died away, the line of monks parted to reveal the Head Lama, Tashi Thubten, sitting on a raised dais at the head of the room.

The elderly lama eyed the visitors through wizened eyes. He motioned for them to step forward. Hesitating only slightly, Bonvalot led his companions through the sea of monks until they were directly facing Tashi Thubten. Following Lobsang's cue, they bowed low before the head lama.

"Thank you, Excellency, for your hospitality," said Bonvalot. "We are grateful for all the food and the gifts you have given us. After traveling so far with little in the way of proper food and shelter, we greatly appreciate it."

"This is the minimum that should be done by one who is skilled in goodness and who knows the path of peace," said Tashi Thubten. "You honor us with your presence. My attendants inform me that among you is a royal prince. May I meet this young man?"

Prince Henri stepped forward and bowed before the elderly lama. Tashi Thubten smiled at the blond, blue-eyed prince and shook his hand warmly. Afterward, Bonvalot presented Father Dedeken and Camille Dancourt, explaining that Camille had come to Tibet to search for her missing husband.

"This husband of yours, what is his name?"

"Armand Dancourt, Excellency," said Camille. "I have his picture here." She removed the photograph from her pocket and handed it to the Head Lama, who studied it solemnly.

"I know this man," said Tashi Thubten. "He came here many months ago. He begged me to teach him the Middle Way but his stay here was brief. After achieving a high level of enlightenment his soul fled like a lark to the heavens. Of men like your husband, the teachers say, 'the pure-hearted one, having clarity of vision, being freed from all sense desires, is not born again into this world.' I believe he has reached a state of true Nirvana, but his life on earth was difficult, indeed.

"By the time he reached us he was already ill. A frightful case of dysentery. Naturally, we prayed for him and our doctor lama treated him in the usual manner by writing the remedy on a scrap of paper which he fed to the patient for his benefit, but there was nothing we could do. It was too late to save him."

Camille's face turned white. She burst into tears and buried her head in Bonvalot's chest, sobbing. Nevertheless, Tashi Thubten continued. "Like most seekers, your husband came here seeking enlightenment and I believe he died content, having achieved a state of almost perfect bliss. True liberation."

Bonvalot stroked Camille's head. "As far as we know, he came to Tibet seeking gold, but somewhere along the way changed his mind and joined a caravan that was heading south to Lhasa. By some miracle we managed to track his movements here. His wife traveled here all the way from France to find her husband."

"When I met your husband," continued the Chief Lama. "He was very unhappy, fearful, melancholic. Empty inside, like a vase with no water. But after studying and praying here in the lamasery, he began to change. He reached a state of inner peace. Your husband learned compassion and forgiveness, and soon his heart was free to accept the gifts of the Buddha. He learned to follow the noble eightfold path."

"Did he ever mention his wife?" said Camille.

Tashi Thubten called to one of his attendants, who brought over a juniper box from one of the altars. Inside there was another, smaller, box which he opened and removed a gold pocket watch and a letter.

"He did not speak about personal matters, but he gave us these things before he died. He asked us to keep them safe for whoever would come searching for him. I believe he meant for you to have them."

Camille reached out with trembling hands and accepted the gifts.

"This was the watch I gave Armand on our wedding day," she said, tearfully.

Tashi Thubten spoke solemnly to Camille, "If you keep fear and distrust inside of you, you will live a life of loneliness. Your husband was yours for only a short time, now he has gone to his next migration. But you are still here. We don't know what will happen in the next life but you must learn to live your present life fully and without regret."

Camille nodded. Beside her, Bonvalot squeezed her hand and smiled. With humility and graciousness, Camille thanked the Chief Lama and begged to be excused. Father Dedeken rose and escorted Camille back to her quarters, leaving Bonvalot and Prince Henri behind to speak at length with Tashi Thubten about mystical matters. They later learned from the Chief Lama that Princess Pema had reached the Potala Palace in good health. She was now fulfilling her destiny to serve the Dalai Lama as his private tutor and maidservant. With her return, the scholars in Lhasa believed she had fulfilled an ancient prophecy.

"We believe the daughter of the Panchen Lama, the girl known as Pema, is the reincarnation of the goddess Kali, the consort of the god Siva. This is an auspicious sign. It means that Tibet will be free of the yoke of its Chinese masters. The golden bird has finally come back to its nest."

"How did your scholars reach this conclusion?" said Bonvalot.

"It is written in this scroll here," said Tashi Thubten, opening up a second box of juniper wood and extracting a scroll written in ancient Tibetan script.

Bonvalot examined the precious document with wonder.

"In Paris we have scholars who are very knowledgeable about such matters. I would very much like to bring back a copy of this scroll so that they may see for themselves that the prophecy concerning the goddess Kali has been fulfilled."

Tashi Thubten considered his request. "You may certainly have a copy for your lamas. What matters to us is that the daughter of the Panchen Lama is the living embodiment of the prophecy. She will remain in the Potala Palace all the days of her present incarnation."

From somewhere in the lamasery, a gong reverberated. The weary travelers stood up and bowed before the venerable lama and retired to their rooms.

After snuffing out their butter lamps for the night, Bonvalot and his companions lay in their straw beds listening to the monks blowing their trumpets in deep, sonorous waves, blending with the gentle clanging of cymbals, the occasional humming from unseen lips, and the soft pitter patter of mice scurrying across the floor, which the monks had referred to as the reincarnations of monks and nuns from days long past, the sounds mingling seamlessly with the thoughts in their heads until they fell into a deep, contented slumber.

CHAPTER 54

The next morning after a breakfast of tsampa and butter tea, the monks from the Sok Lamasery escorted the travelers to their yaks and helped them load their baggage. Camille joined them in the courtyard looking renewed after a good night's sleep and a proper bath. Her face shone with the radiance of youth and her azure eyes sparkled under the glaring sun. Bonvalot was grateful the worst was over and Camille was free to live her life.

"Are you feeling well enough to travel today?" he said.

"I'm perfectly fine," said Camille. "The Chief Lama answered all my questions about Armand. I feel as though he's finally buried. I'm glad he didn't die alone like that poor Englishman we found on the Chang Tang. Armand had his reasons for coming to Tibet, which I may never understand, and he met his fate in this isolated lamasery. I'm just grateful it's over."

"It's not exactly over," said Bonvalot. "We still have to make it down to Hanoi in one piece. I hate to have to tell you this, but the territory we're about to cross is crawling with bandits, smugglers, and assassins."

"Perhaps you shouldn't have told me."

"Rachmed taught you how to shoot, didn't he?"

"Yes, but shooting bottles is one thing. Shooting robbers is something else entirely."

Bonvalot handed her a revolver. "Here is your insurance policy. Keep it in your saddle bag in case of unexpected company."

To assist them on their journey to Batang, Tashi Thubten presented the travelers with six lamas who would act as guides, yak drivers, and porters, as well as numerous sheep, bags of rice, and tsampa. In turn, Bonvalot presented the Chief Lama and his attendants with gifts of magnifying glasses, silver watches, pocket mirrors, and silver rupees, which they graciously accepted.

Bonvalot embraced Lama Tashi Thubten and thanked him for his hospitality, then the riders mounted their horses to start the next stage of the journey, which would take them to Batang, the last town under the rule of the Dalai Lama.

Tashi Thubten and Lobsang stood at the center of a large entourage of lamas waving goodbye. "*Kah-leh phe.* May good luck and fortune follow you."

Bonvalot and his caravan men waved goodbye, engraving the moment forever in their memories.

After bidding the lamas farewell the caravan started out down the rock-strewn path. Out of nowhere, a sudden gust of wind blew the hood away from one of the lamas who was traveling with them. When Bonvalot got a glimpse of his face, he froze, then his heart pounded with fear. *Prejevalsky.* The hallucination that had plagued him since Paris was back. A foreboding sense of dread came over Bonvalot. Was it too late to stop these terrifying visions? Would he be haunted by Prejevalsky for the rest of his life?

Prince Henri came up alongside him. "Bonvalot, what do you say about making another attempt at Lhasa next year?"

"I don't think so," said Bonvalot. "Perhaps it's best we left the Roof of the World to its own savage beauty. It's time I moved on to new challenges." He winked at Camille. "Don't you agree, Madame Dancourt?"

"Absolutely," she said, trotting alongside him. "I think you've given the Tibetans enough trouble for awhile. But does it pain you that we didn't make it to Lhasa?"

"I've come to the conclusion, Madame Dancourt, that Tibet is best left to the Tibetans. There are some mysteries in the world that should remain as such, and let the rest of mankind dream their dream of Lhasa. In that way, the dream will live on forever."

"What about you, Father Dedeken?" said Camille. "Do you hope to return to Tibet some day?"

"My job is to go where the Almighty sends me," said Father Dedeken, patting his horse's neck. "Which I pray is not quite so far away as Tibet."

"Monsieur Bonvalot," said Camille. "Thank you again for everything. I feel as though you've given me the most precious gift of all, the gift of life."

Bonvalot took Camille's hand. "I'll admit getting you out of Tibet alive became a personal objective of mine. And now that you've landed on your own two feet, all I ask is that you let go of the past and enjoy the journey. According to the Chief Lama, you have a lifetime of happiness ahead of you. I'll be sorry when we finally go our separate ways."

"I share your sentiments," said Camille. "I shall remember this journey for the rest of my life."

Father Dedeken pulled out a pipe with great ceremony and lit it with a match.

"Look what I have here," said Dedeken. "I've been saving this tobacco for months. Now that we've reached an altitude of only 12,000 feet, I feel it's finally safe enough to indulge in the favorite consolation of the traveler and the sailor, namely smoking. Care to join me in a smoke?"

"I thought you'd never ask," said Bonvalot, grabbing the pipe out of Dedeken's hand. He took a few deep puffs he said, "Ah, what a pleasure that is. Thank you for reminding me how good it feels to have a smoke."

"It makes me feel like I'm in another world," said Father Dedeken, surveying the jagged peaks of violet-tinted mountains bathed in the warm glow of sunlight that stretched before them like a mirage. "With the open road straight ahead, and new blood flowing in my veins, I'm a new man. What say you Bonvalot?"

Bonvalot thought about the sinister hooded lama who seemed to be following him, but he refused to be hounded by these maddening visions. He gleamed mischievously at Dedeken. "I say it's time we moved on to the next stage of our journey. We have many miles ahead of us until we reach the coast."

Kicking his horse's side, Bonvalot galloped down the rocky stretch of road. "Onward to Batang!" he called out as his band of intrepid explorers raced after him.

CHAPTER 55

By June of 1890 the explorers reached Ta-Chien-lu, a town on the frontier between China and Tibet whose streets were so filthy, they reeked of sewage, and dirty pigs and yelping dogs could be seen running wild. They found the accommodations equally bad as the streets, being little more than decrepit, opium-infused inns where robbers and addicts were known to consort and the food was abysmal.

To their relief, they were greeted by a party of French missionaries who regaled the travelers in true Gallic fashion, with food, wine, and song after which Bonvalot and his cohorts regaled the brothers with harrowing tales about their journey across Tibet. After their welcoming feast, Bonvalot thought it prudent to leave Camille with the missionaries for her own safety while he took Prince Henri, Father Dedeken, Rachmed, and Bartholomeus to the local mandarin for an obligatory visit. As they were led in to see the official, Bonvalot found himself in the uncomfortable position of having to explain to his Excellency why he was escorting a royal prince through China without so much as a passport let alone a royal entourage.

The mandarin received the European visitors guardedly. He looked askance at their disheveled appearance, overgrown beards, dirty faces, and scruffy sheepskin caps, quite certain that they were frauds. Not believing that the young blond man was a royal prince, the mandarin decided to put him to a test.

Without flinching, the mandarin ordered Prince Henri to behead one of his subjects on the spot. When the young man recoiled with disgust, refusing on principle to behead an innocent the mandarin smiled slyly, positive he was a charlatan. After screaming every insult he could think of, the mandarin promptly threw the foreign devils out.

Later, when Bonvalot and his companions returned to the inn, they were accosted by a gang of armed robbers who demanded all their money and valuables. A gunfight ensued. Aided by a cache of 2,000 cartridges at their disposal, Bonvalot never doubted their ability to shoot their way out of Ta-Chien-lu, but he worried that their valuable Tibetan artifacts, photographs, and biological collection would be pilfered, lost, or shot to pieces. After calling a hasty truce aided by a generous bribe, the intrepid travelers fled Ta-Chien-lu with the assistance of an English Naturalist, who promised to ship their treasures to the nearest French Embassy.

Hastening across the Sichuan and Yunnan provinces, they sought respite where they may, and after resting from their ordeal, embarked by canoe down the Red River, following it all the way south to Hanoi. When they reached this French outpost, Bonvalot, Father Dedeken, Prince Henri, and Camille Dancourt rejoiced at seeing the Tricolor flying freely and gloriously from the theater and all the colonial government buildings, while the soldiers proudly wore their blue tunics, white breeches, and tropical pith helmets as they marched through the streets.

After resting in Hanoi for a month, the travelers embarked by steamer to Hong Kong, where Bartholomeus disembarked for the last time. With undying loyalty, he bid his master *adieu,* vowing to continue their missionary work from his ancestral village in Kansou. From Hong Kong, the travelers continued on to Saigon, Singapore, Ceylon, and the Suez Canal.

When they reached Port Said Abdullah disembarked with a great outpouring of emotion, vowing to remember Bonvalot and the gallant Prince Henri all of his days. As he stood on the wharf, Abdullah waved to them and wished them luck for the remainder of their journey home. "Aziz, I'm coming home to you!" he cried, as tears streamed down his face. Bonvalot waved a final goodbye to Abdullah and wished him Godspeed. From the desert sands of Africa, Abdullah began the long journey back to Chinese Turkestan where he planned to pick up his former profession of squirrel dealer. He had no plans to work in a caravan ever again.

For his part, Rachmed was hoping to see Paris. He had missed his chance to see the Expo, but he had high hopes he would still be able to climb the Eiffel Tower and pay a visit to the Moulin Rouge. Bolstered by the thought of a much-needed holiday, he continued on to Marseilles with the others where he spent the remainder of the sea voyage stalking the steamer's decks, grumbling about the food, and prostrating himself in the fashion of Mohammedans. On more than one occasion, he was asked to sit for photographs with the captain and the officers, and with several of the crew as well. A man of the steppe, Rachmed felt entirely unsuited to life on the ocean.

When a quiet moment came, Bonvalot found Camille alone on deck. She was sitting in a lounge chair sipping a hot cup of tea as she watched the waves rise and fall, surging and swelling and occasionally crashing against the deck. She had changed out of her traveling clothes and into a proper dress; her luxurious hair, now radiant after a proper washing, was covered by a scarf. She looked so calm, Bonvalot almost didn't recognize her.

"Hello there," he said. "May I join you?"

"Of course, I didn't see you at lunch today."

"I ate in my stateroom. I had piles of correspondence to catch up on. I promised our benefactor, the Duke of Chartres, that I would keep him informed about our progress. So tell me, how does it feel like to finally be going home?"

"It's not what I expected," she said. "I truly thought we would find Armand alive and whole, and that I would return to Lyon with him. Still, we're here and we're alive; it's like a dream. So many times I thought we'd never make it out of that dreadful place. So many times I lost all hope. And what about you, Monsieur Bonvalot? What are your plans now?"

"Oh, I don't know, after I rest awhile and write my memoirs, perhaps I'll go to Ethiopia or Madagascar. They say the flora and fauna of Madagascar is like nowhere else on earth. There are species of birds, mammals, and reptiles that have yet to be discovered. After the frigid cold of the Chang Tang I'm looking forward to spending some time in a more tropical zone."

"So you never get tired of this exploration business?"

"No, never," he said. "Rachmed claims I'm a *saya*, a person who is doomed to wander the land forever. Truth be told, I never tire of discovering the beauty, the wonder, and the majesty of our planet. There's so much of our world that's yet to be discovered. I only hope I'm lucky enough to continue doing what I love best."

"Your eyes glow when you talk about exploration," she said.

"Is that so?"

"Indeed," she said. "Perhaps one day I'll accompany you."

"Come again?"

Camille looked thoughtful. "Actually, Monsieur Bonvalot, I've grown quite fond of this life of exploration. In any case, I'll be very sorry when we finally go our separate ways. After spending so much time at each other's side, I feel I've gotten to know you rather well. Almost as well as Rachmed."

"Be careful, Rachmed's the jealous type."

She laughed. "In all seriousness, I don't think I can go back to my old life. Not any more, not after so much has changed. I feel like a ship without a rudder."

"Don't worry. Things will settle down once you get back to Lyon. You'll meet someone new, perhaps a banker, and life will go on as before. You'll cook his supper, raise his children, keep his house, and this little excursion to the Roof of the World will soon become a distant memory. Besides, I would feel terribly guilty if I thought I had somehow disturbed your karma."

"I assure you Monsieur Bonvalot, you could never disturb my karma. But you'd better be careful or you'll risk coming back in your next life as a yak."

"Now there's a frightful thought," said Bonvalot. "Damned beasts are about as unpredictable as Henri after a night of drinking."

Camille laughed and Bonvalot took her hand in his as they sat watching the rolling blue waves and the tiny ships moving across the horizon. The cool breeze tickled their faces and invigorated them. After a moment of reflective silence, Camille said, "I meant what I said, Monsieur Bonvalot. I would love to be your traveling partner again."

Bonvalot tenderly stroked her face. "I would be honored to have you along, Madame Dancourt."

After disembarking at the port of Marseilles, the travelers transferred to the railway station for the remainder of the journey back to Paris. During the trip there was much laughing, singing, and celebrating as the passengers showered the returning explorers with endless bottles of champagne congratulations, toasting them for completing so arduous and momentous a journey.

When they reached the Gare du Nord, Camille headed straight to the telegraph office to announce her arrival to her family while Bonvalot, Prince Henri, Father Dedeken, and Rachmed decided to partake of a hot meal in a café, after which they escorted Father Dedeken to his train bound for Brussels. Once their Belgian companion's luggage was stowed, they stood on the platform to savor the sights, smells, and sounds of Paris—and the enjoyment of each others' company—for one last time.

Bonvalot set his rucksack down on the platform and hugged his friend. "Thank you Constant for placing so much confidence in me. It was a daring scheme, I'll admit, but the odds were against us reaching Lhasa. Under the circumstances, I don't think we fared too poorly."

"You're being modest," said Dedeken, smiling. "We came closer to reaching Lhasa than any other explorer in the modern age. We saw sights no other European has ever seen. I would have expected no less from a man of your caliber, Gabriel. I predict that it will take a veritable army to beat your record. I daresay you and Prince Henri are France's best bets for this year's gold medal. If I haven't left for my next assignment, I would like very much to join you at the ceremony." Dedeken turned to Prince Henri. "Your Highness, it was a great honor and a privilege to accompany you on this momentous journey. I wish you Godspeed and I hope you will always remember me."

Prince Henri reached out to shake Father Dedeken's hand, but after several seconds, broke down and hugged him. Next, Father Dedeken turned to Rachmed.

"And to you, Rachmed, I feel as though I owe you my life. Without you, we never would have made it out of Tibet alive. *Asalaam Alaikum.*"

"*Alaikum asalaam,*" said Rachmed, bowing to Father Dedeken. "You are the bravest and boldest missionary I have ever met. And the best marksman as well. May Allah the all merciful guide you all the days of your life."

"Good-bye Father," said Bonvalot. "And thank you for taking this little detour to Tibet with us. Without your experience, knowledge of Chinese, and cheerful disposition, I'm sure we'd still be stuck at 16,000 feet without a Bible or a prayer."

"On the contrary," said Father Dedeken. "It is I who should thank you for showing me the spirit of adventure and the meaning of courage. You and Prince Henri are a true credit to the Republic. I'm sure the memory of our expedition will live long after all of us are gone. *Adieu mes frères.*"

The train whistle blew and steam hissed from the locomotive, prompting Father Dedeken to take his leave. They watched their brave Belgian companion board the train and wave a final goodbye, his eyes cloudy behind a pair of thick spectacles. They waved in return as the train pulled out of the station and disappeared in a cloud of smoke.

Bonvalot turned to Prince Henri. "With your permission, I shall take my leave. I have a little unfinished business I must attend to before I return home."

"Don't remind me about home," said Prince Henri. "Let's see: home to father's grumbling, my mother's nagging, my uncle's griping over money woes. If I had my choice, I'd rather be stumbling along at 18,000 feet half dead—but free of all the petty squabbles and constant haranguing of home. In any case, I'll be expecting you for dinner on Sunday. Maman and Papa will demand a full report about our travels to Tibet. But do me a favor chap, don't mention anything about Pema to Papa, will you? I made an agreement with him that I would stay out of trouble for a year. Wouldn't want to cause any unnecessary strife."

"I understand perfectly," said Bonvalot.

"And do me another favor," said Henri, lowering his voice to a whisper. "Destroy all the photographs we took of her."

Bonvalot was stunned. "What? Are you certain? I don't understand. You were quite taken with the girl. Why would you—"

"I don't want to risk Papa finding out about her. It could complicate matters if I'm to remain in his will. I have to get back in his good graces."

"Oh, I see," said Bonvalot, taken aback. "Very well, if that is your wish I will honor it. I'm sure the lovely Tibetan princess will live on in your memory until you are reunited with her in your next incarnation. Until then, I believe she's safe." Bonvalot turned to Rachmed. "Rachmed, do me a favor. I've got something important to attend to. Stay here with the luggage for a few minutes until I return, and then we'll take a cab home." Bonvalot doffed the brim of his hat. "Then I shall see you on Sunday, your Highness. Please give my regards to your parents."

Dodging horse carriages and delivery wagons, Bonvalot crossed the Rue de Saint-Quentin and entered the lobby of the Hôtel de Saint Quentin, which was bustling with tourists. He jostled his way through the crowd, his heart beating rapidly, until he found what he was looking for.

Camille Dancourt was sitting on a divan situated under a palm tree, her reddish-gold hair coiled on top of her head as she fanned herself copiously, more from nerves than from the heat. When she saw Bonvalot weaving through the lobby, she beamed and dropped her fan.

"*Enfin,*" he said, approaching her. "Thank goodness you're still here. I was afraid I had missed you."

"After all we've been through? How could I leave without saying a proper goodbye. I had to see you one last time and thank you again from the bottom of my heart. My brother should be arriving shortly to pick me up."

"I know we don't have much time," said Bonvalot. "But there's something I very much wish to tell you."

"Before you say anything," Camille opened her purse and withdrew a stack of bank notes. "I believe we have a little unfinished business to attend. There's the matter of the two thousand francs—"

Bonvalot pushed her hand away. "There's no need for that. I've already spoken to Prince Henri about the matter. His Excellency, the Duke of Chartres will cover all your expenses. Please keep your money and use it to rebuild the next chapter of your life."

"Then please tell his Excellency I'm most grateful for his generosity," said Camille. "As well as yours. You know, Monsieur Bonvalot, I can never repay you for everything you've done for me."

Before she could say anything more, Bonvalot held a finger to her lips.

"If you'll permit me," he said. "I have something important that I've been meaning to tell you for some time. During these past few months I've found myself growing closer to you than I've been with any other woman in my life. You should know I'm quite fond of you. Please forgive my directness, but after your mourning period has ended, I would very much like to call upon you properly. That is, if you'll agree."

Camille beamed with happiness. "I can think of nothing more splendid, "she said, slipping her arm into his. "Now, concerning that expedition to Madagascar, I have a few ideas I'd like to discuss with you."

CHAPTER 56

Paris, France
December 15, 1903

The news of the invasion of Tibet reached Gabriel Bonvalot on a crisp December morning in Paris. Having given up the life of an explorer and after recently being elected by unanimous vote as a deputy of the 10th Arrondissement to the National Assembly, Bonvalot detested his new life as a cog in the wheel of French politics. Drawing on his years dodging hostile border guards, bandits, and deceitful Chinese Ambans, Bonvalot steered clear of all the intrigue, scandals, and mud-slinging that characterized parliamentary life and sought refuge in the one place he considered his home away from home: Café Tortoni.

Whenever he needed a respite, Bonvalot would steal away for an hour or two to dine with colleagues and old friends or just sit in quiet solitude working on his true love: *La France de Demain*, the journal he founded to support his ideas of French nationalism and colonialism. Most of the time he reminisced about the old days, recalling the highlights of his long and prolific career as an explorer.

One of his most precious memories was the time he presented a rare and valuable Tibetan manuscript to Professor Philippe Édouard Foucaux, one of the world's foremost Tibetologists. The manuscript represented the culmination of the professor's life's work by confirming that the ancient prophecy concerning the reincarnation of Kali, the consort of the god Siva, had been fulfilled. The daughter of the Panchen Lama had returned as this earthly incarnate, and when Bonvalot helped save her life, he had set a cosmic wheel in motion with ramifications too astounding and too auspicious to be neglected. Professor Foucaux had assured

Bonvalot that by confirming this prophecy, he had helped an old man reach a state of pure bliss. It meant that his life's work had not been in vain, and that one day he too would be reunited with his beautiful lotus flower somewhere on the slopes of the Himalayas. But that was so many years ago, and the professor died not too long afterward. Bonvalot did not know if the old man ever saw his beloved lotus flower again.

Escaping from the Palais Bourbon one particularly cold and windy afternoon, Bonvalot headed to Café Tortoni to work on his latest article. He was so engrossed in his thoughts that he never took notice of the beggar that had followed him into the café and was making his way toward him. Bundled in a tattered overcoat, the beggar's head was shrouded by a hood. When he reached Bonvalot's table he muttered just loud enough to grab the famed politician's attention.

"Is anyone sitting here?"

Startled, Bonvalot looked up, and when he caught a glimpse of the wretched man's face, he recoiled. A memory came flooding back, a memory from years past that occasionally still haunted him. His eyes widened in disbelief. *Prejevalsky?*

"You," said Bonvalot. "What the devil are you doing here after all these years? I thought you were gone for good."

"You're not happy to see your old friend?" said Prejevalsky.

"An old friend that tried to kill me," said Bonvalot. "Did you come here to kill me now?"

"You insult me," said Prejevalsky. "Why would I do such an uncivilized thing? I came to show you something important. If you don't mind, I'll have a seat."

Prejevalsky heaved his bulky frame into a chair and at the same time threw a muddied newspaper down on the table. "Have a look at this," he said. "You may find it interesting."

Bonvalot unfolded the newspaper and when he scanned the blaring headline, he stared at it in shock:

INVASION OF TIBET BEGUN

The slaughter in Tibet has roused much feeling in Great Britain, and it is possible that Colonel Younghusband, the political agent of the Indian Government, will not be allowed to proceed further with the expedition. He has seventy-five miles

more to travel before he reaches Gyangtse, where he has been ordered to stop and parley before demanding entrance into ancient Lhasa. It can be taken for granted that the Government will do everything in its power to prevent a repetition of the bloody scene at Guru. The extreme Liberal papers characterize the slaughter as one of the worst blots on the history of England. In the meantime, Col. Younghusband's escort is prepared for all eventualities, and if the step is considered advisable the force is probably quite strong enough to reach Lhasa.

Bonvalot read the article in disbelief, adjusting his reading monocle to make sure he'd got it correct. Yes, there was no doubt. The British, under the leadership of Colonel Younghusband, had invaded Tibet and were on their way to Lhasa. Thousands of innocent Tibetans had been slaughtered protecting their homeland, and without a doubt countless more would be joining their battered and bloody corpses on the frozen ground. He wanted to call Prince Henri d'Orléans on the telephone and tell him about this tragic occurrence, but he remembered the prince had died two years ago while on expedition in Indochina.

"Good heavens," said Bonvalot. "It's a veritable slaughter."

"That appears to be true," said Prejevalsky.

"So why did you come now?"

"Many years ago you called me a failure," said Prejevalsky, smiling ironically. "And I objected to that on the grounds that I had ventured further into Tibet than any other explorer in modern times. My explorations yielded valuable collections and I had gained the trust of the Dalai Lama's tutor. He was going to arrange a meeting for me with the pontiff. But all that's in the past now. When it was your turn to go, I willingly offered my services yet you refused me with the stubbornness of fools. Still I persisted because it's in my nature to assist other scientific expeditions. And what was the result? You failed and now our British friends have all the glory."

"But the dead..." said Bonvalot. "All those innocent dead. Where is the glory of that?"

"And what of it?" said Prejevalsky. "Hasn't bloodshed been the price of conquest for thousands of years? I have no doubt that had you followed my plan you would have achieved all the fame and glory you desired. Every door in Europe and America would have opened for you. But you sacrificed it all in the name of your stupid idealism. Glory, you said, will not come at the price of bloodshed. And now the Englishman Younghusband has all the glory."

"You're wrong," said Bonvalot, locking his eyes with his Russian rival. "We don't belong there. Nobody belongs there."

"Poppycock."

"Tibet is a land of mystery and it should remain as such: unknowable and unconquerable. Tibet was never ours to take. That's the lesson the English failed to learn. That's the lesson you failed to learn."

His rival's eyes blazed with fury. "You ungrateful bastard. I should have done away with you when I had the chance."

"That's impossible," said Bonvalot. "You're just a figment of my imagination, a manifestation of my doubts and fears, an insidious hallucination. I have no regrets, no regrets at all."

"I have one final message for you, from an old friend of yours." From his breast pocket Prejevalsky produced a small white flower which he laid on the table. "This is the last you shall be hearing from me." Then Prejevalsky rose and fled the café.

Bonvalot picked up the flower. It was a pure white lotus flower. A Himalayan snow lotus. In a split second, an old memory came flooding back, that of an old man with a snow-white beard and kind, expressive eyes. A long lost love in the mountains of Sikkim. When the realization struck Bonvalot, his eyes went wide. He cried out, "Wait a minute, stop. Who gave this to you? Come back at once!"

But the beggar was gone.

Bonvalot raced after him but it was too late. He watched as the beggar dashed out to the bustling boulevard, pushed his way through the crowd of pedestrians, then headed straight for a line of swift-moving carriages...and *disappeared.*

For several minutes Bonvalot stood on the sidewalk cupping the lotus flower in his hand as he tried to make sense of it all. Then he turned and headed back into the café, the warmth and the smell of food a welcome respite from the blustery cold of the Paris winter.

Postscript

Gabriel Bonvalot

For his expedition to Tibet, Bonvalot was awarded the French Geographical Society's gold medal in 1891. His book about the journey, *"De Paris au Tonkin à travers le Tibet Inconnu,"* and its English translation, "Across Thibet," were huge bestsellers. In 1898, Bonvalot launched his final expedition to Ethiopia where he planned to join the Marchand expedition at Fachoda, but after failing to obtain the cooperation of the Ethiopian emperor, Menilek II, Bonvalot quit before reaching the Sudan. He served in the French Parliament from 1902 to 1906, and from 1912 to 1920, served as the mayor of Brienne-le-Château, where a bust was erected in his honor in a square named after him. Bonvalot died in Paris a national hero on Dec. 10, 1933 at the age of 80. He never returned to Asia.

Prince Henri d'Orléans

For his expedition to Tibet with Gabriel Bonvalot, Prince Henri earned the Gold Medal of the Geographical Society of Paris in 1891. In 1892 the prince made another journey of exploration in Central Africa and two years later he visited Madagascar. In 1895 he returned to Tonkin where he explored the sources of the Irrawaddy River for which he earned another Gold Medal in addition to the Cross of the Legion of Honor. In 1897, while visiting Abyssinia, Prince Henri made disparaging comments about the conduct of the Italian soldiers which led to a duel with the Count of Turin, Vittorio Emanuele. The duel was widely covered in the press, and even made the cover of *Le Petit Journal*. During the duel, which lasted 26 minutes, Henri received a serious wound to his right abdomen, putting him in an obvious state of inferiority and making the Count of Turin famous throughout Europe. In 1901, while on a trip to Annam, Prince Henri died of a tropical malady in Saigon. He was 33 years old.

Father Constant Dedeken

In 1891, Father Dedeken published a travelogue of his journey to Tibet called *"A Travers l'Asie."* After recuperating from the strenuous journey at his parents' home in Belgium, Father Dedeken traveled to the Belgian Congo in 1892 to continue his missionary work. In the Fall of 1894, he returned to Brussels to visit his parents and, despite his failing health, Father Dedeken returned to the Congo in November of 1895 where he died on March 3rd, 1896, a few days shy of his 44th birthday. A statue dedicated to Father Dedeken was erected in Wilrijk, and another one in Antwerp. He was made a Knight of the Order of Leopold.

Professor Philippe Édouard Foucaux

In 1858 Professor Foucaux published the first Tibetan grammar in French and occupied the first chair of Tibetan studies in Europe. Born in 1811 to a merchant family, he left for Paris at age 27 to study Indology as well as the Tibetan language. Afterwards he was appointed a Tibetan teacher at the *École des Langues Orientales* and was known as Europe's first Tibetan teacher. Foucaux died in 1894.

13th Dalai Lama

Thubten Gyatso, the 13th Dalai Lama, was born on February 12th, 1876 and was recognized as the reincarnation of the Dalai Lama in 1878. He was escorted to Lhasa and given his pre-novice vows by the Panchen Lama, Tenpai Wangchuk. Thubten Gyatso was an intelligent reformer who proved himself a skillful politician when Tibet became a pawn in the Great Game between Russia and Great Britain. He was responsible for countering the British expedition to Tibet, restoring discipline in monastic life, and increasing the number of lay official to avoid excessive power being placed in the hands of monks. He predicted the (Chinese) invasion of Tibet and announced he would die early so that his successor would be old enough to act as a leader for the Tibetan people at the time of the invasion. He died a few months later in Lhasa in December, 1933.

Author's Note: the story behind *Race to Tibet*

The idea for writing *Race to Tibet* came about in an unusual manner. While I was researching my first book, a historical novel set in the Danish West Indies, I came across an obscure, outspoken Danish princess whose life story gripped me. Princess Marie Valdemar was born in 1865 as Princess Marie d'Orléans, the daughter of Prince Robert, Duke of Chartres, a Grandson of King Louis-Philippe of France and a Pretender to the French throne.

Through her marriage to Prince Valdemar (the youngest son of Christian IX of Denmark), Princess Marie developed a great love of Denmark and the Danish people. In addition, she strongly opposed the sale of the Danish West Indies to the United States. Out of curiosity, I began to look into the life of Princess Marie d'Orléans, and was struck by how tragic and poignant it was, and how much it paralleled the life of Princess Diana with its tale of unrequited love and early death. Before long I decided to write a novel about her life, but after months of knocking on doors, I realized I would never be able to gain access to the Royal Danish Archives where the obscure details of her life lay locked up. Instead of giving up, I started searching for other sources. I made a list of all her relatives and searched for any diaries or memoirs they might have left behind, anything to fill in the missing gaps in her tragic life. As it turned out, the only relative of Princess Marie's who wrote an extensive number of books was her younger brother, Prince Henri d'Orléans, a notable French explorer who died at the age of thirty-three.

During his brief life, Prince Henri earned a reputation as a ladies' man, a dilettante, and a hot-headed dueler, but he earned the Gold Medal of the French Geographical Society twice, once in 1891 for a daring expedition to Tibet he made with the French explorer, Gabriel Bonvalot, and again in 1896 for his expedition from the Gulf of Tonkin to the Gulf of Bengal. The more I read about his expedition to Tibet, the more I became enthralled with the story until I found myself studying it in great depth. Not only did I focus on the expedition, I also threw myself into the study of the Great Game, Central Asian history and geography, famous explorers, and the history of Europe's obsession with Tibet.

Gradually, my focus changed from writing about Princess Marie's life to writing about Prince Henri d'Orléans and Gabriel Bonvalot's expedition to Tibet. To this end, I researched this famous journey both in the original French and in the English translation. But still there were many unanswered questions about what really happened to these hardy explorers on the Roof of the World. Victorian writers are known more for the details they left out than for what they chose to tell; this was an era when propriety and discretion were at their zenith. Luckily, after months and months of unrelenting searching and digging, I came upon another version of the events, this one written by Father Constant de Deken, a Belgian missionary who had accompanied the famous explorers. I had struck gold.

Unusual for his generation, Father Constant de Deken was fluent in Chinese and wrote about his experiences with uncharacteristic candor, telling details that would have raised eyebrows in polite society. His input added a whole new dimension to the story, filling it with more danger and suspense, and for that I am eternally grateful. By combining both versions and adding some fictional elements of my own, the end result is this account of an historic journey into mysterious Tibet. But it only came about because of this tragic Danish princess and her sad, poignant life. And so, I owe this lovely lady all the gratitude in the world for leading me to this fascinating story. Without Princess Marie d'Orléans, *Race to Tibet* would not have been possible.

Bibliography

Bonvalot, Gabriel. 1889. *Du Caucase aux Indes à travers Le Pamir.* Paris: E. Plon Nourrit et Cie., Imprimeurs-Éditeurs and *Through the Heart of Asia* (English translation in 2 Volumes, also 1889) London: Chapman & Hall, Ltd.

Bonvalot, Gabriel. 1892. *De Paris au Tonkin à travers le Tibet Inconnu.* Paris: Librairie Hachette et Cie. and *Across Thibet* (English translation in 2 Volumes, 1892) London: Cassell & Company, Ltd.

Bower, Hamilton. 1894. *Diary of a Journey Across Tibet.* London: Rivington, Percival and Co.

Burnaby, Fred. 1877. *A Ride to Khiva: Travels and Adventures in Central Asia.* New York: Harper & Brothers Publishers.

Deken, Constant de. 1894. *À travers l'Asie.* Brussels: Polleunis et Ceuterick, Imprimeurs.

French, Patrick. 2003. *Tibet, Tibet: A Personal History of a Lost Land.* London: Harper Perennial.

French, Patrick. 1994. *Younghusband: The Last Great Imperial Adventurer.* London: Harper Collins Publishers.

Hopkirk, Peter. 1990. *The Great Game: The Struggle for Empire in Central Asia.* New York: Kodansha America, Inc.

Hopkirk, Peter. 1996. *Quest for Kim.* London: John Murray.

Hopkirk, Peter. 1982. *Trespassers on the Roof of the World: The Secret Exploration of Tibet.* New York: Kodansha America, Inc.

Jouneau, Gabriel and Paul Berger. 1939. *Un Grand Français: Gabriel Bonvalot, Explorateur.* Paris: Les Publications Colonials.

Kirchner, Friedrich. 1888. *A Student's Manual of Psychology.* (Adapted from *Katechismus der Psichologie*) London: Swan Sonnenschein Lowrey & Co.

Lansdell, Henry. 1885. *Russian Central Asia, including Kuldja, Bokhara, Khiva and Merv.* Boston: Houghton, Mifflin, & Company.

Meyer, Karl E. and Shareen Blair Brysac. 1999. *Tournament of Shadows: The Great Game and the race for empire in Central Asia.* New York: Basic Books.

Normanton, Simon. 1988. *Tibet: The Lost Civilization.* New York: Viking Penguin, Inc.

Orléans, Henri Philippe Marie (Prince d'). 1894. *Around Tonkin and Siam.* London: Chapman & Hall Ltd.

Orléans, Henri Philippe Marie (Prince d'). 1902. *L'Âme du Voyageur.* Paris: Calmann Lévy, Éditeur.

Orléans, Henri Philippe Marie (Prince d'). 1893. *Le Père Huc et Ses Critiques.* Paris: Calmann Lévy, Éditeur.

Orléans, Henri Philippe Marie (Prince d'). 1889. *Six Mois aux Indes Chassent les Tigres.* Paris: Calmann Lévy, Éditeur.

Parville, Henri de. 1890. *L'Exposition Universelle 1889.* Paris: J. Rothschild, Éditeur.

Prejevalsky, Nikolai. 1879. *From Kulja, across the Tian Shan to Lob Nor.* London: Sampson Low, Marston, Searle, & Rivington.

Prejevalsky, Nikolai. 1876. *Mongolia, the Tangut Country, and the Solitudes of Northern Tibet.* London: Sampson Low, Marston, Searle, and Rivington.

Rayfield, Donald. 1976. *The Dream of Lhasa: The Life of Nikolay Przhevalsky Explorer of Central Asia.* London: Ohio University Press.

Waddell, L. Austine. 1899. *The Buddhism of Tibet: or Lamaism with its mystic cults, symbolism and mythology, and in its relation to Indian Buddhism.* London: Luzac & Co.

Younghusband, Francis Edward. 1910. *India and Tibet.* London: John Murray.

Younghusband, Francis Edward. 1904. *The Heart of a Continent: A Narrative of Travels in Manchuria, Across the Gobi Desert, Through the Himalayas, the Pamirs, and Hunza 1884-1894.* London: John Murray.

Younghusband, Francis Edward. 1924. *Wonders of the Himalaya.* London: John Murray.

25002271R00211

Made in the USA
San Bernardino, CA
14 October 2015